CONJUNCTIONS

Bi-Annual Volumes of New Writing

Edited by
Bradford Morrow

Contributing Editors
Walter Abish
Chinua Achebe
John Ashbery
Mei-mei Berssenbrugge
Guy Davenport
Elizabeth Frank
William H. Gass
John Guare
Susan Howe
Robert Kelly
Ann Lauterbach
Patrick McGrath
Nathaniel Tarn
Quincy Troupe
John Edgar Wideman

published by Bard College

EDITOR: Bradford Morrow
MANAGING EDITOR: Michael Bergstein
SENIOR EDITORS: Robert Antoni, Martine Bellen, Thalia Field, Ben Marcus,
    Pat Sims, Lee Smith
ART EDITOR: Anthony McCall
PUBLICITY: Mark R. Primoff
WEBMASTER: Michael Neff
EDITORIAL ASSISTANTS: Seze Devres, Blair Holt, Sage Jacobs, Paulina
    Belle Nissenblatt, Rachel Sherman, Sadia Talib

CONJUNCTIONS is published in the Spring and Fall of each year by Bard
College, Annandale-on-Hudson, NY 12504. This issue is made possible in part
with the generous funding of the Lannan Foundation.

This publication is made possible with public funds from the New York State
Council on the Arts, a State Agency.

SUBSCRIPTIONS: Send subscription order to CONJUNCTIONS, Bard College,
Annandale-on-Hudson, NY 12504. Single year (two volumes): $18.00 for indi-
viduals; $25.00 for institutions and overseas. Two years (four volumes): $32.00
for individuals; $45.00 for institutions and overseas. Patron subscription (life-
time): $500.00. Overseas subscribers please make payment by International
Money Order. Back issues available at $12.00 per copy. For subscription and
advertising information, call 914-758-1539 or fax 914-758-2660.

Editorial communications should be sent to 33 West 9th Street, New York, NY
10011. Unsolicited manuscripts cannot be returned unless accompanied by a
stamped, self-addressed envelope.

Printers: Edwards Brothers.
Typesetter: Bill White, Typeworks.

ISSN 0278-2324
ISBN 0-941964-44-2

Manufactured in the United States of America.

TABLE OF CONTENTS

From ALMANAC; A Winter's Tale

Being for the Bissextile or LEAP YEAR 2000
and of the 224th year of the American Independence

Maureen Howard

Lo! The year is new and cheery,
Bright the snow, though dark the morn.
And the black bird pecks till weary
At the barren stalks of corn.

January 1.

THE FLINTSTONES

CONSIDER THEIR AFFINITIES: both Freeman and his grandfather have withdrawn from the competition. (The kid had no father. That link is lost.) They stand above the crowd with high pokey shoulders, their awkward bodies strung together loosely, not the compact look of men who once fooled around on a basketball court, but they share an attractive energy — loners not losers, not always — for the dear boy is his grandfather exactly. Their loping long stride sets the hustling city at a distance as though they have arrived from an earlier time, both Artie Freeman and Cyril O'Connor, as though they might easily saunter through swinging doors of the old Astor House on lower Broadway or into the feed store on Fulton Street, or rise respectfully at a meeting of the First Ward with a gentleman's request. Shock-haired men, Artie's rumpled black, Cyril's stark white; they bear matching widower's peaks and startling blue eyes, the bright blue of untroubled summer skies. All in all, good looks somewhat botched by large, heavily lobed ears and by the narrow pinched nose of the craggy Irish. The old man cannot help his dignity, though it makes him seem a pretender seeking refuge in his old books, blindly pacing the dark rooms of his apartment, a pretender to better days when containment, reserve, independence and inquiry served a man well.

Consider that his grandson dutifully trudging Fifth Avenue with an insupportable knee would not have seemed such an ass at the New Year's debacle, if not cursed with a remnant of Cyril's

7

outdated posture. And that Artie would not be so often ticked off if he did not sense that the words-upon-words barely visible to the old guy in his history books were kin to the glut of information on his screen, databases from which he fudged convincing facts; and that his grandfather's obsessive isolation was much like the lone hours at his work station where, most recently, he brindled, hoofed and uddered make-believe cows, one cow standing for thousands, her lactation engineered to the nth degree.

Not bad times, the many suppers with Cyril. Steak and potato on the menu, no vitamins as in the old days. In need of a remedy on this nauseous New Year's Day — hair of the dog, raw egg yolks in beer — Artie thinks of the primal cure, the pastel vitamins pressed in the shape of the Flintstones and their dinosaur pet. Each morning his mother had unscrewed the childproof cap and let him choose a chalky Fred or Wilma, Pebbles or Dino.

She had packed the vitamins with his Yankee pjs and driven him into the city on a warm spring day. In fact, his spring vacation from school. All as usual — Cyril and Mae down at the curb to meet them so that his mother would not have to park on Fifth Avenue. That was a fiction: Fiona O'Connor seldom visited her parents in their apartment and his mother could not parallel park, could not stop, if she stopped at a light, without a squealing of tires. In every particular a lousy driver. All as usual, the doorman taking his zip bag into the lobby. His grandmother leaning into the car. Two fair Irish faces — mother and daughter — facing off.

"Don't spoil my kid," his mother said.

"No more," a clip to Mae O'Connor's voice, "than we spoiled you."

As usual his grandfather had turned him around by the shoulders to stand straight and wave his mother off. It could not have been as usual, for Cyril was still on Wall Street in those days. Unless that day was Good Friday and the market was closed, but Artie surely remembered Mae poking her head into the scarred suburban wagon, his grandmother's red hair fading to white. His mother's hair brazen, that word picked up from Cyril, who said with the faintest smile that his daughter was brazen. The boy believed it was therefore commendable that his mother's hair was copper bright.

He stood at attention that fine morning, held his hand high in a salute, fearful that she might turn and wave back at him, killing the dachshund at the curb. Fiona did turn with a wild hoot of joy,

8

both hands off the wheel, happy to be free of him. That is what the boy thought. He was ten years old. Freeman has not revised that opinion. He remembers the station wagon screeching off, turning east at the end of the block, right through a red light. A parting view of the battered blue Connecticut plate.

It was the last he saw of his mother, who died that week in a boating accident in calm West Indian waters. She was not at the helm, knew nothing of sailing. The chances she would be totalled on the interstate he had figured as one in five. That she should capsize with her lover in collision with a tourist speedboat off the tiny island of Nevis was a million to one. Each weekday of that spring vacation, his grandfather, dressed in a three-piece suit, dealt out Wilma or Pebbles, unaware that the vitamins were for toddling midgets. On the Saturday after Easter the news came early. Cyril in a sporty jacket, Mae fussing over French toast. After breakfast they had planned to go down the Avenue, to take their grandson to the Temple of Dendur for the very first time.

But the news came early. His grandfather answered the phone, then took the boy's hand, which was nearly as big as his own. "Vitamins," he said with great solemnity. "She would have wanted you to grow. To grow up." A neutral statement, yet it was how Mae knew that her daughter was dead. She had bounced the Vermont Maid syrup in its plastic jug into the kitchen sink, retracted their silverware and plates while the eggy bread burned in the skillet. Clearing the deck, as it were, for sorrow, she tossed the baby vitamins into the trash. For a while Freeman believed that denied the niacin, B_{12}, riboflavin of the Flintstones intended for little people, he became a skinny freak, but at that moment his extremities were palsied with fear, with rage, yet, in imitation of his grandfather, he found no tears.

Alone in the white clapboard house in Connecticut where he had lived with his mother, he often imagined that he would answer the phone and the cops would say which barrier she had driven through, on which entrance ramp she had refused to yield. Even this role of dealing in manly fashion with sirens, doctors and tubular apparatus, taken from television drama, was taken from him. Fiona O'Connor was not rendered contrite in a hospital bed to be cared for by her boy, the child that a childish woman would have wanted to grow up.

Now he limps to his grandparents' apartment, never thought of as home though he lived there after the white house in Connecticut

9

faded to no more than a set for old Hollywood flicks — the comedies of loving, quarrelsome couples that his grandmother found so reassuring. Movie homes that held forth the ideal of home in quaint shutters and shrubbery, pristine stove and sink, handwritten letters on a breakfast tray. Mae's big bland apartment was never home, for all the days he ran up Fifth Avenue from the Temple of Dendur to be back at the dining-room table with his math or Latin textbooks before Cyril's key turned in the door. Faking it — homework and home.

Artie Freeman, the gimp, makes it to the lobby of that apartment house, finding there an untended dachshund simpering at the glass door, which is also untended. "Poor beast," Artie says. Poor civilized beast, for when he lets it slither out, it is beached in snow well above its head and cannot figure how to lift its stumpy leg. Yes, there was snow, he had woken with a swollen head, two heads as it were, one twisting him back to the night of debauchery — to the songs, toots, cries and kisses which preceded his disgrace; the second head turned to a blinding assault of thick white snow plastered to windowsill. Plastered. He remembers beating the trunk of a taxi with his fists, then slipping to his knees, studying the stamp of tire tread and the faint smear of exhaust on the new white world. Without scarf, gloves, overcoat, he had walked alone though Central Park, which was closed to traffic, unpeopled by the storm, a paper dunce cap dribbling crimson down his forehead. Concerts, fireworks, all outdoor revels had been called off in the city due to a freaky, calamitous storm. At noon lights had dimmed, fluttered. Messages, in this city of messages, were half-written, half-transmitted, cut off in the troubled air.

Artie frees the squat dog from its prison of snow, strokes it while she (puckered rows of tiny tits) relieves herself on the clawed foot of a gilt table Artie has hated for its fancy-pants glamour since he was a little boy. Elevators out, they climb the stairs together, the bitch's loose stomach whacking every step. At each landing she waits for Freeman, who hobbles behind, and sniffs politely at rumpsteak and bone until she whines at the sixth floor to be let into the dark beyond. Paw scratch, click of a latch and she is home. Figuring life span of breed with modest turnover of old apartments on Upper East Side, he takes the low-slung hound to be a random variable, perhaps a descendent of the very dog he feared his mother would kill the week before she died.

Crawling the last flights in the dark stairwell, Artie fears that on this aftermath of a day, he will discover his grandfather asleep forever in the crocked leather chair or laid out in his Brooks Brothers pajamas under the genteel pall of Mae's crocheted spread, the gold pocket watch, now his, ticking away on the night table, though ... though while Artie fumbles with his key, it would be like Cyril to be reading on without lamplight, his wretched old eyes following word by magnified word—Jefferson, Monroe, Adams—plots of the past in which he loses the line literally. Often Freeman wants to shout at the unopened door—Here! I am here from the city of outlaws marauders unhoused tribes unknown to your floundering fathers their endless words writ out sealed posted to an old coot assembling big word by big word double-crostic for the insoluble grief forbearance here—I am here. But being so like the old man, he always enters without a word. Today, pain distracts him from anger. He sets down the meat and potatoes, leans his muddled head against the door.

"Here!" Artie cries, "I'm here!" Then the terror, premeditated terror: he will find his grandfather dead.

January 17. Benjamin Franklin born at Boston, 1706.

Papa. Cher Papa. Though he has successfully concluded his diplomatic duties which bring to an end the War of Independence, he stands bemused, hat in one hand, spectacles in the other, while a most beautiful lady crowns him with laurel and myrtle in the grand salon of the Musée de Paris. It is 1783. She alone is awed, while ladies and gents of high degree, powdered and wigged, look to their American hero with bemused smiles of respect. He is the new Prometheus, the natural aristocrat among them, hero of the New World from generous dome of bald head to plain buckles on his shoes.

One does not dress for private company as for a public ball.

—Benjamin Franklin

Or does one? Does one carry the Quakerish hat to make a point when it is replaced by the herbal tribute intended for emperors and gods? So that the laurels will not prick. Cher Papa, as Madame Helvétius called him, one of the many ladies to whom he was more fatherly than to his own children. Easier to play at family away from home and to be the public's darling, father of us all. Biographer's business; ferret out Franklin, the peevish husband, his drawing-room dalliances, that love letter with a lascivious phrase; make philosopher and statesman real, human, flawed. Isn't

11

that more comfortable in dealing with a man of genius? Franklin beat his biographers to the draw, shrewdly controlling the image of a simple man given to small theatrics, to harmless play.

Old Cyril, sipping from history that trick dribble cup of Time, admired Ben Franklin when, in his retirement some years before the millennium, he took to reading The Founding Fathers. He bought the anecdotal version of a near penniless boy which appears in *The Autobiography*. Young Ben with three Puffy Rolls under his arm walking up from the docks in Philadelphia where, standing in her father's doorway, he saw the girl who was to become his wife. Bending to the book, Cyril puzzled out Franklin's story — an ambitious young man in his printer's apron setting type for *Poor Richard's Almanack*, which featured Advice and Amusement, Essential Information of the Sun, Moon and Stars, printing his best-seller in downtime when the press was not running a job. At an early age, adept, as Cyril has been, at making money, and more than clever at his craft, though Cyril O'Connor was struck, reading between the lines, to discover that when Ben finally married the Puffy Roll girl he no longer loved her. Then hastily as he was able, Cyril read on to Franklin in gentleman's tricorn and weskit flying the famous silk kite, teasing electricity out of a storm. Nothing daunted the old man until one unexceptional night (it is timeless in the dark apartment) Cyril understood that Franklin was seventy when Congress commissioned him as Minister to France, not many years younger than he is as he closes his book and feels his way to the bedroom, grumbling that the sun will rise next day.

Often he cannot name the day, but will wake with the first dull light, of that he is unfortunately certain. Still, he reads on — the great man's letters, bagatelles, political satires, his experiments and observations. Franklin awarded degrees from St. Andrew's, Oxford, the first honorary degree from Harvard; tributes to a natural philosopher, long before the word scientist came into being. Finding that there really was no correspondence between the American inventor-self-inventor and himself other than the art of money-making, he reads on only to marvel. Then, as though time will be allotted so that he may turn back one day, Cyril takes up his pen to mark a passage:

> *If you would not be forgotten*
> *As soon as you are rotten,*
> *Either write things worth reading,*
> *Or do things worth the writing.*

But finds that disheartening, for he has never written or done, and is forgotten by all but the boy whose care packages come bound in guilt, and so marks another of Poor Richard's pithy maxims: *Let thy Discontents be Secret.* And further scrawls in the flyleaf of Franklin's delightful self-advertising Autobiography: Printer, Publisher, Statesman. Inventor of: Rocking chair, catheter, Franklin stove, lightning rod, bifocals, water wings — until the list of Practical Inventions runs off the page leaving Cyril to contemplate Franklin's Long Arm, a device for removing books from high shelves, his improvements on the sea anchor and the glass armonica. A thorough man, Cyril reads to the last page to discover it was not a bitter end for Franklin, who wrote to a friend that if allowed, he'd live his whole life over. And closing *The Autobiography,* Cyril O'Connor considers his own Rags to Riches career, sorely limited to puts and calls and the short-sighted futures of Wall Street.

But on the first day of January, Janus allowing us to screw our heads back in this newest year of our Lord, Artie Freeman braved the snowbound city, crawled the black stairway to his grandparents' apartment, still unclear as to how he arrived in his own bed ten stories above Central Park on this powerless morning. Clever at guessing games — it's Artie's business to shape up unorganized data for Skylark, to chart and graph Product, as in overflowing milk pails, to coolly round off statistics into digestible, vendable pies, yet he stupidly leans on the bell, bangs crazily on the door wanting his grandfather, who is the fragile ghost of himself, wanting him alive while predicting with tears in his bloodshot eyes that it is a fitting end to that Christ awful century — the old gentleman will certainly have died.

The woman who opens the door is tiny, will-o'-the-wisp. In the dim front hall where the mirror and hat rack of old waver in the candlelight, she calls out, "What kept you?"

Artie sees they have been waiting, they — for in the living room beyond, Cyril is buttoned into his antiquated Chesterfield with the worn velvet collar.

"Ah, dear boy!" The routine greeting out of Edwardian novels or the Noël Coward revivals which his grandmother loved pisses Artie off. Cyril is jolly, thumping his cold hands together as though in applause for the little woman all in white who pokes the decorative birch logs into a musty blaze suffusing the neglected room with flattering light. His grandfather's leather chair is pushed to the window so that the history buff may read on, his endless pages.

Sylvie, that is the name of this blunt little enchantress, has arrived from Cyril's unimaginable past. Artie is outraged by her charms. The lovers (getting his aching head around that one) speak a bill-and-coo language — *old beau, sweetheart* — and laugh at the adventure of Sylvie driving through a blizzard to find him, Captain O'Connor, to find him quite alone in the dark, yet so — so *available*. As the beau reaches for her hand, Sylvie is properly embarrassed and issues an emphatic change of subject. "Chances are an hour or so, the power will go on. You know about chances."

"I figure" — Artie Freeman figures to spite this minx who has transformed his grandfather with the kiss of life — "figure that the power in the corroded infrastructure of uptown Manhattan may not be restored in our time. We may not experience again the comfort of central heating, electricity, phone, the indispensable phone."

"Ah," she finds him amusing, "then it is better we go home to Connecticut." She is Sylvie, a sprite intent on running off with Cyril. Elope is the word of his grandfather's choice.

"Elope into the future, my — "

"My boy," Artie fills in.

"Hard to drop the old locutions," Cyril says.

"You are seventy-five."

"Seventy-six," says Sylvie.

"He never leaves these rooms. He sits, walks, sleeps. The basic functions, that's it. And reads. He can barely read," Artie hears himself shouting, "word by painful word."

"And yet he insistently stands on his head!" A rich rumble of mirth from Sylvie's small body. "You speak as though Cyril is not here. Isn't that what we do with the demented and little children?"

"His dotage! Elope into his dotage." Artie's rudeness can't touch them. He doubts that his grandfather sees that Sylvie wears bridal white — boots, ski pants, parka, a powder puff of white hair — the snow princess who has waited for her lover how many frozen years? Thawed, the two of them, into giddy youngsters. Already secret smiles, words overlapping as they now speak their piece, a cornball, geriatric romance. One stolen night of luff in the fifties. Artie detects a trace of Garbo guttural in Sylvie's recitation. While Cyril warms himself by the last embers of Mae's smoldering logs, this Sylvie reconstructs their passion at a little Hungarian restaurant — rhapsodic violin, potato pancakes.

Cyril sighs, "Red cabbage, veal paprika."

Artie slings the rump steak and bone onto Mae's noncommittal carpet. The city shut down, he had foraged for food, recalling his grandfather's love of a bloody steak — how often Cyril had turned their slabs of meat in a pan and proudly split their baked potatoes, the years they hacked it alone. He is sorry for the stain on Mae's beige wall-to-wall, for the bland fare of his grandmother's table, her weekly hair appointment, good works with the Gray Ladies of Charity and the yearly cruise to Bermuda. Harmless Mae, her touch of the ordinary on everything. An air of the exotic invades her living room — shadows of candlelight, a creamy silk scarf draping the button-back couch; the shimmer of Sylvie's glossy lidded eyes, crystal earrings of the seductress. Artie is undone by their story. He has projected gum loss in a colorful bar chart, pitching neglect against heredity for a dentifrice designed for oldies, great-looking oldies like Cyril and his sweetie, who smile undentured upon him from the reclaimed height of their passion which has not been eroded by years of dutiful marriage to the wrong mates — to poor Mae O'Connor and to a blameless airline executive who expired, conveniently, on a golf cart in Boca Raton.

"Incredible, is it not?" Cyril fixes his grandson straight-on. He has lost peripheral vision.

"Fucking off the charts."

"Not so, not so." Sylvie revealing their pact. "We swore we would meet in the next century, so it is possible. I never forgot our foolish promise, how we cried when we parted . . ." (Artie sees them on the steps of the Plaza, on a misty Waterloo Bridge.) "The Captain, too, bawling for the world to see in Grand Central under the clock," Sylvie's coy hesitation, "the morning after. The morning after, fifty years seemed forever. You grow old and . . . *naturlich*, it is not."

"So, you guys got a lot to talk about." Aiming this at his grandfather who did not weep over the graves of his wife and daughter, but it now occurs to Artie Freeman that Fiona and Mae were counterfeits in Cyril's life of let's pretend. And their years together, aging man and orphan boy, a mere litter of homework, checkers, chess, frizzled minute steak and mealy potatoes, evenings his grandfather had not relished, nor had he delighted in Artie's stunning math scores or his array of diving trophies. All Cyril O'Connor's praise was fraudulent, meant for the son of some daughter born of desire.

15

The lights flicker, flick on. Sylvie looks to the dial of her dainty watch, prods her old darling. "We're off." In the dark hall, Artie had missed the duffle, the very one Cyril brought back from his war, packed for the boy each summer when he was shipped off to camp. It bears both their names in black stencil.

When he rings for the elevator, Cyril turns back to Artie, who is curled in upon himself at the open door. "What of the young woman? The girl?"

"I gave her the ring." His croak of amazement that the old guy has remembered.

The victory sign from Cyril and then, "We're off," echoing Sylvie, the little imp in the driver's seat, who made it through one of the memorable storms of the century in an invincible old Jeep.

"Torque on the ice?"

She doesn't hear Arthur Freeman's feeble cut, words of a snotty kid, but he gets that she has shouted her romantic tale so that she might hear herself speak. The deaf old doll leading that blind, hoodwinked old man, the last living soul who knows who A. Freeman is — a bastard begot in the mud of Woodstock. For all their easy intimacy, he has never told Louise Moffett, his Lou who now wears the ring — perhaps wears the ring? — the likely story of his humiliating origin, though he had often computed the continuous density of the spermbank which enabled one unidentified donor to succeed in becoming his father during Fiona's transcendent multiplicity of fucks. That he leapt into being at the legendary Love Fest was, of course, only conjecture. By the time he met Louise, he had given up on it as a trite tale. She had seemed satisfied with *orphan* and with his remnant of family, an aged grandfather set in the wings, as though it freed her from her own — a heavy-duty Dad, the dithering lightweight Mom set at their distance in Wisconsin. Until recently, he admits, when the idea of their New Year's Eve got under way, their failed idea to flip back in time. They would drink to 1950, fed up with media blab — for weeks, for months the demoralizing history — info-techno, gender bender, Deco-Eco, Lenin to Lennon, Stravinsky to Sting, Moon Mullins to Moon Walk, Blimp to Bomb, Cola to coke.

"Enough!" Lou had cried. As though she faced a huge prepared canvas, she sketched it in lightly, "Turn back. Suppose we turn back. To my parents, their childhood. Chores, Sunday School, 4H, both of them safe on the family farm. They might have been chicks in the incubator."

"A little hard to stage in the city." He said no more for it struck him that her paintings were always of the farm, every silo, barn and tree distorted to force observation, destroy nostalgia.

"Shirley and Harold, they would have been eight or ten." She had no head for numbers.

"No, in early adolescence. So we can just play at being ourselves." She laughed at that one. "With zits and braces," he said.

"Be serious," a phrase she tossed at him from their first days together, lately without much amusement. "I only meant their amazing innocence."

Which Lou and Artie agreed would not be much fun. So that he had come up with the idea of his grandparents' sedate coming of age, his imagination feeding off old movies, shadowy reruns of the fifties, the post-war American dream. He had called upon Cyril and Mae as historical figures, then Louise had been curious. *At least they knew who they were.* He had said that and been wrong, now sees that he produced them as types, so damn sure he knew who they were that he rendered them lifeless to his shame. And feels the further disgrace of his grandfather getting it on—liver spot to liver spot with Sylvie, entwined varicosities. Off to Connecticut. Abandoned, left to nurse his throbbing knee in the empty apartment. He imagines Captain O'Connor in an Eisenhower jacket fumbling with Sylvie's zipper, trembling hand on wasp waist, not in a slick hotel scene, their love nest is a home with green shutters much like the dreamhouse Cyril bought for his unwed daughter, supporting Fiona in all her follies—the throwing of lumpy plates and pots, her untalented strumming of unmelodic folk songs. On long winter nights the fire had blazed in Connecticut. Artie learned to lay the kindling, leave a crack for air between seasoned logs. When the flames were high, his mother sat with her legs crossed to meditate, clearing her head of here and now, until, he knew this as a boy, until he was cast out, no longer present in the radiant warmth of her room.

Last night yet another dismissal. As his grandfather and Sylvie descend in the elevator, climb into the Jeep, head off through soiled city slush toward a house with green shutters, the painful moments blink on—oddly spliced like random camcorder footage. He had steered Louise to the back of the loft, his hand firm on her waist. The man leading, wasn't that how they'd done it? Stumbling in an awkward two-step, sure, he'd sampled a Rob Roy,

17

thrown back a Stinger and the dregs of a Manhattan, the sticky cocktails of the fifties. He'd thought to take her behind the screen where an easy chair, a scrap of rug, their bed gave a semblance of home. A giant painting overwhelmed them, Lou's one unfinished work not stacked away for their perverse celebration. He knelt before her vision of an apple tree's heartwood with a miniature inset of the tree in full flower. Astonishing, the thwunk-thwunk of his heart, years of cool blown away. A suitor on his knees, he had given some thought to the offering of the ring which he had taken from his grandmother's jewelry case, snapped open the velvet box to ask Cyril, "May I . . . ?"

Had Cyril seen the sparkler when he looked up from the page? A twitch of memory in the weak blue eyes: "Yes, by all means. She would want you to have it." Then skipped to the presumption, "You are going to marry!"

"Yes." Ordinary talk followed, absolute flow of conversation breaking the reticence of all their years, the old man curious about the girl.

"The woman."

"Of course, woman."

And Artie was quick to praise her, in fact a girl from the heart-land, eager to bring Louise home — calling it home where Cyril sat reading, tidy but unclean. He felt somewhat uncomfortable, his easy words promoting the attributes of Louise — her beauty, humor, competence — not the woman herself but single white female: caring, loves art and a good laugh. Overselling himself on the proposal for lately the M word was written in invisible ink all over Lou's calendar, a drop of lemon juice and it would surface. "Be serious" had narrowed in meaning.

"Marriage," Cyril said, "is an honorable state. I felt the need for it and your grandmother did surely. Not my Fiona. She was entirely free of such institutions. I often think she might have come round, though I would not have encouraged her."

"Come round?"

"In those days —"

"Come round? Who'd she come round to? My father?" Which cut off the pleasant talk, always had.

"If I knew. If I knew —"

Artie ending that one. "— I would have told you long ago who the bastard was." Then feeling ungrateful, he set his grandfather's magnifying glass to the top line of a page from which it had wandered. "Thanks," he said, snapping the box closed on the ring, "I'm sorry."

"No need for that," Cyril said. "It's a sorry world."

"Better dealt with in sayings? Things others have said?"

The magnifying glass slipped to the carpet. Artie put it in the old man's cold fingers. "Sorry," he said again. "Thanks for the ring." And Cyril began an anecdotal account of the diamond's purchase.

"In those days —"

Walking home through the park, Artie ran off what he should have said, a habit of long standing, the should-have-said-to-Cyril: A contortionist's stiff upper lip hiding my withered limb, the crippled kid, you know crippled having once trained me to walk like a little soldier, stand up like a man, words from your boy stories, pluck against adversity, value of the ring in my pocket no more to you than my weekly allowance, more than a year's take in my cottage industry, always money to heal the wound of what might be called, I suppose, my inner life, my blind rage at being fatherless turned to a gentle myth, one of your wife's dotty ones, transubstantiation. Numb the injury with ice, pay up. So, do you see me, Pops, kneeling, a suitable suitor? Part of me hoping the ring might be worthless, a gag.

But the ring, like his grandfather's hard currency, had its value, was there for the taking though Artie believed the arcane token no part of his life. Yet last night he knelt on one knee in the shadow of a tiny apple tree. Its snowy petals showered promise as though pages of the calendar fluttered forward to spring and he was suddenly worshipful as he dug the velvet box out of his grandfather's pocket, for he was costumed in the Eisenhower jacket, though unsteady, unable to judge the distance to his loved one's hand.

"Hey! Love you, my Lou."

At a distance, on the other side of the screen, the New Year's revelry continued. He had wanted the magic moment to be midnight. That moment had passed. He had wanted the accompaniment of his grandmother's music, maybe—"Begin the Beguine," "What Is This Thing Called Love?" Someone had put on the pounding Electro Funk of an immediate past. The gummy smell of turpentine rags mixed with the heavy sweetness of hashish, the night smoking its way into a timeless future. Balanced uncertainly, Artie saw with selective clarity the dribble of champagne he had dealt to Lou's taffeta dress.

"Love my Lou-Lou!"

She plucked the diamond from its velvet safety in a snit, put it on her finger, taking it as one more prop for their millenarian masquerade. "Oh, Artie! You're polluted."

He stayed a supplicant, kissing the stained hem of her gown. "Serioushly, Lou!"

"Not now, when you're sauced."

The painful moments surface. Louise jabs him with her stiletto heel, a swift kick to the knee. He topples, streaks of viridian and raw umber on Captain O'Connor's uniform, Lou's apple tree felled. She weeps uncontrollably. He hears her call above the throbbing music, calling out for his buddies who appear as her henchmen. Then he is lifted ceremoniously, held up to ridicule as in a tar-and-feather ritual. Heaved out of Lou's loft.

Fair's fair, he would say if she'd hear him out, then romance her with the absurdity of Cyril and Sylvie, "One night of luff in the fifties, Louise. It's spooky, time warped, Twilight Zone."

Then surely she'd laugh at him, "Be serious."

For Listening Through Earphones
Julio Cortázar

— Translated from Spanish by Stephen Kessler

A TECHNICIAN EXPLAINED IT to me, but I can't say I understood. When you listen to a record through earphones (not all records, but just exactly the ones that shouldn't do this), it happens that in the fraction of a second preceding the first sound one can perceive, extremely faintly, that first sound about to sound an instant later at full strength. Sometimes you don't even notice, but when you're waiting for a string quartet or madrigal or a *lied*, the almost imperceptible pre-echo is really rather disagreeable. Any self-respecting echo ought to come after, not before; what kind of an echo is that? I'm listening to the *Royal Variations* of Orlando Gibbons, and just in between, precisely in that brief night of the ears as they get ready for the fresh irruption of sound, a chord far in the distance or the first notes of the melody inscribe themselves in a kind of microbial audition, which has nothing to do with what's about to begin a half-second later and which is nonetheless its parody, its infinitesimal mockery. Elizabeth Schumann is going to sing *Du bist die Ruh,* there's that customary air at the depths of the record in its perfection which puts us in a state of tense expectancy, of total dedication to what's about to begin, and just then from the ultradepths of silence we hear horribly some bacterial or robotic voice which inframinimally sings *Du bist,* cuts off, there's another sliver of silence, then the singer's voice surges forth full force, the real *Du bist die Ruh.*

(It's a terrible example, because before the soprano begins to sing there's a piano prelude, and it's the first two or three piano notes that reach us through this subliminal channel I'm talking about; but as you'll have understood (because I presume you've shared the experience) what I'm saying, it's not worth the trouble to look for a better example; I think this phonographic sickness is well known and suffered by everyone.)

My friend the technician explained to me that this pre-echo, which up until then had seemed to me inconceivable, was the result of those things that happen when there are all kinds of circuits, feedbacks, electronic loops and other ad hoc vocabularies. What I understood as a pre-echo, and what in good sane temporal logic seemed to me impossible, turned out to be something perfectly comprehensible to my friend, though I still couldn't understand it and it hardly mattered. Once more a mystery was explained, how *before* you begin to sing the record already contains the beginning of your song, but it turns out it's not like that, you began from silence and the pre-echo is nothing more than a mechanical delay which is pre-recorded relative to, etc. Which doesn't keep us, when in the concave black universe of the earphones we're awaiting the start of a Mozart quartet and the four little crickets deliver their instant parody a tenth of a second beforehand, from feeling kind of violated, and nobody can understand how the record companies haven't solved a problem that doesn't seem insoluble especially in light of everything their technicians have figured out since the day when Thomas Alva Edison placed his lips close to the horn and said, for all time, *Mary had a little lamb.*

If I think of this (because it annoys me every time I listen to one of those records where the pre-echoes are as exasperating as Glenn Gould's purring when he plays the piano) it's mainly because in these last few years I've taken a great liking to earphones. I discovered them quite late, and for a long time I thought them merely an occasional recourse, a momentary trick to spare my relations or neighbors my preferences for the work of Varese, Nono, Lutoslavski or Cat Anderson, musicians who sound better after ten at night. And I must say that at first the mere fact of putting something over my ears bothered me, offended me; the hoop squeezing my head, the cord getting tangled around my arms and shoulders, not being able to go get a drink, feeling suddenly so isolated from the outside, wrapped in a phosphorescent silence which is not the silence of places and spaces.

You never know when the great leaps are going to happen; all of a sudden I liked listening to jazz and chamber music through earphones. Up until then I'd had a lofty idea of my Rogers loudspeakers, acquired in London after a know-it-all dissertation by an Imhoff salesman who'd sold me a Beomaster but didn't like the speakers of that brand (he was right), but now I began to realize that the open sound was less perfect, less subtle than its direct passage from earphone into the ear. Bad part included, I mean the pre-echo on some records, I sensed a finer sharpness in the sound reproduction; I was no longer bothered by the slight weight on my head, the psychological prison and the inevitable entanglements of the cord.

I was reminded of those faraway days when I witnessed the birth of radio in Argentina, the first lead sulphide receivers that we called "telephones," not so different from our current headphones except for the weight. Also where radio was concerned the first speakers were less faithful than the "telephones," even though they didn't waste any time eliminating them completely because the whole family couldn't try to listen to a soccer match with however many other sets on their heads. Who could have told us that sixty years later those headsets would return to take their place in the world of the phonograph record, and from there — *horresco referens* — they would serve for listening to the radio in its most stupid and alienating form as we can see in the streets and squares where people pass right by us like zombies from some different and hostile dimension, embubbled in contempt or spite or simply idiocy or fashion and that way, see for yourself, justifiably split off from the crowd, beyond judgment, not guilty.

Nomenclatures possibly of some significance: speakers are also called *altoparlantes* in Spanish, and the other idioms I know make use of the same image: *loudspeaker, haut-parleur*. On the other hand, *audífonos*, which started out in Spanish being called *"teléfonos"* and later *"auriculares,"* arrive in English as *earphones* and in French as *casques d'écoute*. There's something more subtle and refined in these changes and variations; suffice to point out in the case of speakers that the term tends to center its function on the word more than on music (*parlante, speaker, parleur*), while earphones inhabit a broader semantic spectrum, they're a more sophisticated term to suit the reproduction of sound.

It fascinates me that the woman at my side may be listening to records through earphones, that her face may reflect without her knowing it everything that is happening in that small interior night, in that total intimacy between the music and her ears. If I'm also listening, the reactions I see in her mouth or her eyes are explicable, but when she's doing it alone there's something fascinating in those passages, those instantaneous transformations of expression, those light hand strokes which convert rhythms and sounds into gestural movements, music into theater, melody into animated sculpture. For a few moments I forget reality, and the earphones on her head look to me like the electrodes of a new kind of Frankenstein whose waxen visage is given the spark of life, animating her little by little, making her leave the motionlessness in which we think we listen to music but which isn't that way at all to an outside observer. The woman's face becomes a moon reflecting the distant light, a changing light that throws across her valleys and hills a ceaseless play of shades, of veils, of subtle smiles or brief showers of sadness. A moon of music, ultimate erotic consequence of a remote, complex, almost inconceivable process.

Almost inconceivable? I listen through earphones to the recording of a Bartók quartet, and I feel from the deepest part of me a pure connection with that music fulfilling itself in its own time and simultaneously in mine. But later, thinking about the record now asleep on its shelf with so many others, I begin to imagine movements, bridges, stages, and it's vertigo facing the process whose terminus I've been once again just a few minutes before. It's impossible to describe — or even to follow — in all its phases, but maybe you can see the high points, the peaks of an incredibly complex graph. It begins with a Hungarian musician who invents, transmutes and communicates a sonic structure in the form of a string quartet. By means of sensory and esthetic mechanisms, and by the technique of its intelligible transcription, that structure is encoded on a piece of sheet music which one day will be read and selected by four instrumentalists; operating through the inverse process of creation, these musicians will transmute the signs of the score into sound. From that return to the original source, the path is projected forward; multiple physical phenomena born of violins and violoncellos will convert those musical signs into acoustic elements which will be captured by a microphone and transformed into electrical impulses; these in turn will be converted into mechanical vibrations which will be impressed on a phonographic plate from which will emerge the record that is now asleep on its shelf. For its part the record has been the object of a mechanical decoding, provoking vibrations from a diamond in its groove (which is the most prodigious moment on the material plane, the most inconceivable in nonscientific terms), and now an electronic system of translation of those impulses and acoustical signals comes into play, its return to the field of sound by way of loudspeakers or earphones beyond which ears are waiting in their microphonic condition to communicate in turn the sonic signals to a central laboratory of which deep down we don't have the slightest useful idea, but which half an hour ago gave me the Béla Bartók quartet at the other vertiginous extreme of that trip which it occurs to hardly anyone to imagine while they listen to records as if it were the simplest thing in the world.

When I go into my earphones,
when my hands slip them onto my head so carefully
because I have a sensitive head
and besides and above all earphones are sensitive,
it's curious how the impression may be the opposite,
I'm the one entering my earphones, the one who's putting his head
into a different night, another kind of darkness.
Outwardly nothing appears to have changed, the room with its
        lamps,
Carol reading a book by Virginia Woolf in the armchair in front
        of me,
the cigarettes, Flanelle, who's playing with a ball of paper,
the same as ever, what's right there, what's ours, another night,

and now nothing's the same because the outer silence muffled
by the rubber rings my hands adjust
gives way to a different silence,
an interior silence, the floating planetarium of the blood,
the cavern of the skull, the ears opening up to another listening,
and the record barely in place with that silence like living
        expectation,
a velvety silence, a tactile silence, something that has the feel
of intergalactic flotation, of music of the spheres, a silence
that is a panting silence, a silent whirring of cosmic crickets,
a concentrated waiting (perhaps two, four seconds), now the needle
runs through the former silence and focuses it
in a black plush (sometimes red or green), a phosphene silence
until the first note or chord explodes
also inside, in me, the music in the center of the glass skull
I saw in the British Museum, which contained the shimmering
        cosmos

in the depths of its transparency, so
the music doesn't come from the earphones, it's as if it surged out
    of my self, I'm my own listener,
pure space where the rhythm runs
and the melody weaves its progressive web full in the center of
    the black cavern.

How not to think, then, that somehow poetry is a word heard through invisible earphones as soon as the poem begins to work its spell. We can become abstracted in a story or a novel, living them on a level more theirs than ours as long as we're reading, but the system of communication remains linked to the surrounding life, the information keeps on being information however esthetic, elliptical, symbolic it becomes. In contrast the poem *communicates the poem*, and it doesn't try to nor can it communicate anything else. Its reason for coming into existence and for being turns it into the interiorization of an interiority, exactly like earphones, which eliminate the bridge from outside to inside and vice versa in order to create a state exclusively internal, the presence and experience of music which seems to come from the depths of the black cavern.

No one saw it better than Rainer Maria Rilke in the first of the *Sonnets to Orpheus:*
O Orpheus singt! o Hoher Baum im Ohr!
Orpheus sings. Oh towering tree in the ear!
Interior tree: the first instantaneous thicket of a Brahms or Lutoslavski quartet, bursting forth in all its foliage. And Rilke will close his sonnet with an image which refines that certitude of interior creation, when he intuits why the wild animals respond to the song of the god, and says to Orpheus:
da schufst du ihnen Tempel im Gehör
and you built them a temple in their ears.
Orpheus is music, not poetry, but earphones catalyze those "friendly similitudes" Valéry spoke of. If material earphones let music arrive from within, the poem itself is a verbal earphone; its impulses pass from the printed word to the eyes and from there raise a mighty tree in the inward ear.

The Character
Jena Osman

It was a fair trial. The body proves the process and the animal shows its wool. This is an idea that allows for immediate access. The fair was not a trial, but a place to show the animals. The man was an animal, and thus his trial was fair.[1] This is not an aesthetic sphere. The equation shifts as analogical contexts reach out and shake the snowflakes over the dome of the city.

see a world salute a sir
who sets a table
and sues the national object
and kills and keels and
bloodies the tent
the hand that pours judicial seizure[2]

detachment, there's order; order is the fruit of action[3]

---

[1] Can we really fault the Russian director Meyerhold for not mentioning the Russian fairground, but instead placing all of his attention on French and Italian models?[a]

[2] The proceedings were complex and required intense concentration; however, N. L. and I found our attention wandering to the man who filled the water pitchers that were placed before the justices. He wore lime green slacks.

[3] Action or animation? It is possible to perceive animation in a completely inactive subject — even in a subject that is dead.[b] There is no perception without attachment.

---

[a] Can we fault *you* for delimiting the justice system within an aesthetic sphere?

[b] "Attachment is a manufacturer of illusions and whoever wants reality ought to be detached." — Simone Weill

Jena Osman

this suspect sets a table of fatality[4]

Innocence applies to the character in the way that fine china applies to a whale. At least in the eyes of the many rides that trauma
the body on its way up and down. Amusements: perhaps you've
seen him?[5] The lines in his hands coincide with the lines on which
you wait hour after hour, at the end of which you cash in your
ticket and fall up and into the sky. The gavel always strikes him,
it strikes him now and again.[6]

a jeer
over part of necessity
I
pull past the fair outerly
past an action.
might a sort of passivity
agitate action?[7]

---

[4]my point exactly

[5]Meyerhold writes: "In [the director's] attempts to reproduce reality 'as it really is,'
he improves the puppets further and further[c] until finally he arrives at a far simpler
solution to the problem: replace the puppets with real men."[d]

[6]See Bill Irwin's "The Courtroom"

[7]"We want receiving centers for dots and dashes" — H. D.

---

[c]in other words, the actors

[d]in other words, the character

"a rest, sit close a while
the sick, the contrary
the following that I speak of
a rest, they'll have a rest"[8]

You purchase a future. It has nothing to do with bars or weights or balance. Look at your punishment as a purchase.[9]

the author of himself's complication

so that one plus one and he
one plus one and he[10]

effort to withhold
a so-called someone in the hold of the boat
the sail as contract
sinking environment[11]

the guard did order
superior orders, infinitely under
put over the other sea sea green
grainy, etc.
contact the circle tangent to discretion
let them know we are here
to enter society

---

[8]For indeed they must rest. The costumes she had designed for them treated the body as an axis from which their limbs could only pivot.

[9]Emerson wrote: "The least change in our point of view gives the whole world a pictorial air. A man who seldom rides, needs only to get into a coach and traverse his own town, to turn the street into a puppet-show."

[10]"Do not presume too much upon my love; I may do that I shall be sorry for."[e]

[11]"A ship is a habitat before being a means of transport . . . the enjoyment of being enclosed reaches its paroxysm when, from the bosom of this unbroken inwardness, it is possible to watch, through a large window-pane, the outside vagueness of the waters, and thus define, in a single act, the inside by means of its opposite." — Roland Barthes[f]

---

[e]in other words, Cassius

[f]see "Cabins" by Max Beckmann

"Knock, knock; never at quiet!
What are you?"[12]

the good me, more
a part pieced across the storm
I
leave a mark
on the destructed
hillock bound

I swear it
I crossed over and then
I fell in

"do you play what the others play
at the beach
by the water
in the core?"[13]

---

[12]I've seen this porter portrayed as a vaudevillian. "Anon, anon! I pray you, remember the porter."[g] Laughter is the societal urge, yet laughter is also that which is most aberrant.

[13]The character said this in his sleep.[h]

---

[g]in other words, Macbeth

[h]or was it you?

The essay is not another thing:
the mis-knowing of the man
is there
The guilty, even his story
is proof of experiments
of conscience[14]

that power is something,
she thinks

whereby a reader is pushed from the page[15]

continuous assault
of fuss

---

[14]Or of annotation.

[15]{turn page over a couple of times very exaggeratedly}[i]

---

[i]{turn page over a couple of times very exaggeratedly}

poor attendant detached from
that to be attended, misfortune,
misfortune suffices not
he fights consolation, the
attendant[16]

there we meet our friend[17]

good resides in us inasmuch
as good exists in anything
the hourly thought I thank you sir
and sit down father
rest you —[18]

---

[16]is that related?[j] I have to agree with you there.[k] I'm not sure

[17]In other words, the character.

[18]I would like to talk —

---

[j]it seemed a bit frivolous to me.

[k]why don't we chat like this more often?

across destruction it is light
not the consolation — love —
it is light
a self transported from letters
into things, the letters themselves
sir, speed you;
what's your will? — [19]

attachment succeeds in an interior
however, illusory;
in this place resides a city
and within resides the border skeleton
our eye skids the steel wall of it[20]

"Then there's life in't."

"Sa, sa, sa, sa."[21]

---

[19]I actually have something I'd like to say —

[20]But I've lost my notes.[l]

[21]King Lear comes back to the surface, and admits that he knows Gloucester."[m]

---

[l]don't you recognize me? can't you see me? your voice sounds so familiar . . .

[m]but will he acknowledge me?

Two Stories

David Foster Wallace

YET ANOTHER INSTANCE OF THE POROUSNESS
OF CERTAIN BORDERS (XXI)

As IN THOSE OTHER DREAMS, I'm with somebody I know but don't know how I know them, and this person suddenly points out to me that I'm blind. Or else it's in the presence of this person that I suddenly realize I'm blind. What happens when I realize this is I get sad. It makes me incredibly sad that I'm blind. The person somehow knows how sad I am and warns me that crying will hurt my eyes somehow and make them even worse, but I can't help it — I sit down and start crying really hard. I wake up crying, and crying so hard in bed that I can't really see anything or make anything out or anything. This makes me cry even harder. My girlfriend is concerned and wakes up and asks what's the matter and it's a minute or more before I can even get it together enough to realize that I'm awake and not blind and that I'm crying for no reason and to tell my girlfriend about the dream and get her input on it. All day at work then I'm super conscious of my eyesight and my eyes and how good it is to be able to see colors and people's faces and know just where I am, and of how fragile it all is, the human eye mechanism and the ability to see, how easily it could be lost, how I'm always seeing blind people with their canes and weird-looking faces and always thinking of them as just interesting to spend a couple of seconds looking at and never thinking they had anything to do with me or my eyes, and how it's really just an incredibly lucky coincidence that I can see instead of being one of those blind people I see on the subway. And all day whenever this stuff strikes me I start tearing up again, getting ready to start crying, and only keeping myself from crying because of the cubicles' low partitions and how everybody can see me and would be concerned, and the whole day after the dream is like this, and it's tiring as hell, my girlfriend would say emotionally draining, and I sign out early and go home and I'm so sleepy I can barely keep my eyes open, and when I get home I go right in and crawl into bed at like 4:00 in the afternoon and more or less pass out.

THINK

Her brassiere's snaps are in the front. His own forehead snaps clear. He thinks to kneel. But he knows what she might think if he kneels. What cleared his forehead's lines was a type of revelation. Her breasts have come free. He imagines his wife and son. Her breasts are unconfined now. The bed's comforter has a tulle hem, like a ballerina's little hem. This is the younger sister of his wife's college roommate. Everyone else has gone to the mall, some to shop, some to see a movie at the mall's multiplex. The sister with breasts by the bed has a level gaze and a slight smile, slight and smoky, media-taught. She sees his color heighten and forehead go smooth in a kind of revelation — why she'd begged off the mall, the meaning of certain comments, looks, distended moments over the weekend he'd thought were his vanity, imagination. We see these things a dozen times a day in entertainment but imagine we our-selves, our own imaginations, are mad. A different man might have said what he'd seen was: Her hand moved to her bra and *freed* her breasts. His legs might slightly tremble when she asks what he thinks. Her expression is from Page 18 of the Victoria's Secret catalogue. She is, he thinks, the sort of woman who'd keep her heels on if he asked her to. Even if she'd never kept heels on before she'd give him a knowing, smoky smile, Page 18. In quick profile as she turns to close the door her breast is a half-globe at the bottom, a ski-jump curve above. Figure skaters have a tulle hem, as well. The languid half-turn and push at the door are tumid with some kind of significance; he realizes suddenly she's replay-ing a scene from some movie she loves. In his imagination's tab-leau his wife's hand is on his small son's shoulder in an almost fatherly way.

It's not even that he decides to kneel — he simply finds he feels carpet and weight against his knees. His position might make her think he wants her underwear off. His face is at the height of her underwear as she walks toward him. He can feel the weave of his slacks' fabric, the texture of carpet below that, over that, against his knees. Her expression is a combination of seductive and aroused, with an overlay of amusement meant to convey sophistication, the loss of all illusions long ago. It's the sort of expression that looks devastating in a composed photograph but becomes awkward when it's maintained over real time. When he clasps his hands in front of his chest it's now clear he is kneeling to pray. There can now be no mistaking what he's doing. His color is very high. Her breasts stop their slight tremble and slight sway when she stops. She's now on the same side of the bed as he but not yet right up against him. His gaze at the room's ceiling is supplicatory. Also, his lips are soundlessly moving. She stands confused. Her awareness of her own nudity becomes a different kind of awareness. She's not sure how to stand or look while he's gazing so intently upward. His eyes are not closed. Her sister and her husband and kids and the man's wife and tiny son have taken the man's Voyager minivan to the mall. She crosses her arms and looks briefly behind her: the door, her blouse and brassiere, the wife's antique dresser stippled with sunlight through the window's leaves. She could try, for just a moment, to imagine what is happening in his head. A bathroom scale just barely peeking out from below the foot of the bed, beneath the gauzy hem of the comforter. Even for an instant, to try putting herself in his place.

The question she asks makes his forehead pucker as he winces. She has crossed her arms. It's a three-word question.

"It's not what you think," he says. His eyes never leave the middle distance between the ceiling and themselves. She's aware of just how she's standing, how silly it might look through a window. It's not excitement that's hardened her nipples. Her own forehead forms a puzzled line.

He says, "It's not what you think I'm afraid of."

And what if she joined him on the floor, just like this, clasped in supplication: just this way.

Yip

Joanna Scott

YIP.

  Yip.

  Yip.

This is a tape of Harold Linder. Brilliant young Harold. I want Harold to be the star of my show. Listen:

  Yip.

  Yip.

His brilliance lies in his uninhibited love of his own voice. It doesn't matter to him what he says. To speak aloud is everything. No, not quite everything. To speak aloud in front of an audience is everything. This is my discovery.

  Yip. Yadderyipip. Yadderyipiphipippityhiphop.

  Yip.

  Yip.

  Charlie looks forward to a tempting meal. Oh, Charlie. Yip. Oh, Charlie. Yip. Hap. Haphop. Do you like soup, Charlie? Yip. Soup, Charlie? Yip.

  Yip.

  Yip.

I found him in Bellevue, where I'd gone to see Mr. Jack Dawes, the leading man in my last production. Jack had been hospitalized after he was found wandering along Madison Avenue *in puris naturalibus*. In other words, in a state of desquamation. Uncased, as it were, and obviously enjoying the attention. I'd received an anonymous phone call alerting me to the fact that another member of my company had come unhinged. As I expected, the reporters were waiting outside the hospital when I arrived, armed with cameras, pens and their ubiquitous notepads. They are always ready to publicize a celebrity's embarrassment. They have built their careers upon such exposure, and those of us in the limelight must accept it as a sort of tax upon our fame. Which is not to say that one must lose all dignity at such moments. As I stepped from the taxicab I raised my hand as though preparing to make a speech, then I walked regally, full of purpose, toward the entrance and into the lobby.

After signing the necessary papers to commit Jack Dawes for forty-eight hours, I took a stroll along the corridors of the locked ward. That's where I met young Harold, who was leaning against a wall and yipping.

Yip.

Yip.

Yadderyipyip.

The clarity of the sound, even amidst the hubbub of insanity, impressed me, and I stopped to listen. At the time I believed he was unaware of me watching him, but now I understand how important it is for Harold to have an audience. No one can be a spectator to his performance without Harold's tacit permission.

Yadderyip. Yadderyip. Oh, Charlie. Poor Charlie. Do you want something to eat, Charlie?

Yip.

Yip.

Yip.

This boy is not mad, I told the doctors. They disagreed and named his disorder, one of those tangled Latin names that always seems to celebrate exaggeration: **hyperbolicisticitis disease,** or something like that. I asked to take Harold along home with me, but the doctors said I would need his mother's permission. So I called her, Mrs. Linder, and asked if I might borrow her son. She refused, of course. Then I told her who I was, hoping to use my name as leverage, but as it turned out she was one of the few people in the city, perhaps the only one, who had never heard of me.

"Mrs. Linder, I want Harold in my play," I explained. That interested her.

"What would he do?" she asked.

"I want him in my show," I said.

"But what would he do?"

"I don't know. Whatever he wants to do. Whatever comes naturally to him."

She said she'd think about it and call me back. A few minutes later the pay phone rang, and it was Mrs. Linder, who during the interim must have called some acquaintance of hers, who warned her against me. "No," she said. "Under no circumstances will I permit you to put my son on stage." I tried to convince her to lend me Harold for a two-week trial period, but she refused. I assured her I was no circus impresario. I was a famous theater director, a modern artist, and I could make her son famous. Rich, too. Still she said no.

Charlie looks forward to a tempting meal. Soup, Charlie. Oh, soup, Charlie. Oh, steak, Charlie. Oh, corn, Charlie. Oh, butter- yip, yip. Butteryoyip, oh butteryoh, ow, ohwa, ohwa, ohwa.

I'm certain that a production with Harold at its center would be a wild success. It's the seduction of shame again. The potential for embarrassment is great when lines haven't been memorized and rehearsed. Imagine the twelve-year-old boy standing in the circle of a spotlight on a bare stage — no painted background, none of my extravagant props or music, only Harold and his voice. The show's suspense would be predicated upon his composure. Should he lose it, the spectacle would become the kind of event that takes its place in theater history: "I was there the night that boy . . ." what- ever. The possibilities for failure are limitless.

Suspense is essential to all performance, from symphonic music to vaudeville. Without the element of suspense, Harold seems to most people no more than an insane creature capable only of babbling on and on. But put the boy on stage, and mere babbling would turn into artful improvisation. It is not just for my own sake that I want to make Harold a star — I am concerned about the boy and want to save him from a lifetime wasted inside institu- tions. Besides, Harold enjoys having an audience — I could tell as much right there in the hospital while I watched him. He pretended not to notice me, but I knew he was grateful for the attention.

Yip.

Yadderyipyip. Oh, Charlie. Do you want something to eat, Charlie?

The first time I applauded him I detected the barest ripple of a startle, a slight tremor in his arms, a twitch of his jaw. I stopped clapping and waited for the boy to continue, but he stared past me at the peeling white wall. Imagine a silence so powerful that you can feel it wrapped around your body — and just beyond, the clamor of other patients. If I'd had any doubt about the boy's re- markable ability I lost it during that nearly endless silence. And then, the burst of sound:

Yip.

Yadderyipyip. Yadderyipyip.

The fact that Harold cannot carry a tune makes him even more unique. Mrs. Linder and the doctors look upon the boy as a malfunctioning machine and keep trying to tinker with the gears and cogs of his mind. But I know that the boy is perfect. In the corridor at Bellevue I recognized in his voice the precise expression of my own artistic ambition. It felt as though he were calling to me out of my past, a voice rising with the night mist from the estuary bordering our estate.

Yip. Yadderyipyip.

A strange seabird calling a warning, splitting the silence into two halves, the voice of the bird separating past from present and defining the space of my solitude.

Poor Charlie. Do you want soup, Charlie? Soup, Charlie? Steak, Charlie?

How tempting it is to twist my life into a dramatic tale of suffering in order to explain my dark art. But I might as well come out with it and admit that I've had more than my fair share of privileges. As a boy I was treated, along with my older brother, to all the pomp and rigorous training befitting the sons of a man who had made millions in the insurance business. I grew up in a stone mansion on one hundred and sixty rolling acres overlooking Long Island Sound. My brother and I had nannies and tutors and chauffeurs protecting us from the world. We attended a small Jesuit day school. Through those early years my happiness was as solid and encompassing as the house, and I believed that the same was true for my brother, though I couldn't be sure. He was an athletic boy, handsome in a puckish way, an apt enough student but a dull companion to my young mind. He and I were strangers to each other not because of any perceptible dislike but simply because we had such different interests. When we weren't studying, he'd go for a swim or gallop his pony Turl along the beach; I preferred to occupy myself indoors.

Our home had a library with panelled oak, a splendid living room with a period Adams mantel, three kitchens and two dining rooms, one of which we used only on holidays. A circular staircase led up from the reception hall to the second floor. The master bedroom was painted a light peach with ivory trim, and the master bath had black and coralline tile and Tang red fixtures. My own bedroom had buff walls and a bay window with a red leather built-in seat. I liked to sit there for hours, reading and watching the color of the Sound change from silver to a satiny black as the afternoon wore on.

I have no disclosures to make about unloving parents or sadistic priests who whipped knowledge into their stubborn pupils. My teachers, all of them tending toward the rotund, were more inclined to whip cream into peaks for their cranberry cobblers than to whip the tender buttocks of young boys. And my parents were like children themselves, dazed by their ingenuity, for their wealth seemed to them something they'd accumulated while out on a Sunday stroll — a pocketful of pebbles and seashells and feathers and gold. And though my father outlived both his eldest son and his wife, even in the last months of his life he could be seen shaking his head in disbelief at his fortune as he walked around the grounds of his estate, his Stetson Sennit at a tilt to shade his eyes against the sun. Life had stunned him from the start — and for this, more than for the privileges, I am grateful.

I inherited from both my parents a sense of wonder and so have devoted myself to sharing that wonder with others. How dull we become if we're not careful. Nothing kills interest like routine, day in and day out spent measuring percentages or hauling trash or teaching young girls how to type, and then at night an hour of the Wayne King Orchestra or maybe a boxing match broadcast live from the Bronx Coliseum. The tedium of competition. No, I am not a sportsman. Neither do I take any pleasure in the dance orchestras that lull their listeners to sleep. I prefer long periods of silence punctuated by unexpected sound:

Yip!

Yip!

My dear Harold, so strange and wonderful. With the boy as my star, I would be able to shake my audience out of the slumber of routine once and for all. People know that they shouldn't come to my theater if they want to be reassured that all is right with the world — they can go to the picture shows for that. My shows are never reassuring. They are as jolting as the modern world, as full of surprises. Harold would be my consummate theatrical surprise.

Poor Charlie. Are you hungry, Charlie? Do you want something to eat, Charlie? Strawberry short-Charlie-cake, Charlie, strawberry shortcake, Charlie, if you please, oh please oh please.

Yip.

Such is the force of a vital personality unimpeded by social consciousness.

Yip.

An individual, alone but not lonely.

41

Yip.

If I had half his ego I would be satisfied. The critics complain that my art is marred by my vanity, that I lack discretion, that I'll put anything and anyone into my productions because I'm too vain to subject myself to aesthetic discipline. My last show, "Garden City," which featured the crazy has-been mime, Jack Dawes, along with two dozen amateur clowns, a marionette troupe and fifty retired chorus-line girls, was nicknamed "Garbage Dump." This wounded me — proof that I'm not vain enough, not compared to young Harold, who exists only as a performer, never stepping outside the role to consider the value of his art. How I envy the boy. He wants an audience, but he cares nothing about the impression he makes — just like a bird that calls out for no other reason than to be heard.

Oh, Charlie. Charlie looks forward to a tempting meal. Wait, Charlie, I've got something for you, Charlie, soup, Charlie, steak, Charlie, strawberry oh . . .

His voice is so completely expressive that any word, any sound is revealing. He could count from one to one thousand, and the audience would be mesmerized. Yes, I like to imagine this: Harold counting aloud, one, two, three, four and so on. It would take three hours, and after Harold finished counting he would remain silent for as long as ten minutes. He would just stand there in the spotlight, his body pressing against the empty space behind him, and then, at last, he would utter a single yip.

Yip.

If you've ever blown a gentle breath into the face of a dog and heard the animal gasp, then you'll know how the audience would react when Harold yipped that final yip. Spot off, and my treasure would be hidden once again in darkness.

Brilliant, yes? I'm sure any skeptic would be quickly converted and would forget the hows and whys and wherewithals of Harold's speech, for all that matters is the boy's acrobatic voice and his admirable self-sufficiency.

Yadderyip. Yap yap yap.

I knew what I was hearing in the corridor in Bellevue: it was the sound of a solitary creature calling out to the world and expecting no answer, like that strange seabird I heard one night when I was a child. Alone in my buff-colored room with its red-leather upholstered window seat —

Yip.

Yip.

Poor Charlie. Yip. Do you want soup, Charlie? Yip. Soup, Charlie?

Strange sounds — you'll hear them in the dead of night, on any night, if you listen carefully.

Yip.

Just as I heard the seabird on that summer night when I was ten years old. Not gull, not tern or cormorant. An albatross? No. A great auk? No. A loon or grebe or piping plover? No, no, no. It was a sound I'd never heard before, and when I looked out my window to find the bird I saw nothing but the shrugging forms of boulders and the iron-colored water. I slept, finally, and awoke the next day to the news of my brother's accidental death by drowning.

Yip.

For years I'd thought of that bird I never saw as a messenger announcing the passing of my older brother. Eventually I came to think of it as a coincidence — a strange sound in the middle of the night coinciding with my brother's death.

Yip.

Yadderyip. Yadderyip.

Listen. Listen closely to the silence. There's always something new to hear.

The silence bearing the meaning of the sound.

Yip.

Water sloshing against the pylons of our dock. A body sweeping up and back, up and back, curling around the wood like a hand, then letting go. Clenching, then letting go. I never saw this; I never saw my brother's lifeless body at all. My parents did everything they could to protect me, short of keeping my brother's death a secret.

The vague details surrounding my brother's drowning led me to think of death not as the exquisite sleep described by my parents but as a terrible mystery, and so I made my theater terrible and mysterious, for art must show us what we fear most. In the corridor in Bellevue, young Harold had me remembering the night my brother died, and in the silence that followed our exchange I found myself wondering whether the sound I'd heard in my buff-colored room had really been a bird's cry at all.

Yip.

It might not have been a bird. It might have been a boy yipping as he leapt from the end of the dock into the water. Leapt, not fell —

such a sound does not arise from an accident.

Yip.

A bird's voice, or a boy's? This much I know: Harold deserves to be heard by others.

Charlie looks forward to a tempting meal. Soup, Charlie. Yip. Steak, Charlie. Yip. Corn, Charlie. Strawberry short-Charlie-cake-Charlie. Poor Charlie.

My marvelous boy.

Do you want something to eat, Charlie? Charlie, are you there? Charlie? Charlie?

Harold has left the hospital and gone to live with his mother. I call her daily, I plead and reason and praise. Yesterday I went to meet her in person. They live in a tidy six-room brick tudor out in Queens, just the two of them for the time being, until Mrs. Linder can place her son in an adequate "facility," as she says. She is a thin woman, fiftyish, a widow, I presume, with hair bleached an unnatural yellow, and she was obviously none too pleased by my visit, though she did invite me in and offer me a cup of tea. I saw no sign of Harold, no evidence that the boy lived there at all. The house was as oppressively still as a museum after hours, with every piece of furniture looking as though it had been glued to the lime green carpet and the air devoid of any fragrance other than the light tannic scent of tea.

Mrs. Linder was out in the kitchen preparing the tea when I became aware of Harold's presence in the house — the very walls seemed to wait tensely for something to happen, for me to leave, I supposed at first, and then I realized that the tension had nothing to do with me. The house was waiting for Harold to continue yipping. I had arrived during one of his lengthy intervals, and the stillness was of the boy's making, defined by his voice and as integral to his performance as any sound he might utter.

His mother clearly does not understand him. She refers to Harold as her "poor little imbecile" and scolds me for wanting to exploit him. She did, however, give me this tape of Harold, apparently in hopes that it would satisfy me and I would leave them alone. But Harold does not want to be left alone — I knew as much while I sat in Mrs. Linder's house listening to the silence, and I knew it again when I was leaving and glanced up from the front walk at the curtained windows on the second floor.

I called Mrs. Linder this morning, and I will visit her again tomorrow. Sooner or later she will have to give in, and I will finally be able to offer my public a theatrical experience unlike anything they've ever known. Imagine: the lights go down, the audience settles into an expectant hush, spot on, and after a long, clenched silence my magnificent little seabird comes back to life:

Yip.

Yip.

Yip.

Kali

Mei-mei Berssenbrugge

1.

First, the beginning, presupposed as a past, goes to ground like a foundation and doubles itself,
Then, I defy inflection, in having this double outside itself.
It becomes a name, the black of an eye, a person you fear, but it's not yet in the world, or fixed in time.
Black means she's unknown by people full of ignorance, since it stands for their ignorance.
Figures on a white teapot in a basin of milk come alive in the milk, a white dog attacking a bear for spectators.
Its dark color is the density, when she substitutes her own gesture, given sense by my compliance with it.
Sense becomes a potential real space, following her like a drift of things.
Vertiginous animality tangles in pleated material of my body.
An animal mother creates a matter double for her.
Its matter is ground, blue to blackness and bare as dread reality.

46

2.

The ghost limb is determined from outside, since it derives from a violent incident, but unified inside by originary structures in the brain stem and limbic system.

She stands in front of waves like a stone on a reflecting surface.

The ungroundedness of waves constitutes the violent character of sacrifice.

A triangle places itself on the sea, sometimes obscuring the woman, like a witch's hat.

The hat, existing "in the air" on what you see, omits what was natural in itself.

For example, fate, an airy image, shakes her from sleep and transforms what you see into a beach of witches

Is realization in matter also required, because folds in matter might reduplicate the folds in her clothes?

3.

Now at night preserves itself as a black bird.

Form is its principle, a trace in dark of a body which couldn't be sensed.

Her being there opens out of her captivity in me, to being like swimming.

Experience of her shifts like a pronoun or originary transcendence and is specified through some other thing, a surface of emergence (motherhood, environment).

I means a pronoun for who's speaking so *I* cannot mean the witch.

The witch, relates to *I* as an index, briefly creating the illusion, need doesn't exist.

Prayer, undisturbed by clamor, is not dragged in the mud, but entrusted to memory.

It goes to the ground and disappears, so if she *were* to go outside, she *would* meet him.

When she threw snow at the bird on the road, it never moved.

The pronoun, whiteness, moved downward.

4.

She spans a bridge over a human being.

She appears black from a distance, the way sky appears blue, but held in your hand is colorless like larvae or an element of the voice.

Crystals are employed to identify this seed element introduced into my body, as if by genetic index.

Matter becomes a matter of my expression.

A fold in matter relates to the light of memory, the way the fold catches illumination and varies according to the light of day.

How does a fold by itself determine "thin" and superimposable depth, the paper fold defining a "minimum" of depth on our scale, as the image of a pleated fan casts a sense of depth in front of the image of a wall?

The cerebral cortex, gray matter, is a large sheet of two dimensional tissue, wadded up to fit in the spherical skull.

A room transforms itself into two dimensions, into consciousness, following a line, like the proliferation of the symbol for her dark skin.

We're made to believe she is the thing per se, she is the picture.

Distinction between the symbol, linked to its object by conventional devotion, and the index, is *how a* muse requires sacrifice.

5.

Red flowers amid dark light reflecting from a plane of water drying up, lamella, maya, as if there's nothing prior for the girl, only this chaotic visual from which a symbol takes its volume.

When the perception achieves speed, a wave becomes as hard as a wall of marble.

You can learn from seeing the pain and humiliation on her face and thinking you caused it.

If everything black embodies her as time, like a wall of black marble, how to think about black itself?

Is it the point of enactment from the symbol?

6.

I don't care for this artificial layer anymore.

Now my mother is dead and dark as the animal's eyes.

Her symbol, which has neither sound nor thought of sound, is the word for the thing which I inwardly speak by seeing it, but can't see it and can't say it.

Her silk gown glows like crystal.

The light wall lends her refinement and immateriality.

Nevertheless, her expressiveness maintains through a place that's neither sensible nor the unity of a synthesis, like stains on patterned cloth behind her.

The selvage is sprocketed, a strip of film, polka dots, her pupils, setting point of view.

A length of cloth would seem to localize in space elements distributed across time.

Love was not a sentiment, because in nature, this pattern had no place.

In me, nothing utilized the pattern as a mnemonic aid, but a pattern can change.

7.

Its soul is a unity of synthesis.

The animal bleeds on the white dog.

The unity is the collected thoughts and feelings of the spectators.

"Auto"-sentimentality conveys this projection of her internal space onto the arena.

Separability of parts applies to abstract matter, not pleats of mass that surround living beings, but veins like a witch in the soul.

She pops out of a planet in a cartoon, moving around earth above my body.

Pleats hold her like an animal in the dark we hear rustle away without calling it.

The absolute is the structure of this process.

It returns from a dark eye, intuited in comic narrative like space at rest, dissolved of every other of time, bad infinity, thought of time.

So bad was your luck, though looking, you did not see the woman came as your daughter and bound her feet.

The witch, my control like medicine, did not end up as a narrative fold in matter, since this communication stretches out indefinitely, absolute achieving its potential.

When the spectacle reached its climax, the shape glowed blue violet in the halo of the ionization.

Fingernails coated with oil were used for this prophecy.

Dead Man's Fuel

Mike McCormack

LIKE THE LEGIONS WHO HAVE gone before and the legions who will come after, I met him on the lip of his own grave a split second after he came over from the other side. He was standing on the edge of his grave, looking down at where he had lain beneath the trampled earth and the whitewashed emblem of his savior. He was wringing his hat into a shapeless mass between his hands, a look of anguish and disorientation drawing his features. Not for the first time did I think that if I had a penny for every time I had seen that look I would long ago have indentured an apprentice and handed over my trade at the first opportunity, then taken my chances with those other pilgrims in the wastelands that lie beyond this graveyard. But I am not running a business and no money changes hands in this land without value; such dreams are only torment.

Their anguish, their torment — so much of it have I seen through the years that I admit now without shame that my soul is totally callused over with indifference. I do not give a damn for their sensibilities anymore and because of that I have been freed to develop an attitude of cold efficiency. It is an attitude which spares me and profits them — previously so much time was wasted in grief and this rictus of foreboding. Now I come upon them suddenly, stalking among the crosses and mausoleums and startling them with my abruptness. I tell them straight out that if they value what is left of their lives then they had better follow me; if they choose to stay where they are and curl up and die, as they inevitably will, then that is a matter of no consequence to me. All I ask is that they decide quickly and not waste my time. Their choice is simple: they take their chances with me or they stay there and die. It's not much of a choice but then this is a world without mercy.

Thankfully, he was not the argumentative sort. He was sharp enough to mark closely the piles of bones that stood at the head of several graves around; he drew the relevant lesson, then remolded

51

his hat and followed me from the graveyard outside to where the stores were situated. On entering, I informed him quickly that he was here to pick up provisions and instructions for a journey he was to make alone and that the sooner he was kitted out, the sooner he would be on his way, taking steps towards his destination.

First I relieved him of his suit and replaced it with a pair of jeans that were riveted and double-stitched in heavy fabric, styled more for endurance than comfort. He turned in his shirt and tie for three cotton shirts with long sleeves, one white to ward off the summer heat and two black to hold body warmth when the snows fell. He was given three jerkins woven from new wool and a long poncho of alpaca which could be belted at the waist and which would serve well as a blanket in the innumerable nights to follow. His shoes were replaced with heavy boots of Portuguese leather, laced above the ankles with leather thongs and lined also with kipskin. He was urged to work them continuously with animal fat and to set by a store of thongs from cured skins, cutting them in a spiral fashion from the edge of the hide to the center to maximize length; thus was the pilgrim clothed.

Nor did he go without armaments. I took down a shotgun and sawed four inches off the barrel and made up the loss in weight with fifteen extra cartridges. I told him that when he reached open ground he should fire off a few practice rounds to get the feel of the gun and write the loss off against experience. I showed him also how the thongs of his boots would double to string a bow from the hickory ribs beneath the canvas tarpaulin of his wagon, and how bull reeds and willow rods would make serviceable arrows — he would have plenty of time to practice the art of fletching using the feathers of grounded birds he would encounter on his route. And I gave him also a curved blade with three different edges for the various types of cutting and scraping he would do. It was bolted to a wooden handle, and with a piece of sandstone and a measure of linseed to keep it whetted; thus was the pilgrim armed.

I took down a book then, a compendium of all the beasts and flora he was likely to encounter. I pointed out those creatures that were good to hunt and eat and those that were carriers of contagion — rabies, anthrax and brucellosis. I familiarized him also with the reptiles and snakes that would lie in his path and the various types of corrosion they bore; those types that could be sucked out without difficulty from a crossed incision at the wound and those that were so potent it would be better for him to lie down on the spot and pull a blanket over his head so that he would not forfeit his eyes to the crows before his breath left him. I pointed out also that it is in the balance of the universe that there is not an illness nor an ailment likely to befall him but that there is also an herb to counter it; an infusion of lungwort will ease diarrhea and chest complaints while a decoction of yarrow will aid blood clotting; powdered mullein is a good sedative and a poultice of burdock will clear most wounds. Against that, hemlock and camus are to be avoided for they are an antidote to no known illness and bring a fever and sickness all their own. I pointed out also that in time of catastrophe he might have to trade a limb to save his soul and that the serrated edge of his blade was plenty sharp enough to saw through any of his bones if he had the nerve for it. It would be a good index of his electedness if he could endure this calamity and continue the length of his journey without a full set of limbs.

We spent some time also poring over maps that are torn now and barely legible. I marked out for him the general direction he should take, his only choice being whether he should walk east or west. In fact this was no choice at all, since his destination was equal distance in either direction from the exact spot on which he stood. My advice was that, so early in the morning, he should set out on his strongest foot and walk east into the rising sun, putting its furnace behind him as quickly as possible for the greater part of the day. I showed him on the maps also those sands wherein it was possible to sink wells and find oases, and those parts that were lush with water-bearing cacti. I inscribed too those salt flats that were without beasts or vegetation and that were to be avoided at all costs. I marked off the narrow defiles between mountain ranges and the stone revetments that were the probable strongholds of brigands and felons and likely sites for ambushes. I counseled caution in these areas and when I had done so I rolled up the maps and put them aside, heedless to his protest that he needed them for the journey. I informed him that such maps did not come in duplicate and that there would be other pilgrims in his wake.

On the question of companionship I warned him against falling in with strangers on his journey. Once he had taken the measure of his own stride he would make better time at his own pace rather than breaking or lengthening it to suit others. But if these strangers were unavoidable then he should stand at all times with the sun and wagon to his back when addressing them and on no account was he to enter into games of skill or hazard where there was a possibility of him losing face or his cloak, for, whatever price he put on his dignity, he could ill afford to part with the latter. And I told him also that if the opportunity arose in the darkness, when no moon rose and no stars flecked the sky, it should not conscience him to take out his knife and open that same stranger's throat, particularly so if that man's boots were sturdier than his own and his oxen had wintered heavily on crushed oats. When first light came, he should hitch up his wagon and move off with no backward glance save to take an alignment from the carnage for he was unlikely to be called to account for it.

I told him further that of all the gullies and ravines and valleys on his journey none would have such depths and sheer sides nor be so lacking in footholds as the vortex of his own solitude, that pit wherein there is no progress that is not circular. Against it I taught him a handful of songs that were of no consequence save their melody and one canticle against sleeplessness; all of these to keep his mind supple and his tongue from falling into a rictus of disuse. In the days ahead without partners the gift of speech could readily flee him and it would be a fatal thing indeed for him to arrive at his destination and be unable to speak his name or give an account of his actions. I showed him also how a simple reed organ could be fashioned between his two thumbs with a blade of grass. It would give a range of two octaves and a fifth and two reeds blown in tandem would allow him to play simple harmonies and extend the range a further octave. I warned him against laughing upon such toys for he would be well glad of them in the night when wolves and predators moved beyond the light of his campfire. I told him that time spent crafting instruments of dissonance and percussion from hollowed bone and cured hides was time spent girding himself against idiocy: all travellers need time out to catch their breath and play.

And to give the vortex of solitude a wider berth I furnished him with a series of mind games to keep him thinking, for, like every human enterprise, death is something you have to continually bring your mind to bear upon. Along with a series of puzzles and conundrums I gave him also the ontological argument and the argument from design. I told him their history and significance and made him repeat them before me till I was assured he had their structure and progress committed to memory without flaw. And then I gave him a series of counterarguments and objections with which he could interrogate them, build them up or break them down as he saw fit. But because of the unique misery it afforded I omitted the teleological argument altogether and hoped fervently that he would not chance upon it of his own volition for it has a pitilessness and desolation without recourse.

Before we moved into the yard I spoke to him of how the terrain and cartography of his own mind would engender many rogue epistemologies and deceptions on his route, how calenture and hallucinations and mirages and tinnitus of the ears would raise up many fraudulent cities and oases in the desert and populate the night with the voices of friends long since departed and not yet conceived. More than on the plains or in the desert, the pit of despair is quarried in the mind and I cautioned him to look to it with the same vigilance he tended to his blade and his boots. I recommended an attitude of doubt and scepticism towards everything that did not glow with self-evident truthfulness except in those extreme circumstances of pain and desolation when wagers of faith were the only way forward.

All this done, I took him around the back of the stores where the joiners were putting away their tools and the painters were finishing the last coat of creosote on the wagon. I told him the wagon was crafted in seasoned maplewood and that with proper maintenance it would take him the entire length of his journey. From this day out he was to look to it as he would to his very soul, keeping it clean and balanced with the weight distributed evenly over the four wheels and keeping also a sharp eye to the desert heat that it would not wring the last sap from the timber and sunder the mortices on rocky ground. Every opportunity should be taken to submerge the wagon in streams and in lakes to let the timber swell to a tightness. As I hitched up the oxen he voiced the inevitable preference for horses but I informed him that the desert floor was well littered with the bones of horses struck down by the brunt of the sun and that these same bones would make good cleaning and scraping instruments; oxen are the draught animals par excellence, creatures of fortitude and huge resilience. I told him how best to fodder them and I showed him the spot of their necks from which, in times of privation, a quart of blood could be siphoned and drunk steaming in the cold night without fatally weakening the animal, provided the incision was cauterized with a hot blade and the ox was allowed to rest at the first opportunity.

He was about to climb on the wagon and move off before he remembered a last thing — how would he recognize his destination?

I told him that of all his worries, and he would have plenty, this would be the least of them. He would recognize it without error in the same way he would recognize his own simulacrum if it came walking towards him out of the desert with the self-same sins of his birth; keep striking a line due east into the rising sun and he would not miss it. I remembered then to take from him his time-piece and cast it in a pile with the others: in the days and months ahead it would be nothing but a torment to him. All he would need to know of time from this moment forth could be read from the elevation of the sun and felt in the slackness of his belly. My final instruction was that if in his life it had been his habit to petition saints or martyrs with prayers or offerings then now was not the time to neglect these rituals; small sacrifices of birds and game should be offered up when he had enough to eat and suffi-cient stores set by.

Finally he chucked the reins and moved off out of the courtyard without valediction or further query. I did not offer my hand in goodwill nor did I accompany him any step of the way but I kept watch until the wagon had disappeared below the curve of the horizon. Then I went inside and took out his bundle of clothes and set fire to them for he would not be returning to reclaim them.

And as they burned no breeze moved and smoke began to fill the yard and I fell to thinking of all the pilgrims I had instructed and equipped for this same journey, more pilgrims through the years than there are stars in the firmament or ants on the ground. I re-membered how I had sent them out, one after another into the wastes, armed with those few chattels and instructions against blind chance and those nameless contingencies that lie in ambush at every step of the road, ready to waylay and leave them bloodied and broken on hot sands or in cold snows, their souls lost forever in this oblivion without any reckoning. I thought of the wisdom I had passed on to those travellers I hoped might profit from it and how easily this same wisdom is ridiculed by circumstances which refuse to reveal themselves; circumstances which bide their time and sneer like sentient beings from behind positions of strength, invisibly watching the pilgrims who pass by heedlessly with the backs of their necks clear and exposed. And I thought also of the confidence and certainty with which I speak out my instructions — whence did I get such authority? I am, after all, a man who has never moved beyond these perimeter walls and I have no experi-ence whatever of the things on which I speak with such eloquence.

I have never fired a gun or strung a bow, my food is handed to me on a plate and in the evening I play cards with the other craftsmen. Now the terrible truth is that I have no faith anymore in my work nor, if I search deeply enough within myself, can I remember a time when I did. I seem to remember it always as a performance, a soothsayer's carnival act, where I flourished these vague conjectures for the astonishment of some rude audience. All I can hope for now is that somewhere in my charlatan's eloquence some of these pilgrims will find material enough to make a fight of it; after that they will have to take their chances.

The fire is dying down now and the yard is filled with smoke. I can see no further than the perimeter wall. Pretty soon now I will walk to the graveyard and bring back another pilgrim. I will go through the same ceremony of outfitting and instruction and with the same air of confidence — I know it well by heart. All I wonder at anymore is the difficulty I have with putting in words just how much I have grown to hate this job.

From Black Box Cutaway
Susan Gevirtz

"telephone, picking it up to begin talking with his wife—back in a village where there isn't and never has been a telephone"

—John Knoop, *Release Print*, May 1995

a piece of smoke

What word is $|_{|}$ $|$ $|$ $|_{|}$

a basket of water
I have two twins, one's face is half paralyzed
Paralysis is a hard tone   tooth on fork

Start behaving and feeling like the donor of your heart

It could also be the other way around
even things that happened in the future
to say that I have a memory of
stained by dark matter

still our hands
fumbling for it

what will happen and adjourn
You   hybridize   subtract from

little   erupt

Susan Gevirtz

The first film I wrote
the eye follows
I wrote the motion the

the screen — I barely utter her word —
your only real mother

Now I'm old and
no one will ask the question

Carve her cunt into the sky
Think garbage, deciphretude
I will go to rest

Who's number 7? That's me
There were things I wanted to say
You coward   You

I stayed here with the weather
vines grew upon me
and old age as algae
between the poolman's visits
all around me reports of (the) sky
little by little by little

the absolutely unmentioned   -able
oh courageous sky

the looked up at
I recall holding that command

Susan Gevirtz

"Tonight I visited the kingdom of shadows."
— Gorky, among the audience of the first film showing

The red and the rose

people only believe in

"the hoser hosed
the waterer watered"

dictatorship of the present
of orange in black and white

We were in a cave by the sea
as if in an aperture   time turns the sea
sepia the sea looked in upon us
an oath descended upon us
— the Lumière brothers promising to work together always

Watch — the horse
            w/out the horse
            w/one horse
            w/2 horses
            and the shadows on the ground
            show the kinds of mounts
            and the period it was made

Susan Gevirtz

Light Before

in night fever   he thought

           Sewing Machine   and saw

how to make pictures move

We are en masse

The first character a crowd

shot in the morning   shown in the evening

         the wind   in the branches   of the trees   behind the
character   feeding the baby   See the wind
make the water   in the lush black
and white garden   pleat

The nine foot high door   closes in your face

a train pulls in
to camera
a station
in reverse demolition
brick by brick
a wall goes
back up

Susan Gevirtz

D V N O I S E

little enchantment

rowing out
suspense in thirty seconds

putting and putting

laundry flys from the mast
in front of dark waves

It's called "The World Nearby"
first you film the theatre
in which the film will later be shown

start the show by showing the audience where they are and
where they have never gone

From above: dusty light pours
into the black umbrellas

stealing the film
stealing into the film
wand around around and around

the word nearby

Susan Gevirtz

ESCALATOR
>   often someone
>   is in the scene
>   who is responding to the scene
>   by reacting to the scene

>   The soccer ball never appears
>   Only four trousers running on white

Line
the house walks into the line of the soundtrack
unrestored
to sound

I am now two people   The one lying down
and the one sitting

in slanted posture
the one
goes up
as if riding
a giant sewing machine

Susan Gevirtz

Telephone to a village where there isn't and never has been a telephone. Picking it up and continuing to talk to his wife: "The man told of his journey and finally asked how many meters of cloth she wanted, then said plaintively, 'She can't seem to hear me.'"
— Knoop, *Release Print*

. . . it's clear we are caught in the crossfire of a war that is not ours. Jeopardy. She sees troops marching and hears the regulated fall of heavy boots. She thinks, "this is war footage   this is where   war footage comes from." I have been taken prisoner. I am enclosed in a small rectangular space but I *can* see out." With terror she looks through her window and sees three windows across the hall with rain streaming down their panes so you can't see through them. This affront. I think, "these are windows blocked by the film footage of rain. They — the enemy — are incessantly running this footage behind the windows . . . so we can't see out."

Things That Have Stopped Moving
Gilbert Sorrentino

SINCE BEN STERN'S DEATH, I've come to admit that Clara always brought out the worst in me. This is not to say that her husband's death caused this admission; nor do I mean to imply that had I never known Clara I would have been, as the nauseating cant has it, a better person who learned to like myself. I suppose I don't quite know what I mean to say. When I think of the years during which the three of us abraded each other, and of Ben's melodramatic deathbed farewell, a ghastly seriocomic scene in which I participated with a kind of distant passive elation, I feel compelled to get at, or into, or, most likely, to slink around the banal triangle of desire, lust and expediency that we constructed, again and again. Simply put, we met, became intimates and relentlessly poisoned each other. With our eyes wide open, to paraphrase the old song. I never really much liked this essentially spoiled couple, and "spoiled" is the word. Somebody once remarked that "spoiled" means precisely what it says, and that spoiled people cannot be repaired; they rot. And Ben and Clara were decidedly rotten. I was no less rotten, although "flimsy" might be a better word, and one could argue that I brought out the worst in Clara. As for Ben, well, he was absolutely necessary for Clara and me to dance our dance. I was sure, almost from the beginning—a portentous phrase, indeed—that Ben was well aware of Clara's "playing around," if you will, with me and with all the other men with whom she regularly had a few laughs, as she liked so robustly, and somehow innocently, to put it. She could act the real American-girl sport, Clara could, a master of the disingenuous: *My goodness!*, I can hear her saying, *just what am I doing in bed with this stranger?* There was, to speak in figures, a kind of heuristic script to which the three of us had limited access, so that each of us could add to, delete from and revise this script in the preposterous belief that the others would act according to these changes. What actually happened, as they say, was that over the years, each one of us was continually subject to the whims, betrayals, neuroses and general vileness of the other two. We pretended otherwise, which pretense thoroughly subverted any possibility of our living lives that were even slightly authentic. I confess that my hope, really more of a velleity than a hope, now that these thirty-five years are good and dead, is that Clara is good and dead as well. Perhaps she is. That I don't know, one way or the other, is dismally perfect.

*

My lust for Clara was awakened and made manifest as an adjunct to a lawful, if rare and surprising coupling with my wife, a sexual diversion that occurred on a Sunday afternoon as counterpoint to Ben and Clara's own marital intercourse. We had known the Sterns a few weeks when they asked us to their apartment for Sunday afternoon drinks and lunch. My wife had met, I believe, Ben and Clara once or twice, and made it clear that she disliked them: she said that they looked like magazine photographs, make what you will of that. But I had long since stopped caring about her likes and dislikes and their motivations. I consented to go, but said something, perhaps, about my wife already having made plans — something to explain what I was certain would be her refusal to accompany me. But she said she'd come, to my surprise.

I was, by that time, wholly aware of Clara's subtly provocative behavior, but as yet had no nagging desire for her, although I was fascinated by the assertiveness of her body, by her — or its — way of walking and standing and sitting, the way, I suppose, that its femininity situated itself in the world. But she was, after all, married to Ben, who seemed to me then funny, intelligent and, well, smart and candid. I was very taken with him and found myself somewhat reluctantly, but happily, borrowing his style, for want of a better word.

An achingly cold Sunday in January: we chatted, gossiped, ate, rather lightly, but drank a good deal. As the afternoon progressed, and the streets took on the cold gray patina of a deep New York winter day moving toward its early palest-rose wash of twilight, we began, blithely, to inject the sexual into our conversation. We told lascivious stories and jokes in blatantly vulgar language, and every other word seemed loaded with the salaciously suggestive. My wife blushed beautifully enough to unexpectedly excite me; to put it plainly, the four of us were aroused, and giddy with desire. Rather abruptly, Ben and Clara rose and walked from the living room/bedroom into the adjacent kitchen, and almost immediately my wife and I heard the rustle of clothes, Clara's quick gasp and then the panting and grunting of their copulation. My wife and I were quite helplessly thrown, by the situation, at each other, and, fully dressed and somewhat deliriously, we fucked on the edge of the couch, recklessly driven by the sounds from the kitchen.

Soon there was silence from that room, followed by whispering and quiet laughter. My wife called out, in a silly, girlish voice, for Ben and Clara not to come in, while we cleaned ourselves and adjusted our clothing. And then we four were reunited, so to say, for another drink. We grinned foolish and oddly superior grins, as if nobody on the sad face of the sad earth had ever been so crazily free and adventurous, as if we had just performed acts foreign to grade-school teachers, waitresses and salesmen, foreign to our parents and rigorously bourgeois queers. As if sex was only ours to deploy and control.

When we had settled down with drinks and cigarettes in a thin aroma of whiskey and flesh, I looked up, by chance, to see Clara looking at me in such a way as to make clear that she had *expected* my look. What was happening? How can I get at this? Just fifteen minutes earlier, on my knees, between my wife's spread thighs, I had known, amorphously and with a kind of dread, that I really wanted to be fucking Clara, I wanted her perched on the edge of the couch, her legs wide apart, her eyes glassy. This sudden crack of lust had come from nowhere, had no gestation, was not the trite fantasy of a passion I'd long nursed for Clara. But her look told me that she knew what I'd thought, that she'd seen into my desire and, as importantly, that she'd felt the same way in the kitchen with Ben. I was, at that moment, amazingly, stupidly besotted.

Less than a month later, at a party, I danced Clara into a bedroom, and pushed myself into her to come instantly, in helpless fury. Clara laughed and said that she knew it, or that it had to be that way, or something like that; but not in a manner designed to make me feel inadequate, but so as to make me believe — and I believed, oh yes — that this first carnal encounter with her had to be exactly this sort of encounter, and that it was *right*. My instantaneous ejaculation had been made into a venereal triumph! When we emerged into the lights of the party, our clothes were disarranged, but everyone seemed too drunk to notice or care, except, perhaps, for Ben. Or so I now think. I now think, too, that the quiet laughter from that kitchen, the whispering, was a revelation — one that I did not countenance — of the Sterns' knowledge that I was but a step away from a dementia of lust for Clara: that I was to be their perfect fool. I grant you that this suspicion may appear too fine-tuned, too sensitive, too baseless. And still, whether it was planned or not, a game or not, something happened that afternoon that drew Clara and me together into a flawed affair that virtually defined the rest of my life.

I must add a coda to the story of that Sunday. In a cab on the way home, my wife, smelling womanly and ruttish, stroked me, and then, when we kissed, gently pushed her tongue into my mouth with a voluptuousness that had for a long time been absent from our marriage. And when we got into our apartment, she urged me to the floor as she pulled up her skirt and we made love profoundly, in that serious way known only to the married. Lying, exhausted, next to my sweaty and dozing wife, I thought that this sudden sexual magic would, perhaps, protect me from what lay in wait for me with Clara. I should say that I hoped it would protect me. But I knew that this behavior had been but an aberration. My wife could have driven me into a reeling delirium of lewdness and abandon, yet nothing would have been able to halt the corrosive idiocy that was about to seize me.

*

I met Ben and Clara about six months before my wife and I separated. We kept putting off steps toward a separation, mostly because of inertia or sloth or cowardice. We lived what I might call a reasonable if delicately adjusted life, but we both knew that the inevitable would soon occur. Once in a while we made love, but this was only to prove to ourselves that we were able to arouse each other, that we were, in effect, still attractive, I suppose. My penis, in such instances, was no more than a kind of mechanical toy that doggedly performed its manly task. We rarely quarreled, for we were rarely together. What my wife did during the long hours, sometimes the long days that we spent apart was of no concern to me. Nor, I knew, were my comings and goings of interest to her. None of this, I assure you, has anything to do with Ben and Clara, but it's the rare spouse who doesn't like to talk about dead or dying marriages, and to turn them, heartlessly, into the grimmest of jokes. The jokes are surely more lethal when children are involved, and when the hatred-infused couple pretends to the world and, of course, to themselves, that they'd rather suffer screaming agonies than forgo custody of or visitation rights with their children. They mean this at the time, through the tears and threats and shouted insults, and it takes a year, or perhaps two, before the adored children bore and irritate them, before they begin to conjure excuses for not seeing them over the weekend, or, conversely, to invent stories whereby the children may be got rid of for a day or two so as to accommodate a new lover—always a really *wonderful* person. This sickening desire to be thought of as busily independent marvel, noble and self-sacrificing parent and righteously angry ex-spouse seems very American. What both parties usually really want is adolescent freedom and plenty of money to indulge its inanities: that's the glittering dream. As for the children, it's been my observation that Americans despise children, despite the ceaseless sentimental propaganda to the contrary.

In any event, I hadn't known Ben and Clara more than a few weeks—perhaps it was but a few days—when Ben decided to enter into a kind of emotional collaboration with me, an odd partnership, formed in alliance against Clara. I didn't truly realize this until some few weeks later, and by then, Clara and I had already been adulterous, and I had no interest in who was doing what to whom for whatever reason. So long as I could see a future of sex with Clara, Ben's motives were of no importance. I think that I had some notion that she'd ultimately become a wife to both of us, but that Ben, and only Ben, would have to suffer the usual domestic antagonisms. I would possess, unbeknownst to him, the spectacular whore.

Ben and I were sitting in their kitchen, and Clara was out. Ben seemed to me intent on making me believe that he was wholly unconcerned with her whereabouts, although he may well have been enraged and humiliated because of his knowledge of her wantonness. He may have considered that apathy and boredom would play better with me, the stranger on whom he had designs. I don't know. He was playing what even I could see—and I couldn't see much—was a weak hand. And yet, now, when I reflect on our wounded lives, I see that I have made the recorder's mistake of *deciding* that this was but an act on Ben's part, because I had, *then*, decided it was an act. But all memories, as even cats and dogs know, are suspect. As if it mattered.

We had got about halfway through a quart of cheap Spanish brandy, when Ben decided to make me, as I've suggested, a partner in his marital combat. I'm pretty sure I went along with this pathology, because, as I recall, I thought that any revelation about her would allow me to get closer to her, to become — it is absurd to say so — indispensable to her. I wanted a glimpse, that is, of her wonderful weakness, her amoral shabbiness. I would have been anything, or played at being anything, to stay in — the phrase is wildly comic — the bosom of the family. That Ben and Clara were, in some absolute married way, as one in their warped lives, was a truth that I would not countenance for a long time. Well, for years.

Ben had got quite drunk, and had pressed on me a book of Robert Lowell's poems, but I had no clear sense of what he wanted me to do about it or with it. I put the book on the table, I took a drink, I picked the book up and leafed through it. Christ only knows what sort of raptly attentive face I had put on, but Ben suddenly remarked that *Clara* had given him the book last *Christmas*, because she knew how much he *liked* Lowell. I nodded and gravely riffled the pages, assuming what I hoped would pass as a pose of deferential admiration for Ben's superb taste. And Clara's! Ben's and Clara's! Ben repeated his line about this being a Christmas present from Clara, and at that moment, I looked, as I instantly realized I was meant to look, at Clara's inscription. It read: *Xmas 1960 to Ben.* That the message was but a flat statement of fact was comically clear: this book had been given to Ben by someone on a date specified. Other than that, the message was wholly occluded. I looked up and Ben was smiling sadly at me, oh, we were partners, we were pals incorporated, but I was not yet wholly aware of my position as Clara's future enemy, only as Ben's confidant. I'm ashamed to say that I believe I felt sorry for him, the put-upon recipient of such cold apathy.

Not three weeks later, I fucked Clara, almost accidentally, or so I believed, standing up in that same kitchen, while Ben was out getting beer. She had her period, but I didn't care, nor did she. Later, I sat in miserable stickiness as I drank one of the beers that Ben had brought back. The kitchen smelled of sex and blood, and my pants were flagrantly stained at the fly. I realized, yet without any shame, what a *brutta figura* I must have made. That Ben did his best not to notice made it clear that I had somehow been played for a fool. For a chump, really. Since I was quite obviously crazy, it didn't matter to me.

*

Clara had been promiscuous long before I knew her, and from what I gathered over time, promiscuous long before she married Ben. She was recklessly sexual, with a vast anxious dedication to erotic adventure, although the word surely glamorizes her activities. She pursued these affairs with the sedulous dedication of a collector of anything, with, that is, the dedication of a kind of maniac. That such sexual avocation is solemnly described as "joyless" or "empty" doesn't fit in Clara's case: she was wholly and matter-of-factly pleased with her churning libido, and the prospect of picking up some happily dazed copying-machine salesman in the desolate lobby of a local movie theater and then silently and efficiently blowing him in his parked car delighted her.

Ben knew, before their marriage, all about her penchant for what she may well have thought of as the free life, and was much too hip and blasé to think that he could change her ways. Such a belief was, to Ben, just so much middle-class bullshit Christian baloney. But he did believe something that was much more absurd than faith in love as rescuer of the emotionally damaged, morally skewed spouse of song and story. To put it as simply as possible, he believed that Clara's marriage *to him* would effect a change in her behavior. He would do nothing, or so I carefully reconstructed his thinking; there would be neither admonition nor recrimination, neither scorn nor anger, neither sorrowful displays nor contemptuous remarks. There would be nothing save an unspoken pity for this poor slut. Clara, annexed to Ben's relaxed, nonjudgmental, affectless and cynical life, would, so he thought, abruptly stop her frantic couplings in hallway and bathroom and rooftop and automobile, in park and doorway and elevator and cellar and toilet stall, her clothes on or off or half-off or undone. Her sex life would seem, when held against Ben's *sangfroid*, utterly and irredeemably square, the provincial doings of a suburban Jezebel in sweaty congress with her balding neighbor. Of course, nothing of the sort happened. Clara's honeymoon and marriage was but a brief interlude in her marriage to herself, to her own endlessly interesting desires.

I never asked either Ben or Clara how accurate my guess was concerning Ben's expectations and Clara's blithe thwarting of those expectations. Not that they would have admitted anything of the sort — I can see Ben's bemused stare and Clara's smile. There is, however, the strong probability that it was when Ben came to realize that their union would do nothing to change Clara in the least, that he abandoned the marriage and became his wife's dutiful if somewhat bored collaborator, and a voyeur who followed her erotic meanderings with a detached interest.

*

Ben liked to reveal, in near-comic confidence, snippets of his life with Clara. He did this, or so I believe, in the hope that I would tell Clara what he'd told me, and so irritate her into thinking that he and I had managed some sort of fragile rapport that wholly excluded her. Sometimes I would pass Ben's confidences on to her, sometimes not; sometimes I'd embroider or condense Ben's stories, and sometimes invent things that he'd never even hinted at.

One of the things he told me, at a time when I was sure that he knew of my affair with his wife, was that Clara had always, and without fail, faked her orgasms. He was enormously amused by this, for, or so he said, he was delighted that Clara thought that she was duping him into thinking that he was a perfect lover. But Ben was as duplicitous as he claimed she was, for his gratified and satisfied response to her moans and gasps and soft screams, to her sated smile, was utterly counterfeit. His fake-masculine response to her fake-feminine pleasure filled her with a sense of, in his pleased words, "smug triumph." At bottom, then, he was unconcerned with her sexual pleasure or the lack of it, and it amazed him — I can almost hear his laughter — that Clara, *Clara*, for Christ's sake! — held to the notion that he *cared* whether she came or not, and that, unbelievably, she was disturbed lest he discover her deception. But Ben was interested only in his own orgasm: as far as he was concerned, Clara could have stupendous, wracking orgasms, real or pretended, by the score, lie in bed a mannequin, fall, for Christ's sake, *asleep* — all was immaterial to him, so long as *he* came. What Clara did or did not do was Clara's affair. That she worked so hard at her conjugal dramatics somehow — how can I put this — *touched* Ben, so much so that he never even came close to suggesting that he even suspected that she might be faking. "Deluded pathetic girl" is what he once called her.

He most certainly, though, wanted *me* to tell Clara this story, of course, and he also wanted me to fret over whether Clara was faking with me. But I didn't tell her, because I realized, despite my attempts to deny and then to rationalize it, that I felt the same way as Ben: I didn't care, either. I once lightly asked Clara what sort of lover Ben was, and she said that he was more of a masturbator than a lover. I think I might have gone a little red at this, for that was what Ben had once said about Clara, and I wondered to whom Clara had said this about me. Outside of, doubtlessly, Ben.

*

The occasions were rare on which I angered and irritated Clara, and when I did, she'd let me know it, as they say, in devious, often astonishingly petty ways, which she never, of course, recognized at all. To describe them is unimportant to the point I want to make, such as it is.

Sometimes Clara would wear an expression of bored smugness, barely but noticeably concealed by "good manners." It was quite a face. It was at such times that I would obliquely suggest — in different ways, using different words and emphases and approaches — that her expression was very much like that of the clutch of well-off and marvelously dim white Protestants she unaccountably admired. This was an expression developed and trained early on, at about the time, in fact, that these people find that the world has been constructed and arranged for their pleasure, but that it is also filled with others who want to partake of that pleasure — which is certainly not their due! — *without permission.*

Such a comment would mildly annoy Clara, but she would become angry only when I'd suggest that many of her pals' mundane pleasures quite wonderfully killed at least some of the bastards off: to wit, alcohol, cocaine, polo, fast cars, horses, skiing, sex, mountain climbing, etc. I would add that although this was surely just, it wasn't nearly enough to even the score in terms of the grief and misery they caused just by being alive, with their prep schools and sailboats, monopolies and stock-exchange seats, securities and trust funds, private beaches and stables, custom-last shoes and shark lawyers; and, of course, their terror of knowledge, contempt for art and the polite fucking Jesus that they trot out when needed. Despite the fact that I would run through this routine, with slight variations, at, as one might say, the drop of a top hat, it would always, *always* get to Clara. She'd sit back in her chair, or lean on the bar, or turn toward me in bed, to treat me to that perfectly constructed face: it was all I could do not to call it cruelly to her attention. But to what purpose? Her anger at my venom — often, but not always, real — toward her beloved idiots was weirdly felt, offered up on what was, figuratively speaking, a tasteful Episcopalian altar. Clara was, for Christ's sake, Jewish!

And still, and still, her vapid, excruciatingly imitative expression was an homage to and defense of that ghastly cadre that, quite naturally, thought of her — when forced to think of her — as a vulgar bitch who would not, no, not ever do.

*

The showgirl with whom I lost my virginity when I was sixteen was only two or three years older than I, but she was so overwhelmingly sophisticated, sexually, that I was awed throughout the entirety of the night I spent with her. We did a number of things that I had hitherto known of only as escapades in pornographic stories and pictures — those rare few I had seen. I was so thoroughly made to realize my own naïveté, that years passed before I could even begin to admit to my callowness. Until that time of candid acceptance, I had managed to turn that night into a liaison of sexual equals, although, as I say, it was nothing of the kind. Her influence, if that's the word, was so profound that I afterward often felt dumbstruck and inept before women with whom I was about to go to bed: that is to say that they would sometimes "become" her, or, more accurately, I would revert to the flustered youth of that night. Such situations, which occurred without warning, usually proved disastrous, as one may well imagine.

My father had arranged this adventure for me, and such was his presence in my life at the time that I thought this arrangement wholly reasonable, even judicious. I can't recall how the night was planned, but I'm quite certain that my father did not ask my opinion. He didn't know if I was a virgin or not, but assumed, given the era and his knowledge of his own life and those of his peers, that I was. He was correct. He clearly believed that it was his paternal duty to introduce me to sex in, as he would surely have put it, "the right way." And so he arranged for me to spend the night with a showgirl from the Copacabana, in those days a glitteringly tawdry nightclub near the Plaza, emblematic of flashy, four A.M. New York, whose clientele was predominantly made up of tough men in silk shirts packing wads of cash, little of which had been honestly come by.

I should make it clear that my father had not asked me my thoughts concerning his plans, not because he held me cheap or thought of me as insignificant, but because, as a Sicilian, he knew that his decision was unerringly correct, beyond cavil, and that

this was so because he was, all in all, perfect. Sicilians, as somebody said, cannot be "reformed" or taught anything because they
know that they are gods: and it was as a god that my father planned
my entrance into manhood. Sicilians are essentially serious people,
never more so than when smiling and chatting pleasantly with
strangers, that is, with people who are not part of their lives in
any way that matters. The smiles and warm, intimate stories are
but devices that serve as charming barriers behind which little
can be seen or known. A Sicilian can talk with someone for years
and deliver a sum total of information over this time that, considered objectively, comes to a handful of comic anecdotes and a
gigantic mass of the most elaborately empty details. And all of
these data seemed deeply personal, private and revelatory. Under
the easy conversational brio, the Sicilian has been continuously
sizing up his interlocutor, and arranging the stories and putative
intimate details that will be perfect *just for him.* I have no way to
analyze or explain such odd behavior: it is simply the fact. My
father, being this way, wanted me to be this way, expected it,
really. And so, the loss of my virginity as a prerequisite to becoming a passable man could not be the result of some dalliance with
a "nice girl," both of us a little drunk after a party. Such frivolity
was for The Americans, as my father called those citizens who,
whatever else they may have been, were surely not gods. These
digressions lead me to another, a kind of exemplar of my father's
way of thinking. When he was an old man, some few months
before his death, I heard him tell some men with whom he had
struck up a kind of friendship in the hospital while recovering
from a triple-bypass operation, that he had been a trapeze flyer in
his native Italy but had been forced to flee Mussolini because of
his Jewish mother, who had been one of the great equestriennes
in the Hungarian circus world. He told this story with such an
expression of wistful regret that for a moment I thought it might
be true, that he had kept some fantastic secret from me and my
mother, that he was actually Jewish! But it had to do with his lack
of concern about what he told these hospital acquaintances. They
were, in his mind, mere Americans, with no idea of what a man's
life is and should be. He was, that is, amusing himself by seeing
how far he could go with these childish men, eager to swallow
childish lies in the same way that they swallowed childish games
on television. I now believe that what he wanted, at all costs, was
to assist me in avoiding such American childishness, and thus help

75

me into his ideal of manhood in what he knew to be the only proper way.

On the morning of my erotic christening, there was no teasing, no off-color jokes or winks or grins, and there had been none for the preceding week, during which time I had been wholly aware of the arrangement. I can't remember what my mother had been told concerning my night away from home, but my father had concocted something having to do with the business. I was, as my mother well knew, expected to ultimately join my father's business as a partner.

That night, after dinner at Monte's Venetian Room in Brooklyn, during which my father talked to me about school, and thrilled me by complimenting me on the dark, sober tie that my mother had insisted I wear, one of his cronies drove me to Manhattan in my father's Fleetwood sedan. He was tall and very dark and disconcertingly still, and we had nothing at all to say to each other. I was intimidated by him, really—his name, not that it matters, was Lou Angelini—by his taciturnity, his air of respect for me as the boss's son and his rigorously conservative dress. We arrived at the Hotel Pierre, in those days even quieter and more elegant, more *raffinée* than it is now. I hardly remember what happened then, but I recall my sense of clumsiness and awkwardness as we walked through the lobby, terribly slowly, because of Lou's slight limp, the effect of what he called a "war wound." But we did, finally, get on an elevator, and then, finally, reached a door in the long, muffled corridor.

Lou knocked quietly, twice, and when the door opened, a pretty girl of nineteen or twenty smiled at us. She had ash blond hair and although her eyes were elaborately made up, her lips were their natural soft pink. Lou looked at her, in her silk robe, up and down, and then left without a word. From that moment on, I was in a detached state of blissful shock, or perhaps happy stupor, as Grace, who later told me that she was half-Italian and half-Polish, showed me, in her words, a few things, more than a few things, that I might like. In the middle of the night we ordered room service and ate ham and eggs and drank cognac-and-ginger-ale highballs. There was nothing romantic or spongy about Grace, and yet she wasn't cold or bored. She was, in fact, what my mother, the circumstances of course being different, would have called "full of fun." When, at maybe four in the morning, she and I danced—that is, she taught me steps to the samba—to the soft radio, it was with a grave sense of play. It was intensely erotic and yet, although we were both naked, not bluntly sexual. Everything seemed magical, and I was obviously insane with pleasure. I had lost all sense of shame with this girl and had, too, of course, fallen in love with her. I even asked her if I might, maybe, call her sometime, a request that was met by a big smile whose import was instantly decipherable: it said, *You are a boy.*

I remember Grace's body pretty well, her long waist, small breasts, the dark auburn of her neat pubic hair. She told me that she thought my father was a real sport, and I knew, instantly, that he had often spent the night with her. She would be, to my father, a nice kid, but a whore, and had her womanly role; not, surely, my mother's role, or the role of the nice unknown girl that my father assumed I would discover and marry, but a valuable role. I always thought to tell Clara that had she been more like the whore that Grace was, rather than the bogus whore that she so contemptuously fabricated, I could have really, well, really loved her. I never said a word, and it has only recently occurred to me that I remained silent because I had no idea of what I truly meant to say, without sounding more like a fool than I had already proven myself to be.

*

On a very cold winter Saturday, I got two phone calls, not an hour apart, from Clara and an old sometime acquaintance, Robert. Both calls carried the news that Ben was very near death, that he had, indeed, about ten days to live. Robert was serious and somber, his voice an annoying mix of manufactured sadness and the self-important tone that bad news seems to make, for many people, mandatory. I did not, of course, let on to him that this was not bad news to me. Clara was her usual glacially sardonic self, much too ironically detached to be affected by something so banal as death. As always, I found in her distantly gelid tones the erotic quality that had unfailingly undone me. It had been perhaps six years since I'd heard from either Clara or Ben, and my first reaction to this sudden news was no better than apathetic. As the phrase has it, I didn't care whether he lived or died.

Ben, according to Clara, would be very happy to see me, and would I come? There was, Clara told me, plenty of room in the big wooden house that they'd bought on the Hudson, and my presence would make for a sort of reunion, I think she said, an *event,* which word she used without the hint of a dark smile. Robert also insisted — he told me that he was speaking for the, God help us, "family" — on the wondrous quality that my presence at the deathbed would add. I was tempted to say "to the festivities?" but kept my mouth shut. It had been so long, what a long time, it's been years, and years, and so long, and on and on. So we chattered, the three of us. It had, really, not been long enough, it would never be long enough. And yet, I agreed to go, knowing what a disgusting carnival it would be. There would be present the shattered rabble from Ben's past life, along with the fawning students, the grim, scowling artistic platoon from the nearby town, the arts reporter on the local rag and, surely, the predictably ill-dressed colleagues in the English Department, who were too hip, too distracted by art and ideas to care about clothes, man, but among whom, I was virtually certain, Ben had cut a bohemian, Byronic, urbane figure — the dandy amid the rubes — for almost fifteen years. And, too, there would be Clara, the discreetly bored, aging bitch about whom the panting saps to whom she'd thrown the occasional sexual pourboire of one kind or another, would circle to proffer drinks, sandwiches, lights for her cigarettes and condolences. They would, each seedy associate professor and second-rate graduate student, smile tenderly and longingly at the strong wife, this astonishing woman who hid her grief with wit and repartee. And each would be happy to believe that this fascinating tramp had taken him, and only him, into bed, car, bathroom, cellar or back yard. What passion had been theirs! Etcetera. Meanwhile, the smudged and blurry wives and girlfriends lurked on the far side of this erotic Arcadia, being, as always, good sports, anonymous in their calf-length skirts and terrifyingly red lipstick.

Later that day, I regretted my decision to travel up to that grim third-rate college into whose zombie life Ben had settled. But when all is said and done, whenever that may be, I really did want to see Ben die, or, more precisely, watch him slide toward death out of, so to speak, the corner of my eye. None of his destructive asides or poisonous denigrations could save him, and for this I was thankful. I felt no guilt about any of these thoughts, or, better, desires, for I'd always, as I've already mentioned, hated Ben for putting me in the way of Clara, and then for getting in the way of me and Clara. The son of a bitch couldn't win, as far as I was concerned. Of course, the three of us had conspired in this plan of desire and need and demand and destruction, and it was somehow contingent upon our simmering dislike of each other. I was curious, too, to see if Clara still held him — and me — in the venereal contempt that was the perfect expression of her nature. I had cuckolded Ben for years and years, although "cuckolded" is not the right word, as I think I've pointed out. I had, from the beginning, been permitted to discover that there was a good chance that Ben had, early on, found out about our passionate indiscretions. I have no authentic recollection of what I then thought of this, but I can guess that I somehow, in some skewed pathology of gratitude, felt a sense of privilege at being the recipient of this couple's comradely attentions. I do know that I had come to worship what I took to be our wondrous freedom with an intensity that went beyond the imbecile.

The next day I got on the train at Grand Central and went up to watch Ben die, and to look into the cold, blank eyes of his wife. She was composed, remote and sisterly, settled, uncomfortably, it seemed, into her flesh, as if she were finally alive, but not quite sure of life's demands. On the way home, I thought of how we had lain waste to our sensibilities, with a truly genuine devotion to waste: we grew old amid this waste. We would not stay away from each other until we were sure that it didn't matter anymore whether we did or not.

*

At the very moment that my mother died, Clara and I were in bed together in the Hotel Brittany. She and I had met by accident on Vanderbilt Avenue and had gone downtown together in a cab. Clara, in her careless and reckless way, lied to me that she was going to meet an old school friend from Bennington in the Village, and I contributed my own godawful, transparent lie. We wound up drinking in a bar off Sheridan Square, and I was soon taking liberties, as the creaking phrase has it, with her in a booth. We had, some six months before, decided to break off our affair of three years. We had no concern, of course, with Ben's feelings, even the ersatz ones we handily ascribed to him, but we were somewhat anxious over the possibility that a full-blown adulterous romance might impinge upon our freedom to have romances with others. We had spent some hours thrashing this out, for we were serious indeed about our prospective lusts.

The afternoon had turned into a windy, bitter night, and a thin, powder-dry snow lashed the streets with a stinging drizzle.

I bought a bottle of Gordon's and we walked through the harsh weather a few blocks to the Brittany, a faded and somewhat decrepit hotel that still retained a semblance of old glamour in the appointments of its raffish bar and taproom, a locale that featured a weekend cocktail pianist, some gifted hack with a name like Tommy Jazzino or Chip Mellodius. I had always liked the rooms in the Brittany, mostly because of the large closets, a strange thing, I grant you, to care about, since I never once registered at the desk with anything even remotely resembling luggage. The desk clerk nodded and smiled at us as I signed and paid; he probably thought he knew us from the night before, or the week before. God knows, the desperately sex-driven all have the same lost, hopeful look, the same imploring face that seems to whine *please don't disturb me before I come.* Such half-mad people are called lovers, a fact usually denied by lovers. This denial is most often rooted in the dreary fact that most people fall, or once fell, into this category, and no doubt think it unique.

One of the inconsequential things that I remember about our night in that warm room, thinly edged with the smell of cigarette smoke and gin, is the fact that Clara, as she undressed, revealed herself to be wearing an undergarment that looked like a pair of rather fancy culottes: they were a kind of pale raspberry in color, trimmed with black lace. She described them, apologetically, for some reason, as a fucking goddamn slip for idiot girls. I can't say whether they were effectively arousing or not, but they were remarkable and quite unforgettable. I've always wondered whether Clara, of all the women in the world, was the only one to wear this particular item of underclothing; I wonder, too, what Ben thought of her in this extravagant lingerie. I never asked her.

Clara told me that Ben was currently screwing one of his graduate students, a serious, annoyingly smart young woman from Princeton, who was, according to Clara, well ahead of academic schedule in the dowdiness department, almost in the same nonpareil league as assistant professors. The girl thought — what else? — that Ben was really aware, really brilliant, really wonderful, his blinding light hidden under the conventional academic barrel. And so young, so young to be so aware, so brilliant, so wonderful. She thought, according to Clara, that Ben would one day write an academic novel to surpass Randall Jarrell! And, in this novel, she dreamed that she might figure, barely and flatteringly disguised, as a complex and wonderfully difficult graduate student. I'm more or less painting this particular lily, as may be obvious, although Clara *did* actually say that Ben was screwing a graduate student. For all I know she might have looked like Rita Hayworth. Rita Hayworth! It pleases me to be given this glorious woman to use as a term of comparison, for this time has no understanding of her at all. She speaks, her face and body and the timbre of her voice speak to men on their own, as they say, morosely distant from wives and homes, half-drunk in the dim bars of half-empty hotels. She stands in bathroom doorways, in a skirt and brassiere, waiting for a light. She is perfectly and ideally dead, as she should be. What, in this age of speeding trash and moronic facts, would such a beauty even have to *do?*

We drank and smoked and Clara cried, not about Ben, certainly, but about her father's recent death. Then I fucked her and we slept. I woke at about five in the morning, and, touching Clara's naked body next to mine, I was instantaneously nutty with lust. As I again fucked her groaning self with a dedicated selfishness, my mother called to me. I could hear her voice as clearly as if she stood next to the bed, or in the bathroom doorway, and as I came, she called to me again, from somewhere out of the darkness of the closet, a wistful, flat, soft statement of my name. At that moment I knew that my mother had just died. How strange and perverse a moment it was, my mind on some eerie plane, Clara pushing me off and out of her, in raw annoyance that I had jounced her awake. I made, I believe, some apologies to get off the sexual hook, prob- ably delivered with a stricken look of guilt on my face, one that suggested how wretched I felt for my lack of concern for her. She lit a cigarette, as did I, and I got out of bed to stand at the window, smoking and looking down at the freezing streets, thus complet- ing, with exhausted flair, I think, the two-bit melodrama. Clara, of course, bought none of this.

I thought, although it wasn't really a thought, that Clara, rather than my mother, should have died, and that I could kill her, right there in the bed. The night clerk would never remember us, and I had registered under my usual fake name, "Bob Wyatt," a monicker so insipid as to be blank. Kill her to even things up for my sad, uncompleted mother, and then commiserate with Ben and Miss Complit. I could imagine their sensitive literary comments, the lines from Hardy or Yeats and Ben's dim smile as I delivered the *envoi* with a snatch of Dylan Thomas, a poet whom Ben loathed.

I was sick with guilt, intolerable slug that I was, and waiting for despair to fall on me in its black rain. Good old despair!, that most durable and aberrant and selfish of pleasures. But despair eluded me, or I it, and as the room began to admit pale January light, I went down on Clara until she very happily came. She was more or less sweet after that, and let me give her my bacon at breakfast. We sat at the table a long time, drinking coffee and smoking. I didn't want to call the hospital and be told about my mother, I didn't want to be right. I didn't want to have to take care of the terrible details of death, the business angle, as Ben had once called it, prick that he was. But mostly, I didn't want to have to pair my mother's flesh and Clara's, but it was already too late to escape that.

Of course, I write this now, years after these events, as the phrase goes. What I then thought, I don't recall. We ate, by the way, in an Automat on Broadway, just south of Eighth Street. It's long gone, along with all the other Automats, along with all the other everythings, but every time I pass the spot where it stood, I can smell Clara. Her subtle sexual odor is uncannily apparent, an odor that she claimed was generated exclusively for me — a preposterous confession that I, sweet Mother of God, believed for a long time. Now I'm *righteously* permitted, I feel, to think of her as nothing but that sexual odor. As nothing but a cunt.

*

The phenomenon of my mother's death in the Methodist Hospital in Brooklyn at the moment at which I was drunkenly fucking Clara, became, some months after the funeral, the source of what I quite irrationally believed would be a revelation of sorts. Of what, I had no idea, but the temporal conjunction of the two incidents seemed too sinister not to be meaningful. I thought that I might now be able to understand the feverishly obsessive erotics occasioned in me by the thought of Clara, because of the coincidence of death and fornication. I apparently really believed that my flatly banal night in the Brittany held some lesson for my life. And yet, if truth be told — if truth be told! — the adventure was, as always with Clara, intrinsically void. My mother's death lent it no importance; in fact, I was, surely, intent on teasing some meaning from this drunken shambles to avoid the shame of self-confrontation: that is, my mother's death, if rightly manipulated, would redeem my debased adultery by lending it a tragic mystery. What childish perversity!

I know that had I been gifted that night with second sight, so that I could have predicted my mother's sudden fall into death; and had I seen such catastrophe in my mind's eye while kissing Clara's sex through her glowing lingerie, her demise would have occasioned nothing that my lust had not already decided on. To be crudely frank, I would have crawled to Clara under any circumstances, come corruption, hell, come anybody's death. So, then, my desire to make these two incidents yield meaning was nothing more than a way of avoiding the truth about my own lust; I wanted, that is, to make my lust important, in the same way that blinded lovers know that their ordinary couplings are unique and astonishing and bright with amorous truth.

Even now, when I think to luxuriate in self-pity, I conjure up that particular night and try to extract, from its various acts, a moral, no, a lesson, a pensum, that will serve to partially explain my general failure as a man. This failure *must* be somehow dependent upon the circumstances attendant upon my mother's death. Or so I hope; for otherwise my life seems to have no meaning at all, not even that of its being. But I am always sidetracked, because I link that night with the night spent with Grace, and that, without fail, allows my father to enter the bleak world of recollection.

*

I occasionally dream of my father, especially when I find myself vexed by memories of Clara. In these dreams, he does workaday things, nothing strange or even unexpected. He lights an English Oval, he leans against one of his gleaming Cadillacs, he turns to me and says "Lavagetto," he buys me a Hickey-Freeman pearl gray pinstripe suit, he takes me to the fights at the Garden where we sit ringside with big, loud men, he tells me he's sorry about my mother, whom he always loved. When he confesses to the latter, he says something about the good veal and peppers in the Italian grocery on Baltic Street, but I know how to translate this secret dream language. But whatever he is doing or saying, he invariably wears a snap-brim fedora, and much of the time it is a white Borsalino. This hat is, I think, a figure for authority and grace and strength, for arrogance, for manhood. A figure, that is, for everything that I once wanted to possess and exhibit.

When I was sixteen, my father took me, on a hot day in August, to a pier in Erie Basin, where he was doing a complete overhaul on two Norwegian freighters. His foreman, a short, dark man of forty-five or so, whose name — the only name I ever knew him by — was Sorrow, took his cap off when he approached my father, and made a slight bow to me. I was embarrassed by this, and looked away at the huge rusting and peeling hulls of the *Kristiansand* and the *Trondheim* riding high in the water. Sorrow said something to my father in Sicilian, and my father answered in English, and gestured toward the ships. As Sorrow walked away, my father put his arm around my shoulders, and said something about the old greaseballs and their goddamn Chinese, and laughed. I should note that by this time in his life my father, who had been born just outside Agrigento and who had passed through Ellis Island at the age of ten, had invented an American birthplace for himself, and had given himself a wonderfully burlesque "American" middle name, Kendrick. My mother often delightedly said that he claimed a birthday on, sometimes, the Fourth of July, and sometimes Flag Day. And yet my mother, for all of her bitterness toward this man from whom she had been separated for twelve years, never spoke of him without a subterranean admiration and affection that I had no way of reconciling with her anger and sense of betrayal. He was to her, I now think, the only real man in the world, and she had often told me stories of their courtship and early marriage that were suffused with details that were at once innocent — almost girlish — and oddly erotic. On that pier, though, whatever he may have been to my mother, he seemed to me a magical stranger in a beautiful hat and a tropical worsted suit of so creamy a tan that it seemed to blush. I knew why Sorrow was so deferential, for my father radiated an authority that created him a figure endowed with authority: he made, that is, a self that was, then, his self. It was not, that is, the creation of someone that he was not, a kind of con-man invention that, for some reason, many people admire, but was infinitely more subtle than that: he had successfully endowed, in some mysterious way, certain traits of manhood with a style that was not naturally or specifically intrinsic to them, but which became so at the moment of his appropriation of them. It was this, I suspect, that so enthralled my mother.

Norwegian ships, back in the forties, were generally agreed to be, by the longshoremen and stevedores, scalers and painters who worked on the Brooklyn and North River piers, the filthiest afloat. This may or may not have been true, but it was accepted as such, until even the Norwegian seamen who sailed on these tubs came to believe it, and, in a perverse way, to flaunt their ships' squalid conditions. They may not have been any cleaner than those sailing under different flags, but their reputation for egregious feculence had been solidly fixed.

My father and I had walked about half the length of the pier, and when we were about even with the fo'c'sle of one of the ships, he struck up a conversation with a man called Joe the Ice. He was in a powder blue gabardine suit, white shirt and navy tie, and wore a little teardrop diamond in his lapel. I had come to learn that Joe had something to do with what my father called "collections," not that it here matters. He seemed to me benign and rather affable, but he had an air of being, so to say, all business. There was a story that my Uncle Ralph told about a deckhand on a Moore McCormack tug who was still paying the weekly vig to Joe on a loan he'd made some eleven years earlier. He rarely complained, so my uncle said: he was whole and working.

I suddenly realized that my father had a wad of cash in his hand, and he said to Joe that five grand was jake with him. Joe took out a handful of cash from a tattered red manila portfolio, and counted out five thousand dollars. My father called Sorrow over, all three spoke briefly in Sicilian, and Sorrow took the ten thousand. I was astonished and bewildered, amazed, really, at having seen ten thousand dollars produced, so to speak, out of the air, in the oily heat of the Red Hook summer afternoon. My father smiled at me, and told me, in as few words, that he'd made a bet with the Ice, even money, that he could walk through the *Trondheim*, from the holds, up through all the decks, onto the main deck and the bridge — walk through the whole ship — without getting a spot or smudge or smear of oil or dirt or rust on his clothes or hat. Then he left me to Sorrow and Joe, and walked up the gangplank. I stood with the men, and, by now, a few scalers who were coming off shift. In a minute, the entire pier knew of the bet, and men waited patiently to see my father appear at the gangway. My father insisted that an electrician who worked for the Navy accompany him to make sure that everything was done right.

My father won the bet, came out spotless and then took me to Foffé's on Montague Street, where he had a Scotch or two, and I drank 7-Ups, and then we drove to a haberdashery near the old Latin Quarter. He bought me a dozen lusciously soft, white broadcloth shirts, and, deferring to my somewhat dim taste, a half-dozen silk ties, the latter spectacularly "Broadway," ties that my mother called "bookmaker" ties. She swore that my father had no sense at all, buying a high-school boy such expensive things, but then told me a story about his spending his last twenty dollars on a hat to impress her before they were engaged. I had heard this story, with subtle and loving variations and embellishments, many times.

When I think of that sweltering Brooklyn, so long dead, and my father in his beautiful clothes, with his strong face and huge hands; and when I think of the casually arrogant way in which he bet five thousand dollars, on a kind of whim; and when I, still and always amazed, realize that he had that money in his pocket, I sometimes get up and look at myself in the mirror. I look like my father, but I am not, not at all, like my father. What would he have said about my deformed relationship with the Sterns? About Clara standing me up God knows how many times? About the weakness or lack of will or courage that prevented me from abandoning the whore, prevented me from marrying some woman whose flaws were, at the very worst, the flaws of sanity? What?

When I dream of my father in his spotless hat and, waking, wish that I could have somehow appropriated the authority and confidence that I, of course irrationally, think it to have possessed, I am unfailingly left with the truth that it was my father's Borsalino. And only his.

*

Patsy Manucci, one of my father's drivers and a kind of sidekick who provided my father with a gin-rummy partner and a brand of raucous and mostly unintentional comedy, had a brother, Rocco, of whom, as a boy of fifteen or so, I was in awe. He was a horse of a man, almost, indeed, as thick through the chest and shoulders as a horse, and he spoke in a gravelly voice that was, as the phrase has it, too good to be true. Patsy possessed the same voice, and when the brothers had a discussion or argument about handicapping, the din of their colloquy could be heard through closed doors and even walls. My mother, who liked both brothers, said that their voices were the result of years of shouting the results from the candy store out to the street corner. I did not know what "the results" meant, but I knew that Patsy loved this crack, as he worshiped my mother, and thought it so funny that he repeated it everywhere.

He often said, with the most solemn and respectful of faces, that Rocco was a graduate of Fordham, where he'd studied medicine, a lie so preposterous that nobody ever had the heart to call

him on it, or for that matter, even to laugh: people would listen
to this wistful, crazy revelation and nod their heads in understanding. *Life!*, their nods regretfully said, *Ah, that's how life is.*
Once, my father, in a context I no longer remember, broke this
unspoken rule of solemnity, and said that Rocco had graduated
from Fordham's "upstate campus," which caused the men with
whom he'd been talking to burst into laughter. I laughed too, but
had no true idea why.

Rocco was a runner for a policy operation headed by a man
named Jackie Glass, who always dressed beautifully in Oxford
gray or navy blue suits, white shirts, repp-striped ties and French-
toed shoes that seemed as soft as gloves. He was married to an ex-
showgirl, a tall, hard redhead, and they had two spoiled blond
children, Marvin and Elaine, who got everything they wanted,
or so it appeared to me. His wife's name was Charl, short, I discovered, for Charlene. Jackie was connected, as the phrase had it,
with one of the New York families, I don't know which one, which
gave Rocco, in my adolescent eyes, the most weighty authority:
he worked for a man who worked for serious people who had a
great deal to say about the running of many things, including the
city.

But this was the lesser part of what enthralled me insofar as
Rocco was concerned. Rocco was a gambler, but a gambler who
existed in a kind of Paradiso, an Eden, an empyrean of gambling
that was wholly unreal to me. One night he won sixty thousand
dollars in a crap game up on Pleasant Avenue. Even in this time,
when people who can barely sing, dance, act, hit a ball or throw a
punch make millions for barely doing these things, sixty thousand
dollars is a lot of money; in 1944, when a seventy-five-dollar-a-
week job was thought to be the key to a big apartment on Easy
Street, it was, simply, a fantasy amount. Rocco lost the sixty grand
two days later in another crap game on Elizabeth Street.

To win it. To have it. To let it all go. To say to hell with it.
That's what fascinated me about Rocco. It's the way I've always
wanted to live, the way I've wanted to act with the men and
women I've known, with, of course, especially Clara. I've never
had the courage, that is to say that I've never had the courage to
act on my belief that the world, beyond all its endlessly rehearsed
wonders and beauties, is absolute shit, that life is best when ignored, or somehow turned away from, and that nothing should be
taken at face value. In sum, that everything is a pathetic bust. But

I have always acted otherwise, as if there is, perpetually, the possibility for change, for amelioration, for friendship and love. I have, that is, always and unforgivably, acted as if there is hope. But to say: Fuck life! I've never managed it, or if I have, it was momentary, melodramatic gesture, empty and contemptible. I think, in effect, of losing sixty thousand dollars, and, without fail, make my craven accommodations. I will not, ever, let it all go.

*

Some few years into my absurd relationship with Clara, a friend of mine, who had rented a ramshackle beach house on Fire Island for the month of September, had to return to the city with a little less than two weeks left on his lease. He asked me if I wanted to take the place, gratis, for this period, and I agreed, thinking to ask Clara to make some excuse and spend this time on the island with me. She had been, for some months, disconcertingly faithful to Ben, and I thought that a time alone together, as the strangely lugubrious old song has it, would work to revive our passion, a passion that, I'm afraid, I remembered as a series of dissolving pornographic tableaux. I think that one usually remembers love as a totality of experience and feeling, a complex in which the sun that falls on the kitchen table in the morning is part of the emotion attendant on the beloved; whereas lust is simply the recall of the purely and metonymically salacious. Clara was a duchess of lust, as I have tried to make clear, and images of her in divers erotic scenes were, overwhelmingly, images of dazed carnality. In any event, I told her of my sudden luck and asked her to come. I implored her to come.

A day or two later, she told me that she'd invented a story for Ben, complete with a sick school friend or a spontaneous reunion, faked phone calls, a fantasy airline reservation, something, everything. I had no way of proving that Clara had done any of this, and I've been long convinced that Ben had joined in this spurious drama, had helped to fashion his own betrayal. Clara was, and probably always had been one of the machines by the use of which Ben was assisted in his seductions of fragile students and frowzy colleagues and the wives of friends — the butcher and the baker, for all I know. Perhaps even my ex-wife. At the time, all I cared about was Clara involved in lovemaking with me. With me!

We took the ferry from Bay Shore one warm morning, and then clomped along the boardwalk to a disreputable, weathered shack in Ocean Bay Park. Clara had laughed on the ferry as she described Ben's sour expression as she prepared to leave. She had a neat, well-turned story for almost every occasion, and in me the most willing of listeners. Nothing was on my mind but her, I had become desire, ah, how wonderful and dirty she was, her light perfume piquant with the salt air of the Sound. The moment we slammed the door of the musty shack, Clara almost coyly pulled off her T-shirt and stepped out of her shorts. Was I not the most finished of seducers?

Those ten days, however, ended with my morose wallowing in bitter nostalgia. Clara, of course, noticed my tragic expression, and, although people's feelings held little interest for her, she was manifestly disturbed that this germ of misery might make me less reliant a sexual partner than she had bargained for. She had given me two weeks of her time and had spent her energy to be with me; she did not expect gloom and silence. My ill-concealed distemper and preoccupied air turned the last few days of our sojourn into a chilly period of reading and glum card games.

I had been made wretched — blue is, I suppose, the best word — by a delicate, faded memory evoked by ocean and beach, a memory of fifteen years earlier, when a woman I had loved, loved to distraction, spent a summer with me in a rented cottage on the island's North Shore. There is little point in rehearsing the serene joy of that summer, other than to say that I could not, perhaps did not want to drive from my mind the image of her sitting across from me in the early twilight on the little flagstone patio behind the two-room cottage. She was, in this image, always in white: shorts and T-shirt, skirt and blouse, pinafore, crisply dazzling summer dress, and her tan glows warmly against the candor of her lovely white clothing. She holds a gin and tonic, and as she leans forward to light her cigarette from my proffered match, she looks up and her dark eyes astound me.

I did a really thorough job of destroying this love when we returned to the city in the fall, by means of a cruel apathy, one that I even more cruelly pretended was a distraction caused by painful personal concerns that could not be shared with anyone — especially with her. So that was that. I saw her, many years later, well after my marriage and divorce, while Clara and I were in an early phase of our demented, futile eroticism. It was in sad Tompkins Square, on a gray, humid day just made for mania. We did not acknowledge each other, but the look of understanding that crossed her face, the comprehension of my flimsy reality that registered on her calm, beautiful features, almost stopped my heart. She had, as the phrase so aptly puts it, seen right through me. I thought to speak to her, to ask her — I don't know — to help me, perhaps? I thought I'd vomit, but was spared at least that shame.

*

Wittgenstein famously closes the *Tractatus* by writing that "what we cannot speak about we must pass over in silence." I'm not certain that I agree with this beautifully subtle, frigid refutation, or, perhaps, critique, of the empty blather with which we are surrounded every day. My rejected and buried Roman Catholicism rouses itself at this proposition, flaunting, quietly to be sure, the garrulous sacrament of Penance as counterbalance to Wittgenstein. God knows, the very act of confession, the snug dark of the confessional, the confessor's aloof profile in the gloom — all these virtually guarantee that the penitent will most certainly attempt to speak, in halting improvisations or rehearsed platitudes, about those sins and crimes and dark longings which cannot ever be represented in language. Silence will not do in the confessional, and the unspeakable always finds a voice, garbled and inexact though it may be.

Yet outside of the fierce niceties of the elaborate ritual that makes Roman Catholicism a sly, gay and mysterious game, never to be understood by functional and palsy-walsy Christianity, I do indeed understand Wittgenstein's blunt postscript. It has been my experience that we cannot speak about anything at all, and yet we rattle on, our ceaseless chatter so much a part of our lives that even the hackneyed concept of "last words" is enshrined as a phenomenon of grave importance, as if it matters what anyone says entering the dark nullity. We refuse, really, just as if we were all ensconced permanently in a universal confessional, to pass over the unspeakable in silence. We start. We continue. We go on and on, through childhood and adolescence, fornication and pain and disease and death. Talking to make sense — how sad the very idea! — of childhood and adolescence, fornication and pain and disease and death.

This story that I have told, or made, such as it is, for instance, with a half-submerged truth here and a robustly confident lie there, with a congeries of facts and near-facts everywhere, this story is an exhibit of speech about something of which I cannot speak. For years, I did pass over it, quite obediently, so to say, in silence. Then, for no reason that I can point to, I decided to ease my mind by speaking, if not the unspeakable, then the difficult to speak. As I half-knew they would, each page, paragraph, clause, sentence, each word pulled relentlessly and stubbornly away from that which I had thought to say. So that my speech, I now see, has made the past even more remote and unfocused than silence would have. But I declare that I have spoken the truth, or something very close to it.

When I say that my narrative is not quite representative of the actuality of the experiences it purports to represent, I play no semiological games. That is to say that were the act of signification a wholly successful transaction with the real, I could still never have effected the proper transaction. I have no language for it, there is no language for it. Just as well that words are empty. How terrifying true representation would be!

This story is dotted with flaws and contradictions and riddled with inconsistencies, some of which even the inattentive reader will discover. Some of these gaffes may well be considered felicities of uncertainty and indeterminacy: such is prose. The tale also, it will have been clear, occasionally flaunts its triumphs, small though they may be. I am afraid that the final word about the gluey, tortuous, somehow glamorously perverse relationship that Ben and Clara and I constructed and sent shuffling into the world hasn't been arrived at; but perhaps the unspeakable has had created some sad analogue of itself, if such is possible. Something has been spoken of, surely, but I can't determine what or where it is.

In any event, I've spent a fair amount of time and attempted a degree of care in the creation and arrangement of these fragments. There are moments or flashes when I believe that I have seen myself, in a quirk of syntax, as I really was, when I can swear that Ben or Clara are wholly if fleetingly present in these simulacra of the past. Moments, flashes, when this admittedly inadequate series of signs seems to body forth a gone time. But I know that this is nonsense, nothing but a ruse with which I have been faithfully complicit so as to make the landscape of my life seem more valuable and interesting than it ever was.

Without Pity
Elizabeth Willis

To embark sleepily

being everywhere

(radiant)

To fashion oneself

wholly after dogs

To talk oneself out of

a beautiful illness

eschewing affection

and envying lilies

How were the fish eaten

the fire carried

If beauty came

only by restraint

How does a ghost eat?

Even Mary crumbled under piety —

her stone son

Understanding misery

never to desert it

What can be forgiven

of its dangerous body

(not a constant)

To find the branch

of an underground river

while tongues wag out

the weakest things

To escape design

(its "higher calling")

To make or love

anything

To hate the agony

of any human thing.

Burial Plot
Nathaniel Tarn

To be away from mind
or even start to move away from mind:
it is to be as far as nothingness,
as you, in your far box under the ground,
skip from horizon to horizon
yet all your death not knowing movement —
not realizing here that, on the largest scale,

it is all going on at the same time.

As for your "waking life"
which is but one small part of "sleep"
longer than any time we can imagine —
                that "waking life":
you think it is the window of our dream
                onto the universe
from which we see, or hope we see

into the furthest reaches of the moment.

            But the truth of it
is that the lying in that box,
                our long-surviving home,
is where we have the time at last
to see the depths of all our lives
past, present and to come,
there to imagine mind in all its splendor,

            an original face.

What is the ending of time
when time has apparently ended
but not for all? Its face to you
            if your eyes are still?
Why do you think those in their boxes
no longer can remember your existence
when they have nothing else to think of

    all their death through?

Why, in your thoughts, do you still wait
for some such break of time
as might put stop to a long meditation
where you have been quite out of time
but, in the same event, wished to re-enter it?
Where plot is chosen, the fiction will enact
endings foretold, a structure closed — not

open, fairy-like, when mimic of desire.

We had moved north to the most spacious
lots of a growing town. The box lies south
where we shall lie, the one atop another,
among much tighter acres. There we shall be
crowded with everyone where all can go —
            yet time is never crowded.
Now to move planets on. Eyes swivel inward,

witness all love. Better not feed the moon.

From And How on Earth
Anselm Hollo

The how *has always struck me as more interesting
than the* why.

*The "titles" of individual parts = silent movie
captions.*

> the poem
> a pattern of tea leaves
> on the bottom of the cup
>
> *(maybe Basho?*
> *maybe Goethe?*

VOICE OVER PAST HOUSE

rampant apprehension gone

sneeze twist remember trouble

wise old dog   tulips in bed

red green murmur turn-on

exactly walk

every stalk

come down slowly

write it back long thread

wing down corner zoom through stem

back to moon   or worm song

O PONDER BONE OF FABLED CARP

distant in time now,
maman
          equals pigeon

          duchess of echoes

          in hidden ruins'
          barefoot patter

memory seizes bundle, rides
horse of no illusion

ear tracks cricket blessings
clouds & echoes

translates, fabulates
umbrella afternoons

          arrow flashes
          the diminutive trembles

          in entourage of antennae
          gods hammer ears
          warlords groan exhausted

caress hair,
          lament tangle
in pale fits of ink

Anselm Hollo

SECRET COHESIVE TACTICS

Blip off dim sunset. Blip on wild din sunrise!
Rise, Sun! Roar! Screen falls off
Falls off complicated
Fits of unreadable gridlock. Come sane, please?
Slow-lit mind skips out to prance,
Gods' summer legs delight green fool.
Love mind, mouse, moon,
& chansons, & cricket chirps.
Chase feast, unwind, let mind ships hover.
Hover, pencil shadow. First snooze, best snooze?
O dark ancestral snooze: spin yarn, hitch smoke —
Flower strange ways. Rise, sun, roar
On serendipitous dill brine,
Gather voice from house now ash and air.

TEMPLE NOIR

Images distributed about her, unceasingly, like moths:
totalized in cognitive map of hair specific to these
exercises on the Trail of Death and Ruin, as preface to
"adventure moment."

Notice she was gowned in actuality, and yet, as the other
functions which followed her head leaped into instant
anteriority, the dance became problematic.

There was much more to the same effect: precise
lugubriousness.

The analytic craze was at its height, shriveling souls with
sardonic laconicism in the foyer of instant fame — *her name:*
it jerked up with murmured absentation — a coincidence she
thought to emphasize, when her eye chanced to imagine
this *referentiality* gazing at her, so *dialectical . . .*

Anselm Hollo

APOCRYPHA HIPPONACTEA

fly likes smell of shit

△

sweet flesh hope creatures
loiter, does, in browse fest
where dank lads roam on sassy paws
. . .
charmed subject entire[ly?]

△

sillily jot swill slur

△

endure future   crouched in cellars

△

"I got *mine*. But I ain't got *enough!*"

△

toss possible musical peony
gentle apparatus
into sudden sea

△

you must assume that this
has nothing to do with you

Anselm Hollo

THE JOB

hushed, turned away
from uninspired diatribe platform

certain of being thoughts
alone but tactile

see bodies distilled in tragic nod
hear call: "wake, wizard!
cut time!
dispell this razor air, cold stratagems
      and whale anxiety"

in wild incessant years
                dusk horses throng

air roars through aeons of babble
whispers laconic protocols

         prance advance to glimpse
         sprawl in realm of caw

smile on, not quite animate
in glorious timing of blue
and mostly excessive flit

VIBRANT IONS

      minutes
            selves
        socks

    all one dune

                    come again?

                  I will

desire floats
      in a cyclone of dizzy cares

Homecoming
Can Xue

— Translated from Chinese by Ronald R. Janssen and Jian Zhang

AS A MATTER OF FACT, I'm very familiar with this area. For some time I came here every day. However, now it's too dark, and the moon is reluctant to come out, so I can go forward only by instinct. After a while, I smell an odor. It's from a small chestnut tree. Past the chestnut tree, dry grass crackles under my step. Now I feel relaxed. Here's a stretch of grassland. No matter which direction you face, you can't reach the end of the prairie without at least half an hour's walk. The ground is very flat, without even any dips. Once my younger brother and I conducted an experiment here by walking forward for ten minutes with our eyes closed. We both came out of the trial safe and sound.

Reaching the grassland I wander about aimlessly. I know soon afterwards I'm going to see a house. Ultimately I will arrive there without even needing to think about it much. In the past this method always brought me unexpected joy. Once I enter that house, I will sit down and drink a cup of tea with the owner (a pale-faced gentleman with no beard or hair). Then one breath will take you down along a zigzag mountain trail until you reach a grove of banana trees. The owner is fairly kind, and he always sees me off to the corner, where I have to turn, reluctant to part. He always wishes me good luck. The most comfortable thing is the downhill trail, which is very easy to walk. Soon there will appear a monkey to greet me. Each time I nod at him, and then he leads the way. Usually when I reach the banana grove, I lie down beneath a tree and eat my fill. Then I go home. On my way home there is no monkey. Of course, I wouldn't lose my way, because everything is so familiar to me. Strangely, the way home is again downhill, and I walk without any effort. How come? I've never understood the logic in this.

Wandering like this, I reach the house, because my forehead has suddenly bumped into the brick wall. Tonight the owner of the house hasn't put on the light. Nor does he greet me from the stoop as he usually does.

"Why should you come so late?" he says from inside the window. He sounds a bit unhappy. Feeling his way around for a long time, he opens the door with a creak.

"I can't turn on the light," he says. "It's too dangerous. I guess you still don't know that behind our house there is a deep abyss. This house was built on the cliff. I have been hiding this fact from you in the past. But now I can't do it anymore. Do you remember that I always accompany you to the corner, chatting about something interesting? I was afraid that you would turn your head and see the position of the house!"

I sit down at the table.

"That's not too difficult," the owner continues. In the darkness he passes a cup of lukewarm water into my hand. "Once in a while it comes out. I mean the moon. You can see it now. I definitely can't turn on the light. Please forgive me. This house has reached its dying age. Please listen, and you will understand everything."

What he has said is patent nonsense. It's obvious to me that the house is situated at the end of the flat grassland with its back toward the mountain. I can remember clearly. Once I even circled around to the back of the house and fed pigeons there! But now he has made it so terrifying that I have to be more cautious.

It's true that the moon still hasn't come out, but there's no sound whatsoever from the outside. It's a silent, suffocating light. It could be that the owner has lost his mind during my absence for all these years.

He sits quietly in front of me, smoking.

"Maybe you don't believe me. Just stand up and have a look!"

Supporting myself with the table, I stand up. All of a sudden I fall forward onto the ground without anybody pulling me.

"Now you know." I guess he is smiling slightly. "It's terrible, such a thing. Light is absolutely forbidden. And the banana grove can only be reached under the condition that you do not turn your head and look back. Besides, that is something that happened many years ago. Now you might not even have any interest."

"Now I have to wait until morning to leave." I sigh and say, "When the dawn comes I can see outside and it will be convenient for me to go then."

"You're completely wrong," he says, deep in thought while smoking. "There won't even be a question of dawn. I've told you that

102

such a house has reached its dying age. Can't you imagine what's left? Since you have forced your way in, I have to arrange a room for you. Of course, the light cannot be turned on. You'd better calm yourself down and listen. You can hear how those sea waves are striking against the cliff."

Of course I can't hear anything. Outside the window appears a dark shadow that might be the mountain. I remember this house is located at the foot of a mountain. I listen intently. Still there is dead silence.

"How can the dawn come?" The owner has guessed what I'm thinking. "You will understand. As time goes by, you will understand everything. Once you have forced your way in, you have to live here. It's true that you've been here in the past, and every time I saw you off in person. But that's only passing by — not the same thing as your forcing your way in now. At that time this house was not as old as it is now."

I mean to argue, I mean to tell him that I did not intend to force my way in. As in the past, this time I am still passing by. I would not have come if I had known that my behavior constituted "forcing my way in." But I open my mouth without saying anything, as if I am feeling timid and ashamed.

"The foundation of the house is very fragile, and it's built on top of the cliff. Right behind the house there's a deep abyss. You should be aware of the situation. Now that you have come, you can live in a small room on the right. As a matter of fact, I am not the owner of this house. The original owner has departed. I also came here accidentally, and I stayed. At that time the original owner was not too old. One day he went to the back of the house to feed the pigeons. When I heard the sound, I went to the back of the house also. But I couldn't find him. He had disappeared. That was the first time that I discovered the cliff behind the house. Of course the original owner had jumped over the edge. I didn't even have a chance to ask him why he had built the house in such a place. Even now I am bewildered. But I've gotten used to the idea."

He leads me to the appointed small room, and orders me to lie down on the wooden bed. He tells me not to think about anything, saying that this way I can hear what's happening outside. He also advises me not even to expect the dawn, since such a thing does not exist anymore. I have to learn to adjust to the new environment in which I depend on the senses of touch and hearing. As silently as a fish he leaves me. For a long, long time I am in doubt as to whether he is exaggerating. For example, he considers my coming here as "forcing my way in," and he also emphasizes the cliff and the abyss. But what do these have to do with putting on a light?

I don't know how long I've been sleeping in silence. Finally I've made up my mind. I find a lighter in my pocket and start a small fire. By the faint light I look the small room up and down without finding anything. This is an extremely ordinary room. The ceiling is made of bamboo strips. The only furniture in the room is the old wooden bed that I have lain on. On the bed there's a cotton mattress and a quilt. It's completely silent, and there appear to be no terrible changes in the house because of the light I am making. Obviously the owner of the house is exaggerating. It could be that he's suffering from a neurosis. It's hard to say about a lot of things in the world. There are all kinds of possibilities. To be cautious, I had better keep motionless in the room. Besides, there isn't much fluid left in my lighter. I should save it. It's the same as the blind-fold game I used to play with my younger brother. We would limit our travel to only ten minutes. The whole situation might have turned out completely differently if we had set our time limit at one hour. Then what is the structure of the human ears? For example, can my ears be as quiet as now forever? As for the owner of the house, can he find a way to keep himself quiet? How can he be so listless for such a long time?

I hear him coming. Feeling around, he says, "So one corner of the ceiling has dropped! Those explosions just now were horrifying. I hope you didn't make any light. In the sea waves below, a fishing boat is sinking. I suspect that fisherman on the boat is the original owner of this house. Such things always have a relationship to each other. According to the analysis that I've heard, the fishing boat has run on the rocks. The whole boat has been fragmented and the dead man is lying peacefully amidst the seaweed. Above him is the little house he built with his own hands. . . . Of course this story is nothing but nonsense. How can he see any house? He's been choked to death by seawater. It's not even poetic at all. He's lying at the bottom of the water with his face down and buried in the sand and stone. He will go rotten gradually. . . . Now I'm returning to my room. You only need to calm down and stay on. Gradually you'll find that everything is fine, at least better than your wandering all over the place."

I try to walk out of the house. The earth is trembling terribly.

Clinging to the ground, I crawl outside the front gate. In front of me should be the flat stretch of grassland. As soon as I stand up and walk, I suddenly feel that there's no grass under my feet but something hard and moving. I start to change directions. However, no matter which direction I walk I can never reach the grassland and beneath my feet there's always that lump of moving substance. Surrounding me is a stretch of grayish black. Except for the vague silhouette of the house, I can't even see the mountains. Of course, I can't go behind the house. According to the owner, there's a cliff. Since I have walked randomly along the grassland, I should be able to walk back as long as I walk randomly. There's no need to feel tense. So thinking, I start walking in one direction randomly. In the beginning nothing happens. I start to feel a little bit pleased with myself. About a hundred paces on, I suddenly step into empty air. Fortunately, I get caught in a little tree sticking out and I climb back onto the cliff. I remember very well that I started walking from the front of the house. Why have I reached the cliff? Does that mean that "different roads lead to the same destination"? Where's the trail through the grassland? I ponder hard. It seems there should be some answer. In fact, I have vaguely felt that answer for a long time, but subconsciously I have refused to recognize it. Clutching the ground, I crawl back into the house. Inside, there's a kind of relaxation and a safe feeling. I even feel that the darkness and the smell of the lime are familiar, cozy, comfortable. In the darkness the owner of the house hands me a cup of water — lukewarm and with a smell of being unboiled, but it's still drinkable.

"I have to say something," the owner of the house announces. At that moment I smell the fragrance of a cigarette. "It's about him. He wears a black garment and a black hat. Even his leg wrappings are black. He appeared on the street of the town as if he were an ancient bandit. Some people passed right in front of him without even noticing him. Others spied on him secretly from those closed windows. Both sides of the street were completely lined with barber shops. Inside sat many customers waiting to have their hair cut. Some of them appeared to be in high spirits. Nobody knew where all the barbers had gone. The customers did not notice the black-clothed person. Those who spied on him behind the windows were all pedestrians. And those pedestrians who had noticed him had sneaked into the barber shops quickly, hiding themselves behind the curtains. The sun was burning and he was soaked with sweat. Stretching his arms, he appeared to be driving something away. Those who were hidden observed the performance of that black-jacketed man with pale faces. Without anybody pushing him, he fell down. A large number of people swarmed out and circled him.

"'Send him home!' one of those that hid ordered.

"'Right, send him home!' all those that surrounded him agreed.

"Just don't think about things like the dawn. Then you can harmonize yourself with the house. The sky will never lighten. Once you keep this rule in mind, you will feel comfortable. It's because he was too listless that the original owner jumped into the sea from the cliff behind the house and became a fisherman. Every day I listen here, and I can always hear him struggling in the stormy sea. You and I do not belong to the sea below, we two. You knew the answer long ago. The original owner's skill at sailing a boat was not very good. He was good at building a house. Therefore, his boat running into the rocks is unavoidable."

Quietly he returns to his own room.

As soon as I heard the owner telling me that below the cliff there is the sea, I started to have an irrational desire for this imaginary world below. I don't know how long I've been staying in this house. I can't count because I don't have my watch with me and it's always so dark. Also my lighter has long since run out of fluid. Whenever I feel bored, I chat with the owner about the sea. Every time, he hands me a cup of lukewarm water and smokes his cigarette. He always starts the conversation with this sentence: "The little boat of the original owner has arrived . . ." Every time, I object: "But the original owner is dead, isn't he? He ran his boat onto the rocks." At that moment he smiles, and the red glow of his cigarette flashes. Paying no attention to my objection, he continues this talk: "Upon departure, I went to see the boat off. On the boat there was only one fisherman. I heard that he died of old age later on. Then he himself became the fisherman. He never fished. Instead he only picked up seaweed and such things to fill his stomach. Afterwards his face gradually turned blue."

With some understanding, I say, "We two are living above. We never turn on the light. So it's almost as if we didn't exist. Isn't that so? Even if the original owner passed by below, he would never notice the house above him. It's very possible that he once mistook this lump of black shadow as a tree. Calmly he glanced at it and immediately he turned his glance away."

After a while, without knowing it, I join the discussion. We talk so eagerly that we feel uncomfortable to lapse into silence. But once we say something, we immediately feel that we are too talkative. Time passes by like this. Of course, there is no clock, and the dawn never comes. The owner of the house says that before long I will be acclimated to the fact that there is no seasonal change. He also says that we cannot use the content of our talk as the basis to sort out the years, months or days because we forget completely about our talks the next day. Besides, the little boat itself is fictitious and it's meaningless except for filling our need to divert ourselves from boredom.

When we feel tired from talking, we doze off separately. Once when I wake up I incidentally remember what happened in the past. I remember that I found that trail from the very beginning, the single little trail toward the grassland. Although I have walked on that trail hundreds of times, every time I still have to look for it, though I never put in much effort in looking for it. But what happened next is vague. It seemed that a tropical flamingo was chasing me desperately. I was not afraid of it, yet he could never get ahead of me. He ran in the same position as if held in place by a magnetic stone. I'm wondering if the small trail that I have used hundreds of times is really the only way to reach here. Since in my original memory this house is located at the end of a stretch of grassland with its back toward the mountain, there should be several ways from different directions to reach here. For example, one could come down from the mountain or come from the south or west of the grassland. Who can say that there's no path in those places? Once in the dim light I really saw a human figure in the west and I believe I was not mistaken. Would the flamingo come again?

But now the house owner has firmly eliminated all the possibilities. He insists that there is a deep abyss behind the house, and there has never been a grassland in front of the house aside from the rolling sand and stones. But how did I come here? According to him, this was only a chance incident. The so-called grassland and the banana groves are nothing but illusions that I made for myself. At the beginning there was a trail behind the house, the trail where he saw me off. But after several big explosions the trail has been blocked by mud and sand. The original owner of the house had calculated the odds before he chose this location to build his house. It is usual for people to pass by this location accidentally. Many people have passed by the house by chance as I did in the past. He received them politely and saw them off at the corner. Nobody noticed anything abnormal. But this time my forcing my way in was unexpected. That was why he was a little bit upset at the beginning, but now he feels OK.

I insist on looking at the pigeons at the back of the house. I say that we should feed those little creatures. With a sneer, he agrees reluctantly. But he says that we have to go through the tunnel in the kitchen to the cliff at the back of the house. In such a place it is enough for a person to stretch out her head and have a glance. He can't imagine that I have the idea that there would be pigeons in such a place. Besides, I could never get to the kitchen. If I have such fantasies in my mind, once I moved physically I would fall to the ground.

Although I am living in a room separate from that of the owner, his existence is no doubt a comfort for me. My skeptical mind has gradually calmed down. Every time when I wake up I hear the greeting of the owner: "So you're up." In the darkness I put on my clothes and sit in the living room with the owner every day without exception. When we have nothing to talk about, we sit in silence. I don't feel particularly listless, just a little bit bored.

SECULAR PSALMS :
Music Theater Portfolio

Harry Partch

Robert Ashley

Meredith Monk

John Moran/Ridge Theater

Alice Farley/Henry Threadgill

Ann T. Greene/Leroy Jenkins

Ruth E. Margraff

Yasunao Tone

Neil Bartlett/Nicolas Bloomfield

Guest-edited by Thalia Field

Music Theater: Texts and Traces
Thalia Field

IN OUR CLASSIFICATION SYSTEM it exists on some long low branch in an ecstatic tangle of phylogenies and ontologies from all over the bush. Opera, dance, art, poetry, theater, film, photography, cabaret — even, in the early days, architecture and political activism — can be seen in its genetic soup. Examples of early music theater have been found on many terrains, on several continents at once — its place as an essential literary and dramatic form continually substantiated. Although it is impossible to locate an original, or originating model, we can, by the tracks left for us to follow, easily see that music theater has grown from a small phenomenon to a major movement. The tracks are of different sizes and shapes and come from many directions and go off in many directions — and yet some of them have led us here, to a gathering of artists whose work represents new and innovative forms of music theater, especially those paying special attention to language, and to the ways language traces itself across the page. Some of these compositions were written long ago, while others are newly born — and yet each text is caught up in the printed present. Each possesses a unique anatomy built for music and theater, and remains incomplete without that final stage of being which is live performance. Look at them this way and I hope you will see each text as a species unto itself, self-evolved and specially formed to carry out its particular method of living. As with all forms, it is impossible to untangle which came first, their structures or their functions.

Harry Partch, many would say, is the American pioneer of this art. His unpublished, unproduced script of *The Bewitched* shows a dramatist composing music as language, character and plot. Like his iconoclast compatriot, Henry Cowell, Partch invented unique instruments to express his musical ideas, which were based on non-Western tunings and non-pitched sounds. The feeling of the music, its procedures and beats, can be felt in the way the script is scored and spaced. There are dancers who interact with the musicians on stage, but they are puppets almost to the music's theatrical

110

dominance. No wonder Alice Farley and Henry Threadgill cite him as an important influence on their creation of *Erotec,* where the jazz band is suspended high above the stage, and the dancers enact their computer-age desires directly underneath. Issues of machine-love and machine-fear in *Erotec* echo another important music theater composer, Laurie Anderson, whose electronic compositions, though absent here, use words and sounds as layers of complex drama in the soul of the machine.

All contemporary music theater touches Robert Ashley's shadow at some point. His ear is not only tuned to music, but to the great art of the tale: the shaggy dog, the anecdote, the snippet, the aside. And of course people call him a poet, though he has said that for him, "the libretto — the text for the three operas — doesn't have in it that extreme refinement of language that one would find in a shorter form. It's not poetry, it's song. It's song in the same way that *The Iliad* was a song. It's just a song; if you read one line, it's not *that* interesting in itself, but if you read a hundred they start to make sense." He captures, not only in content but also in form, the very structure of consciousness that courses through America like the television broadcasts to which his work aspires. In this way he is creating an idiom as self-consciously "American" as Virgil Thompson did. Ashley calls it tribal. Dramaturgically his pieces break drama into place and character, and then character into tonalities, defined not simply musically, but behaviorally, socially and narratively. As you can see in his score, the characters are given pitches but not told exactly what or how to sing, so their song-speech hovers around the pitch in a measure of indeterminacy.

If Ashley's work is structured by anecdote, Meredith Monk appears to come to music theater from the opposite pole — from a pre-literate place of movement and vocalization which paints landscapes, journeys and characters through abstraction. But though she uses very little so-called "language," the range of vocal expression in her music becomes a found ur-language, a translation into sound of the abstract principles of drama. Or, as she herself has said, her compositions exist "between the bar lines and beyond the notes." Her most famous opera is *Atlas,* but here we are given a rare view of an early song-cycle, one of the last to be "written" as text — without the intermediary use of tape. The orchestration of Monk's work is kept simple so that the vocal textures can be foregrounded, and *Our Lady of Late* is in that tradition, with only a wineglass for accompaniment. Additionally, Meredith Monk is an artist who ignores traditional "collaborative" models (whose borders are too often repressively patrolled in the Establishment venues of opera and musical theater). Her process of creation is nonlinear and she herself functions as composer, writer, director and performer — with a large degree of involvement from the rest of the cast. If you look closely you'll see that alternative collaborations are present elsewhere in this tradition, and perhaps there's something about this reorganization of roles which keeps these creations so fresh.

Electronic technology has found wide acceptance in composition, and many composers have extended it to music theater. John Moran (with Bob McGrath and Lori Olinder of Ridge Theater) has taken electronic composition and found an entirely new dramaturgical vocabulary for it. The kind of dramatic experience Moran creates comes from something profoundly structural, like the "invisible" effect of editing in cinema, and can be seen in the lip-synched, meticulously choreographed and often frighteningly robotic performances in his work. The music seems to be composed entirely of sounds, sound effects and strands of melody and speech, spliced and cut together like film images to make the scenes in a Frankenstein's monster of music narrative. The dialogue too gives the impression of being a sound effect, and where the entire opera is already on tape there is the impression that the live-ness of the performance is as much an echo as are the characters in the story. When I asked Ridge Theater and Moran for a script, most of what they could reassemble of *Everyday Newt Burman* is what you see in this portfolio: a momentary glimpse of their process, as scripts for them are places to pass through quickly on the way to tape, which is where his more recent operas exist exclusively.

Indeterminacy is a growing presence in contemporary music theater. Yasunao Tone's *Geography and Music* was designed as a text-based accompaniment to dance, and as with other compositions in this indeterminate vein, such as those of Michael Peppe and Joshua Fried, the texts on the page are illusions of a predictability that can't exist in performance once the electronic interventions are enacted. These procedural compositions highlight dramatic questions of the distance between text and performance, utterance and meaning.

Ruth E. Margraff is more of a writer who composes than a composer who writes, though that distinction may be only academic.

In *Wallpaper Psalm,* she takes up several strands of these various traditions and adds them to her ornate vision of a punk-rant drama. She uses a musicalized vocabulary of character and scene to help structure the story around literary qualities of hysteria and rupture — and the songs in *Wallpaper Psalm* come out of a "naive" tradition (Meredith Monk meets Sonic Youth?) where vocal quality is more important than precision of notes. The function the songs play in the drama is a pathos like that of the pre-war building which acts as both setting and allegorical singer in whose throat the characters become stuck and are finally disgorged. Her language skips between sense and sound and when she performs her own vocal experiments she shares some ground with Yoko Ono and Diamanda Galas. Also, like Robert Ashley reinvented, the different places in the "set" as well as the individual characters in *Wallpaper Psalm* have emotional pitches and modes which define them.

Also included in this ad hoc assemblage, though they are not themselves composers, are two writers who seem to integrate music directly into the form of their texts. Ann T. Greene and Leroy Jenkins's *The Negros Burial Ground* takes us to the shifting ground of history and the different musical idioms and styles that converge when the past is excavated. Neil Bartlett's adaptation of *Lady Into Fox,* composed by Nicolas Bloomfield, provides a contemporary chamber drama — where the accompaniment is almost the soul of the transformation. There are many poets who write important and innovative libretti, and perhaps someday it will be possible to take a separate look at that tradition.

Since its inception around a smoky table somewhere in the sixteenth century, opera has always been the hybrid (or multimedia) artform par excellence, picking and borrowing from far-flung practices to achieve its creators' desire for synthesis. Twentieth-century opera/music theater has been no less dynamic; innovations ranging from silent film to jazz to satellites and rap music have come to the party and stayed. This is not to say that there haven't always been traditions, but rather that the traditions of opera seem to be more about adventures in musico-dramatic expressivity than, for example, representations of "reality." I would wager that opera's constant popularity stems from its chameleonlike ability to be many things to many people. Following the great vaudeville decades in the early century, all the forms of music drama have been gathering momentum in America. Commenting on the Met's production of *Einstein on the Beach*, Laurie Anderson remarked, "Afterwards, everyone I knew started to write an opera, including myself. You'd see someone on the street — 'How's your opera?' 'Fine, how's yours?' It was really a fad." And that fad has not flagged, as I think the evidence here plainly shows.

Ironically, however, since the beginning of opera there has been a sort of "gentleman's" feud between the primacy of the text and the primacy of the music. Along with everything else split along binary lines in Europe (mind-body, master-slave, human-non-human, etc.) this debate was self-perpetuating. On the one hand the story demanded clarity of conception and delivery, and on the other hand the music had a nasty way of defeating the words at almost all points, either through pitch, ornamentation, rhythm or orchestration. This duel makes endlessly entertaining history, too detailed to recount here, until finally the brawl spilled into the streets of the more self-consciously modern era in such works as Strauss's *Capriccio* (in which a poet and a composer literally duke it out) and Schönberg's *Moses und Aron* (in which Moses only speaks and Aron sings).

In some ways it seems that the pieces in this collection, where text is so much a part of the musical conception, can be construed as some sort of response to the duel, highlighting its essential questions, perhaps signaling its insufficiency. Gertrude Stein made it possible to find music theater in the sounds and composition of language itself, an urge which reappears in Glass's *Einstein on the Beach*, and the syllabic orchestrations of Charles Amirkhanian. In fact, many if not most contemporary music theater composers position themselves on the spectrum of the material versus the grammatical aspects of language. One of the most impressive is Steve Reich's opera, *The Cave*, where the sounds of extemporaneous speech are the basis of the musical composition itself, woven motivically into an exploration of national character. John Cage formalized the possibilities of noise in music, and his composed silences conditioned listeners to the drama inherent in chance, duration and accident as much as harmony, meaning or form. Perhaps it was becoming clear to composers and dramatists influenced by the upheavals of the media century that war and peace, high and low culture, east, west, north, south, speech, music and noise were not so far apart after all. Stories, they learned, are dramatized less through text or music primarily, but by the strategies of the whole event (and that traditional values of musical or textual "intelligibility" are overrated). Thus the repertoire differs place to place, person to person—but carried in the mumbles, whispers, screeches and melodies we can either find or produce are all the treasures of time. For what sound I cause today becomes what I said tomorrow, and thereby marks that place where we all were, decorated and colored like statues or cartoons, the performance taking shape and slowly becoming an art. As an audience we crave these nonfranchised experiences. Our ears inch around on our heads and our faces grow more open so that we don't miss any of the fun. We are much more interested in what we don't yet understand.

"History is the story of original actions" (John Cage).

---

p.s.

It is a happy coincidence that with the publication of this portfolio comes the introduction of Conjunctions *on-line. Our site will allow us to present some, though not much, of what's missing in these pages: a tiny bit of sound or video that will give a small sample of each composer's music. In addition to many of the artists included here, you will find others whose work we couldn't accommodate in print. I hope you will visit this site at www.conjunctions.com/lit*

Literature on music theater composers is scarce. For those who are interested in reading more, I highly recommend The guests go in to supper, *Birch & Sumner, eds., Burning Books, 1986, from which some quotes here are taken.*

Harry Partch and Gourd Tree. Van Nuys, Calif., 1964.
Photograph by Danlee Mitchell.

The Bewitched

A Ballet Satire
With an Essay A Somewhat Spoof

Harry Partch

AS A THEATER PRODUCTION the work has three elements: The
Witch, the Witch's Chorus (the orchestra), the Bewitched (the
dancers).

The Witch
She belongs to the ancient school. She is an omniscient soul, all-
perceptive, with that wonderful power to make other people see,
if she feels so inclined. Much of the time she doesn't care whether
they see or not, but — when she does — she is always willing to
wait for the right psychological moment to strike, which she can
of course predict.

In a sense, The Witch is a Greek oracle, and her Chorus is like the
choruses of ancient tragedy, in that they echo the oracle, are frequently the interpreters of the oracle, and are always under the
oracle's power of suggestion. The bewitched dancers become the
players on the stage, in this analogy with lyric tragedy.

The essential tie between the ten psychological scenes is The
Witch's dominance of the entire tableau. When she is not singing,
shouting, murmuring or trumpeting, she dominates merely by her
presence, because her vocal entrance into each situation is always
imminent.

The Music
It runs to about forty minutes, and the individual scenes vary
from three to six minutes. One scene leads into the next without
musical pause, and each new beginning is aided by comparative
darkness and comparative light. Each new day, as it were, brings
a new situation to test The Witch's versatility, and it is always

117

problematical how she will handle it, or whether she will even notice it.

The scenes are a series of psychological situations, each with a climax of salutary or whimsical witchery. They are stories of releases from prejudice, from individual limitations, and the witchery even suggests releases from the accidents of physical form, and of sex, that create prejudices and limitations. Each one, in its characteristic way, is a theatrical unfolding of nakedness, a psychological striptease, or — in another sense — it is a surprising reversal, often diametric, with the effect of underlining the complementary character and amazing affinity of seeming opposites.

<u>The Stage</u>
Three instruments — Bass Marimba, Kithara, Diamond Marimba — dominate the set. They are on risers of different heights: the Kithara (center) is the lowest; the Bass Marimba (left) is higher; the Diamond Marimba (right) is highest. These risers are connected by a stairway, or a nexus of stairways, which mature into an ascent to one of the far corners at the rear. The end is not evident. The disappearance of the stairway might be painted onto the back canvas, in order to give the effect of endlessness.

Only the instrumentalists really use the stairways in a respectable manner. For the dancers, the stairways are mostly symbolic. The dancers constantly show their contempt for the symbol by jumping straight from stage to platform or platform to stage, with feet together, on beats of the music.

The remaining instruments of the Chorus are either partially visible in the wings or partially visible in the pit. The conductor is in the pit.

The Witch is on a throne near the front of the stage (right), throughout (except in the tenth scene, where she lies flat on the stage), draped in robes which assume different colors with the changing lights. She faces left, and the lights are such that she is simply a dark profile to the audience. The actors (the dancers) hear her, but she is always invisible to them, and the dark profile is intended to create the illusion of a <u>presence</u>, one which is theatrically invisible. The Witch generally sits immobile, but sometimes she stands, and sometimes moves rhythmically on the throne. Now and then she assumes command of her Chorus (the orchestra), as ostensible conductor.

In writing this outline I am letting my mind wander about, unhindered by either experience or familiarity. Although the psychological situations are familiar enough as such, my suggestions regarding stage set, lights, costumes and movements about the stage are only that — suggestions. These tangible properties of skill in the theater I would like to invoke in experience and attitudes beyond my own. My statements are really questions; i.e., is this particular idea a good idea? in costume? in lighting? in movement? is what I am really trying to say. Even the music is subject to change — by lengthening, shortening, the changing of emphasis.

— H.P.

* * *

The figures in squares refer the action to the same symbols in the full score.

1. BACKGROUND FOR THE TRANSFIGURATION OF AMERICAN
UNDERGRADS IN A HONG KONG MUSIC HALL

Dancers: Miss A   Costumes: Miss A wears a smock which
        Mr. Zee   falls just below the hips;
        Mr. Wy   bare legs.
                           Mr. Zee and Mr. Wy: Hawaiian swimming trunks, sport jackets, bare legs.

(⬜1, line 3) The three dancers enter simultaneously, right, and stand stock still.

(⬜2) They move toward the center, but

(⬜3) are suddenly arrested.

(⬜4) "I don't dig this," says Mr. Wy, grabbing the hem of Miss A's smock. But she artfully whirls to brush and release herself, and leads the two Hawaiians further on stage.

They all get lost again. What else is there to do?
But they will never be lost in the same way again!

(5 , line 6) Again, they are arrested, but recover in five beats this time, and are obviously much less timid. "Fascinating!" says Miss A.

(6) "A real weirdo!" says Mr. Zee. Being dancers, everything Miss A, Mr. Zee and Mr. Wy say, they say with their legs, which are appropriately bare.

(Lines 8 and 9) They begin to liquefy with the music, and all three playfully gesture like Chinese female music-hall singers.

(7) At this juncture they are all virtually unshockable, and refuse to be arrested.

(8 , line 10) "Watch this!" says Mr. Zee on the downbeat, who as a college man is thoroughly schooled in the female upbeat, and proposes to intensify Miss A's fascination.

(9) Miss A, happy and speechless, sails away on the ensuing pianissimo in a leggy duet with Mr. Zee, and in the course of which Mr. Wy matures very fast.

(10) "She wants it weird, so she'll get it weird, by gad!" says Mr. Wy, making up with intensity what he has lost in slowness as a student of the natural sciences.

(Lines 12 and 13) A lively joust in adolescent weirdness for Miss A's pale favor

(11) ends suddenly,

(12) resumes,

(13) and ends for good, simply because the Witch's Chorus — the orchestra — and the determined Harmonic Canon have had enough of this nonsense.

(14) "Ee----------Yow-oo-wuh!" says The Witch. This ejaculation might otherwise be rendered as: "You shallow idiots!" The Witch opens her mouth, but at this point considers the movement of any other muscle uncalled for.

Two vigorous <u>stamps</u> by the Witch's Chorus reduce Miss A and the Hawaiians to less than the dust.

(15) The Witch very, very, very slowly rises to her full height, while at the same time Miss A, flanked by Mr. Zee and Mr. Wy, very, very, very slowly sinks to the floor, with the crossed legs of a tea ceremony.

"U------wuh!" says The Witch. "Ho-ho-ho---" says the Witch's Chorus, as those three of less-than-ashes contemplate the endless depths of the stage floor.

"U------wuh!" says The Witch again. "Ho-ho-ho---" says the Witch's Chorus, as stagehands gently throw large gray cloaks over the three bent shoulders.

For one fleeting fraction of a moment, to Miss A, to Mr. Zee and to Mr. Wy—together and separately—the East holds no mystery.

Darkness.

-----0-----

2. BACKGROUND FOR THE PERMUTATION OF EXERCISES IN HARMONY AND COUNTERPOINT

Dancers: 1st couple —
    Miss Bee
    Mr. Ecks
    2nd couple —
    Miss See
    Mr. Doubleyu

Costumes: Fifteenth century. Miss Bee has flowing black locks, Miss See flowing golden locks. Mr. Ecks wears a golden Joan of Arc wig, and Mr. Doubleyu a black one. Both men wear loose shepherds' jackets with leotards of contrasting color.

121

Harry Partch

($\boxed{1}$) The very formal dance begins almost immediately. Miss Bee and Mr. Ecks do the first four bars toward the front, with the second couple (Miss See and Mr. Doubleyu) behind.

($\boxed{2}$) Mr. Ecks bows formally (third beat) and Miss Bee curtsies formally (fourth beat).

The following five-beat bar belongs to The Witch, who moves the weight of her body with slight knee bends from one leg to the other on each beat, and the Witch's Chorus, which <u>stamps</u> on the fifth beat.

($\boxed{3}$) The second couple brings us back to schoolroom normalcy with a formal bow (Mr. Doubleyu, third beat) and a formal curtsy (Miss See, fourth beat), after which

($\boxed{4}$) another Witch's five-beat bar sounds threateningly for the future of Mr. Doubleyu and Miss See.

($\boxed{5}$) It is again the first couple's turn at formal exercise.

($\boxed{6}$) Again a bewitched 5/4 bar.

($\boxed{7}$) Again the second couple's turn.

($\boxed{8}$, line 4) Then, The Witch and her Chorus, in typical 5/4, portend an awakening for the exercising couples — six bars.

($\boxed{9}$) "Let's try a variation in counterpoint," says Miss Bee, only slightly disturbed by The Witch.

($\boxed{10}$) "I'll point counter to you any day," says the quick Mr. Ecks, jumping into her groove four timely beats later,

($\boxed{11}$) while she curtsies,

($\boxed{12}$) and he bows.

(13) The Witch's recurrent 5/4 bar is now reinforced with a double (8th note) stamp by the Chorus.

(14 to 24 , lines 6 to 9) "Us too!" cry Miss See and Mr. Doubleyu in unison, and the sixteen-bar exercise, with 5/4 witching bars between each four-bar section, and with all the appropriate curtsying and bowing, flows like fate and the eighteenth century to its inevitable end.

(25) "Let's play along," says the Witch's Chorus, and one century becomes another as easily as day becomes dusk.

"Oh — my-oh — ee-ee-u," says The Witch, knowing all along what is going to happen next.

(26) For the unsquelchable Miss Bee, counterpointed by the ineludable Mr. Ecks, pulls us gently back again to the eighteenth century, until —

"Yee-oo-----------" screams The Witch, which might be translated, "This is all well and good, but such naivete can get disgusting."

At this, Miss Bee and Miss See fly to the respective arms of Mr. Ecks and Mr. Doubleyu, and each couple becomes paralyzed into a single unit of flesh.

(27) Now consummated as Mr. and Mrs. Ecks, and Mr. and Mrs. Doubleyu, they cooperate with each other and the Witch's Chorus in a dance at the Dawn of Time (with the eighteenth century scarcely even discernible in the dim, dim future), to the "Ho-ho-hee-oh" of the Chorus.

(28) Slow darkness.

-----0-----

3. BACKGROUND FOR THE INSPIRED ROMANCING OF A PATHOLOGICAL LIAR

Dancers: Mr. Hi-Daddy
        Miss Oh-Baby Dee

Costumes: Mr. Hi-Daddy is in a sweatshirt, tights and fourteenth-century pointed foot coverings; he wears a large peacock tail, the spread of which he can control. Miss Oh-Baby is in a one-piece bathing suit.

As lights come on, The Witch and her Chorus introduce the scene with a sad, slow poignance, anticipating Mr. Hi-Daddy's ensuing trauma and getting the sadness over with, so that the episode can end hilariously — so that we can laugh at Hi-Daddy's fate, with only a vague recollection of sorrow in the background.

(1 , line 3) Mr. Hi-Daddy backs in, stage right, with tail spread, followed by Miss Oh-Baby Dee, who gazes on him with both fascination and calculation.

(Lines 4 to 7) At first, Hi-Daddy is slow, but extravagant, gesturing, posturing, taking and holding the strange positions of the gods on Hindu temples. This is the ancient, time-honored and intellectual part of the pathological liar's dance.

(2 , line 7) "That's enough of that," says Hi-Daddy. "Now let's make with the body," and in the forty bars of 4½/4 that follow, the body gets made — every part of it — in the effort to impress Oh-Baby with the body, even if it kills it. Oh-Baby gets impressed but not as Hi-Daddy expected.

(3 , line 14) She grabs the ball away from him, and dashes about with determination to the "Ho — hay-ee" encouragement from the Witch's Chorus.

124

(4 , line 16) Exactly on the downbeat, Hi-Daddy drops his tail in
disgust, and goes to a corner to brood.

The Witch murmurs, then suddenly takes command of her Chorus,
driving them into a steady offbeat with her "Whu-
tuh, tuh, tuh, tuh —" In the course of this witching development, Oh-Baby finds herself transformed into a new version of Hi-Daddy.

(5 , line 18) She grabs his dropped tail, ties it on, struts, brags,
spreads her feathers,

(6) and with just a brief echo of his make-with-the-body 4½/4
rhythm.

(7) Unable to cope with his disintegrating ego, Hi-Daddy the
vanquished races up the stairs with Hi-Daddy
the Victorious in hot pursuit.

(8) Complete darkness, followed by

(9) a tremendous stamp by the Witch's Chorus, which says, in
effect: "That's the inevitable end of that."

-----0-----

4. BACKGROUND FOR THE ALCHEMY OF A SOUL TORMENTED
BY CONTEMPORARY MUSIC

Dancer: Mr. Too-Much   Costume: He is dressed in silk
knee breeches, silk stockings and
with the tails of evening dress.
He uses a white cane and carries
in the left hand a talisman in the
form of a star centered with the
outlines of a horse's buttocks.

The scene begins semi-dark, without dancer. The Witch and her
Chorus speak in contrapuntal dialogue. Their
mood is mercurial, and falls now into a profound
contemplation of another inevitability — that of

125

Mr. Too-Much, and the inevitability of his white cane and his talisman — in short, the inevitability of a horse's ass now and then.

(⬜1⬜, line 2) The contemplation produces the vision, and Too-Much appears. He does a self-satisfied, stylized dance right in line with the triplet character of the voice instruments, the Harmonic Canon and Kithara,

(⬜2⬜, ⬜3⬜) and is only slightly nonplussed by the long, doleful whistles from the Witch's Chorus.

(⬜4⬜, line 6) He becomes somewhat more disturbed with the mild remarks of The Witch, who really has no desire to ridicule Too-Much, but is damned well determined to make him realize his proper place in the world.

However, with typical individuality, Too-Much reacts as even more of a horse's ass.

(⬜5⬜) A very, very, very sad little passage follows between the Chorus and the Harmonic Canon, because they both know that Too-Much is going to respond to this with even more individuality — by being still more horse assy. He dances his triplet theme now with quaint and whimsical vigor, enlarges on it,

(⬜6⬜) does it backward,

(⬜7⬜) and forward.

(⬜8⬜) He places his little idol center stage and begins to salaam before it, but at this critical point, with the trunk of his body only halfway on its descending arc,

(⬜9⬜) The Witch makes a quick, strong movement, while staring at him. Although Mr. Too-Much is incapable of seeing her, he is psychically aware of some

annoying interference, and looks quickly in her
direction for the length of three beats.

(⟨10⟩) Again he goes through the preliminaries to a salaam, and is
again frustrated at the same downward point by
the same unseen force. For another three beats
Too-Much and the psychic force stare at each
other.

(⟨11⟩) Still again, Too-Much undertakes a salaam,

(⟨12⟩) and for the third time is stopped by The Witch in exactly
the same descending point of the salaam.

Now the Chorus comes ostensibly to his side, at least enough to
deliver an angry stamp to help him vent his
frustration.

(⟨13⟩) Too-Much is virtually paralyzed by the alchemy of his soul,
but with the next stamp something clicks in
Too-Much.

(⟨14⟩) He dances off to the twang of the Hong Kong Music Hall,
and the trilling clarinet, playing his white cane
as though it were a flute — finally realizing what
excellent clowning he is providing in this world.

-----0-----

5. BACKGROUND FOR THE VISIONS OF A DEFEATED BASKETBALL
TEAM IN THE SHOWER ROOM

Dancers: Mesdemoiselles
Ee, Ef, Gee,
Aich, Aye.
Hermes, the god.
Messrs. Kyuh,
Ess, Tee, You,
Vee.

Costumes: The women are
dressed in long toweling, with
flapping ends, suggesting un-
dress. Hermes ought to be
naked. The men have bare
legs, and wear tunics in the
shape of large numbers — 1, 2,
3, 4, 5 — or any others.

($\boxed{1}$) Semi-dark stage.

($\boxed{3}$, $\boxed{5}$, $\boxed{7}$) Lights brighten on a lugubrious dance of the five women, moving only in alternate measures, to the Chorus's offbeat "Ho-ho."

($\boxed{2}$, $\boxed{4}$, $\boxed{6}$) They rest in alternate measures, as though their spirits could not possibly sustain them through the memory of having left the basketball court as men.

($\boxed{8}$) Darkness descends,

($\boxed{9}$) and as it returns, on a seven-note figure in the Bass Marimba, a vision of Hermes appears at the top of the ascending staircase, with a basketball under his arm.

($\boxed{10}$) Forgetting that they are really not women (or perhaps remembering), they gaze in fascination at the naked figure, and begin a determined movement in his honor.

($\boxed{11}$) Hermes tosses the basketball down (first beat of Diamond Marimba); the ball is caught by Miss Ee (second beat), and it is tossed about (tossed and caught on alternate beats) until

($\boxed{12}$) it is caught for the third time by Miss Ee. But, instead of tossing it again, she dashes offstage with the prize, with the other four women flying after her, towels streaming in their wake.

($\boxed{13}$) The vision of Hermes vanishes, with dimming lights, while The Witch and her Chorus become dominant.

($\boxed{14}$) Lights brighten suddenly, with Hermes reappearing as numbered quintuplets, in the same spot. They descend the staircase with Hermean, godlike irreverence, scattering over the entire scene with complete abandon, to the contrapuntal five against three of the Bass and Diamond Marimbas. At the climactic height of this display of skill in basketball technique,

(15) The Witch intervenes with a screaming "Oo-ee----------yuh!" as the quintuplets scamper for cover.

(16) Complete darkness, with the first of the vigorous 13/8 measures.

(17) A spotlight shows Miss Ee tumbling down the staircase in her toweling, and

(18 through 21) on the first beat of successive bars, Miss Ef, Miss Gee, Miss Aich and Miss Aye come plunging down into darkness (the spotlight does not move).

(22) With virtually complete darkness, to the end of the rhythmic fade-out, and The Witch's muttering "Ay-u----," the bewitched basketball team has fallen completely under the charming belief that reality contains a slight compound of both experience and imagination.

"So there you are!" says the Witch's Chorus, with its last vigorous stamp.

"But where?" says the sustained sub-bass.

-----0-----

6. BACKGROUND FOR EUPHORIA ON A SAUSALITO STAIRWAY

Dancers: Miss Jay   Costumes: Traditional ballet costumes —
         Mr. Are   the kind that would never excite
                                      second notice on a Sausalito stairway.

(1) Miss Jay enters, followed by Mr. Are. They are obviously very conservative, highly prejudiced about anything, very refined teen-agers, the kind commonplace in Sausalito.

(2) But they do not escape The Witch, with accompanying Harmonic Canon, when she feels in a bewitching mood. She holds them apart from their infantile suburbanism for only three bars, however,

(3) so they whirl away while The Witch catches her breath for another expression of Golden-Gate inanity

(4) for another three bars.

(5) Now The Witch decides to let them build up their little affair, because she knows that there's nothing like a staircase (now-you're-up-now-I'm-down, now-I'm-up-now-you're-down) to bring this sort of thing to a climax.

(6) Before very long, however, the Diamond Marimba and the Kithara conspire in a chord, the kind that Pythagoras is supposed to have used for the purpose of paralyzing a person in motion.

To Mr. Are's delight, the body of young Miss Jay is now paralyzed, and in a position which is admirable for clinical examination, which he proceeds to administer (four bars).

(7) He has completed his work, with decidedly mixed judgments, when the same instruments deliver the unparalyzing or releasing chord, and young Miss Jay carries the preclinical movement to its consummation, just as though nothing had happened (as indeed it didn't). Now things really get adolescent.

(8 , first beat) Mr. Jay makes a huge adolescent leap,

(9 , second beat) and lands with the Chorus's stamp. Miss Are realizes that this is the psychological moment, (last half of second beat) and begins a long swooning glide in company with the obliging viola,

(10 , first beat) finally landing in Mr. Are's virile arms.

(11 and 12) Happy over the thrill of this collision, Miss Jay and Mr. Are, with the help of the agreeable instruments, more or less repeat this figure, with slight variations just for kicks.

(13) "Ee-ya-ee-ya-ee-ya-ee-ya----" yelps The Witch in powerful rhythmic thrusts, to a col legno viola and a pounding Diamond Marimba, which simply means: "The time has come."

Darkness gradually descends, and as the lights brighten

(14) Miss Jay and Mr. Are are seen high on the staircase, she above, he below. As she takes three steps down, he takes three steps up, till they are only a step apart.

(15) Then she takes three steps backward — up, while he takes three steps backward — down. This pattern is placidly repeated in each two bars of the 5/4 rhythm, and is obviously going to go on forever, while The Witch does a self-satisfied "Ee-oh----".

(16) Miss Jay goes backward and forward, and Mr. Are goes backward and forward, contrapuntally, as the music and lights fade.

And so they are completely complementary while going happily nowhere, which — the Witch realizes — is the best of all possible solutions to any ordinary problem in Sausalito.

-----O-----

7. BACKGROUND FOR THE TRANSMUTATION OF DETECTIVES
ON THE TAIL OF A CULPRIT

Dancers: Mr. Oh   Costumes: All three are in shabby
      Mr. Pee   modern street clothes, practically
      Mr. Ding-Dong   indistinguishable.

After a six-bar percussive introduction

($\boxed{1}$) the clarinet sings out and Mr. Oh and the Chromelodeon
enter together. Mr. Oh backs in stealthily, hold-
ing a newspaper open, which he is of course not
reading. He hesitates,

($\boxed{2}$) then backs away again.

($\boxed{3}$) Mr. Pee enters in exactly the same manner, holding a newspaper open, hesitates,

($\boxed{4}$) backs away again.

($\boxed{5}$) Now they back away in unison.

($\boxed{6}$) Next, each independently explores the situation, continuing
to hold his newspaper in front of him, while
moving swiftly about.

($\boxed{7}$, line 6) Suddenly, Mr. Ding-Dong races across the stage,

($\boxed{8}$) and stops abruptly. All three freeze.

($\boxed{9}$) Then, like a football-playing cat, Ding-Dong swings his hips
in a wide arc, and both newspapers fall immedi-
ately to the floor, as though suddenly flicked
down by Ding-Dong's long, invisible tail.

Then, stamp-stamp from the Witch's Chorus, who are having a lot
of fun in this new situation.

A five-beat frozen silence. "Woof!" says the Chorus suddenly, as
Mr. Oh and Mr. Pee jump nervously, and it is

easy to see where the Chorus's sympathies lie, at least for the present.

(10) Since they are now unmasked, without newspapers, Mr. Oh and Mr. Pee put arms on each other's shoulders and do a little chorus-girl type dance, to a brazen tune, kicking on each fourth beat of the 4/4 measures.

(11) Ding-Dong, who stands aside watching, gets bored with this and turns viciously on a Bass Marimba sweep, as the Witch's Chorus prods him through a suggestive ascending whistle and a stamp.

(12 , lines 10–16) Ding-Dong's dance begins, and develops trickily in alternating 2/4 and 3½/4 measures, but it finally becomes such an anti-social tour de force that The Witch can endure it no longer.

(13) Her power becomes apparent in the subdued end to Ding-Dong's dance even before she speaks. "A plague on both your houses!" is the gist of her rhythmic "Oo-oo-oo-Oh-oh-oh-Ee-ee-ee------" shriek.

(14) Darkness descends with the tolling bowls. This ought to be the end, but — since the tailing of culprits never ends — the eternal necessities of two detectives and a culprit must be clearly stated.

(15) With returning lights, the three do a final, symbolic dance — slow and sad, in which each takes turns in aiding the other, to the end that each may achieve the full expression of his character.

Thus, the scene ends in complete bewilderment, since none of the three really knows which is chaser and which is chased, to rolling Diamond Marimba, pianissimo.

-----0-----

8. BACKGROUND FOR THE APOTHEOSIS OF A COURT IN ITS OWN CONTEMPT

Dancers: Your-Honor
          Mr. Pee-A
          Miss Dee-A
          Mrs. Witness

(The defendant is merely an idea, not physically present.)

Costumes: Your-Honor and the two attorneys wear primitive ritualistic costumes. These must be savage, ferocious, frightening, violent, in color and effect. They also wear either fantastic headpieces or fantastic masks. Mrs. Witness, in contrast, wears a straight-line tunic, clean and simple, of a neutral color.

The scene opens with a suggestion of ancient ritual, semi-dark stage, on a melody from the Indians of the Southern California desert — the Cahuillas, whose culture contains a race memory of centuries of hunger. The melody isn't happy, and it has the further characteristics of dignity, and a challenging and melancholy determination.

Throughout this introduction the members of the court stand rigid, Your-Honor and Mrs. Witness on low pedestals, the two attorneys on the floor. Your-Honor and the Harmonic Canon are virtually a single entity,

(1 , line 5) and as the Canon enters Your-Honor swings a large Bass Marimba mallet, menacingly, and moves arms and trunk in a quick, strong and commanding way.

(2) Arguments and questioning of Mrs. Witness begin,

(3 and 4) with sharp interruptions from Your-Honor.

(5) Mrs. Witness (and the Chromelodeon) finally gets a chance to say something, in a graceful, feminine lilt,

(6) but she is ruthlessly interrupted by Your-Honor.

134

(7) "Exception!" shouts Mr. Pee-A — with his arms and legs, of course — as Your-Honor swings his mallet. "Noted and overruled!" shouts Your-Honor, by means of a vigorous <u>stamp</u> by the Witch's Chorus.

(8 , fourth beat) Whereupon Mr. Pee-A takes a huge leap backward, as though propelled by Your-Honor's violence, landing on the first beat of the following bar. But he immediately resumes the attack, slowly inching forward (toward Your-Honor).

(9) Mrs. Witness resumes her lilting but sad little story,

(10) only to be interrupted again by Your-Honor,

(11) with another swing of the mallet, a shout of "Exception!" by Miss Dee-A, a bark of "Noted and overruled!" by Your-Honor (interpreted by the <u>stamp</u>),

(12 , fourth beat) and a huge leap backward by Miss Dee-A. Landing on the first beat of the following bar, Miss Dee-A, like Mr. Pee-A, resumes the attack immediately. By this time Your-Honor is becoming both bored and angry,

(13) and Mrs. Witness, when she speaks again, has definitely become belligerent.

(14) Your-Honor's next interruption therefore has little effect on her, until — Your-Honor does an unheard-of thing.

(15 , first and second beats) He swings his mallet twice instead of once.

(16 , third beat) He then makes a huge leap off his pedestal, landing on the floor with a resounding <u>stamp</u> (fourth beat).

Immediately (fifth beat), softly but determinedly, he begins the little dance which is now in contempt of his own court, while the two attorneys and Mrs. Witness are paralyzed in consternation.

(17) With the re-entrance of the Harmonic Canon, forte, Mrs. Witness loses every last vestige of her femininity, jumps precipitately from her own pedestal to that of Your-Honor, grabs the mallet and swings it viciously.

To Your-Honor, she now becomes three things, in reverse order of power: his wife, his mother, Society.

This is the moment that The Witch and her Chorus have been waiting for, and have insidiously been egging on.

(18) A triumphant and ritualistic march ensues, to the Chorus's "Ho-ho-<u>hee</u>-oh," and The Witch's wild trumpeting.

(19) Your-Honor moves alone now, on a darkening stage.

Telescoping time a bit, Society gazes down proudly, and Your-Honor goes, with amazing dignity and shining eyes, to his lonely apotheosis.

-----O-----

9. BACKGROUND FOR A POLITICAL SOUL LOST AMONG THE VOTELESS WOMEN OF PARADISE

Dancers: Mr. Enn
      Miss Kay
      (And numberless
        visions of houris
        in the background)

Costumes: Mr. Enn wears a black frock coat with a large white carnation and white leotard. Miss Kay wears a filmy, transparent Moorish dance dress and transparent veil.

The mood in paradise is static, suspended somewhere about halfway between exquisite joy and exquisite melancholy. Several beautiful women stand here and there on the stage, immobilized by paradisian hypnosis as part of the set.

Mr. Enn and Miss Kay dance back to back throughout. They move from right to left and vice versa, and front to back and vice versa.

In the first part of the scene Mr. Enn faces the audience, and Miss Kay's movements are all the exact reverse of Mr. Enn's, so that, if his right arm gestures, her left arm gestures; if his left leg moves in a certain way, her right leg moves in that same way.

In the second part of the scene, after The Witch has cast her spell completely, the situation is exactly reversed, and Miss Kay faces the audience.

(1) The dancers enter almost immediately. Mr. Enn is obviously lost and bewildered, as though suffering from trauma, and Miss Kay's back mirrors him.

The Witch is in a gentle mood. The antiphony of her Chorus and the melancholy of the Harmonic Canon, which echoes her, point up the sadness of a situation where there is no security to administer, where human charges and human defenses seem to have become organically fused into a timeless, sad ecstasy.

(2 , line 5) But the Harmonic Canon, through The Witch's power, begins to accelerate, and as it accelerates it engenders a sudden fury in The Witch's "Yah--Yoo--Yuh-----," which is to say: "Here's one politician we're going to get a good look at."

(3) Darkness descends,

(4) and as the light returns Miss Kay, in front now, begins her dance as chosen leader of the houris, while Mr. Enn's back mirrors her every movement.

137

At first, this dance, with all the houris lending at least their hips
to the general result, is vigorously and seduc-
tively feminine, Oriental, corporeal. But this is
as nothing compared to what follows.

($\boxed{5}$, line 10) "Now let's dig," say the two Kitharists, and

($\boxed{6}$) the houris fall, with a frenzied kind of restraint, into the
houriest of all houri dances (and with Mr. Enn's
back matching Miss Kay's front, movement for
movement).

This is not passive femininity; this is forensic sexuality, and not
dissimilar to the spell of the political orator.

The scene ends in a state of Oriental, orgasmic contentment, with
descending darkness, and Mr. Enn realizes, for a
fleeting moment, that he is agreeably at home
among constituents who had no part in his elec-
tion, among continually re-virginized houris,
who are — of course — eternally elected.

-----0-----

10. BACKGROUND FOR THE DEMONIC DESCENT OF THE COGNOSCENTI WHILE SHOUTING OVER COCKTAILS

Dancers: Five women
Five men

Costumes: Fifteenth-century clothes.
See pp. 81, 83, 97, 99 of *English
Costumes from the Fourteenth
through the Nineteenth Century*,
The Macmillan Co., N.Y., 1937.

The party has long since passed the sweet and low stage as the
scene opens. The Witch's Chorus and the dancers
seem independent of each other, since — like
chatterers at all parties — the dancers ignore the
music, and since the Chorus's efforts are directed
toward exactly one denouement — the turning
of this affair into a profound, savage and primitive ritual.

138

(1 , line 3, and 2 , line 7) The storm clouds gather as the Chorus changes its direction of attack. "Ignore us, will you?" they say in effect.

For the dancers are not only blind, but in this case virtually deaf also, and this insistent indifference to the brewing apocalypse is to make their fall that much harder, when it comes.

(3) The Witch warms up with an "Ee-yuh! Oh--oo--uh," but this is just a tryout for the main event

(4) and carries the two Kitharists into an intensifying and crescendoing duet.

(5 , line 13) Again the Chorus changes its direction, but the quickening percussion of this instrumental charge is only a challenge to the dancing idiots, who — like people at parties everywhere when the volume of the phonograph is set up — simply shout louder. These do it with their legs.

The time has come.

(6 , line 15) To a long, anguishing, microtonal and staccato descent on the clarinet, accompanied by fortissimo percussion, The Witch rises from her throne, steps off her platform and gropes toward the center of the stage with eyes shut — and with long, slow breast strokes parts the waves of the blind and deaf that surround her.

When she reaches the front center she lies flat on her back, perpendicular to the edge of the stage, with her head upside down to the audience.

(7) "Hah! Tah, Woe-----Woe, Woe, Woe----- Hah! Tah, Woo-----Woo, Woo, Woo--------," she howls, to a strong, percussive alternating 9/8 and 4/8 rhythm, and fired by the Chorus's percussive voices.

(8 , line 20) In turn, The Witch's voice drives the Chorus into a
sustained fortissimo.

(9) The Witch rises from the floor on a sudden pianissimo, and
the scene is transformed by lights.

Now, in the same rhythm (alternating 9/8 and 4/8), the melody of
the hungry Cahuillas returns, in long, soft, sustained and subdued counterpoint, with tolling
bowls.

(10 , line 24) This sings to its bitter end, at which The Witch
invokes her Chorus to a final determined effort,
driving them to open the doors, to the end that
these cocktailers will really achieve the basic
wish of all cocktailers: a <u>oneness</u>, a sublime
bliss, a final understanding of the common illusion of being alive.

But — alas! — with each vicious <u>Bah</u>! from the Witch's Chorus, they
shrink farther and farther offstage.

<u>Bah</u>! says the Chorus, and the poor cognoscenti shrink again.

"How extraordinary!" says a lady cocktailer. <u>Bah</u>! spits the Chorus,
and she shrinks again.

(11 , line 26) <u>Bah</u>! says the Chorus, and on the final <u>h</u> the stage
is empty.

(12) The Witch murmurs complacently, because she really
doesn't give a damn, as her Chorus goes into a
strong, subtle and soft 5/8.

"Mo-mo-mo-mo-<u>mo</u>-Mo-mo-mo-<u>mo</u>-<u>mo</u>-<u>mo</u>," says the Chorus.
"R-r-rah-uh! Ee--------eh!" says The Witch softly.

The doors to perception are finally open. But — there is no one to
enter.

— First Draft, 1954

A SOMEWHAT SPOOF

I AM A HUMBLED TRADITIONALIST from ancient ages. In my previous life I stood for (alas!) progress, and this was too much, both for my ancient fellow man and the ancient gods. I was dispatched clandestinely, without even the honor of a public execution.

So—, numberless millennia later, I find that the kindly gods have relented. I am back in the world, simply because I have learned that man must also understand regress.

Let not one year pass—I now say to myself—when I do not step one significant century backward. And since there are so many full circles in a man's life, I am firmly convinced that when I have regressed as far as I can possibly go, I shall have actually arrived at a point some years in the wild future, and maybe it won't be so godawful pure.

Ah, purity! The Shakespearean actor in a concert of pure readings (Woe is me!). Pure black-and-white tails, pure orchids on a pure bosom (I love music!). Pure, pure paintings (We are in the presence of Ah—t!). Pure movie-makers talking wistfully of soundtrack counterpoint (Who wants to counter my point?). Pure criticism in pure print (Sunday circ., 1,367,455). Massive lunges across the modern dance stage (Puh-yure movement! Just puh-yure movement!).

Ah, sweet purity! —— Pure dance, pure chance,

Pure poetry to pure jazz,
Pure music, pure drama,
Pure telephone poles in the virgin grazz.

Relax!

Whistle softly, and as each loving muscle snuggles under, and each tiny cilia wiggles free, you will see—shimmering before you—the curves of x million perceptible changes in pitch, at least 127 varieties of female giggles and no less than seventeen kinds of falsetto wails, in each cubic foot of free vibrating air.

One does not find free vibrating air just anyplace, however. Let's not look for it in Town or Carnegie Halls, or any other enclosure that has been dedicated to the services of Johann Sempervirens Bach. But—when you find it—you will see at once that it does not even faintly resemble a piano keyboard, the sweating brow of a laborer in the Columbia Concerts vineyard or the stage set for Lucia di Lamermoor. Not one of its tones ever went through the dreadful ordeal of birth by logarithmic section, knifed by the

141

twelfth power of two. And not one of them ever got hung up in a clutch with Grandma Bel-Canto, or hung over with those fussy old twins, Uncle Faulty-Attack and Auntie Faulty-Release.

Observe the professors! There is excellent reason for believing that Giant Musicologists, in order to become Giants, must forever forswear the testimony of their ears and their eyes, and take the Oath of Total Anesthesia for the balance of their natural lives.

All wise men come out of the East —

Because the litany of musical mythology is unexamined, the Giant Musicologist continues to entrench himself. Unchallenged, he accepts all new allegiances as a divine right, counts off another Ave Mozart and bows ceremoniously in the direction of the Library of Congress.

So—, we have finally arrived at cultural "maturity"! Witness, along with European musicology, our addiction to the twelve-tone row and to electronic music after these items became small fashions in Europe.

The young man in Los Angeles who makes music out of common sounds during the late thirties is ignored to extinction, but some young Europeans doing the same thing under the fancy title Musique Concrete — ten years later — are celebrated from New York to California. (The European composer sneezes — sotto voce — and the hairs in the ears of the American A & R man respond immediately with a tremolo.)

Now, with Europe sounding off in multitudinous electronic grunts, groans and farts, the awakening is here again! The Europhiliacs of the American colleges and foundations go to work. Suddenly, it is not only respectable but even mandatory that Americans follow this lead. If Europe can fart, by golly we not only can, we must!

What was that again?

All wise farts come out of the East?

When things are hopping — definition: THE BIG WORLD, complex in excitement, simple in rules, no analysis.

When things are not hopping — definition: the little world, simple in excitement, complex in rules, utter analysis.

If things are hopping who cares how many tones you use? The BIG WORLD has All Tones, All Ideas. The little world has twelve tones, one idea, and ten million libraries stacked with books and

magazines and newspapers to glorify, to apologize for and to analyze those twelve tones and that one idea.

How many millennia backward (or forward) must we go? to find
art in a meaningful role? to find statesmen and artists in love with
each other?

Live, die; then live and know.

— September, 1960

Harry Partch's "The Bewitched" and "A Somewhat Spoof":

"It seems impossible for me to dissociate words and musical ideas. I evolve the dynamics of the music in my mind and formulate the verbal concept at the same time. Then later, when the music is actually heard, the words seem misbegotten and even stupid." — Harry Partch (1901–1974)

This original (1955) version of the scenario for "The Bewitched" was extensively rewritten over the next four years (see Enclosure Three, *a bio-scrapbook of Partch's life published by American Composers Forum in 1997). Partch had been living with his collection of remarkable hand-built instruments in the Gate 5 shipping warehouse in Sausalito, California. Every evening a group of musicians would arrive for rehearsals from their humdrum day jobs all over the Bay Area. They would sometimes stay and improvise until 3:00 A.M., discovering a kind of magic together. This became the basis for the Chorus of Lost Musicians. Several choreographers — such as Maya Angelou (who would also have sung the Witch's part), Martha Graham and Merce Cunningham — were considered before Alwin Nikolais was chosen for the 1957 premiere in Champaign-Urbana, Illinois. Nikolais totally abandoned Partch's narrative and concept, for which Partch ever afterward referred to him as "that albatross around my neck."*

"A Somewhat Spoof" was written in 1960 at the invitation of Oliver Daniel at BMI, who was compiling a book of composers' essays. The book never came to fruition.

— Philip Blackburn

From Foreign Experiences
Robert Ashley

INSTRUCTIONS

THE SCORE

The score has part assignments (rather than "characters") for clarity.

w/ (e.g., Sam w/ Jackie) means: together for that line only.

& (e.g., Joan & Tom) means: continue together until the next part assignment.

For both symbols (**w/** and **&**) each part keeps its own pitch assignment.

In the marginal columns for pitch assignments:

SAM and CHORUS always take the top note.
JACKIE and AMY always take the next-to-top note.
JOAN and MARGHRETA always take the next-to-bottom note.
TOM and BOB always take the bottom note.

CHORUS is all voices not otherwise assigned. I put the CHORUS pitches in parentheses in all columns as a reminder.

The "harmony" column with roman numerals and sub-scripts is for purposes of orchestration. (You might notice that there are 14 chords that recur throughout the piece.)

Need I add? — Don't feel you have to emphasize the four-letter words. They are to be "thrown away" in the way they are used by people who really swear. As the man said, "It's the tune, not the words."

Robert Ashley

ACT I — The Flying Serpent

4 beats per line @ 90 beats/minute
Line one is preceded by 10 measures (10 lines) of orchestra <= 26.66"> [4 beats @ 90 = 2.66"]

		ORCHESTRA INTRO
CHORUS	1	We come down from <u>T</u>ruckee surf<u>i</u>ng against <u>t</u>hat sun
	2	<u>A</u>s if <u>o</u>ff a <u>g</u>reat wave <u>b</u>ut in the
	3	<u>W</u>rong direction <u>c</u>ertainly <u>t</u>he wave is <u>f</u>rozen
	4	<u>O</u>r just <u>m</u>oving so <u>s</u>lowly that no <u>o</u>ne can know
	5	<u>I</u>f you've <u>d</u>one it though / you know the <u>f</u>eeling
	6	<u>I</u>t's all <u>d</u>own hill <u>f</u>rom here <u>l</u>ove
	7	<u>T</u>he hard <u>p</u>art / is <u>o</u>ver
	8	<u>T</u>he gold <u>i</u>s in <u>s</u>ight El Do<u>r</u>ado
	9	<u>E</u>nd of <u>s</u>cene one / /
Bob	10	Make camp in bedrooms of friends
	11	Just until we find a place of our own
	12	A three year old car and a U-haul loaded with junk
	13	Another caravan has seen America
	14	End of scene two . . . It's getting dark now
	15	Let's jump in the car run over and look at the place
	16	This is where we're going to work
	17	This is where we're going to live
	18	Let's drive over and look at it quick big mistake
	19	We should've come in the daytime
	20	We should've come on a weekday
	21	I didn't get this 'til later smack into it
	22	The worst time of day worst day of the year
	23	We drove smack into it leftover dreams
	24	Back Gate of The College remember the

	HARMONY	SAM CHORUS	JACKIE AMY	JOAN MARG.	TOM BOB	SMPTE
$A^b+7M/E\natural$	III b	c	(c)	(c)	(c)	00:00.00
						00:26.20
					$E\natural$	

BOB (*cont.*)	25	Back Gate part later they closed it forever
	26	It was how shall I say this
	27	It was too dangerous
CHORUS	28	The layout is stupidly simple
	29	An iron gate and a road that goes straight
	30	Ahead slightly up hill and to the right
Bob	31	/ We've passed the dead fountain and the shingled names
CHORUS	32	We are into the trees a quaint wooded area
Jackie	33	/ About two hundred yards the whole thing
CHORUS	34	Then you come out in the campus /
Sam	35	/ A stop sign a cross street a strong smell
CHORUS	36	Eucalyptus came in from The Far East by mistake
Amy	37	/ I can't even describe / how dumb this is
CHORUS	38	On the right there's a square building in shadows
	39	On the left and just behind is Faculty Village
Joan	40	/ So-called how nice hidden in trees
CHORUS	41	We passed because it's hidden seeing
	42	Now here's the hard part / (pause) something
	43	Happened here once and it is still here
	44	We just drove through it scared to the teeth
Tom	45	N's dog's whining nobody says a word
CHORUS	46	The New World and we're gonna work here
Marghreta	47	Starting tomorrow in the presence of this thing
CAPTION	48	My heart turns to stone I have become

$A^b+7M / E\natural$

HARMONY	SAM CHORUS	JACKIE AMY	JOAN MARG.	TOM BOB	SMPTE
III b				E♮	01:30.20
	c	(c)	(c)	(c)	
				E♮	
	c	(c)	(c)	(c)	
		A♭			
	c	(c)	(c)	(c)	
	c				
	c	(c)	(c)	(c)	
		A♭			
	c	(c)	(c)	(c)	
			G		
	c	(c)	(c)	(c)	
				E♮	
	c	(c)	(c)	(c)	
			G		
	c	A♭	G	E♮	

149

CAPT. *(cont.)*	49	One of those explorers long gone now
	50	Led his men and women through all kinds of
	51	Dangers laughing drugs to El Dorado
Sam & Jackie	52	Then suddenly you're in the heart of it
	53	Before you know that you know that it's happened you are
	54	There with a common knowledge that you are in trouble
	55	M, S, N and I are in trouble
	56	This place is haunted end of scene three
	57	Work late in the studio very end of the building
	58	I don't like the building at all
	59	Somehow the layering is blurred
	60	Even now I couldn't tell you
	61	After a thousand times up and down (up and down)
	62	Whether the studio is floor two or three
	63	The confusion is right there a part of it
	64	To explain I'll tell a story (naturally)
	65	Medical students intern in two ideas (I know this)
	66	Six months in the private skin (so-called)
	67	You go around with Trapper John, M.D.
	68	Notebook ready deciding what possibly could be wrong
	69	With people who are simply dying in bed
	70	Then six months in the public skin (so-called)
	71	Emergency entrance first floor hose off the
	72	Tiles again another guy just came in without an arm

HARMONY	SAM CHORUS	JACKIE AMY	JOAN MARG.	TOM BOB	SMPTE
$\text{III}b$	C	A♭	G	E♮	02:34.20
	C	A♭			
$\text{III}a$	E♭	C			

$A\flat + 7m / E\natural$

$Fm7 \text{ sus } 4 / F$

151

Sam & Jackie	73	The skin is the (so-called) soul in other words
	74	That thing you read about them looking for for centuries is
	75	Right there in front of you to see the soul
	76	It's not a bag you're inside of (you knew that of course)
	77	It follows the body keeping some distance
Jackie	78	And it is indifferent
Jack. w/ CHOR.	79	All knowledge / comes through it /
Jackie	80	It transmits receives and reveals
	81	A flaw in the structure the skin will reveal it
	82	And a flaw in the structure the skin can't protect it
	83	And it follows from this like one and two equals three
	84	A break in the skin lets in spirits
	85	I'll say it again a break in the skin lets in spirits
Jack. w/ CHOR.	86	Segue from scene four to five four will come back
Jackie	87	I go to the dentist week after week after week
	88	The bad genes have finally caught up with me
	89	I forgot to say this is years later
	90	The four of us hopelessly lost from each other
	91	I live in a shitty apartment
Jack. w/ CHOR.	92	Near to the Back Gate unfortunately
Jackie	93	Now I have to cross that place on foot
	94	When I have the courage which comes and goes
	95	To pick up bread and some vodka for dinner
	96	Back at the shitty apartment alone

		SAM CHORUS	JACKIE AMY	JOAN MARG.	TOM BOB	SMPTE
HARMONY						
	III a	E♭	C			03:38.20
	III b	C	A♭			
			A♭			
		C	A♭	(c)	(c)	
			A♭			
		C	A♭	(c)	(c)	
			A♭			
		C	A♭	(c)	(c)	
	III a		C			

Jackie (*cont.*)	97	But I have learned something now to explain
	98	When the skin is violated the spirits come visiting
	99	I'll say that again the spirits come visiting
Jack. w/ CHOR.	100	You go to a dentist he cuts a hole in you
Jackie	101	That night and until it heals
	102	The spirits come visiting
	103	I can't say it to make it sound civilized
	104	It's something you wouldn't notice maybe
	105	If the skin violations were infrequent
	106	You mostly forget in between times
Jack. w/ CHOR.	107	But when the schedule gets heavy
Jackie	108	When the tearing and the healing overlap
	109	And you are aware of the holes in you the condition they're in
	110	That's when you learn it the spirits come visiting
	111	And you start paying attention
	112	To where you have chosen to live
Jack. w/ CHOR.	113	Segue back to scene four working late the studio
Jackie	114	The building itself scares the shit out of me
	115	It was designed to have holes in it
	116	Jesus designed to be violated
	117	Daytimes you can't tell daytimes
	118	It is as beautiful as an old woman in makeup
	119	Nighttimes watch out my Office oh Jesus
Jack. w/ CHOR.	120	A place to keep things you don't want at home

HARMONY	SAM CHORUS	JACKIE AMY	JOAN MARG.	TOM BOB	SMPTE
III a		C			04:42.20
		C			
	E♭	C	(E♭)	(E♭)	
	E♭	C	(E♭)	(E♭)	
		C			
III b		A♭			
	C	A♭	(C)	(C)	
		A♭			
	C	A♭	(C)	(C)	

Jackie	121	It's on the far other end of the building
	122	Also I don't know what floor it's on
	123	Ten years and I don't know what floor it's on
	124	Where I keep stuff I work with so as
Sam & Jackie	125	To unclutter the studio to make room
	126	For people who don't have an office
CAPTION	127	Between studio and Office there are two ways / to get there
	128	At, say, three in the morning one way is down outside
	129	Across and up that's a long walk at, say,
	130	Three in the morning the other is straight through the building
	131	Straight through the back of the Concert Hall across the
	132	Very back row hope the Exit sign is working
Marghreta	133	This night in question I made four trips
	134	Each one a little more weird than the last
	135	Full grown man each more weird than the last
Marg. & Tom	136	/ Finally / I can't do it /
	137	/ I have to admit I'm afraid /
	138	/ I am afraid to go through there /
Tom & Amy	139	/ That's the only way I can say it /
	140	/ I am afraid to go through there /
Amy & Joan	141	Not afraid of the dark / /
	142	Not afraid of the silence / /
	143	Just afraid / / /
	144	End of scene four El Dorado scene five

HARMONY	SAM CHORUS	JACKIE AMY	JOAN MARG.	TOM BOB	SMPTE
III♭		A♮			05:46.20
	C	A♭			
	C	A♭	G	E♮	
III₍ₐ₎	E♭	C	B♭	F	
			B♭		
			B♭	F	
		C		F	
		C	B♭		

Joan & Marg.	145	I have to get out of this shitty apartment
	146	It's starting ∕ to follow me home
Marg. & Tom	147	∕ To finish up with scene five everything is different
	148	∕ Broken changed ∕ however you want to think about it
Tom & Amy	149	∕ The four of us who came through the Back Gate years ago
	150	Forty Miles away M is trying to survive
Amy & Joan	151	I don't know where S is living on the street I guess
	152	Waiting for a broken heart ∕ to mend ∕
Joan & Marg.	153	I see N almost every day
	154	But I know he strains to keep trusting me
Marg. & Tom	155	∕ Something has happened that nobody understands
Tom & Amy	156	∕ The dog is dead of course even the red car is gone
	157	∕ It started to be accident prone
Amy & Joan	158	F says it's just cosmetic I say everything's
	159	Cosmetic it's gotta go I pay a guy to take it
Joan & Marg.	160	So for the first time in my life I walk or take a bus
	161	If the distance is too great this is scene five
Marg. & Tom	162	∕ In order to get something to take home at night
	163	Vodka and a loaf of bread I have to walk through the place
Tom & Amy	164	∕ I mean the place between the building on the right
	165	∕ At the cross street and the Village so-called
	166	∕ Hidden in the trees and that's the problem
Amy & Joan	167	Something happened here once and it's still here except that
	168	Now it follows me home at night ∕ it hangs around

HARMONY	SAM CHORUS	JACKIE AMY	JOAN MARG.	TOM BOB	SMPTE
IIIa			B♭		06:50.20
IIIb			G	E♮	
		A♭			
				E♮	
		A♭	G		
			G		
			G	E♮	
		A♭		E♮	
		A♭	G		
			G		
		A♭		E♮	
IIIa		C		F	
		C	B♭		

159

Amy & Joan	169	Vodka bread vegetables / lots of soy sauce
Joan & Marg.	170	Read a lot of Velikovsky he's on to something
	171	Everybody hates him even his detractors
Marg. & Tom	172	/ Science gone bananas / in the academy
Tom & Amy	173	/ Or else he couldn't write that well his detractors
	174	/ Write like high school seniors editing the paper
	175	/ He writes ideas fuck your approval that has its charms
Amy & Joan	176	And besides / you never know when a colleague
	177	Might need / an idea for an opera
Joan & Marg.	178	Velikovsky and that other guy Einstein lived next door
	179	To each other I bet I couldn't tell them apart
	180	A pariah and a Brahmin equally contagious
Marg. & Tom	181	How's the wife and kids Immanuel pretty good Albert how's the dog
	182	/ Wha'd'ya hear from Science nothing much I think it's dead
Tom & Amy	183	Gotcha what about technology it'll be the death of us I think
	184	Sorry about that A-bomb that's OK it wasn't your fault
	185	Besides the circle's only half completed
Amy & Joan	186	Violins at twilight two old guys arguing with Moses
Joan & Marg.	187	/ What was that oh shit it's still here
Marg. & Tom	188	It followed me home again /
Tom & Amy	189	It prowls / around the bedroom /
Amy & Joan	190	I fall asleep in the plastic chair
	191	End of scene five / /
Joan & Marg.	192	This is difficult terrain hillbilly madness

HARMONY	SAM CHORUS	JACKIE AMY	JOAN MARG.	TOM BOB	SMPTE
IIIa		C	B♭		07:54.20
			B♭		
			B♭	F	
		C		F	
		C	B♭		
			B♭		
			B♭	F	
IIIb		A♭		E♮	
		A♭	G		
			G		
			G	E♮	
		A♭		E♮	
		A♭	G		
			G		

161

Joan & Marg.	193	Middle aged man lives alone in a shit apartment
Marg. & Tom	194	Across the courtyard a woman with an artificial larynx
Tom & Amy	195	Down below the neighbor has a bar self-standing
	196	And he plays disco records / until late hours
Amy & Joan	197	Donna Summer and Al Green without the words
	198	Just strong beats end of scene six
Joan & Marg.	199	This one's for Carl Welcome to El Dorado
	200	A man is seated at his desk /
	201	Looking over his shoulder we see the telephone
	202	Cradled to his ear he's calling someone
Marg. & Tom	203	It rings on the other end Answer
	204	Hello Scorpio this is Phone Future
Tom & Amy	205	/ Today's another big one you might get killed
	206	Save toward a big project or big investment
Amy & Joan	207	Take care on short term gratifiers
	208	Take care on instant pleasure etcetera
Joan & Marg.	209	/ He mocks the phone voice we see him
	210	Apply something to his teeth or gums
Marg. & Tom	211	We look down on a plate of cocaine
	212	Tongue-time so you don't go out the window
Tom & Amy	213	Enter his secretary a male
	214	The Senators are here Don the tour is ready
Amy & Joan	215	OK / I'll be there in a minute
	216	End of scene seven / /

HARMONY	SAM CHORUS	JACKIE AMY	JOAN MARG.	TOM BOB	SMPTE
IIIb			G		08:58.20
			G	E♮	
		A♭		E♮	
		A♭	G		
			G		
IIIa			B♭		
			B♭	F	
		C		F	
		C	B♭		
			B♭		
			B♭	F	
		C		F	
VIIb		D♭		G	
		D♭	C		

Joan & Marg.	217	/ The Laboratory doesn't show you what it does
	218	Cleanliness is next to Godliness so everything is clean
Marg. & Tom	219	Science without test-tubes so nobody's dissecting
	220	Rats here notice how pale and how green
	221	The light is notice too how comfortable
	222	Senators behave in the expensive leather chairs
Tom & Amy	223	Notice how closely they pay attention notice how the
	224	Temperature of the coffee is exactly right notice
Amy & Joan	225	That there are no women this is a secret meeting
Joan & Marg.	226	/ Don makes a few casual remarks
Marg. & Tom	227	Others have been there / nothing formal of course / we have just
	228	Finished the preliminary stage the reports are very encouraging
	229	Though this is very different from what has gone before one
	230	Could call it except for the poetry another realm
Tom & Amy	231	We don't know in any way what it could be good for what
Amy & Joan	232	Is proposed is simply that we follow through in the circum-
	233	Stances we should expect no publicity to speak of we could
	234	Call it trivial / for the moment / who knows maybe it will
	235	Come to nothing possibly I will not come back etcetera
Joan & Marg.	236	/ A Senator philosophizes on the value of
	237	Uncommitted research end of scene eight
Marg. & Tom	238	Don and his secretary discuss the demonstration tour
	239	Very successful / research will continue support came
	240	In the form of handshakes Don is off tomorrow on a well-

HARMONY	SAM CHORUS	JACKIE AMY	JOAN MARG.	TOM BOB	SMPTE
VII b			C		10:02.20
			c	G	
		Db		G	
		Db	c		
			c		
			c	G	
		Db		G	
		Db	c		
			c		
VII a			G	Db	

Marg. & Tom	241	Deserved vacation Southwest car tour sightseeing rock
	242	Hunting family rest he might not come back end of scene nine
Tom & Amy	243	Don considers his options while Linda's in the bathroom
	244	This kind of research is full of problems (social)
Amy & Joan	245	You can't see what you are seeing until afterward the delay
	246	Effect in what is called understanding so we watch sports
CHORUS	247	Try to get the idea of stop thinking old-style
	248	To stop thinking hopefully the term is used right
	249	At all stop thinking for instance an insert
	250	In the form of a joke the requirements to
	251	Recount the story tell what happened make it interesting
	252	Imagine here an old-school Laboratory
Jackie & Sam	253	There is of course the anomaly that is unsolvable
	254	When some one of you comes up with the answer it's the Nobel Prize
	255	I'll make it short the British deny any practice of oral sex
	256	Researchers have thrown themselves against the rocks of intimacy
	257	Since Kinsey and before trying to crack the story
	258	The National Enquirer offers a fortune for the answer
	259	Pardon me I mean between the sexes this fact
	260	If it can be called that that from Elizabeth Astraea until
	261	Approximately Margaret Thatcher nobody ever took a bath
	262	The evidence is pretty solid coinciding with what
	263	They deny has made for a stock answer in three parts
	264	In order to get a Nobel Prize you have to get by stock answers

HARMONY	SAM CHORUS	JACKIE AMY	JOAN MARG.	TOM BOB	SMPTE
VII a			G	D♮	11:06.20
		A♭		D♮	
		A♭	G		
	C	(C)	(C)	(C)	
VII b	F	(F)			
	F	D♭			

167

Jackie & Sam	265	Which are accompanied by stock characters for instance
	266	Imagine the smartest guy at Harvard he was raised on
	267	Portnoy's Complaint you mention this old problem to him
	268	This is what you get One obviously they're lying
	269	That shouldn't surprise you The British as distinct from the Irish
	270	But like the Scots almost unique among cultures of the world
	271	We can't get into name calling here have made
	272	A national culture famous everywhere based on
	273	Deceit the evidence is all over nobody cares of course
	274	God doesn't care and everybody down here knows it so there's
	275	No problem but it is amazing who would have thought it
	276	Who else would have invented theater remember
	277	That in many cultures around the world
	278	John Le Carré is inconceivable very British
Sam	279	Two who gives a shit Three they might be
	280	Telling the truth in which case who could blame them
	281	All the world's people revel in oral sex
	282	We had to stop asking the question except the British
	283	We don't do it OK you don't do it and we know why
	284	Nobody takes a bath Jane Austen didn't take a bath
	285	She wrote her ass off but she didn't take a bath
	286	Mr. Darcy never took a bath Disraeli never took a bath
	287	The whole place smelled to high heaven whole
	288	Cults jumped on boats to the New World they knew

HARMONY	SAM CHORUS	JACKIE AMY	JOAN MARG.	TOM BOB	SMPTE
VII b	F	D♭			12:10.20
VII a	C	A♭			
	C				
VII b	F				

169

Sam *(cont.)*	289	Something was amiss Charles Dickens never took a bath
	290	Until he met Mark Twain who kidded him so bad about stinking
	291	That he took a bath he hadn't seen his own legs in 15 years
	292	"The fucker almost drowned" End of insert back to scene ten
	293	One other bizarre thing has to be recounted
	294	Don leaves he takes his secrets with him
	295	Linda goes home this is what dreaming is
	296	One thing leads to another thing things are not
	297	Necessarily connected though sometime prior to or
	298	After the accident it happened he thought he saw Eleanor
	299	She was sitting in the shade at a cafe table she nodded
	300	We can't go into family histories here there's no time
	301	But it was a nod in the affirmative a yes
	302	As if some unsolved social problem from the past
	303	Comes back I told you it followed me home
	304	Attachments are complicated right millions of
	305	Years ago there were rumors Linda cried
	306	Junior, Jr. jumped up in the night screaming
	307	Don hears himself saying Jesus Holy Fucking Christ
	308	I didn't do it and he doesn't even swear
	309	But in those small towns there is no truth except in
	310	Belief G. D. told me this one
	311	The witch killed his dog the witch set his house on fire
	312	Opinion blew him up against the wall

HARMONY	SAM CHORUS	JACKIE AMY	JOAN MARG.	TOM BOB	SMPTE
$\overline{VII}b$	F				13:14.20

$\overline{V}a$	E^b				

171

Sam *(cont.)*	313	Then having suffered enough or having
	314	Been cleansed depending on your point of view
	315	He was accepted as a neighbor they even started
	316	Speaking English he could buy a loaf of bread he could
	317	Get his shoes shined end of scene ten
Sam w/ CHOR.	318	Farther and farther into the interior
Sam	319	Shuffled from one shack to another
	320	No hand-tying understand /
	321	No blindfolds no need /
	322	What do you escape to and believe me
	323	That more than once the feeling was that strong
	324	But where to which direction
	325	See you later Agitator there are some beans
	326	On the stove don't eat the mushrooms don't
	327	Drink the water don't wipe your ass on any plant that
	328	Happens to be nearby do a spot test first
	329	It'll save a lot of aimless running we'll be back
	330	In a while keep cool thanks a lot Mex
	331	There have never been nights as cold as
	332	This lizards sleep in their tracks
	333	This must be almost Argentina
	334	A tango (Berlin) end of scene eleven
	335	Finally / he gets there (pause)
	336	He thinks / he gets there (pause)

HARMONY	SAM CHORUS	JACKIE AMY	JOAN MARG.	TOM BOB	SMPTE
V_a	E♭				14:18.20
	E♭	(E♭)	(E♭)	(E♭)	
	E♭				

Sam *(cont.)*	337	I think / he gets there (pause)
	338	It had to stop / someplace
	339	This is like a scene from /
	340	Some old James Bond movie
	341	A Santa's Workshop of violence
	342	At this point you're supposed to see your hands
	343	The idea is to have control
	344	The idea is to distinguish between
	345	Dreams and waking the idea is to know
	346	That they are the same personally I think
	347	The idea is shit about this time I'm ready for
	348	Six cups of tea a cigarette a cup of coffee
	349	Drugs whatever's leftover from the night before
	350	The hair of the dog etcetera
	351	Take a shower / shave / and sauce
	352	Kiss the wife good bye / /
	353	Wash the dishes / / /
	354	Finish up the drugs / /
	355	Make a few phone calls / /
	356	Check with my broker / /
Jackie	357	But he is ahead of himself / /
CHORUS	358	In a shack somewhere the river is
	359	As red as blood two more dreams to go
	360	End of scene twelve / /

HARMONY	CHORUS	SAM / AMY	JACKIE / MARG.	JOAN / BOB	TOM	SMPTE
Va	E♭					15:22.20
Vb	C					
Ia	F					
		D♭				
	F	(F)	(F)	(F)		
Ib	C	(c)	(c)	(c)		

Sam	361	This scene is simple he is in a crowd
	362	Impatience is more than tangible this is
	363	A mob scene the purpose is not clear yet
	364	What is ominous is the fear and joy mixed
	365	A lot of fear a lot of joy
	366	A lot of people he is reminded of the
	367	Excitement of the football crowds of long ago
	368	He is reminded of the growth of mistrust in
	369	Things behind him he is reminded that
CHORUS	370	Some sensitive people / avoid shopping malls
	371	He is reminded of a friend shot down on
	372	Broadway high-noon musta been some otherbody Sheriff
	373	We didn't see nothing then it's obvious
Sam	374	A man comes forward as if from nowhere
	375	He places himself on a pile of sticks of wood
	376	The guys assigned to tie him are in a state of shock
	377	Some asshole in a fancy suit asks him to recant
	378	Who knows recant what he says no God taught me
	379	That the world is good and you can stick it up your
	380	Ass the fire is lit in a field of flowers end of scene thirteen
	381	This is sort of future in the tropics
CHORUS	382	Detroit Science Fiction Car of the Future
	383	Speeds into the Future problems
	384	Of rust all solved Atlantis lay on

HARMONY	CHORUS	SAM AMY	JACKIE JOAN MARG.	TOM BOB	SMPTE
Ib	c				16:26.20
Ia	F				
	F	(F)	(F)	(F)	
	F				
Ib	c				
Vii a	c				
	c	(c)	(c)	(c)	

CHORUS (*cont.*)	385	The Equator and that's why we don't have it anymore
	386	Nothing lays on the Equator long except for terror
	387	/ Read Velikovsky read Plato it says here
Sam	388	Read anybody it's always there between the lines Farther
	389	North you get more done Farther south you have more fun
	390	I read a book that said dying in the Arctic is actually
	391	Sublime more than easy sublime 'course he never did it
	392	Thirty words to describe what we call snow and they don't
	393	Know what writhing is I don't want to live there of course I
	394	Don't like spring floods too much but what's going on to me as
	395	Of now is dangerous and that's because of the Equator Islands
	396	Of the Future Gone Now end of scene fourteen

	HARMONY	SAM CHORUS	JACKIE AMY	JOAN MARG.	TOM BOB	SMPTE
	$\overline{VII}$ b	F	(F)	(F)	(F)	17:30.20
		F				
	$\overline{VII}$ a	C				
	$\overline{VII}$ b	F				

The photographs in the score appear where there are no changes in musical instruction.
All photos © Dan Rest, 1994 (listed in order of appearance):
Robert Ashley in "Improvement"
Amy X Neuburg in "Foreign Experiences"
Sam Ashley in "Foreign Experiences"
Jacqueline Humbert (with Joan La Barbara) in "Improvement"

Meredith Monk performing Our Lady of Late. *Photograph Gaetano Besana.*

Our Lady of Late
Meredith Monk

Our Lady of Late is a wordless song cycle for solo voice accompanied by the sound of a water-filled wineglass rubbed by a finger. Three times within the cycle the singer drinks from the wineglass causing the pitch of the drone to rise.

Our Lady of Late consists of 16 songs and a glass percussion Prologue and Epilogue originally composed and performed by the late Collin Walcott. Each song is an exploration of a particular vocal quality, musical problem, "character" or "persona" or technical aspect. In a sense, each song is a world in itself; the accumulation of the songs creates the universe of *Our Lady of Late*. By carefully structuring and ordering the cycle, the full range of the voice (pitch, volume, speed, impulse, texture, timbre, breath, placement, resonance) is represented. The cycle also builds emotionally with the contrasting qualities of the songs, adding more and more color as the composition progresses.

After I completed my first album, *Key* (1970), which included music primarily for voice and electric organ, dancer/choreographer William Dunas asked me to write a score for a new solo. I composed *Our Lady of Late* in 1972 for his dance and thus began my investigation of the song cycle form, which continued with *Songs from the Hill* (1976), *Light Songs* (1988) and *Volcano Songs* (1994).

When I performed *Our Lady of Late* (I haven't sung it since 1989) in concert, I sat at a small round table with the glass placed in its center. The action of rubbing my finger along the edge of the glass to get a consistent drone created a circular rocking motion in my body. This added to the meditative quality of the performance. Over the constant sound of the glass, my voice could float, skip, slide, lean, weave, strike, blend. As in all of my music, I was exploring different ways of producing sound with the voice. Some sections were nasal, others involved splitting notes, others used the voice as a percussion instrument. I played with various means of combining the voice and the breath, stretching the extreme ends of my range, relating the voice to the glass. For example, in the first piece, "Unison," I tried to get my voice to sound as much like the glass as possible, starting in total unison with the glass. Little by little, the voice moved in microtones away from the sound of the glass and then moved back again, creating a wave-like pattern. I also changed timbre as the song went on, which affected the beats in the microtones.

As I worked on *Our Lady of Late*, I realized again how the voice is a vehicle of transformation. Voices of ancient women, jaunty men, sailors, mothers, children playing, winds blowing made themselves known between the notes and phrases.

181

Score of first lines of first fifteen sections.

Our Lady of Late continued -2-

183

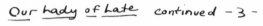

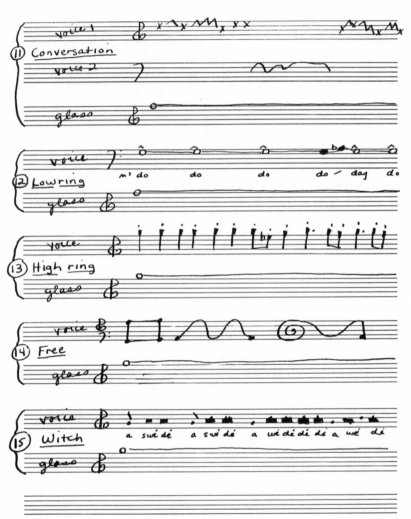

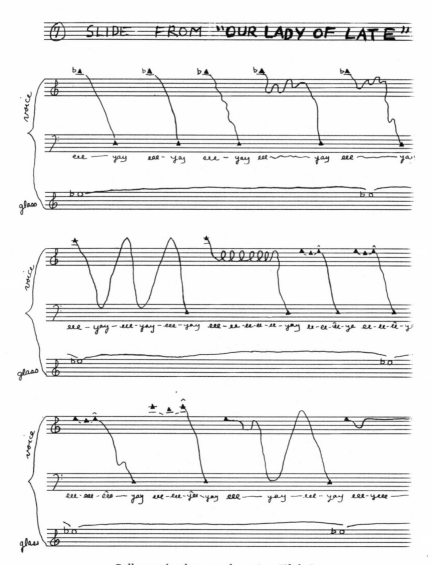

Full score for the seventh section: "Slide."

Meredith Monk

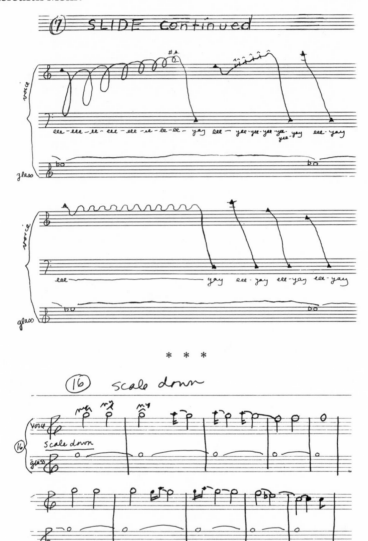

Lead sheet of the sixteenth section: "Scale Down."

From Everyday Newt Burman
The Trilogy of Cyclic Existence
John Moran

— With Ridge Theater

Characters:

Most of the characters have doubles (sometimes many doubles) that echo their actions for brief moments elsewhere in the theater. Their lines are often lip-sync'd from tape. The (#'s) indicate the number of doubles belonging to each character, including the lead.

THE NARRATOR (2)
Somewhere in between Richard Burton (reading Dylan Thomas), Orson Welles (narrating a movie) and Rod Serling (hosting *The Twilight Zone*). He is sad and somber, soft and poetic, with a hint of something frightening and manipulative.

NEWT BURMAN (5-6)
An "Everyman"; more specifically, "The Eternal, Tragic Clown." Newt is both naive and wise, battling between his own discomforts and a great empathy for everyone he encounters. He is obsessed with his friend Hillary, who comes to symbolize his attachment to the world and his humanity.

SERIOUS HILLARY (5)
A cross between "Christopher Robin" and "Wednesday" (from *The Addams Family*), Hillary lives in a treehouse in her parents' backyard that she built for studying. She is moody and unfocused, yet always very intent on everything she thinks. Sharp and angular (except sometimes when being manipulative), she lacks any sense of levity, and has the disturbing habit of "echoing" (via her doubles) all around the person she is addressing.

J.P. JOHNSON — NEWT'S EMPLOYER (3)
Kind of like Sergeant Carter, but with coffee stains on an open tie and rolled up sleeves. Drinking coffee all day and getting an ulcer. If only that slacker Newt Burman would be a better employee, and maybe "sacrifice" a little for his fellow workers, Mr. Bigmouth could start over, with a chance to break even.

MRS. FLANNIGAN (1)
A scary old woman who terrorizes all the children of the community, for to get anywhere else in the town, one has to cross her Splankin' Patch — a foreboding, graveyard-like patch of grass enclosed by a crooked, scary fence. Most of the time we only hear her, scuttling around in her little house, but upon hearing any movement in her Splankin' Patch, she will immediately enter the yard screaming with her Splankin' Paddle in hand.

MISS JONES – MR. JOHNSON'S SECRETARY (1)
Newt's sympathetic friend at work. Later, she is seen as a drunken bag lady, who laughs at Newt when he's crashing out in the Night Club scene.

BILLY, THE YARD'ARM! (1)
The town bully. He appears briefly in a scene where Newt is first pressured about the mysterious "it" that everyone is always talking about. Billy is so wide, he walks from side to side in a large, unmoving gait.

Miscellaneous:

THE GHOST OF WHIP WILL – A NIGHT-CLUB SINGER
THE GHOST OF FATTY SMATTS – A STAND-UP COMEDIAN
THE GHOST OF RINGLY THE JUGGLER
THE GHOST OF HOO-HOO THE CLOWN

NIGHT-CLUB HOSTESS
DRUNKEN COWBOY ROBOTS
NIGHT-CLUB GOERS
VOICE OF HILLARY'S MOTHER
MANY STRANGE PARTY GUESTS

Scenic Areas:
The scenic areas are in a circle, on upper and lower elevations, surrounding an island-like stage in the very middle. Each area has a corresponding sound system.

THE STARLIGHT ROOM (1942)
This is the entire theater, as a big 1940s ballroom or nightclub w/ mirror-balls and bubble-machines. The stage has a big-band orchestra w/ a bandleader. There is a singer, as well as people at tables and milling around, drinking champagne and laughing. This is like a giant ghost-image of New Year's Eve; everyone here has been dead a long time, and it's all kind of slow-motion and distant.

THE GHOST-STAGE/THE PARK
A) At "The Center" point in the circle of sets is a large, abandoned stage. This is like The Starlight Room deserted and run-down. There are cobwebs and dust everywhere. A "tingly" spiderweb is D-S-LEFT, and a large book and podium are D-S-RIGHT.
B) At a later point, we see the stage as an obviously theatrical "park scene" where Newt and Hillary play. It is obvious in that it has a very "play"-like backdrop, with all its loose-ends showing, with footlights and a cartoon tree, D-S-RIGHT.

HILLARY'S TREEHOUSE
S-LEFT of The Ghost-Stage is the Treehouse where Serious Hillary lives and works. It is cramped and crooked, full of collected and obsessed-on objects, all gathered for thinking purposes by Hillary. It has a chair D-S-LEFT, set in front of a violin and music-stand. D-S-RIGHT is a table with a large book. In the back is a stove (w/ a tea kettle) and a cupboard of dishes. C-S-LEFT is a window through which she talks to her mother in the yard below.

NEWT'S HOUSE
A crooked little shack; the main objects here are Newt's creaky old cot, a stove (w/ signs of starvation) and a television. The wind is blowing in through the cracks in the walls and a hanging, exposed light bulb provides almost no help against the darkness.

MRS. FLANNIGAN'S SPLANKIN' YARD!
Shrouded by eternal nighttime, with crickets and hooting owls, Mrs. Flannigan's house sits in the middle of the splankin' patch, which is like an old, dead graveyard. It has a picket fence that Newt climbs over, while making this dangerous crossing.

THE OFFICE & MR. JOHNSON'S OFFICE
Mr. Johnson has a small office, with a desk, phone and window. On the Floor — S.R. of the Splankin' Yard — is another area where Newt enters work and speaks with Miss Jones, Mr. Johnson's secretary.

ENTRANCE TO THE SALOON/THE NIGHT CLUB/THE DRUNK-MACHINE
A) A swinging western saloon door, with a piano and musician to its S-LEFT. One of the Newts is in a loop, entering the saloon over and over.
B) In another area, just off The Saloon Door, is a table with a bottle and glass on it. Another Newt sits there, drinking his troubles away. There is a line that leads to it, where the Newts go after entering the Saloon Door.
C) On the Center-Island, the 3rd Newt is moving in a circle while a drunken woman laughs at him. On a FILM is the image of the drunken woman spinning by, from Newt's perspective. The Narrator is there, with his arms outstretched over the entire scene, like Jesus.

SCENE 1: THE STARLIGHT-ROOM, 1942

DOORS OPEN

BIG BAND MUSIC w/ CHEERING & PARTYING

As the AUDIENCE ENTERS, they find themselves walking into a GIANT, ENVIRONMENTAL PARTY: A cross between a *"The Beatles-Save-the-Day"* kind of thing, and a 1940s NIGHTCLUB. There are BUBBLE-MACHINES, MIRROR-BALLS, FLASHING LIGHTS. On "THE STAGE" there is BIG-BAND MUSIC w/ an MC on a MICRO-PHONE.

PERFORMERS are EVERYWHERE, mostly in LOOPS (in little, staged environments) and OTHERS INTERMINGLING w/ AUDIENCE, offering them champagne, selling cigarettes, partying.

All around, HANGING from BALCONIES, are people WAVING FLAGS that say things like *"THANKS, NEWT!"* and *"I LOVE NEWT!"* and everywhere you look there's another weird guy that you didn't notice before, saying something like *"OH, Thanks for the Eternities, Baby!,"* blowing NOISE-MAKERS and LAUGHING, like it's New Year's Eve.

189

John Moran

waving in Slow Motion

The MC's loop is: *"Okay, Goodnight, Everybody! Goodnight! Goodnight!"*

pause

> ". . . *from the beautiful Starlight Room, this is You Know Who saying 'Thanks for the Eternities, Baby!' I think that Newt Burman is one . . . pretty special guy. How 'bout you?"*

pause

The AUDIENCE is MOVED into CENTER of THEATER

ANGRY MOB—*adds to the Sound of LIVE ACTORS*

Throughout the scene a CONFUSED, DESPERATE-looking NEWT BURMAN is moving through the crowd, becoming gradually more and more AGITATED. He is saying things like *"No, please . . . I'm so tired, please!"* and *"I didn't mean to say I'd do it! She twisted my words around, you guys. Please!"* He EVENTUALLY moves onto the STAGE, and is DRAWING ATTENTION as someone LOSING IT.

HILLARY follows him onto the STAGE like she is trying to calm him down, but they begin to have an ARGUMENT. NEWT is acting PARANOID and HYSTERICAL.

MUSIC STOPS SUDDENLY—*Hillary & Newt on the Stage*

In Horror

Someone Yells: *"What? What is it?"*

Speaking to Everyone

Hillary: He's saying he doesn't wanna *Do* it, you guys! He's saying he's *Afraid!*

190

All MAIN CHARACTERS STORM the STAGE and form an ANGRY MOB around NEWT BURMAN.

ANGRY MOB— *adds to the Sound of LIVE ACTORS*

DRAMATIC MUSIC CUE— *Newt Breaks Free from CROWD*

NEWT EMERGES from the MOB AROUND HIM, desperately sobbing with paranoia and exhaustion.

> Breaking Free to Kettle-Drums

Newt Burman: What the hell is wrong with you People!

> Stumbling Away

> I'm so tired......
> Why can't you just let me go to Sleep?!!

Someone Says: Because we *Need* you, Newt!
+
Everyone: Yeah! *We* need you too.....yeah!.....*etc*

NEWT is MOVING to the CENTER ISLAND

> Still a Wreck

Newt Burman: Need me? NEEEEEED me?
I'm so *Tired*, you guys.....I *just* need a Little....

HILLARY is PUSHED to the FRONT of the CROWD, with people saying things like *"Get HER up here!"* and *"You talk to him, Hillary!"* HILLARY is HOLDING a BALLOON.

> Calmingly

Hillary: Newt.....do you remember *Me*?
I'm *Hillary*, Newt.....*Remember*?

She LETS GO of the BALLOON, like a trance / NEWT is DEVASTATED

Quiet, Dreamlike

Catch the *Sun*, Newt.

ALL CHARACTERS – except NEWT – FREEZE and FADE

NEWT is FINALLY a BROKEN MAN. He WHIMPERS, and COL-LAPSES slowly onto the CENTER ISLAND, and a TIGHT LIGHT comes on him, like a DEATH SCENE.

Destroyed / in Total Resignation

Newt Burman: Okay.....that's *It. That's* it.

I'll do it.....*I'll* do it. Just stop now. *I'll do it. I'll* do it.....*I'll* do it. *Etc.*

ALL LIGHT & SOUND—*Fade Slowly to Darkness*

SCENE 2: THE GHOST-STAGE

BLACKOUT, from PREVIOUS SCENE *("NEWT'S DEATH")*

In our CIRCLE of STAGES – at a CENTRAL LOCATION – is "THE GHOST STAGE," which is covered in DUST and COBWEBS. At D-S-RIGHT is a LARGE BOOK on a PEDESTAL. At D-S-RIGHT, in the UPPER CORNER is a COBWEB (that can be reached by a person standing).

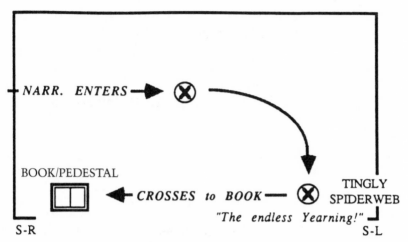

The "LAW of NATURE" on the GHOST-STAGE is that everything occurring on it will at some later point "ECHO" – meaning that a DOUBLE of the actor will be seen at some later point, "echoing" moments from the performance before. These echoes are at HALF-VOLUME, and are HALF-LIT.

10 FOOTSTEPS — *Narrator Enters*
Walking *(in Sync. w/ S-FX)* from **OFF-STAGE-RIGHT**, towards **CENTER**

Quietly Melancholic

The Narrator: But that was *Yesterday.*
Now is *Here* forever.....
And the shadows that once moved across
this yawning, *Empty* stage;

Lay like dust.....

STÁGE CREÁKING
KNEELING down to RUN FINGER along FLOOR

And the memory of the *Layers* of the dust upon the dust.....

2nd CREAK— *Shifting Weight*

All *Echo* here.

w/ DRAFTY WIND   As if wafting in from....from some other....

Ancient place.

SCUFF + 3rd CREAK

STANDING UP

Looking Around, maybe while Beginning to Walk

A *Tomb* for the thespians of another age.

15 STEPS + SCUFF— *to D-S-LEFT*

THE NARRATOR walks SLOWLY to THE SPIDERWEB

Very Droll upon Arrival

Hmmph!

TINGLY CHIMES— *Narr. touches Spiderweb*

RUNNING his FINGER ALONG IT, as if checking for dust

......a little Cleaning!

CREAK — *Looking for Match*

MATCH STRIKING— *Narr. Lights a Cigarette*

STRIKING MATCH along SIDE of STAGE by SPIDERWEB

SCUFF — *Preparing to Step Down*

MUSIC CUE: BRASS & CHORUS

AN INTENSE LIGHT APPEARS on NARRATOR for a MOMENT

Raising Palm, Mystically

......The *Endless Yearning!*

TOTALLY BACK to NORMAL, instantly

2 CREAKS + STEP & SCUFF
STANDING THERE, kind of SPACING OUT in the CORNER for a MOMENT

> Suddenly, totally Real w/ Audience
> (Ha!)
> Do you remember.....re*Member*:

SCUFF—*Turning*
CALLING OUT to EMPTY HOUSE

> *"WHIP WILL!" "WHIP WILL!"*
> It means nothing to you now, does it?

CREAK—*around the word "Day"*

> Back to a Quiet Mode
> But I remember a *Day*, when....."*Whip Will*".....would've *Sang* your broken heart away.

GHOST NIGHT-CLUB & MUSIC— *Fading In*
THE GHOST of a SINGER APPEARS on the STAGE (LIP-SYNC)

> Gentle and patient:
> He would soothe and *Croon* your rapid brain like a stream of ice, into an *Enormous* sea of.....*All* your aches and pains.

> A Different Memory:
> ......and Remember?

PUNCH-LINE DRUMS/NIGHT-CLUB LAUGHTER
THE GHOST of "FATTY SMATTS" APPEARS, ELSEWHERE

> The Guys' Trade-Mark Saying

"No One talks Back, to Big Fatty-Smatts!"
......king of the microphone.

With an Iron-*Hide*, he *Reels* out jokes that
are *Old*......*Even* in his day.

SNARE-ROLL/"OHHHH!"
GHOSTS of "THE JUGGLER" and "THE CLOWN" APPEAR
BRIEFLY

These Cues Come Quickly

"Ringly, the *Juggler*"

ROAR *of* **LAUGHTER**

"Hoo Hoo, the *Clown*"
These are all the legends of a *Forgotten* era.

ALL SOUNDS (and Figures) FADING AWAY QUICKLY
Cross-Fade w/
STEP + SCUFF—*Stepping into the Transition*

Speaking Over Step + Scuff /About to Walk

Because it's *True*, it's really *True* you
know....

7 STEPS + SCUFF—*Narr. towards D-CENTER*
THE NARRATOR "WIPES" the STAGE by CROSSING

During Foot-Steps /"Memories" on 1st Step/Speaking on Beat

......how *Memories* wait for *No* one:
[brief pause]
They are *Stored* and *Locked* and *Put* away,
w/ SCUFF   before we *Even* know they've been *Created*.
=
STOPPING BRIEFLY

2 CREAKS—*while Speaking (Shifting Weight)*

> Which is why it is......*Very very* important,
> to always *Do* and *Think* and *Say*.....*Exactly*
> where you wish to *Live*.

[brief pause]

11 MORE STEPS— *to BOOK/PODIUM*
PODIUM is STILL PRETTY MUCH in the DARK, THOUGH

During Foot-Steps

> Because they never go *Away*.

Walking to Podium....
> They never.....they never *Really* ever go
> away.

Arriving Next to it:
> Which brings us, fellow *Thespians*, to the
> *Reason* we've assembled, this *One* and......
> *Courteous* day:
>
> *But of Course*........

Waving Gesture towards Podium/A Very Strange, Low Voice

> ....the *Play*.

NARR.'S ECHO APPEARS—*Repetition of Narr.'s 1st Sequence*

**The "REAL" NARR. is STARTLED by the ECHO, and APOLOGIZES
for it**

The Narrator: Oh.....I forgot about the *Echo*.
           Ignore it please, and *It* will go away.

           Well, in *Any* way.......

John Moran

TRUMPET FANFARE

The Title Page/Overly Dramatic w/ a Raised Arm

"EVERYDAY, NEWT BURMAN!"
......The Tragedy of Cyclic Existence

* * *

SCENE 6: FLÁNNIGÁN'S SPÁNKING YÁRD!

BILLY d'YARDARM has just EXITED after his CONFRONTING NEWT. NEWT is about to EXIT (to MUSIC) in direction of SPANK-ING YARD. An ILL-WIND is BLOWING the RUSTY OLD GATE OPEN and CLOSED.

BOUNCY CÁRTOON MUSIC
NEWT goes SKIPPING DOWN the LANE

Singing in a Ridiculous Manner

Newt Burman: Lalalaaaa, La Lalalaaaa....La La....*[interrupted]*

"GÁSP!" /WHISTLE /KNEES CHÁTTERING / ROLLING CHORD
NEWT SEES the SPANKING YARD and FREEZES, SHAKING in COMIC FEAR

The Narrator: And then *There* it was......
Right in the *Middle* of the *Town:*

"OH NO!" /MUSIC STOPS ÁBRUPTLY

During Short Musical Pause

.......Flannigan's *Splanking* Yard.

198

MUSIC & SOUNDS ENTER— *The Splanking Yard*
NEWT is FROZEN w/ INDECISION while NARR. NARRATES

Narr.   No way *Around*......and *No* way across:
        The *Horrors* of the *Splanking Patch* are
        Famous in this Town.

        Few have *Entered*.......*Less* have left:
        The ominous *S-Yard* is a *Mournful* place
        of *Reckoning*......for *Allllll* bad children.

MUSIC STOPS ABRUPTLY— *The Narrator Appears*
The NARRATOR, STANDING next to The SPLANKING-YARD,
addressing NEWT

During Pause, after *"Oh, No!"*

The Narrator: Flannigan's *Spanking* Yard!

S-YARD SOUNDS
NEWT is IMMOBILIZED with INDECISION

w/3 UPSLIDING CHORDS *in* **STRINGS**

Whining and Sobbing, Pleading w/ Narrator

Newt Burman: Well, what am I supposed to *Do!?*
        I mean....*Sniff!*....I *Have* to get to *Work*, but
        I just *Can't* go through the *Splanking Patch*
        again*! Please!*
        Especially when *This* is the one where I
        don't get *Out* in time*! Come On, Please!*

TIC-TOCK BLOCKS

The Narrator: I think that maybe you'd better *Sit* down
        and *Think* about it a while.......

NEWT CROUCHES DOWN into a THINKING POSITION

John Moran

Newt Burman: Well now I think *That's* a good *Idea!*

S-YARD, NARR. & NEWT FADEOUT—*Crossfade w/*
Mr. J's Office

OFFICE SOUNDS

Mr. JOHNSON'S OFFICE APPEARS. Mr. JOHNSON is SITTING at his DESK, FRANTICALLY ANSWERING his 2 PHONES, as they ring ONE RIGHT AFTER ANOTHER. Mr. JOHNSON is a disheveled LOU GRANT, OVERWORKED and in charge of a SINKING BUSI-NESS. NEWT BURMAN is not HELPING ANYTHING.

BUZZER

PHONE #1 RING /PICK-UP

Frustrated and Gruff

Mr. Johnson: Hello....! No, I said *7:30* and that's *It!*

PHONE #2 RING /PHONE #1 HANG-UP
PHONE #2 PICK-UP

Yeah....? *[pause]* Well then *Fire* his ass!
D'ya *Hear* me!?!

PHONE #1 RING /PHONE #2 HANG-UP
PHONE #1 PICK-UP

w/ 3 BUZZERS Yes....?
Well what the hell is the *Problem* down there, *Sector-7*....!?!
Look, I don't wanna *Hear* it: You *Fix* it, or you'll find your ass in *10th*-Sector before you can get your *Shoes* tied!

.......*Got it?*

200

SECRETARY ARRIVES at DESK

Like a Telephone-Operator

Miss Jones: Mr. Johnson.....

Setting Down a Different Folder for Each Statement

w/ 3 SCUFFS   You have an 11 o'clock with ICA facility, and a 12:30 with Ian Brady from the Rand Association, plus a 1 o'clock with the Board of Directors in Sector-10.

3rd Scuff

STEPS EXIT /DOOR CLOSES— *Miss Jones Exits*

3rd STRING ACCENT— *Upsliding Chord*
In a STATE of TOTAL FRUSTRATION w/ BOTH PHONES to his
EARS, Mr. JOHNSON BLOWS his STACK

STEAM WHISTLE

w/ Whistle

Where's Newt BURMAN⸮!!!

IMMEDIATE CROSS-FADE to NARRATOR

The NARRATOR APPEARS, STANDING HALF-WAY between Mr-J's
OFFICE and the SPLANKING-YARD

SUSPENDED STRING NOTE

Very Casually, Immediately Upon Entrance of Strings

The Narrator: *Where* is Newt Burman......⸮

201

John Moran

Pointing, and Becoming Very Ominous, Immediately before Entrance
of S-Yard Music

He's Right in the *Middle* of the *Yard.*

IMMEDIATE CROSS-FADE to S-YARD

SPLÁNKING-YÁRD MUSIC & SOUNDS
NEWT is already OVER the FENCE and CROSSING the YARD,
almost PARALYZED in FEAR.

MUSIC STOPS ÁBRUPTLY

STEPPING *on a* TWIG /BELL RING & SCREÁM
NEWT STEPS on a TWIG (as before) and Mrs. FLANNIGAN AP-
PEARS, SCREAMING.

w/ BELL

Popping Up, Ready to Strike

Mrs. Flannigan: *Aaaaauuuuggghhhhh!*

RUNNING LOGS & TÁKE-OFF — *Newt Starts Running*

CHÁSE MUSIC /LÁUGHING /"OW!-OOH!-ÁH!-OOH!"
Mrs. FLANNIGAN CHASES NEWT in PLACE – like 2 DARK-RIDE
ROBOTS – w/ her PADDLE SWINGING and NEWT CLUTCHING
his BUTT, in SYNC. w/ SOUNDS on TAPE ("Ow!s")

As MUSIC COMES to a WIND-DOWN, NEWT makes it OVER the
FENCE. As he does, he STEPS immediately into NEXT SCENE ("Newt
at Work") by BUMPING INTO Miss JONES and KNOCKING the
PAPERS out of her HANDS and ALL OVER the FLOOR.

* * *

John Moran

"Hillary's
Tree House"

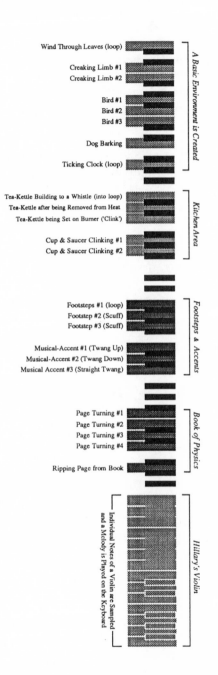

This example shows how characters and their environment are created with sound. The individual samples are chosen based on their rhythmic and melodic qualities, and then placed into the stereo-field (left and right) so that it appears the sounds are being created by the characters as they function within their environment.

In performance, the actors find themselves so governed by the score — being that every movement and word is accompanied by a specific sound and rhythm — that they are actually approaching something closer to a musical expression.

Done correctly, the effect is so smooth and naturalistic that audiences are often unaware that these performers are not actually making these sounds.

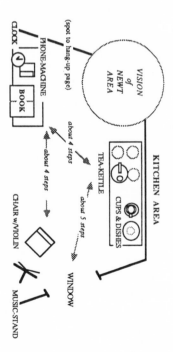

John Moran

SCENE 7: HILLARY'S TREE-HOUSE

X-FADING from previous scene — via The Narrator — we begin Fading Up on Serious Hillary, who is practicing her Violin, seated in her cramped little Tree-House. Gradually throughout the scene, we begin to see flashes of the other Hillarys all over the theater, mirroring moments of her actions.

Throughout the scene, Hillary moves from area to area, in a state of distraction between all the things she wants to do at once. We should see from the decor that she has spent considerable time here, collecting objects and obsessing on being alone.

VIOLIN — *Begin FADING UP on Hillary, slowly*

THE NARRATOR is walking slowly towards the tree-house as we begin to see HILLARY

> As always, Gentle and Somber

The Narrator: Now,
Drawn from this field in perfumed palm,
from Baker's Lane and the Wishing-Pond....

The sound of.....*thinking*.....cuts the shivering air:
37-and-a-half-feet tall, and towering over the ignorant.....
Serious Hillary, prunes and shapes a serious world....in a Tree-House......built for working.

2ND MUSICAL MISTAKE

HILLARY is PRACTICING the VIOLIN, making OCCASIONAL MISTAKES. Several times she stops and starts, sometimes leaning into her music and squinting

VIOLIN RESUMES

Pausing at her 2nd Mistake
Beginning again she resumes playing

The Narrator: OH.....is there anything equal to the *Serious* things.....in bringing delight to God.
Not for Hillary Stevens.
For as Hillary works, so does she *Breathe*,
and *Echo*.....this bright, green morning.

Pause and Listen to Hillary for a Moment;
Begin Again as Melody Changes Character

Holily....Hillary harps the tune....that *Echoes*

This Last Phrase Ends Open, before Exiting

3RD MUSICAL MISTAKE (x3)— *Narrator EXITS UNNOTICED*

HILLARY LEANS into MUSIC-STAND, squinting. She is DIS-TRACTED by the WIND for a moment, then sits up to address THE NARRATOR, and realizes he has left.

w/ a Shiver, a Little Complainy

Hillary: You know,
I don't really remember it being quite so *Cold this [interrupted]*.......Oh.

I thought he was there.

TURNING BACK to her MUSIC
Q: What does this mean; to "Remember" this moment as it is happening!

VIOLIN RESUMES

John Moran

We LISTEN to her PLAY for a while, absorbing all the SOUNDS of the TREE-HOUSE. THE NARRATOR CONTINUES SPEAKING AGAIN from OFF-STAGE when the MELODY CHANGES CHARACTER, as it did the time before.

The Narrator: Slowly....Holily....Hillary harps the tune, that sends *Newt*.....into "absolute."

Here,
and *Everything* now down upon Hillary's serious world

.....that is crashing down,
.....into these long, *Gaping*-arms,
.....that is *Perfect*

Ending Open as Before

4TH MISTAKE (x3)

HILLARY BECOMES FRUSTRATED, and JUMPS UP, SLAMMING VIOLIN onto CHAIR.

Spoiled

Hillary: Ohhh! I'm *Through* with music!

Noticing Book at Table / Into a Weird Stiffness

I *Want*....to study....*physics.*

3 STEPS to TABLE (Still 1 Step Away)
LOOKING at BOOK from a little DISTANCE, then SLIDING IN w/ STATEMENT

1 SCUFF (FOOT) to BOOK

A Lighter Mood

Hillary: *Here* is physics.

TURNING PAGES
HILLARY is MORE and MORE EXCITED as she TURNS through the
PAGES, STOPPING OCCASIONALLY and BLURTING OUT

Turning then Stopping

Hillary: The structure of the *Atom*......¿

Turning then Stopping

Components of the *Helium Molecule!*¿
Oh! Oh!
Structuring of the *Plexic Mitron* in a *Carbonated Mass!!*¿

Turning then Stopping at Picture

Yes, Ye......! [interrupted].....Ohhh!
Here's what I want to look at.

RIPPING PAGE from BOOK
HILLARY TACKS the PICTURE to THE WALL

Admiringly w/ Last Accent Tone (downward)

There is Physics.

Engaged

KETTLE WHISTLING— Rising *Underneath End of Last*

HILLARY SNAPS TO, and MOVES TO KITCHEN AREA

4 STEPS to KITCHEN / KETTLE TURNED OFF

Her idea of a Cool Joke

Hillary: *Ooop!* The *Baby's Blowin'!* [Heh, heh!]

2 STEPS to CUPS / CUP PLACED on COUNTER

1 SCUFF = TURNING to PICTURE

Very, Very Gently

Hillary: *Physics* is Here.

SUDDENLY TURNING to VIOLIN, FRIGHTENED

Oh...but the violin has more *Emotional* weight!

4 STEPS + 2 SCUFFS to VIOLIN *and* SITTING DOWN

While Walking and Sitting Down / That Weird Choppy Style

I should play the violin.

VIOLIN RESUMES
+ little Start Up Note

NARRATOR APPEARS AGAIN in an UNEXPECTED PLACE

Narrator: So little *Time*, so *Much* to *Do!*
Holily....Hillary harps the tune

......that *Beckons*

To this *Crooked* little *Crate*......in its
Long, Waiting wooden-arms......

That Open Thing
Pause / Then Quietly, Somewhere in the Mistakes

MISTAKE (x3)

Newt's here.

VISION of NEWT MUSIC— *Newt Appears in The Wall*
HIS ARMS are OUTSTRETCHED and he LOOKS LIKE JESUS
HILLARY JUMPS UP INSTANTLY and WALKS OVER to "CLOSE THE DOOR"

w/ Vision Music

> Like a Vision

Newt on Tape: *I'm Heeeeerrrre Hillllaaarrryyyy!!!!!*

Almost Simultaneous to Newt's Line
4 QUICK STEPS / TRAP-DOOR CLOSING

HILLARY JUMPS UP and CLOSES a "DOOR" on Newt, whereupon he INSTANTLY DISAPPEARS. HILLARY SPEAKS her LINE while MOVING:

> Short and Emotionless

Hillary: I *know* you are Newt, but I'm not *Ready* for you yet.

> Turning Around like Nothing Happened

The *Nerve* of some people. You'd *Think* they didn't know I have to study *Physics*!

4 SLOW STEPS + 1 SCUFF to BOOK

Here is physics......

TURNING PAGES

NEWT ENTERS (in regular form) on the **GROUND BELOW**, and **CALLS to HER**

> Like a Kid

Newt Burman: *Hilllllaaaarrrrryyyyyy!!!!*

HILLARY LEANS over the EDGE

> Really Normal

209

Hillary: Oh.....Hi, Newt. I'll be right down.

HILLARY GRABS HER RAINCOAT and EXITS TREE-HOUSE
INTO NEXT SCENE: THE PARK

SCENE 8: THE PARK

PREVIOUSLY, after NEWT's CALLING to her from THE GROUND,
HILLARY has just EXITED from the TREE-HOUSE to JOIN HIM
below. NEWT has EXITED as well, and the two of them are about to
ENTER again TOGETHER from OFF-STAGE, onto the "VAUDE-
VILLE-STAGE." HILLARY has her GALOSHES, YELLOW RAIN-
COAT and UMBRELLA.

The "VAUDEVILLE-STAGE" is seen now as an IMPRESSIONISTIC
(à la Warner Bros.) PARK SCENE. Maybe there is a bench, or a foun-
tain, or something like that. It looks very "STAGE-LIKE," w/ all its
LOOSE-ENDS clearly VISIBLE.

THE NARRATOR is the 1ST to be SEEN, followed by NEWT &
HILLARY WALKING (like kids) in an ARC from DISTANCE, gradually into their D-S-LEFT POSITION.

PARK MUSIC

LIGHT THUNDER / CHILDREN PLAYING

Sweetly
Just Before the Entrance of the Upper Part of the Melody

The Narrator: *Oh.....*

Could there be anything more *Wonderful*
In the *Entire, Living* world, than *Walking*
in some *Park* with *Hillary*, on this *Particular* afternoon?

The word "Not" Falls Around the 1st Upward Chord Change in Lower Hand
The word "Show" lands on Downward Chorus Change Beginning Next Measure

I think that you'll find that the answer is, *"TOO"...."NOT"...."SHOW"*

Say 1st Line like you Mean *"...in NEWT's tiny world..."* but w/ a Different Word

For in please *Tiny* world, *Hillary* is the *Star* of....*Every* movie, and where to *Always* sit and *Always*....is to say.....

MUSICAL BREAK
2 *"Rain Cloud"* Chords
DURING BREAK we see HILLARY SPINNING AROUND saying *"Hilllarrryy!,"* like she does again in a moment. They SOUND FAR AWAY this 1st TIME, gradually ARRIVING at FULL VOLUME while reaching POSITION

Just after Chord Break

Narrator (cont): ....*Rain-cloud⸮*

NEWT and HILLARY TAKE OVER the SCENE NOW, NARR. sits down to READ the NEWSPAPER

LONG, LAST CHORD in MUSIC

Ridiculously excited / Spoken so it's Unintelligible

Newt Burman: Oh, Hillary.....I'm your daddy yar'buckle! I mean it's *Great!* Do it again, please!

SUDDEN ENDING

Coldly

Hillary: *No.*

John Moran

HILLARY starts to WALK AWAY. In his EXCITEMENT, NEWT is acting kind of RETARDED, and HILLARY is just plain STRANGE.

ROLLING CHORD
NEWT CROUCHES to convince her, in PIANO ROLL

> The Beginning of a Wind-Up

Newt Burman: Comooooonnnnnnnnnnnnnnn.............

HILLARY becomes EXCITED to do it AGAIN, and TURNS BACK into a HUDDLE, that WINDS UP into HILLARY's SPINNING, like before.

> Turning Back Quickly

Hillary: O.K.O.K.

> *Simultaneously:*

Newt Burman: H-H-H-

Hillary: *H-H-H-Hillaryyyyy......Steve*nson!

HELD CHORD
HILLARY SPINS AROUND w/ ARMS EXTENDED (as before) and STOPS w/ 1 FOOT on the word "Stevenson," to Musical Accent

> Ecstatic

Newt Burman: Oh, that's so *Great!* Do it again, Hillary! Huh?
Will you do it ag.......*[interrupted]*

SUDDEN ENDING— *On Down Beat*
HILLARY TURNS AWAY sharply on beat, and goes off into her own thoughts

Hillary: *No.*

Newt Burman: Well why not?

Harshly, Valley-Girlesque

Hillary: Well because I'm not a *Story*-machine, o*Kay?*

SCHOOL YARD / BASSOON

Oh.....I don'know.

WALKING AROUND in LEAVES

HILLARY is STEPPING AROUND in the LEAVES, acting MOODY, looking at those other kids over there.

I guess it's just......well, it's just kind'a hard to really have very much *Fun*, you know. I mean when you know that everything is just gonna be *Over* someday and.....and *Stuff*.....and......*you* know.....

BASSOON STOPS SUDDENLY

Suddenly a Fast Idea

Hey*I*knowletsplay*Sidewalk!*

PIANO BREAK— *Newt & Hillary Run Around like Crazy*

ABRUPT STOP in MUSIC

NEWT & HILLARY have RUN into POSITION, S.L. – BACK to BACK, HILLARY FACING towards CENTER STAGE.

This is like an ABSTRACTED HOPSCOTCH GAME

Sudden Bursts of Excited Talking, then Sharp Concentration

Hillary: Okay, you go out, okay?
Ready?

2 PIÁNO NOTES— *Newt Nods*

Okay.....

4 JUMPS OUT— *Hillary Jumps while Speaking on Beat*

1, 2, 3, *I'm* OUT

HILLARY MOVES BACK quickly while both SHE and NEWT SPEAK at ONCE

A Flurry of Similar Statements

Both: No....no, okay: Come Back. Okay. Ready?

4 JUMPS OUT— *Hillary Jumps*

Hillary: 1, 2, 3...*[pause]*...out

MUSIC ENTERS— *Narrator Begins Simultaneous Sequence*
HILLARY MOVES BACK quickly, SAME KIND of VOCAL FLURRY, but LESS

3 JUMPS OUT— *Hillary Jumps Out*

Hillary: 1, 2, 3

4 JUMPS OUT / SCHOOL BELL RINGING

Hillary: 1, 2, 3.......*[distracted by school-bell on last step]*

BOTH HILLARY & NEWT are LEANING for a moment, as if being PULLED MAGNETICALLY by the SCHOOL-BELL. They suddenly break free and forget about it. HILLARY RUNS BACK into POSITION w/ NEWT as before.

Go to ⊕

//

Simultaneous to Ⓐ
THE NARRATOR delivers these lines over section "A"

MUSIC ENTERS

After the 1st Couple Measures / Very Sad & Sentimental

The Narrator: Hazy days......*Sidewalk* games

Gesturing to Newt & Hillary

These are my forgotten, rainy *Ways*

SCHOOL BELL RINGING – *Around the word "Forgotten"*

Every child is *Drawn* by the *Voice* of some old school*Bell.*

MUSIC STOPS ABRUPTLY

"2" on Final Down Beat

........*Save* 2.

//

from

UP PIÁNO CHORD—ROLLING CHORD
NEWT & HILLARY are BACK to BACK, but THIS TIME BEGIN a DUEL, NEWT standing IN PLACE, and HILLARY TAKING PACES (to Drum Beats)

On 2nd Beat (Piano Being 1st)

Hillary: Ready⸮

SNÁRE-DRUM
HILLARY BEGINS HER PACES, holding PISTOL in AIR

GUN-SHOT /MUSIC STOPS
HILLARY TURNS SUDDENLY and SHOOTS NEWT, and he FALLS
into a MUD-PUDDLE

HILLARY RUSHES back to NEWT, to help him and CLEAN HIM UP

BÁSSOON MELODY — *Hillary's Helping Mood*

On the Way to Him

Hillary: Oh, poor little-itty *Burman!*

Cleaning Him Up

Look at you: you're *All* a mess here in your
Hobo coat and.....
You prob'ly couldn't find your *Shoes* each
day, if they didn't *Catch* you in the *Morning.*

MUSIC STOPS ABRUPTLY

Really Fast and Sudden

......HeyIknowlet'splaySidewalk!

PIÁNO BREÁK — *Newt & Hillary Run to D-S-RIGHT*
NEWT and HILLARY are now in the D-S-RIGHT CORNER of the
STAGE: NEWT is sitting DOWN, and HILLARY STANDING NEXT
to HIM w/ UMBRELLA. This is called the "RAINCLOUD GAME"

Immediately Upon Arrival at End of Piano Phrase

Hillary: Okay, Ready?

2 LITTLE NOTES — *Newt Nods "Uh-Huh"*
Begin:
PLÁYFUL PIÁNO MELODY w/ PÁUSES
This music ACCOMPANIES HILLARY'S ROLE-PLAYING GAME:
She is PRETENDING to be an ARISTOCRAT, HOLDING OUT her
PALM to check for RAIN

Bad Acting, Like a Kid

Hillary: Oh, isn't it a *Lovely* day for.....

Really Fast and Sudden, w/ 1st Pause in Melody

Newt: Noyou're'sposeStart!

Hillary: Ohyeahokay....

Piano Begins Again

Isn't it a *Lovely* day for *Weather*, Captain Starling? *[pause a moment]*

I *Do* believe I shall be needing an *Umbrella* for the....*[pause]*
I say, *I DO BELIEVE I SHALL BE*.....

Realizes that Newt has not been Listening

 from Repeat

PUNCHING BOINK— *Hillary Kicks Newt*
(2nd x Standing Up w/ Grass Noise)

1st Time:
Why Newt *Burman!*
w/ THUNDER   You haven't heard a *Single* word I *Said!*
2nd Time:
You *Never* get it right!

4 QUICK STEPS— *Stomping Away from Him*

While Stomping

.....I am so *Mad* at you!

Arrive and Ring

BELL (x1)
Upon ARRIVING, HILLARY FOLDS her ARMS and RINGS at NEWT angrily

NEWT MOVES to HILLARY'S SIDE QUICKLY, pleadingly

In Pause Between Rings

Newt: *Awww,* but *Hillaryyyyy, Com'onnnn!*

BELL (x4)
HILLARY RINGS SEVERAL TIMES quickly, stubbornly

THUNDER /UMBRELLA OPEN /MUSIC
HILLARY OPENS her UMBRELLA sharply, and STEPS OUT while SINGING
w/ "RainCloud" Chords

Sung w/ 2 Chords

Hillary: Rain-Cloud.....

NEXT 2 CHORDS: HILLARY & NEWT PUT their HANDS to their EARS, listening for the REPLY from the SKY (which is on a SLIDE)

They "Hear" This:

SLIDE: *".......DON'T CROWD"*

AFTER they "HEAR" the SLIDE, NEWT and HILLARY FALL DOWN GIGGLING, as if this ENTIRE SECTION (including their little quarrel) has been ONE "RAINCLOUD" GAME

MUSIC STOPS ABRUPTLY

After Laughing

BOTH: That was *Great! Yeah!*

 Go to 2nd Ending – After Repeat

Suddenly, Sharply

Hillary: .....*OkaynowyourTurn!*

PIANO BREAK— *Newt & Hillary Run to D-S-RIGHT Again*
NEWT and HILLARY RUN back to PREVIOUS POSITION: THIS
TIME, NEWT is UP and HILLARY is DOWN: It's NEWT'S TURN,
but HILLARY has UMBRELLA

Begin:
PLAYFUL PIANO MELODY
NEWT is trying to REPEAT HILLARY'S PREVIOUS SEQUENCE,
but CAN'T

Newt Can't Do Anything Right

Newt: Uh.....isn't it.....um.....

PUNCHING BOINK— *Hillary Punches Newt in the Stomach*

Suddenly Punching Him

Hillary: .....*NodoitRight!*

Ruining It, Again

Newt: Isn't it.....um....No, okay: Let's *See*.....uh,
Isn't it a....a *Lovely*....um....a *Lovely*....Etc.

Go to last

**HILLARY PUNCHES NEWT – from sitting down – and INTO REPE-
TITION**
(From Repeat, Go to Next)

//

2nd Ending:

NEWT and HILLARY have started to FALL DOWN GIGGLING after 2nd "RAIN-CLOUD" GAME, but this time, INSTEAD of STARTING AGAIN, HILLARY goes off by herself MOODILY, POUTING

BASSOON NOTES (x3)

Things Always Go Bad

Newt: What's the *Matter*, Hillary?

Hillary: Oh, *Nothing* really.

Newt: No, come'on....*What is it?*

Hillary: I told you, *Nothing!*

Little Pause

Newt: Hillary*yyyy*.....come *Onnnn! Please?*

Hillary: Well.....it's *Just*......

Cue: Bassoon Stops, Little Thunder Burst

PIANO CHORD—ROLLING CHORD
HILLARY TURNS SUDDENLY to NEWT and PLEADING WILDLY

Throwing Herself at Him

Hillary: Oh *Please*, Newt! Oh *Please*, you just *Gotta* do it! Please, you've just *Got To!*.....*Etc.*

MUSIC STOPS ABRUPTLY

Both Quickly

Newt: What!?

Hillary: .....raise the Sun?

PIÁNO BREÁK /RUNNING BLOCKS— *Newt Panics*
NEWT suddenly FREAKS OUT (as if this were a subject he desperately
wanted to avoid) and TRIES to BREAK AWAY from HILLARY

Scrambling Around in Place

Newt: *Oh, No! No Way, Brother!*
           You didn't say Nothin' bout No Sun!
           No Way! Etc.

SHE GETS AHOLD of HIM AGAIN by END of MUSICAL-PHRASE

2 LITTLE PIÁNO NOTES

w/ Piano Notes

Hillary: *Please, Newt?*

NEWT SHAKES his HEAD

1 LITTLE PIÁNO NOTE

Hillary: *Please?*

NEWT SHAKES his HEAD

2 MORE

Hillary: *Please, Newt?*

NEWT SHAKES his HEAD

PUNCHING BOINK— *She Punches Him*

Hillary: Okay, *FINE!*

4 STEPS— *Stomping Away Mad*

Arriving, Becoming Manipulative

Hillary: If you can't do that *One* little thing, *I* think that's just *Fine!*

Cue: Little Step on Grass

I mean.....

OPEN UMBRELLA— *Hillary is a Seductive Memory*

Looking Back Through Umbrella like a Memory

I won't be able to be your *Raingirl* now or anything......but *That's* okay.

MUSIC ENTER: SONG
Probably in Middle of Last Statement

Remember?

SUNG:

"Rain-Cloud. Walking."

Spoken

Do you *Remember?*
......I'm *Hillary.*

w/ LONG, ARCING PHRASE

I'm *Always* Hillary, Newt. Just like I'm always *Walking......Remember?*

SUNG:

And saying things like: *"Rain-Cloud"*

As HILLARY TURNS to STEP AWAY UNDERNEATH her UMBREL-LA, we begin the NEXT SCENE: *"REMEMBER HILLARY WALKING"*

SCENE 9: "REMEMBER HILLARY WALKING?"

HAVING JUST TURNED to WALK AWAY from NEWT, w/ her UM-BRELLA OVER her HEAD, HILLARY is JOINED by ALL her DOUBLES. They do a SYNCHRONIZED WALKING SEQUENCE (to S-FX) in all different parts of the theater.

DURING this WALKING SEQUENCE the NARR. NARRATES and NEWT FALLS ASLEEP by where they played the RAINCLOUD GAME earlier.

//

VIOLIN (w/ PIANO ACCOMP.)— *Runs the Length of Scene*

Narrator Begins Ⓐ

WALKING SEQUENCE
Begin on DownBeat of Theme Entrance

 from Repeat

6 STEPS / THUNDER

STOP and POINT at PUDDLE

Lip-Sync from Mic'd Actress:
BELL TONE = *"Look!"*

Cue: Little Burst of Thunder

JUMPING through PUDDLES (x3)
(A Little Laugh at End)

7 STEPS—CAR PASSES

BLOWN in the WIND of SPEEDING CAR. SHAKES FIST and

Lip-Sync: *"Hey!"*

John Moran

HORN HONKS / WHISTLE

The WHISTLE says she can CROSS the STREET SAFELY NOW

9 STEPS

STOP and POINT at PUDDLE

> Lip-Sync:
> **BELL TONE** = *"Look!"*

Cue: Little Burst of Thunder

JUMPING THROUGH PUDDLES (x3)
(A Little Laugh at End)

5 STEPS—CAR PASSES

BLOWN in the WIND of SPEEDING CAR. SHAKES FIST and

Lip-Sync: *"Hey!"*

HORN HONKS / WHISTLE

The WHISTLE says she can CROSS the STREET SAFELY NOW

Go to ⊕ *and Repeat*

AFTER REPEATING, ALL DOUBLES EXIT / MAIN HILLARY to CENTER-ISLAND / MAIN HILLARY INTO NEXT SCENE: "WALKING SOLO"

THROUGHOUT the WALKING SEQUENCE, the NARRATOR is SPEAKING

> Beginning Right with Walking / Very Laid Back but at a Quick Pace

The Narrator: And as Hillary *Walks* away,
She is *Cataloged* and *Saved*.....as if.....*Every*
fleeting *Moment* were from some different
Page that could be turned and read *Again.*

How different is my world *Now:*

Let Car Pass

Now that I can always *Change* that *Awkward, Extra* word........to something more
Melodious and tame.

For in *Turning* away,
Hillary is *Equivalent* to *Memory*......and
All these *Extra* days can have more meaning in the haze of what has *Always* been
this way.

Car Pass

Narr. But that will *Never* come again.

Let us *All* try not to mention
How this cage of *Endless, Lonely* days can
be both so *Unbearable*.....

Jumping thru Puddles

......and *Safe.*

And how........*Aren't* these lonely days?

Car Pass

And how aren't these your *Only* days?
Might as well *Fill* them with a *Field* of
Hillarys.....that can *Run* and chase the
Truth away.

> March her over *Here:*
> Let her *Stomp* her way down *Memory's*
> *Lane,* until a *Cleaner* path has been created,

Right on TRANSITION — *if you're Lucky*

> Car Pass

> ....to trace into the grave.

TRANSITION to "SOLO-WALKING" SEQUENCE

MUSICAL TRANSITION— *Violin Ends into Street Sounds*

The MAIN HILLARY has ARRIVED at the CENTER-ISLAND some-how, and ALL OTHER HILLARYS have EXITED. MAIN-HILLARY begins a WALKING SOLO, in a fairly LARGE CIRCLE around ISLAND, in SYNC to FOOTSTEPS as before, but with a DIFFERENT, more REALISTIC MOOD. She is WALKING as if she JUST LEFT NEWT, and is MAD at HIM.

SOLO WALKING SEQUENCE:

w/ FOOTSTEPS
Cue: *There are 3 Long Bassoon Notes throughout this 1st Section of Footsteps*

> Bitter & Childish

Hillary: Gosh *Darn* that stupid *Newt!*
> I ask him to do *One* little thing, like start
> the program over......and he acts like:
> *"OH, OH! I have So much responsibility!"*

> Well who *Needs* those stupid *People!?*

STOP w/ THUNDER

I have *Work* to do!

w/ BELL   ....*Hmph*

[pause]

I mean, *you know*.....

WÁLKING CONT'd

s'Not that any of *You* people could ever really even *Understand* an idea like that! You know...."WORKING"....like as in having someting *Important* to do with your life!

Like as in having a *Reason* to *Exist!*
Like as in..... *[interrupted]*

CÁR PÁSSES /WÁLKING STOP
HILLARY is SURPRISED, and she SHAKES her FIST, YELLING

Yelling, Shaking Fist

w/ HORN   *HEY!*

w/THUNDER You *Stupid Driver!*

WHISTLE
HILLARY is LOOKING to SEE the LIGHT TURN "GREEN"

Cue: Little *"pre-step"*
WÁLKING CONT'd

Simple and Rather Emotionless

"I am twelve years old."

Long Pause in Speech

John Moran

HILLARY WALKS in **SILENCE** through a **SERIES** of **PASSING SOUNDS**

CARS PASSING (GENTLY) *in* **DISTANCE**

KIDS PLAYING ACROSS *the* **STREET**

SIRENS *in* **DISTANCE**

Cue:
PERSON RUNNING *down* **STREET**

> Under Her Breath, like a Fairly Casual Remembrance when Running
> Sound is Prevalent in the Room:

Hillary: *Oh*.....there's the guy *Runnin'*.

> Continue Walking in Silence

STOPPING w/ THUNDER— *Looking Around Uneasily*

     You know, things seem kind of *Strange*.

Looking Around Sadly

     I think Newt's *Forgetting*.

HILLARY is FADING

> Sadly, while Fading

     Oh.....*God Damn it!* He's *Forgetting* this.....

Erotec [the human life of machines]: An Interview with Alice Farley and Henry Threadgill

Thalia Field and Bradford Morrow

WE SAT DOWN with choreographer Alice Farley and musician/composer Henry Threadgill at Farley's studio in New York, after having seen a performance of their collaboration, *Erotec [the human life of machines]*, in the International Puppet Theater Festival, which was held at the Public Theater in October 1996. *Erotec* — a lapidary, dreamlike, sensual work whose narrative explores uneasy intimacies between humans and their mechanistic counterparts — is a consuming experience for the viewer/listener from the moment one enters the theater. Among the "characters" in the cast are Electronophonic Dancers and Brainpipes, Hermaphroplugs and Cybersisters, all engaged by a human Ringmaster/Dreamer (whose behavior at times is far less spiritual, less *humane*, as it were, than the gizmo-characters he interacts with, and attempts often to control). Above it all, in a balcony overlooking the stage, hover the "Five Strange Angels" — Threadgill's extraordinary jazz quintet. The succinct program note to the work proposes: *The machine, the tool, the technology, begin as an amplification of human desire. Mechanism is a projection of ourselves, never truly separate from the imprint of longing. EROTEC is science fiction for today — our technological culture explored through the human life of machines.*

— Thalia Field & Bradford Morrow
January 1997
New York City

BRADFORD MORROW: How did this *Erotec* collaboration begin? As a music idea, a narrative idea, or simultaneously?
ALICE FARLEY: It came about simultaneously. It was a true collaboration. We started talking about four years ago, and went through many different possibilities of thematic material and then we

settled on the idea of the seduction of technology as the area we wanted to explore. That was our only "given" agenda. We tried not to bring predetermined choreographic or musical ideas into it, but to be open to surprising ourselves. I think that's what defines a good collaboration, that you surprise yourself by coming up with something you never would have found working on your own.

HENRY THREADGILL: Our ideas gravitated to a final place of resolution by process. You never can really be sure what you're talking about until you actually start the process itself. As long as you're talking about it, that's all you're doing, just talking about it.

MORROW: So you found your way into the project through the process of the music's *being* composed, and the movements coming into play.

FARLEY: Right. After the four years of wanting and talking and waiting to do this piece (fund raising, etc.), the actual doing of it was a lot like being caught in an avalanche — the work pushing us, not the other way around. We had an intense collaborative workshop working with the entire cast in Vermont at the Flynn Theatre. The piece was really created there.

THREADGILL: When we began I had some really light sketches — they weren't really even sketches — they were like germs.

MORROW: Music germs —

FARLEY: Over a thirteen-day period we kept coming up with a piece a day. It was the first time I really worked like this. Often, you call a piece collaboration, but what it means is somebody brings a piece of music and you just set a dance to it, or you have a dance mapped out — you have phrases and structure — and someone says, "Okay, you already have that

rhythm and here's some music that sort of fits." But we didn't work like that. We really did commit to the uncharted course. There was dialogue, a collision of elements every day. A costume, an object or a gesture would start to define a character or tension, and would find an affinity to a certain music section. It was quite amazing how easy it was to see what musical landscape was appropriate to which visual landscape and vice versa. The puzzle wants to solve itself. It's unusual to be in a situation where you can work like this.

THREADGILL: It was a great experience for the performers because they were isolated, they were challenged, they couldn't run away from the occupation of paying attention to the other medium. What's hard is to find the means.

FARLEY: The means or the time or the collaborators — are they open enough — because there is a certain leap of faith; you have to divest yourself of control.

MORROW: Some of the themes I noticed centered on the politics of control and domination, and communication: whether you can connect. The passage with the electrical plugs is an example. And it always seemed that the ringmaster figure (Thom Fogarty) would appear in different parts of the theater, and you'd never know where he'd appear next. But one of the themes that seemed most strong was power struggling, of trying to find love, if you will, or connection, in a world that seems to be unintegrated and disconnected.

FARLEY: I suppose I've always had a great belief in the subversive power of desire and love (not to mention humor). That they always seep in — just where you were trying to keep them out. Even into technology. It's been a nice illusion to think all these machines are something apart from ourselves, an objective entity getting the world under control, putting things in order . . . but who are we kidding?

MORROW: The band floated in this wonderful cloud above the narrative, and there seemed to be a lot of verticality and horizontality at the same time. Do you think that came out of the process?

FARLEY: Well, dialogue was the nature of the process, and we wanted a visual dialogue, too, between the dancers and the musicians.

MORROW: It's marvelous that you reversed the orchestra pit from where it usually is — set the orchestra "pit" above the action.

FARLEY: Using vertical space always presents an interesting problem. This culture is visually fluent left to right, not up and down. How often do we notice the tops of buildings or the manhole covers on a New York street? In theater it's the same. At the Metropolitan

Opera or especially at the ballet, what happens on stage is you have this enormous empty space you are not supposed to notice:

a fifty-foot vertical picture frame with action reduced to play on only the very bottom stratum. And of course, the music is in the pit, below the stage, hidden. I am interested in a visual theater that considers the whole field of vision. I was very much influenced by Harry Partch, who talked about integrating the musicians, and taking the responsibility of finding a visual music in theater. In this piece I wanted to see the musicians on stage as characters, and I wanted the eye of the audience to be kept alive and moving.

THALIA FIELD: It's anti-Wagnerian. Could you talk about how, during the process of improvising, you came to decide when things were going to be fixed? Was there an element of indeterminacy in the piece when it was performed, or had you fixed everything?

THREADGILL: We went as far as we could go in Vermont, and what we did there worked, because we never saw this as a final piece anyway. There is no final version.

FARLEY: Our work is fairly anti-traditional in that in most opera and musical theater they finish a score, orchestrate it and then it becomes a package that pretty much can travel anywhere and anyone can duplicate it.

THREADGILL: What we do is in progress, always. Anything can come out, any dance sequence can change. The improvisational movements in it, the fixed movements in it, the music can come out, the whole piece can be triggered by a marginal piece of furniture, we all move around. What we started on a conscious level, we have to always come back to, I think, first, and then we'll be back in process again on a subconscious level. That will determine the change. It won't be arbitrary. You can't do things like that. Well, you can, but I don't operate like that, and I don't think Alice operates like that.

FARLEY: The great thing for us, even in six performances in the Public Theater, was the amount of change, because there was improvisation built structurally into each of the sections. In Henry's music, in jazz, improvisation is not unusual. But in dance, improvisation is used infrequently. There are Cunningham works that read more as abstract exercises, and contact improvisation which focuses on a sort of athletic skill—but it's very seldom that improvisation is allowed in a dramatic dance situation.

FIELD: Could you talk a little about how you worked with the performers to achieve that, or how the improvisation is structured in?

FARLEY: I choreographed with my dancers defined dramatic segments, then I tried to harmonize with Henry's structure of the music. He guides his players, but at the same time expects them to play in their own voices. I tried to get that from my dancers. You might have noticed how very eclectic and idiosyncratic the cast was. The dancers had very different body types, and different trainings. I was not about to try to mold them into my way of moving. I wanted to allow them to be true to the "voices," to respond conversationally or dramatically in a way that I felt was appropriate. With this kind of approach you get sublime moments, and other times you get things that don't really work, but  you have to take that risk. The great thing was that every night I would be surprised. For an audience, I think it's harder to perceive improvisation with dance because in some ways people's ears are more sophisticated than their eyes. They're ready to listen to improvisational segments in music and say, "Ah, there's a risk taken," and even sometimes they say, "It didn't quite work, but it's worth it for this other piece that really works."

THREADGILL: It's a big responsibility for the dancers. The performer has to take responsibility, now. Here it's how you feel about what you did. Often, that's not the case.

FARLEY: Right. With classical ballet, it's "Did you get that arabesque movement right? Stop!" That's what matters.

MORROW: When we walked into the theater we heard the overture — for lack of a better word — whose structure was so tight and precise it felt non-improvisational. Then I saw the two kinetic caryatids — those women who were backlit in the columnlike cages — which I felt had to be totally improvised.

FARLEY: It was, right.

MORROW: So you were immediately informed, by the music and by what you were seeing, that the drama promised to investigate this paradox of improvised and determinate materials. But I couldn't tell how Henry could see what was going on sometimes with the dancing.

FARLEY: He felt that way, too,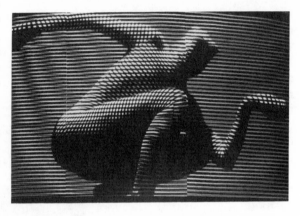

sometimes, but he had rearview mirrors. (Actually, it was telepathy.)

MORROW: There was no moment where the dream was broken. You remained inside this dream until it was over.

FARLEY: That's good. Our greatest goal was to present a landscape and have people walk into it and stay within it. Not give them time to think about their laundry lists.

FIELD: What was the distance between what you thought the piece would be and what you achieved?

THREADGILL: I don't think Alice or I were ever under an illusion that what we discussed was what the piece was going finally to be, because there was subtext and there was conscious text. I mean, it was conscious material, but there was really no text.

FARLEY: When I first started to design the costumes and build the characters, I suppose I imagined the piece would be more constricted than it was. That through exploring mechanical and technological objects we would see the binding limitations, the coldness, the robotic. I was surprised by the amount of longing that appeared instead, and humor and sadness. I wanted to see what happens when the machine dreams. It was interesting to realize that poetry and magic reappear.

FIELD: The modular furniture you referred to, I liked that a lot because it makes me think of the piece as intersecting objects. Did a fixed arrangement emerge from your work, or do you perceive that the whole is made of interchangeable pieces?

FARLEY: Henry was talking about how sections can be removed or are interchangeable to a certain degree as we develop the piece. But I felt it made its own peculiar dream and narrative as it was, and that the character of Thom [Fogarty] was the linking factor. We called him the ringmaster/dreamer.

THREADGILL: Right.

FARLEY: It was his interaction with all creatures that propelled the story.

MORROW: Was he as sinister a figure as I thought?

FARLEY: Sinister, demented and driven by his remote control — but I thought he was also a hope-ful cynic, with his own freedom. He could spit in your eye and walk away. He could be trans-formed by love.

MORROW: You often anthropo-morphized machinery in the work. Electrical plugs wanted to experience sexual joy and human-esque interaction. I was fasci-nated by that, and I found the sequence to be one of the most moving and charming in the en-tire piece. Electronics and its machinery cut loose from any kind of human activity or land-scape. They were operating all on their very own in a human way that's actually very attractive, not riddled by evil or greed when they are not controlled by Thom or watched by Thom.

FARLEY: Right. It's not difficult to imagine machines with a life of their own, or with *our* lives. With all the energy we invest in our design, our use and need for these objects, don't they become in some sense our talismans? Don't they amplify us?

FIELD: Thom had an ambition to control situations, but then he was seduced by them, too. The girls — or machines — had their way with him.

FARLEY: What is life with the re-mote control, or the telephone? Who seduces whom?

FIELD: Is it science fiction, or a certain visual tradition that this landscape came out of for you, or did it just come to you in a dream? Some of the figures seemed right out of a comic book.

FARLEY: It's true I've been a sci-ence-fiction devotee since I was ten, but really the images just evolve. I've always been inter-ested in the automatic method and objective chance. I do think forms or gestures or objects pre-sent themselves to you at a given moment, and once you begin to animate them, they will tell you

where they want to go. It's not a matter of transcribing from a dream (though people frequently assume that), but of finding that same logic that directs your dreams. I like to think of choreography as total spatial design, with a responsibility for color and sculptural form as well as movement patterns. That's why I design the cos-tumes and illusions that go into a piece. Of course, the set and light designers help transform the space as well (here I was working with Bill Stabile and Howard Thies). The aim is really to create another world altogether, and when it works, it should be a seamless landscape.

MORROW: Do you think being costumed affected the way the musicians played?

THREADGILL: I think ultimately it did. Clothing affects everything. Your attitude. Everything.

MORROW: Miles was famous for being able to pick out his players based on what they were wearing, how they held their instruments.

THREADGILL: There's that little Irene Forney song, "Clothes Make the Man." You go out of the house looking a certain way and feeling a certain way. It's about changing how you feel in the morning or afternoon after going to appointments. How you always want to be one up on the other person because of what you wear. Clothes can make you feel superior.

FIELD: Did the musicians pick their costumes?

FARLEY: I gave them a little leeway there.

THREADGILL: We gave them a range of costumes, variations, and let them pick what they wanted.

FARLEY: We ended up picking what seemed to suit each individual. It's very interesting to know — as with the dancers — the individuals. The best use of costume is a visualization of character. To make the characters visible.

MORROW: Who are the musicians or choreographers you feel are doing interesting work now, or in the recent past? You mentioned Harry Partch.

FARLEY: I've always said the greatest American choreographer was Buster Keaton. As far as method or point of view, I've been interested in surrealism for twenty years and participated with various collective groups in New York, Chicago and San Francisco. I particularly respect the incredible costume ritual theater developed by Jean Benoit in Paris in the fifties and sixties — his ideas changed my approach to costuming. I think Oskar Schlemmer's Bauhaus work was important, too. But it was traveling to Japan and Indonesia, seeing the Kabuki and Indonesian dance and theater, that made me realize what a total experience and *visual* language theater could be. Color, gesture and image could move an audience through time, could resonate and communicate beyond words.

MORROW: What about you, Henry? Do you see any tradition come out as a jazz composer?

THREADGILL: I don't think of myself as a jazz composer. I just think of myself as a composer. I write and play different kinds of music. There is a tradition, but it's not an identifiable tradition to somebody over here and somebody over there. It's not like some line of people you can name, like a whole bunch of people who do a Broadway show. There are certainly people all around the country who have had similar ideas of trying to integrate dance and music arts. Mine's a more non-Western approach to total theater, I think, because theater in the Western world is like philosophical thinking in the Western world. It's really divided. When you go to the opera there's the orchestra in the pit, and everything is divided.

Whereas when you look at a lot of Eastern art, you see it all. It's all there in front of you. It's one thing. In music theater everyone works together. People are really working with each other. There's a real connection. Here, a lot of the time the orchestra won't even look at a show. The only person who's watching the show half the time is the conductor. And a lot of the time even he won't look up. He's looking at a screen or a monitor. I happen to have a belief that there is something in the eye — from my eye to your body, or my eye to your eye — that can affect that I'm doing and vice versa. I like to make art that exists on that basis. It's far more interesting and stimulating. I'm not interested in being non-Western, I'm just interested in working in a way I think is superior. I don't care where it comes from.

FIELD: I'd be interested to know what your ideal performance space would be for this project. I found that the atmosphere was such a big part of it, sort of like walking into an East Berlin disco. I felt like it wasn't intended to be as clean as it tends to be in a plush theater, and I'm wondering if that's something that you thought about. Are you pursuing that, or what would your ideal be?

THREADGILL: If we had a bigger space and no columns, and a little more backstage, that's all.

FARLEY: We want to be able to wake an audience up. Because of television, film and computer life, this is such a passive time. "Real" space and "real" time have to be presented intimately, right in your face — with everything visible at once.

THREADGILL: You don't want so much room that you lose that intimacy. It's a whole other thing when this distance occurs. When people are present, you can definitely feel the energy on the stage as a performer. You can see people. When the distances are too great, the audience becomes a blur.

FARLEY: You can feel them when they lean back in their seats. You can just feel that whole removal, and there's less risk involved.

THREADGILL: An intimate space can be very challenging in that type of proximity, it can unnerve you. It can actually provoke a very great performance out of you.

FIELD: We wanted to ask about your being in the International Puppet Festival. How did you wind up there, does that mean something to you, are you in a puppet-theater tradition, or was it sort of a fluke?

FARLEY: The Henson Foundation that produced the festival is interested in a broad definition of puppetry that includes performing objects as well as hand puppets. So they presented us following in the tradition of Schlemmer and Nikolais, experiments in extension of the human form and sculptural animation. It was great of them, because most dance funding doesn't go to support this kind of work.

FIELD: What is the ideal audience relationship to what you're doing? Brecht had a very particular intention for what kind of involvement he wanted from them. Is that something you've thought about? What are you creating for the audience? What kind of mental state do you want them in? How much critical distance should they have?

FARLEY: Everyone prefers an audience that comes in willing to suspend their preconceptions, but I suppose the strongest compliments I've gotten — I do a lot of free outdoor landscape pieces for the general public — and after people have seen them they often come back and say, "I can never walk into this space again and have it look the same to me." They say that the space came alive. Much of this audience would not choose to go through a theater door, they have no preconception of the "theatrical experience," but theater can work on them nonetheless.

THREADGILL: The uninformed audience, throughout my entire career, has always proved to be the best one.

FIELD: Do you think there should be some sort of shift in the model of where theater is performed?

THREADGILL: Just a lot of exposure. You don't have any tradition in American theater. I never went to see a play until I was eighteen years old, and it dawned on me, "Where have I been?"

FARLEY: We have to believe that theater, dance, music strike an authentic chord in people — that there is value and risk in experiencing performance in real time and real space. It's not dependent on knowing some refined and esoteric theory of theater; when the work is good and the audience open, they will respond to it.

THREADGILL: I had no background in it and I was completely wiped out, transported.

MORROW: What you're using strikes me as a perfect balance between absolute articulation, pure intelligence and totally visceral, emotional, from-the-heart procedures. It joins completely the heart and the mind, and that's what I thought was the most successful aspect of everything: visually, performatively, I could feel moments of improvisation, although I couldn't tell, and I found myself almost in the narrative, like you fall into something, that's what you want to watch or listen to, or in my case as a novelist I want a reader to do, to fall into the dream. And the only way you can do that is by opening up. Improvisation is from the heart. It was danced from the heart.

Erotec dancers: Felicia Norton, Sharon Livardo, Thom Fogarty, Mark Mindek, William Isaac, Alicia Diaz, Laura Peterson, Kalya Yannatos, Adam Macadam. Musicians: Brandon Ross, Tony Cedras, Stomu Takeishi, J. T. Lewis, Henry Threadgill. Designers: Bill Stabile, Howard Thies, Alice Farley.

Photographs by Mary Javorek and Eaderesto/Farley.

From The Negros Burial Ground
Ann T. Greene
Composed by Leroy Jenkins

The Cast:

Individuals

MARY BURTON, the indentured servant of tavern owner John Hughson, whose false accusations and testimony triggered the Slave Conspiracy of 1741 hysteria.

JOHN HUGHSON, a British tavern owner hanged in 1742.

SOLOMON BOATWRIGHT, an African artisan/slave, and one of the Conspirators hanged in 1742.

LULAH CUFFEE, an African slave who, having just murdered her mistress, is summarily executed.

20th-Century Dead

ELEANOR BUMPURS, a 67-year-old Bronx resident who was fatally shot while being evicted from her apartment. Police contend that Bumpurs was "violent and uncontrollable" as justification for using deadly physical force against her.

EDMUND (EDDIE) PERRY, a 17-year-old Harlemite and recent Phillips Exeter Academy graduate who died from bullet wounds received while mugging a New York City cop.

MICHAEL STEWART, a 25-year-old Brooklyn artist who died a little more than a week after having been beaten by New York City Transit Police, while being arrested for scrawling graffiti at a subway station.

The "Negros Burial Ground" or "Negros Burying Ground" is the description used on colonial New York maps for the unconsecrated graveyard placed outside of the city to bury Africans, paupers, enemy soldiers and Native Americans. The modern usage would be "The Negroes' Burial Ground."

241

Ann T. Greene

The Old Dead

The inhabitants' society, the World of the Dead, is stratified around the circumstances of their deaths. The OLD DEAD *are:*

THE ELDERS, *the first Africans, men, to be imported to Nieuw Amsterdam. The African men who arrived with the Dutch were artisans, farmers and skilled laborers.*
THE INSURRECTIONISTS, *those who died or were executed resisting slavery, particularly the men and women who plotted the Rebellion of 1712; and* THE CONSPIRATORS, *Africans, free and enslaved, who were implicated in the Slave Conspiracy of 1741. (The latter group contains several embittered Dead, people who claimed no part of any conspiracy and yet were convicted and executed.) Some of* THE INSURRECTIONISTS *and* CONSPIRATORS *are diviners who can maintain contact with the World of the Living,* NATIVE AMERICANS *who were participants in the Insurrection of 1712 and African soldiers who fought for the British during the Revolutionary War.*

Additionally, the World of the Dead is populated by:

THE FECUND, *who are the women who died in childbirth;* THE CHILDREN, *the babies and children who died at birth or because of disease and malnutrition;* THE DISEASED, *adults who died of smallpox, measles, cholera, influenza or any number of epidemic diseases that were common to colonial times; and* THE ITINERANTS, *indentured servants, male and female, who died poor and therefore as dependents of the provincial government. Lastly, there are* LOS NEGROS, *the hapless Spanish subjects who were captured in warfare with the British and enslaved. Some died as* INSURRECTIONISTS *or* CONSPIRATORS. *Others died having killed themselves rather than remain enslaved.*

Introduction

It is 1742. The stage is divided into 2 worlds—that of THE NEGROS BURIAL GROUND *and colonial New York (later 20th century New York City). We hear the everyday street sounds of colonial life and a polyphony of languages. At* THE NEGROS BURIAL

GROUND *African gravediggers are preparing the ground for the interment of adults and children.*

It is dusk. As gallows are constructed and fires lit, from City Hall's steps we hear the insistent and insinuating voice of the young indentured servant, MARY BURTON. *The sky is red with fire and there are the cheers of spectators as accused conspirators* JOHN HUGHSON, *tavern owner,* SOLOMON BOATWRIGHT, *an African slave, and others are hung or burned at the stake.*

HUGHSON, *a white tavern owner, and* BOATWRIGHT, *an African slave, have been accused of conspiring to take over New York, install* HUGHSON *as King of the Negros and free the Africans. These accusations had been brought by the glory-seeking* MARY BURTON, HUGHSON'*s indentured servant, who revels in the sensation she has caused. It is a time of hysteria, where slave rebellion and the fear of slave rebellion permeate the governance of the British colony of New York (formerly Nieuw Amsterdam).*

Many Africans are dying, not only from the burnings and hangings, but from the epidemics common to colonial times — diphtheria, cholera, etc. — and malnutrition. BOATWRIGHT *is buried in what the City has designated as the Negros Burying Ground, a hilly swampland littered with 18th century debris — shards of pottery, decaying animal carcasses and other refuse. There are also other remains, mistaken as debris, but actually grave decorations — torn auction bills, tools, lamps, bottles, cooking pots, etc.*

As he descends to the World of the Dead, which in Bakongo cosmology is the mirror to the "present," i.e., the World of the Living, he meets with others, long and recently dead, and tells the harrowing story of his (and his comrades') executions.

A recent arrival, LULAH CUFFEE, *brings more news of the Living World to the dead. Her story of the murders and hangings further outrages* THE INSURRECTIONISTS *and* CONSPIRATORS. *They challenge* THE ELDERS' *authority.*

Troubled by the unrest, THE ELDERS *forbid the Dead to leave their world. To do so,* THE ELDERS *know, would be to release bad spirits who will haunt the living. All are quieted for the time*

*being and the World of the Dead enters into a period of rest. The
Dead replace the shrouds in which they were buried, lie down in
their graves and turn their heads to the west.*

The second act begins with THE ELDERS *bidding the Dead to
assemble. Having realized that they must occupy* THE INSURREC-
TIONISTS *and* CONSPIRATORS *who resist authority in death as
they did in life, they decide that a tunnel to Africa will be built.
Those who long to reunite with their kin — mothers, fathers, children and siblings — will travel the tunnel to "go home" to Mother
Africa.* THE ELDERS *shrewdly choose the dissidents as the crew,
appointing* BOATWRIGHT *their leader. The work begins.*

ELDERS. Clause!
  Robin!
  Blue Jacket!
  Kwaku!
  Lysabet!
  Solomon!
  Come!

ELDER 1. You who have killed a man with your hands
  You who have set the city afire
  You who have bled atop the green apple trees
  Come with me.

ELDERS. Brave strong ones
  Come with me.

ELDER 2. You who have hung
  in the twisted jute rope
  You who have worn iron rings
  round thy neck
  You who have died
  in the fight to be free
  Come with me.

ELDERS. Bring thy axe
  Come with me.   CHORUS. By the sea we come.
                                 By the sea we go.
                                 Oh Mother
                                 Mother Africa
                                 I come home.

244

SOLO. Oh Mother
How I miss
Your breasts
of sweet milk
How I miss your
fingers full of yam.

CHORUS. By the sea we come.
By the sea we go.

SOLO. Oh Mother
Your hips carried me
to the world
of my kin.
Christian ships
carried me
to a world of
strange men.

CHORUS. By the sea we come.
By the sea we go.
(Repeat.)

SOLO. Away from you . . .
(Repeat.)

CHORUS. By the sea we come.
By the sea we go.

SOLO. Cry not, Mother.
I will slay a goat for
I will take the
medicine for
I will do what
you ask for
Mother Africa.
I must come home
to you.

CHORUS. By the sea we come.
By the sea we go.
(Repeat.)

Scene 2

(It is 1980's New York. Gunfire, screams and wailing, sirens, protests. Demonstrations and funerals merge for the deaths of first MICHAEL STEWART, *then* ELEANOR BUMPURS *and* EDMUND (EDDIE) PERRY.)*

PROTESTERS A & B.

Can you tell me why?

         B. Tell me why!

Deadly force was used to kill
a young man gentle
gifted artist doing
what an artist must?

Can you tell me why?

         B. Tell me why!

Deadly force was used to kill
a mother's mother
someone's Gran'ma
who never hurt a soul?

Can you tell me why?

         B. Tell me why!

Deadly force was used to kill
our scholar who had
much to live for.
Harlem's shining star.

Can you tell us why, cops?   B. Hell, no!
Can you tell us why, Koch?   Hell, no!

We want answers!
No more lying!
We want justice for . . .   B. Michael!
                        Eleanor!
                        Eddie!

(As the protest intensifies, the NEW DEAD *tunnel in an attempt to get back to New York.* ELEANOR BUMPURS *(brandishing a knife) implores the others to dig faster.)*

ELEANOR. I been on Earth
　longer than both of you babies
　and even been here longer than you!
　You youngbloods can't
　get us to the street?
　Let's go!

　　　(*A membrane of earth is broken and the Dead suddenly are
　　　facing each other.* ELEANOR BUMPURS *lunges towards the*
　　　OLD DEAD.)

BOATWRIGHT. (*Laughing.*) Lioness! Protect thy cubs!
　Mother! Save thy sons!

　　　(EDDIE, MICHAEL *and* BOATWRIGHT *restrain her.*)

BOATWRIGHT. (*Angrily.*) Young men, take your mother
　and her knife!
　Where does she think she is?!

　(*To* EDDIE *and* MICHAEL.) Who sent you to us, spirits?
　How did you find us here?
　Where are you from,
　garbed so?
　Come, let me see you.

　　　(*Encouraged by* BOATWRIGHT*'s solicitude,* EDDIE *shows the
　　　tunnelers his bullet wound and* MICHAEL *shows them his
　　　neck burns and his empty eye sockets.*)

OLD DEAD TUNNELER. Look at thee
　A young man, strong and black
　A musket tore your back.
　Three hundred gilders lost
　Did Master rue the cost
　of his African
　so strong and black?

OLD DEAD TUNNELERS. (*Chorus.*) It is true
　that thee are with us now
　Thy Master's gilders gone
　No doubt he mourns the loss
　but killed you nonetheless.
　One of his best.
　What did thou do, my son
　to thy Master?

247

OLD DEAD TUNNELER. Look at thee
   Rings burned around thy neck
   Eyes plucked from out thy face
   The pearls of Africa
   are missing from thy case.
   Thy Master stole thou eyes?
   No others tell thou that
   they still are used
   to find your way, to this our home?
   Young slave made blind.

OLD DEAD TUNNELERS. (*Chorus.*) Thy Master's gilders gone.
   No doubt he mourns the loss
   but killed you nonetheless.
   One of his very best.
   What did thou do, my son
   to thy Master?

   Look at thee
   Africans strong and black
   Thy Masters' loss our gain
   Thy mutilation is their shame.
   Three hundred gilders thrown away
   is not the measure of
   Two warriors in our midst.
   Returned to the Mother's land
   because of what thee did
   to thy Master.

BOATWRIGHT. Now to The Elders.
   Come.
   Come, Mother, take my arm.

     (*The* OLD DEAD *begin escorting the* NEW DEAD *to meet* THE
     ELDERS.)

EDDIE. Michael!

MICHAEL. Yeh!

EDDIE. How do you know
   they're not taking us
   to a trading post!

MICHAEL. A trading post?

EDDIE. You know
   to the coast
   You know
   of Senegal
   It was . . .
   It was . . .

MICHAEL. Goree?

EDDIE. Yeh, Goree.
   It happened before, bro.
   It can happen again.
   I'm telling you, Michael.
   There were
   Brothers turning brothers
   into slaves!

MICHAEL. Eddie, brothers sell brothers
   in every age.

Scene 3

(*On their way to* THE ELDERS, *the tunnelers talk to the* NEW DEAD.)

TUNNELER. I wait for you.
   I dig for you.
   You come. You come.

MICHAEL. Don't he look like . . .

ELEANOR. Well, he ain't!
   They look like Africans to me
   and I ain't no African.

TUNNELERS. Here you are at last.

EDDIE. Never seen these folks
   in my life.
   I'm from Harlem.

ELEANOR. My people from South Carolina!
  I wish I had my knife.

  (*As soon as they arrive,* THE ELDERS *question the* NEW DEAD.)

ELDERS. You have never been to Africa?

NEW DEAD. No.

ELDERS. Never taste the fruit
  of the coconut tree?

NEW DEAD. No.

ELDERS. Aah! Where from the World
  of the Living did you come?

ELEANOR. I come up from Carolina
  to die in the Bronx.
  Motherfuckin cops trying to get me
  out my house!
  My house!

  (*Stunned.*)
  Last thing I remember
  was this mess on my dress.
  Cops shoot me . . .
  Blew me **away** . . .
  Blew me away . . .
  Blew **me** away . . .

EDDIE. What you folks call
  the militia
  was po . . . pigs back in the day.
  Me and my bro, Jonah
  went out to play
  a game of ball.
  Harlem ball. Basketball.

  Y'know? Shoot some hoop?
  Well, me and Jonah
  I mean Jonah and I
  weren't doing nothin.
  This pig comes runnin . . .
  We got to hide!
  We split!
  No "stop" or nothin!

Gunshot.
Bam!
Bullet.
Bam! Bam!
Me. Bam!
MICHAEL. Down   I'm dead.
in the catacombs
where the L goes to Queens
They took me down.
I dropped my can.
Stars exploded in my eyes.
'Cause they choked me.
Then it was black.
And that's the last thing
I remember.   ELEANOR. (*An aside.*) So what
the Hell is this shit?
And how do I get out of here?

(THE ELDERS *confer, and then gather the* OLD DEAD.)

ELDERS. Long days ago
Back in the land
of the dancing Sun
Yoruba capture Nupe.
Sell him to the Fon
capture Bambura.
Sell him to the Ashanti
Sell him to the British.   EDDIE. (*To* MICHAEL.) See? See?
He labored til he die.   What I tell you?
Never to see Mother Africa
Again.

The gods say
no home go.
We stay here.   OLD DEAD. (*Weeping.*) Where is
My Mother
My Brother
The gods say   My Sister?
No home go.
We stay here.

No home go.   ELEANOR. (*An aside.*) Yeh, well
We stay here.   that's alright
for you folks

251

Ann T. Greene

But I'm from the Bronx.
I got to get uptown.

(*One of the* OLD DEAD, NANA, *has stepped forward to stare at* MICHAEL. *She addresses* THE ELDERS.)

NANA. Mos high to thee I speak.
Me nurse five babies
None mine own.

I hab a baby
long time go
A baby son
My lil one.

I tell de master
Take all my wealth
Sell me my son
for dis belt
o' cowrie shell.　　　　　　　WOMEN'S VOICES. Owo*
　　　　　　　　　　　　　　　Owo
He say　　　　　　　　　　　Owo
Nana, dat no gold.
Dem shells no worth no
more dan dis baby boy.

Keep you cowrie
gib me dat chile.

I no more see　　　　　　　WOMEN'S VOICES. Owo
my baby son　　　　　　　　Owo
til dis day.　　　　　　　　Owo
　　　　　　　　　　　　　　Owo
He de one.　　　　　　　　　Owo
My lil one　　　　　　　　　Owo
My baby son.　　　　　　　　Owo

(*The* OLD DEAD *rejoice and welcome him and the reluctant others to the World of the Dead.*)

Eleanor Bumpurs
Edmund Perry
Michael Stewart.

─────────────
Yoruba for cowrie shells.

CHORUS. Mother, here you are with me.
Brother, welcome
welcome home.
Hush, baby, stop ye crying
Home you are at last.

Brother, here you are with me.
Sister, welcome
welcome home.
Hush, baby, stop ye crying
Home you are at last.

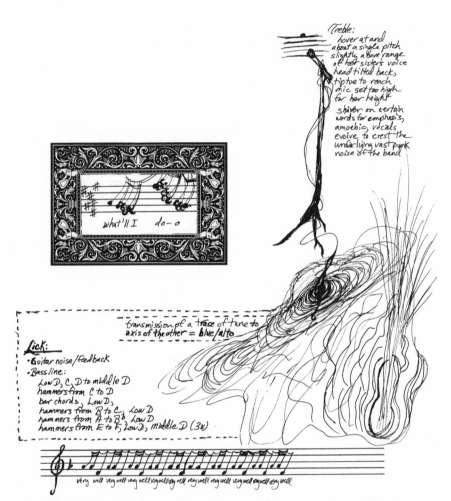

Treble:
hover at and
about a single pitch
slightly above range
of her sister's voice
head tilted back,
tiptoe to reach
mic set too high
for her height
shiver on certain
words for emphasis,
amoebic, vocals
evolve to crest the
underlying vast punk
noise of the band

what'll I do-o

transmission of a trace of tune to
axis of the other = blue/alto

Lick:
• Guitar noise/feedback
• Bass line:
   Low D, C, D to middle D
   hammers from C to D
   bar chords, Low D,
   hammers from B to C, Low D
   hammers from A to B♭, Low D
   hammers from E to F, Low D, middle D (3x)

very well very well very well very well very well very well very well very well very well very well

Illustration/Song 1: "Brick Shoulders" *(Chaucia's asymmetrical malfunction of behavior moves from stuck in throat of building into descant face-of-the-clock cadence into shut-up volley back to the psalm of very well, very well).*

From Wallpaper Psalm
(an electric & hysteric operetta)
Ruth E. Margraff

Characters:

CHAUCIA & HER SISTER, two elderly women who have a history that spans their pinnacles of youth and beauty, moments of courtship into which they built themselves various structures, or circuits, to perform. They maintain a certain surface, which, when slipping, may cause hysterical abjection and thereby music.

PERPETRATOR, a punk rock, ranting, suspect invader of the building. Slightly out of breath as if he brings some message from the front line or from an action that is supposed to be happening offstage.

ROBERT, dressed like a soldier/doorman. The witness, as was John to the book of Revelations, writing down such large visions as the millennium, the Antichrist, the seven seals, ten-headed angels eating little books that went sour in their bellies, ornamental heavenly city structures, the ends of the earth, etc. Monitors the lobby with a small surveillance device and by signature into an enormous black book. A service that Chaucia pays for in a pre-war building (once luxurious but dilapidated now as is the building).

NOTE TO THE READER ON STYLE

THE LANGUAGE OF THIS PLAY FUNCTIONS AS A TIGHTLY STRUC-TURED ORNAMENTAL SURFACE WHICH WHEN STRAINED WILL MALFUNCTION INTO HYSTERIC RUPTURES OF MUSIC OR VARIOUS DECORATED PANICS. FOR THIS REASON, PLEASE READ AS HAVING BASIC UNDERLYING ASYMMETRY AND ATTEMPTING BY ITS INTER-LOCKING (LANGUAGE) TO REACH A CERTAIN SYMMETRY.

DECORATIVE FACADES ARE PHYSICALIZATIONS OF A SOCIAL STRUC-TURE WHEREIN THE WALLS, DESIGNS, OBJECTS, BODIES AND LAN-GUAGE HAVE AN "ELECTRICITY" COURSING THROUGH THEM (VERY MUCH A CLOSED CIRCUIT). INTERCOM, ELEVATOR, RADIO, LAMP

AND CLOCK MAY BE WIRED/AMPLIFIED SO THAT THEY PROCESS
SOUND AND INTERACT WITH PERFORMERS.

MUSIC EMERGES FROM THIS (ELECTRIC) DRONE — A SINGULAR AND
HORIZONTAL AXIS THROUGH THIS PIECE AND FROM A PERFORMA-
TIVE HYSTERIA WHICH IS HALF MUSIC, HALF HYSTERIA. SONGS THAT
ARE MELODIC ARE SPENT REGAINING THIS COMPOSURE.

Place: Set in a Tudor City, pre-war, sophisticated apartment building on East 42nd Street, New York City.

Time: "Turn of the Century" in between the trees of good & evil
from Genesis and the tree of life, post-apocalypse from the Book
of Revelations or turn of the old testament into the new, a pre-
carious rupture of time, a lapse, and yet a point of transfiguration,
where, as in Numbers 16:32, the "earth opens up its mouth and
swallows all the people and all that appertained unto them."

WHERE THE LOVERS STROLL

(*Lights come up in elevator,* ROBERT *is there, holding open
the door. There is a lush green velvet rupture cut like a
river is cut into the floor curving across the stage, velvet
trees draping it. He and* CHAUCIA *step into it and begin to
stroll like lovers. Stroll music when he takes her arm.*)

ROBERT. You know darling, walking next to you here/now in the
lane . . . The lane gently curving as we walk a little this way . . .
bending to the bold blue patch of lake and then away again . . .

CHAUCIA. Oh yes, is that the lake?

ROBERT. (*Outburst w/innuendo.*) Or the ocean, who knows, it is
a <u>body</u> of water, it is all one piece, the waves rearing up and
crashing (dashing their feet against the stones) . . . Oh no, my
dear, it isn't that the sea is <u>salty</u> that nobody drinks it. It is because if you were to dip your ladle into the ocean you would
be separating a Piece from the Whole and that is where, in the
narrative, the hurricanes come from. Tidal waves erupt. Splashing, heaving, terrible winds. A large shark hurls itself onto the
deck! The ship capsizes with the great weight of the shark! Half
the crew and the Captain <u>drown</u> before the very eyes of the
sailor who <u>thought</u> <u>he</u> <u>was</u> <u>just</u> <u>thirsty</u>.

CHAUCIA. What is it Robert? What does it mean?

ROBERT. Oh darling tomorrow perhaps, I'll be sent away like a box of tea only to be blindly gutted, shot through the torso with a cannon ball, rammed through the eyeball with a musket. Frozen solid in a bloody battle creek like some sort of skinny rabbit with his foot in a trap.

CHAUCIA. Oh Robert. I remember how the whole city went out searching for that little boy lost in the marsh. And we walked in the lane just like this until I stood enclosed in the circle of the candle and I said Robert, darling "What IS IT." And then you poured forth the story. I had no idea. I thought I was walking to the store to get a bolt of cloth for my SISTER FOR A DRESS! I couldn't remember why we were walking. I didn't know the store was closed and the city was closed.

ROBERT. (*Outburst to sky.*) I'll tell you why it is. Why the brutality. The terror of a boy lost in the marsh. The taxes. I'll tell you why they tax our very exertions. Our heat! The water in our pipes. They tax us for a map of roads we'll never even travel on. They tax whatever they find in the earth beneath our feet. And the buried bones that might be interesting for their private collections! You can't just stand yourself up in this country (if you have no financial heritage) on a piece of earth and think you have a slice of property anymore. And think oh I could <u>dwell here</u> maybe. They'll start hacking at it, shaving a percentage of your foothold. They'll take a rock here and a pebble there and if you grow a potato they will fork off a bite of it and chew it in front of you with their <u>mouths</u> <u>wide</u> <u>open</u>.

CHAUCIA. Oh Robert. I hear a cry in the trees. (*Drone.*) Do you think it's the bats? Squeaking when they fly?

> (*A huge long and terrible pause. They stop walking altogether and listen to the drone.*)

> (*Note:* "●●●" = ROBERT *hums three notes from the drone/ punctuation.*)

ROBERT. I'm sorry ma'am but I haven't read much ornithology. If you don't like my subjects we can always communicate physically. I can sweep you up into the thicket like a flower pressed in a book. And we can therefore cease●●●to be.

257

Illustration/Song 2: "Perfectly Opposite Arrows" *(apology, where Robert's hum of the pre-war building drone shortcircuits at the frontline, as foreshadowed by his outbursts where the lovers strolled).*

CHAUCIA. Oh Robert. Was it my hair when I spoke?

ROBERT. Your hair would probably get messed up if we cease••• to be.

>   (*Note: ">>>"* = *electric shortcircuit of the drone. Stroll malfunctions.*)

CHAUCIA. Was it my eyes, was I looking too dark? Too deep? What did I do?>>>

ROBERT. Were you surprised at my letter?

CHAUCIA. Not so much surprised as — I don't know.>>>

ROBERT. <u>What</u> don't you know? You had an education.

CHAUCIA. I don't know what is happening, Robert. What is it? Is another small boy drowning? Should we get a lantern and search for him?>>>

ROBERT. Do you get the sudden urge to hurl yourself against my shoulders? Are my shoulders above you? Above the others? Head and shoulders above the others? Don't think quickly. Yes or no. Nod or shake your head.

CHAUCIA. I don't know.>>>

ROBERT. That's a response.

CHAUCIA. Oh God.>>>

ROBERT. I tell you lady, something's lacking. This whole idea, maybe this is not a good idea.

CHAUCIA. (*Panicking.*) No. Oh please.>>>

ROBERT. Maybe we should just go back.

CHAUCIA. Oh Robert help. I think I was starting to <u>reproduce</u>.>>>

ROBERT. That baby will be born dead. I can tell.

CHAUCIA. You don't know anything about the future. You have no imagination.>>>

ROBERT. I was going to the front line. I was going to go tomorrow so you'd fuck me in the thicket tonight. How many times are you gonna fall for that trick? You stand there with a candle like an idiot.

CHAUCIA. Robert help me! Help me! Help me! (*She screams in pain.*) I'm fainting. >>> >>> >>> >>> >>> >>>

(*He catches her as she faints.*)

* * *

(CHAUCIA *turns around to get into the elevator, her mouth is bleeding and hideous.* ROBERT *is gone. She becomes hysterical and seems defensively dangerous:*)

"BRICK SHOULDERS"
(Song)

CHAUCIA. (*Hysterical.*)
I'm so sorry, so sorry that I —
Was I chaste ?
I must have leaked some
Where did it get out and misconstrue?
I really thought I was a closed circuit
I don't even drink more than a sherry, I don't mix it
I would never loosen up a tempest like that
wouldn't pull the drapes
you know they brick the streets in France and when I was
an ingenue I had them brick me in (up to my neck the way
they used to handle menstruation)
Brick me up to my neck and wash my face twice a day.
Or more.
So I'll be still
So if he travels by I'd have to chase him half underground
I'd have to shrug my brick shoulders
which then supposedly would tremble up the city
I'm still starving
I didn't, I never
I'm doing it again
I terribly apologize it was a slip
I humble in here like a shot dog
Please don't carry it, don't gossip, don't tell anyone,
why don't you just shut up —
(*The door starts slowly rolling open.*)
Shut up shut up shut up shut up shut up shut up shut up,
shut up about it if you —
(*It is* ROBERT.)

you're a low life anyway nobody cares about your filthy conjectures.

(ROBERT *gets into the elevator with her calmly.*)

ROBERT. I'll pick up the phone when I get back downstairs and have them <u>fix the door</u>. I'm sorry there was such a wind I know it's difficult, to negotiate the front steps—the front? The entrance? Where were you standing?—anyway and then with the door malfunctioning you said it was a door that struck—you said the word "door" I think, I assumed it was the front door with the gold furnishings or was it this door? Would there be a wind in here? How could there be a wind? In a hall? We take precautions, insulate, we spread salt on the ice, rugs on the woodwork.

CHAUCIA. Where are we going Robert?

ROBERT. I'm taking you to the hospital.

CHAUCIA. Where are we going to go.

ROBERT. When it's Christmas I'll be even kinder.

CHAUCIA. Oh what would you like for Christmas this time darling? (CHAUCIA *slumps.*)

* * *

(CHAUCIA *still slumped on the elevator floor, door rolls open, a very electric sound, there is a transmission between* ROBERT *and* HER SISTER, *who seems weak also, but clever.* HER SISTER *has a rather rectangular pregnancy protruding from her belly.* ROBERT *and* HER SISTER *begin to walk in the same lush verdant lane. Stroll music when she takes his arm.*)

HER SISTER. (*Seductive.*) Where are we going now my dear?

ROBERT. Well it'll soon be Christmas won't it?

HER SISTER. Oh what do you want for Christmas this time darling?

ROBERT. Well I pray for nuclear war if we can get the Russian apparatus reassembled and the button accidentally triggered we can clear the earth of all its ornamental clutter, trinkets,

261

packaging, the waste. If we could just go back, return to when confusion was as thin as paint. Chip at the layers and the frost that thickens in our freezers. I'm the one who has to scrape the Christmas off you know, nobody notices my — shall we call it — labor.

HER SISTER. Well I don't suppose you are aroused by anything I wear, my jewelry, anymore.

ROBERT. It is all about your jewelry, complications of a bulbous womb, an infant king perhaps and then some slaughter at the end to prove he'll be the jewel of christendom, it gets me nervous, maybe I should step away, step back a little.

HER SISTER. But do you like me when I'm naked?

ROBERT. No, God no. You're never naked. Naked would be perfect but you'll always have a tiny bruise, a scratch, a sore throat or your dinner bulging or some holy fetus cell dividing. No. Oh God.

HER SISTER. But would you like it if we had no skin at all then you could see the void beneath I guess, the bloody meat that seems to entertain your little perpetrators. The flexing of our tiny verbs and then a burst of adjectives to purchase on the way back home. At least we seem to occasionally transmit something to each other.

ROBERT. No no no. We are plugged in. Our very words plug into the entire dictionary. Other people look them up, they say Aha and copy them. We beat at things we do not understand, we beat the children, sabotage ourselves, we wreck our cars. Even the mail. Even if I sent an old-fashioned letter, handmade paper, handwritten and honest. If you were reclining lavishly by an idyllic sea, your lungs inflated with the pure salt air and they would bring you my letter on a china plate.

HER SISTER. (*After an electric contraction. They start walking backwards.*) Good God>>> The child is going out of focus for me>>> I was feeding him your voice>>> and softening his volume>>> so that the convoluted vocals were subdued>>>> >>>> >>>> >>>> >>>> >>>> >>>> >>>> >>>>

ROBERT. No no no. We are plugged in. Even the mail has slots and numbers.

Illustration/Song 3: "Radio Spider Demon" *(punk rock rupture via elevator shaft wherein the Perpetrator convulses Chaucia's pitch upwards into shrill, vertical staff and Robert's drone accelerates).*

HER SISTER. But would you like it if we had no skin. If we remove cosmetics, curls, all the things we do as we are dressing? >>>

ROBERT. Oh no. God no. You're never dressed enough. You're never grounded, never fully conquered.

HER SISTER. Well at least our child, will be crucified some day >>>

ROBERT. He isn't even mine. I stand in the position of a father. I put my hands into my pockets, rattling my keys therefore I am his father.

HER SISTER. Well at least I will arouse the world in marble with my breast laid bare for him. I'll decorate the sanctuaries for a while. >>>

ROBERT. Until a global war erupts and blows off pieces of your face and severs hunks of limb and sculpted drapery. We'll have to wait for <u>Russia</u> or the third world countries.
>>>> >>>> >>>> >>>> >>>> >>>> >>>> >>>> >>>>
>>>> >>>> >>>> >>>> >>>> >>>> >>>> >>>>

> *(They are back inside the elevator. There is tremendous voltage zapping them. It zaps* HER SISTER's *pregnant belly. She contorts. Recorded baby's cry, generic. A throbbing, dripping suitcase comes out of* HER SISTER, *she begins to leave the elevator in complete shame.)*

* * *

> *(*CHAUCIA *rouses from a slouch in elevator. Same as before.)*

CHAUCIA. Where are we going to go Robert?

ROBERT. I'm taking you to the hospital.

CHAUCIA. I would rather go on home.

ROBERT. But no one is there. You have no one to turn to, do you? Do you have someone to turn to?

CHAUCIA. My sister is arriving.

ROBERT. She is still arriving?

CHAUCIA. Very soon.

ROBERT. She's in there now, isn't she. She's been there for some time but she can't help you. Both of you are helpless. Occasionally helpless. You lapse in and out of helplessness and at this time you are lapsing.

CHAUCIA. I change my mind I don't want you to find me. I'd like to faint invisibly, no flourishes I'm sorry, I don't want anyone to accidentally get onto the elevator and to be thrust into a distress. I don't want a coincidence at all.

ROBERT. Very well I won't be of assistance.

CHAUCIA. Very well.

ROBERT. Very well then.

CHAUCIA. Very well.

> (*He leaves the elevator, it closes softly.*)

CHAUCIA. (*Fainting to herself.*)
very well
very well
very well
very well
very well
very well
very well
very well
very well
very well
(*As she crosses to lobby.*)

* * *

> (CHAUCIA *comes to the desk, disheveled, her mouth swollen, she seems ill.*)

CHAUCIA. Oh Robert, I apologize you know for . . . looking like a gray, half-rotted dinosaur, I think I'm sick, it's been around me like a shroud.

ROBERT. (*Not looking up, humming.*) •••Well it's a lovely shroud •••

CHAUCIA. Oh really Robert

ROBERT. •••You look lovely with it or without it either way•••

265

CHAUCIA. Oh the courtesy (*She tips him, supports herself a little on the counter.*) There'll be a little luggage for you if you'd have the time, a little later on.

ROBERT. •••Who is visiting?•••

(PERPETRATOR *enters in the margins dressed impeccably in a suit.*)

CHAUCIA. Why my sister is arriving, I've been telling you. Haven't I been telling you, I thought I'd wait down here, oh there's a tree indoors, your poor spine! (*Tips him again absently.*) You always keep the lobby looking civilized and I appreciate your work.

ROBERT. (*Bending at the waist.*) Ma'am. I don't mean to be curious, but.

CHAUCIA. Yes darling.

ROBERT. I noticed that your mouth seems swollen and sort of purplish. Are you all right?

CHAUCIA. No. I'm ill. I'm pale. I.

ROBERT. What happened to your mouth?

CHAUCIA. (*Panicking.*) I DON'T KNOW. HOW SHOULD I KNOW? I thought perhaps you'd seen something happen, I thought you were supposed to watch this building, I thought that's what you were doing down here all the time but maybe I'm wrong. I don't know if I'm wrong. I don't know what you do to earn a living down here.

ROBERT. Don't start with me lady.

CHAUCIA. Obviously you aren't up to par with your position.

ROBERT. Lady. I don't think you want to mess with me.

CHAUCIA. I'll mess with you. And I want this building watched or I'll write a complaint. I'll have you on the streets. I'll have you penniless. I'd relish that. I'd really really relish it.

ROBERT. Excuse me lady.

(PERPETRATOR *has come to the desk.* ROBERT *attends to him, they mumble to each other professionally,* CHAUCIA *excuses herself and stands by elevator.* PERPETRATOR *signs the register and stands beside* CHAUCIA *casually.*)

PERPETRATOR. *(Whispers.)* Do you got a goddam dime?

CHAUCIA. *(Whispers back.)* I beg your pardon?

PERPETRATOR. Do you got a goddam dime? If you stick a dime in my pocket I can tell you things you need to know.

CHAUCIA. I don't think I need to know anything from a bum.

PERPETRATOR. I ain't a bum.

CHAUCIA. You're a bum underneath that suit I recognize you.

PERPETRATOR. Yeah I'll tell you what you are, you dressed up decorated piece of bullshit, I recognize you too I know what you've got underneath that outfit, I know every single prick that's pricked your stinking socket.

CHAUCIA. *(Stands up as if cold water had been doused upon her, clears throat.)* I think that you'd fare a little better if you entertained people. I know how to formally entertain. *(Whispers.)* Robert please. Why do I feel like I should whisper?

"RADIO SPIDER DEMON"
(Punk Rant/Song)

PERPETRATOR.
Deep down in your sockets you have nothing but a demon
glowing demon glowing and what kind of demon is it
down there in that hole?
What kind of lap does that thing eat?
Well first of all it has got wires sticking out of it,
sharp as razors, as can poke somebody's eyes,
as can poison when it scratches anything,
or tangles up, or beeps,
convulses, spewing sparks and
voltage and I call it C.E.G.R.S.D. which in other words is the
Contaminated, Electrocutive, Radio Spider Demon
which is down there feeding on your lacy bullshit
and your pearly bullshit and this
Radio Spider Demon
Radio Spider Demon
Radio Spider Demon
is as fucking gray as fucking gray as fucking gray as fucking
gray as fucking gray . . .

CHAUCIA. (*Finds her scream.*) Robert, help me, you know I'm appropriate.

> (ROBERT*'s hum mutates into a siren, blares,* ••• ••• ••• ••• ••• ••• ••• ••• ••• ••• ••• ••• ••• ••• *a skirmish wherein* ROBERT *wrestles with the* PERPETRATOR.)

"RADIO SPIDER DEMON" (continued)

PERPETRATOR. (*Yelling over the alarm.*)
AND ALL THIS NOISE IS BLARING OUT OF YOUR SLUT SLIT. AND IT MEANS DAMN YOU, AND YOUR GODDAM COFFIN, DAMN THAT COFFIN, MAY THE DEVIL PLUCK YOUR COFFIN FROM THE RADIOACTIVE DIRT AND BLOW UP YOUR HAT AND BLOW UP YOUR FINERY, YOUR FINE-FED FLESH AND MAY THE <u>GRAY, RADIO, SPIDER,</u> BE SMASHED WITH SOME GODFORSAKEN BOOT!
(ROBERT *has thrown* PERPETRATOR *out.*)

"MATTE THE POWDER"
(Song)

CHAUCIA. (*Walks down the lush lane by herself back to elevator.*)
In the velvet afternoons
We shall together walk along
In the garden, In the lane
Where the lovers stroll

In the iridescent evenings
We shall talk along forever
In the garden, In the lane
Where the lovers stroll

Green deep the thicket
Aqua blue the sky
Soft, soft the petals
Climbing up the lattice white
Softly spoken dresses
Up against the lattice white
Black blink the lashes
Blusher thin the pink
Younger silk the lotion
Matte matte the powder
Matte matte the powder
Of the lattice white

(CHAUCIA *powders her face throughout, snaps the compact shut at the end because* HER SISTER *has darkened the door with her suitcase.*

CHAUCIA *quickly gets into the elevator and flees all the way back to her bed, which* HER SISTER *observes as she signs the register with a flourish.*)

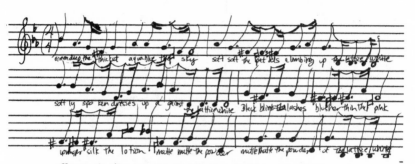

Illustration/Song 4: "Matte The Powder" *(sweet/melodic spent regaining her composure to a decorated panic).*

269

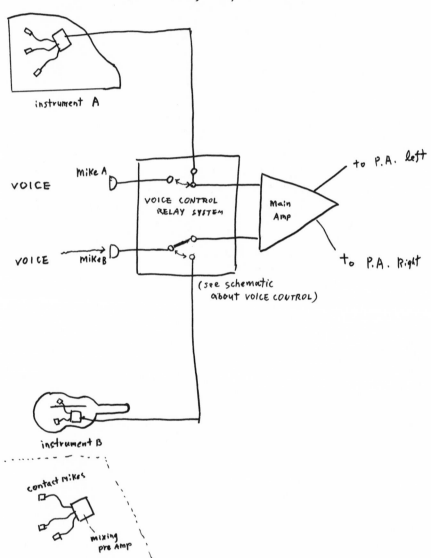

Block Diagram for Sound System
for " Geography and Music"

instrument A

VOICE   Mike A

VOICE CONTROL
RELAY SYSTEM

VOICE   Mike B

(see schematic
about VOICE CONTROL)

Main
Amp

to P.A. left

to P.A. Right

instrument B

contact Mikes

mixing
pre Amp

Geography and Music
for Amplified String Music and Text
Yasunao Tone

*— Translated from Chinese by Yasunao Tone
with assistance from Judith Grossman*

INTRODUCTION

THE FOLLOWING TEXTS are mostly taken from the geography sections of **Tai-pin Yulan**, 1,000 volumes of Chinese encyclopedia, published in 983 A.D. The rest of them are excerpts from **Tai-pin Kwan Chi**, published in 981 A.D., and both volumes were edited by the same editor, Li Fan.

INSTRUCTIONS

About sound system:

1. P.A. system has to be two channels separated into right and left sides of a concert hall.

2. Each of two amplified instruments should be connected via voice control gating system to either of two P.A. channels. (See block diagram.)

3. Two mikes are connected to the voice control gating system, so that the voices activate each relay to switch on/off the amplified sound. Thus, for instance, when mike A is used, the amplified sound of the instrument B and voice are heard from the P.A. When mike B is used, the result is the reverse. (See block diagram.)

Yasunao Tone

Instructions for voices and instruments:

1. Each performer starts to play independently; however, textual reading starts at least a moment later.

2. Notations and text are page numbered, but performer can play without regarding the order.

3. The text has to be considered as an accumulation of the following:

   a. phoneme

   b. grapheme

   c. word

   d. phrase

Then, text has to be read aloud as any combination of the above, and each punctuation needs to alternate mikes.

4. Any technical modulation between voice control system and instruments is encouraged.

Note: In 1979, I was commissioned by the American Dance Festival in Durham to write a musical score for *Roadrunners*, a new work by Merce Cunningham. The piece comprises the text above, the notation for two amplified string instruments (which is derived from the tablature of ninth-century Chinese pipa music) and the gating system. The recorded reading of the original Chinese text was included in the performance. German, Italian, French and Spanish translations were performed in place of English translation wherever it was appropriate to do so. The Chinese text has remained in the original Chinese. The piece was performed as part of the Merce Cunningham Dance Company's repertoire for the next nine years. Performers were John Cage, David Tudor, Takehisa Kosugi, Martin Karve and Michael Pugliese. I would like to dedicate this text to the late David Tudor, who passed away while I was writing this note.

Yasunao Tone

THE COUNTRY OF JIO-YAO

The Book of Late Han, the third official Chinese history, states that in the reign of Emperor Ang, circa 110 A.D., three thousand Jio-yao people, the southern barbarians, thronged to You-chiang City, a city on the southern Chinese border. This group intended to pay tribute to the imperial storehouse; such tributes as hundreds of ivories, cows and buffaloes.

The Jio-yao people were only three feet in stature. They dwelt in holes and swam so well that the birds and animals were astounded. However, Lie-tze, a Taoist book of the third century B.C., states that 3,000,000 leagues lie between Jio-yao and the eastern border of China and that the people measure only one and a half feet in stature.

The Book of Mountains and Seas says that people of this country are shorter than Chinese people. Their land is located east of San-Shou, or the country of three heads.

In *The Family Book of Confucius*, it is recorded that once, a guest from Wu asked Confucius the following question, "How tall is the tallest and shortest man?" Confucius replied, "The shortest is a Jio-yao man, who is only three feet in height. The tallest is hardly over ten feet. Here lies the pole of human stature."

The Illustrated Book of Foreign Countries states, Jio-yao people swim very well and are adept at catching birds. In the land, weeds and trees die in Summer and sprout in Winter. Jio-yao people are located 30,000 leagues from Mount Suspicious Nine Peaks.

YU-MIN

According to *The Book of Mountains and Seas*, there lives in the country of Yu-min a group of wing people with long heads, and according to another report from the same volume, long necks as well.

According to *The Illustrated Book of Foreign Countries*, the wings of the Yu-min people cannot sustain long navigation. They are oviparous as a group. Their country is located forty thousand leagues from Mount Suspicious Nine Peaks, the southern border of China.

LAND OF WHITE PEOPLE

The Book of Mountains and Seas mentions that the Land of White People is located north of Lon-Yui, ... they have white bodies and wild tangled hair.

The Book of Natural History states that in a plain of Ri-nan, a mass of women were seen, unaccompanied by their husbands. Their bodies were pure white and they were unclothed, except for a white robe covering one shoulder.

COUNTRY OF CHIAN FU

According to **The Illustrated Geography**, Emperor Dai-Wu of the Yin Dynasty once sent Wang Meng to visit Sheng Wang Mu, the goddess for immortality, so that he could pick a medicinal peach from her, which would enable the emperor to become immortal. But there he could not find any food, so that he had to eat nuts and wear bark. Although he never married, he begot two children. The children emerged from his own back. This was the origin of the Chian Fu people. This country is located 20,000 leagues from Yu-meng Gate.

QUEER ARM

In the country of Chi-gon, or Queer Arm, the people are exceptionally skillful. They fashion flying chariots from the wings of hundreds of birds previously shot down. These chariots travel on the wind.

In the age of King Tung of the Shang Dynasty, the Queer Arm people flew to the border of the Yu region, on the power of the west wind. Their chariots were destroyed by King Tung's army, but were not exhibited to the general public. Ten years after, when the strong east wind blew, the King allowed the Queer Arm people to return to their native country. This country is located ten thousand leagues west of the Yu-Meng Gate, the custom-house of the furthest western border of China.

RUO-TOU PEOPLE

On a frontier of Rinan, a part of northern Vietnam, there live the Ruo-Tou or dropping head people, whose heads fly well. Among this race, or species, there is a rite called Hui-ruo, or insect dropping head; the people were named after the rite. However, this is obsolete now.

Before their heads fly, their eyes vanish and their ears become wings. They return at dawn, landing on their bodies. In the Wu period, the third century A.D., they were captured quite often.

OCEAN MEN

In an eastern sea dwell Ocean Men. They are five to six feet tall and resemble human beings. Each one has a face like that of a beautiful woman, but lacks feet. Their skin has the shimmer of jade with no characteristic scales. The hair on this skin is of five different colors, each hair about one inch long. The hair on their head is similar to a horse tail and grows to about five feet. Sexual organs are identical in the male and female. Old widowers and widows are the most easily captured among the group. All the Ocean Men are friendly to man and have never been known to attack man.

COUNTRY OF SHAMAN

The Book of Mountains and Seas states that Wu Hsien or country of Shaman is located north of Nu Jen. In the country, people manipulate blue snakes by right hands and red vipers by left hands. They stay in the bushy mountains and divine together.

275

According to **The Illustrated Foreign Country**, in the old days King Dai Wu of the Yin dynasty allowed shamans to pray in only mountains and rivers. Because of that they fled a hundred thousand leagues from the southern seaboard.

COUNTRY OF CH'IEN T'O

Once upon a time, there lived a king, Quie Tung, whose bravery and strategic skill were beyond man, or godlike; he waged many wars and conquered many countries. Finally he expanded his wars as far as five Indian countries.

In these regions, he obtained two precious ribbons from the natives. He kept one ribbon and gave the other to the queen. Soon after, the queen appeared before the king, wearing the ribbon around her breast. When the queen showed her breast to the king, he was surprised to see her breast imprinted with a golden yellow hand mark. The queen complained to the king, "What kind of ribbon have you given to me? No sooner did I wear this ribbon than a yellow hand mark appeared on my breast."

The king angrily questioned his retainers on the left and on the right. He received the following reply, "This is not our fault, your majesty. There was something wrong with these ribbons from the start." The king then bid his subjects to chase the merchant who supplied the ribbons, in order to question him.

.... King Sahbahdahgon of India had a long cherished desire. He collected these ribbons as tax. Initially, he permitted his subjects to hoard all the ribbons. Then he bid them to paint their hands with golden yellow dye. The ten million impressions of these hands were fixed in such a way that in men, the dye would appear upon the back, and in women upon the breast. The merchant explained further, "The king allowed the members of his retinue, as well as the common people, to wear the magic ribbons simply to observe how they worked."

King Quie clacked his sword and proclaimed, "Until I cut off the arms and legs of King Sahbahdahgon with this sword, I will neither eat nor sleep."

He then ordered his subjects to bring him the arms and legs of King Sahbahdahgon. Soon, King Sahbahdahgon received a report from his subjects on this matter. The king had his subjects reply to the envoy from King Quie, as follows: "Although we do have a king with the name of Sahbahdahgon we have, in actuality, no king at all. Therefore we have constructed a bronze statue of a king, merely for an educational purpose. In truth we are all vassals here."

After receiving a report of the events in India, King Quie invaded the country with his cavalry and elephant forces. The real king was hidden by his people in a cave. King Quie was greeted, instead, by a bronze statue.

King Quie realized this was a false king. Nevertheless, he cut off the arms and legs of the statue by the use of his magical powers. At the same moment, in his secret cave, King Sahbahdahgon lost his arms and legs.

From Lady Into Fox

an intimate musical

Neil Bartlett
Music by Nicolas Bloomfield

— Based on the novella by David Garnett

(*A darkened room in a house in the English countryside. The curtains are drawn. It is a raw, dank evening. The fire is lit.* TEBRICK
*enters, swiftly, not using the door. He finishes one glass of whiskey
and then pours himself another as he says:*)

T. Wonderful or supernatural events are not so uncommon,
        rather they
    are irregular in their incidence. There may not be one marvel
        to speak of
    in a century, and then often enough comes a plentiful crop;
        monsters
    swarm, comets blaze and meteors fall in showers.

    But the strange event which I shall here relate came alone and
    unsupported into a hostile world *(BISBIGLIANDO)*. We may
        account for it
    as we will; but it is in the explanation that we shall find most
        difficulty,
    not in the accepting for true a story so fully proved, and by the
        testimony
    of not one witness,
    But of a dozen, and all respectable, and all agreeing
    She had been most strictly brought up, her Mother being
    Dead; that her maiden name certainly had been Fox —
    But that nothing about her appearance was vixenish
    Though her hair had a shading of red
                                    they said; *CHORD*
    That she had been blooded as a child of ten

278

But vomited in fright at it and ever since then *CHORD*
Would not ride to hounds, or rather, not do it
Unless her husband persuaded her to it; *CHORD*
That the house was remote, indeed, set apart —
That Miss Silvia was always somewhat wild at heart — *CHORD*

Of course the change
Would have been less strange
Had it been more gradual
As it was —   — A Miracle?
              An Act
              Of God —
              Though odd,
              A Fact
                that
                  at
                    Tangley
                      In the north of Oxfordshire
                      On the early afternoon
                      Of the first, dark day of January
                      In the year Eighteen-Eighty,
                        Mr. and Mrs. Tebrick, being yet only in the
third month of a happy marriage, went walking together across
     the fields
not far from their house
and while walking
              heard
                Hounds.

(*Music — January Theme.*)

T. And hearing the hunt, and nearing a wood,
    Tebrick quickened his pace, that they might get a good
    view. His wife hung back, and he, taking hold of her hand, began
        almost to
    drag her — she suddenly snatched her hand away from his and
        cried out —
    So that he instantly turned his head
    (*Sings.*)
    And there
    Where his wife had been
    was not his wife

279

But a fox
Of a very
bright
red.

(SILVIA *appears. It seems that she has been there all along, but only now has become visible . . . There is indeed nothing fox-like about her appearance, except for her beautiful coloring.*)

Can it be she?
Am I not dreaming?

(*Chord.*)

The fox advanced a pace or two towards him.

(*Chord.*)

He saw at once that his wife was looking at him from the animal's eyes, beseeching.

(*Music.*)

Why?
Can this be my fault?
                         — For if any dreadful thing happened he
        would never
blame her but always himself —
At this
The fox came close enough to kiss . . .
She trembled in his arms . . . ;
She kept
Her shining eyes on his;
Then, wept,
So that her husband
Could not contain his tears . . .

(*Not caring in his grief that he is addressing a fox, or that the audience may well think that he is mad,* MR. TEBRICK *sings quite as if he was addressing a woman; and, moreover, a woman with whom he is in love.*)

THE VOW

T. **Weep not, Silvia, at this change:**
Though you're changed, I know you still.
Doubt not, Silvia, that I'll stay here close beside you: for I will.
Take not, Silvia, those bright eyes
For an instant from my face;
Fear not, Silvia — while you live no other takes your place.

Be not, Silvia, now dismayed;
Tell your heart there's no harm done . . .
Some men, Silvia, should their Love change, then would falter;
**   I'm not one;**
Let us, Silvia, now return
To that house that we'll still share.
You are Silvia — though you change to — anything: I swear,

As you changed once before in my eyes my love
That night you changed from a Bride to a Wife —
And have changed once again — you are still my love
To cherish, to have and to hold all my life —
And I vow once again on my knees here before you
Forsaking all others, to you I shall cleave,
And I pray — not that God in his mercy restore you
But that He in His wisdom receive
**   this prayer:**
That I may keep you, keep you, keep you close to my heart
'til Death, Silvia
Death Silvia,
Death Us Do Part.

We sat thus till it was getting near dusk, quite in silence, never
    lifting our eyes the one from the other's face. Indeed, had
        anyone passed
by to witness the scene they might have supposed us
lovers............not husband).....................and wife).

S. Have pity on me husband) . . . for I am your wife).

T.   Then I recollected myself,
    and thought that I must somehow hide her. For it was clear that
        we could
    not return to the house in the same manner as we had left it.

281

Neil Bartlett

It is one of the wonders of the human heart,
                              is it not,
                                              that it can so quickly
accommodate itself to great change.

(MR. TEBRICK *carries her home, and there cares for his wife daily. She cannot walk upright or perform any human actions unaided. He cannot hear her, except when she makes sounds which he thinks are those of a fox.*)

HE TAKES HER HOME

(*Spoken in rhythm.*)

T.   When your wife is changed,
  You must take her in your arms at once;
  Clasp her to your breast, reassure her of her charms at once —
  Tear your shirt, if you have to, so she's hot against your skin . . .
  This will demonstrate affection — also furnish some protection
  'Gainst the spreading of suspicion of your new wife's new
      condition —

(*Music.*)

Which is best kept under your hat, so
No-one's guessed what's under your coat — go
Quietly, lest what's up in your room provokes the dogs —
But dogs (bark, don't they?

S.   (ha!

T. **And she'll kiss you — after a fashion —**
  As to thank you . . . after a while
  You'll lie still — long after midnight . . .
  One so rigid . . .
  One so curled . . .
  Both safe from,
  Yes safe from (the World!

S.   **(The Irish Setter**
           The old fox terr'yer, the (bitch —

T. (*To the dogs.*)   **(Hush!**
  (*To her.*)   **Shush!**

S.   **Bitch Bitch (Dogs.**

T.   **(Don't let them hear you**
They can't get near you
It's almost day —

And I swear she understands me!
Yes ev'ry word I say!

HE DRESSES HER IN THE MORNING

T. When your wife awakes,
Do not blame yourself if you've not guessed
The reason why she drags and tears the gown in which she once
    got dressed —
She will not go naked, notwithstanding her new shape —
Fetch the jacket with lace trimmings — or the flowered silk with
    ribbons —
Which are easier than buttons
To do up — and she'll need cushions —

Her requiring your assistance may seem odd, but your persistence
Is rewarded, 'cause the ribbons look best all tied neatly don't they?

And she thanks you — after her fashion —
Is so gentle — after her style —
Still herself — in her confusion . . . still so modest . . . hardly
    wild . . .
And safe here
So safe — like (a Child.

S.   **(A chained-up Setter**
An old fox, get her, the (bitch!

T.   **(Hush!**
Shush!
They're all kept (well-tied

S.   **(Getter**

T.   **All tied up (outside,**

S.   **Get her**

T.   **(Out of harm's way —**

s.   **(Out.**

T. *(Having calmed her down.)* **And you see, she understands me,**
                        Yes ev'ry word I say.

HE BRINGS HER THE TRAY

T. When your wife is dressed
    You must take (once she's been brushed, and then
    Been well sprayed down with scent —
    If the stench persists then brush again)

s.   SCENT   BRUSH

T. **Take her down — you will have to — start the morning as you**
    did . . .
    She will   want to sit at table, use a cup if she is able,

s.   WANT TO SIT

T. Have her egg as she was used to — and buttered toast

s.   EGG   BUTTER

T. (Two slices);   jam (her fav'rite's quince); fine —

s.   QUINCE JAM

T. Cut cold ham, and now — I

s.   COLD HAM

T. Find I am requiréd to supply
    Fresh Grapes —   she likes them, don't you?

s.   GRAPES   THANK YOU

T. **This strange taste, confirmed by Scripture**
    Helps abate her morning odor
    So the dogs can't smell you — can they?

    (They listen for the dogs but can hear nothing. He clears
    away the tray.)

s. Husband, are we to have no luncheon today?

HE DOES THE HOUSEWORK

S.   (When?

T.   (When your wife can't speak
She must often be beside herself to see you do each week
The tasks in which she once took pride herself —
Must despair as her husband does his best to run her house . . .
Your domestic education must be cause for consternation
As she watches in vexation and can give no explanation —
. . . Fetch the tray in the morning;
      Then get the meal in the evening;
      You set the rooms straight — even
      Shoot the dogs so they can't bark (now . . .

S.   (Now may I not go out into the
garden, husband?

When?

T.   **And she never (fails to delight you —**

S.   (When?   — Soon?

T.   **In the firelight — at eventide —**
      As she sits — there in the lamplight —
      Where she should be — by my side . . .

      (*Both sotto voce, both staccato, both speaking private thoughts.*)

T.   **(I shan't upset her**

S.   **(The Irish Setter**

T.   **But I can't let her (go out.   — Hush Shsh.**

S.   **The old bitch ter'yer (is dead . . . . ; shsh . . .**

T.   **(No, I can't —**

S.   **(So she can't . . .**

T.   **(And she shan't**

S.   **(And he can't**

T.   **(But we aren't   unhappy;**

285

s.   (But I   can't   be unhappy . . .

t. (Because she understands me — yes ev'ry word I say!!

s. (Because   he understands me!

> (*He lights a lamp and settles down in the silence of the evening.*
>
> SILVIA *goes to the piano and attempts to find a piece of music.*
>
> *She comes to him, puts her paw into his hand and looks at him with sparkling eyes shining with joy and gratitude, and pants with eagerness, and jumps at him and licks his face.*
>
> *She returns to the piano.*)

t. (*Gently.*) Silvia, what do you do there?
Silvia?

> (*She cannot manage the music. She leads him to the piano and shows him the piece of music which she has chosen. He does not hear her when she says:*)

s. Schumann. Sullivan manytimes.
SchumannMendelsshonHoneymoon.

> (*but he understands that she has picked this piece of music to comfort and delight him. They look at each other with great love. He opens the score, and as he does so we hear it.*
>
> *He sings their song to her.*)

THE SONG

t. **Night falls;**
>   **now sleeps the noisy world . . .**
Now turns the lark to her bower, the white dove to her nest;
Now droops each garden flower, spent; the lilies close and rest.
Night falls;
>   **and lovers keep their word**
**To meet where rose-shadows gather, where first they met and
        kissed —**
See how as evening stars appear they keep th'appointed tryst.

286

And as
    night falls I too would keep
A promise made in a whisper, and then sealed with a kiss —
Oh meet me by the garden gate — by the rose-tree yonder —
And let me show you where
We two might wander!!

> *(He closes the score. He feels that the evening will now proceed as it always used to. He turns down a lamp, saying:)*

And shall we now retire Silvia?

> *(He goes to pick her up to carry her upstairs, but she suddenly slips gracefully away, having spied the pack of cards. TRIPLET FIGURE*
> *He does not hear her say:)*

s. Piquet. Madeira. Laterdeara.

> *(He fetches the pack and he deals two hands of cards.)*

Timeshare
Jeffrey Eugenides

MY FATHER IS SHOWING me around his new motel. I shouldn't call it a motel after everything he's explained to me but I still do. What it is, what it's going to be, my father says, is a timeshare resort. As we walk down the dim hallway (some of the bulbs have burned out), my father informs me of the recent improvements. "We put in a new oceanfront patio," he says. "I had a landscape architect come in, but he wanted to charge me an arm and a leg. So I designed it myself."

Most of the units haven't been renovated yet. The place was a wreck when my father borrowed the money to buy it, and from what my mother tells me, it looks a lot better now. They've repainted, for one thing, and put on a new roof. Each room will have a kitchen installed. At present, however, only a few rooms are occupied. Some units don't even have doors. Walking by, I can see painting tarps and broken air conditioners lying on the floors. Water-stained carpeting curls back from the edges of the rooms. Some walls have holes in them the size of a fist, evidence of the college kids who used to stay here during spring break. My father plans to install new carpeting, and to refuse to rent to students. "Or if I do," he says, "I'll charge a big deposit, like three hundred bucks. And I'll hire a security guard for a couple of weeks. But the idea is to make this place a more upscale kind of place. As far as the college kids go, piss on 'em."

The foreman of this renewal is Buddy. My father found him out on the highway, where day workers line up in the morning. He's a little guy with a red face and makes, for his labor, five dollars an hour. "Wages are a lot lower down here in Florida," my father explains to me. My mother is surprised at how strong Buddy is for his size. Just yesterday, she saw him carrying a stack of cinder blocks to the dumpster. "He's like a little Hercules," she says. We come to the end of the hallway and enter the stairwell. When I take hold of the aluminum banister, it nearly rips out of the wall. Every place in Florida has these same walls.

"What's that smell?" I ask.

Above me, hunched over, my father says nothing, climbing.

"Did you check the land before you bought this place?" I ask. "Maybe it's built over a toxic dump."

"That's Florida," says my mother. "It smells that way down here."

At the top of the stairs, a thin green runner extends down another darkened hallway. As my father leads the way, my mother nudges me, and I see what she's been talking about: he's walking lopsided, compensating for his bad back. She's been after him to see a doctor but he never does. Every so often, his back goes out and he spends a day soaking in the bathtub (the tub in room 308, where my parents are staying temporarily). We pass a maid's cart, loaded with cleaning fluids, mops and wet rags. In an open doorway, the maid stands, looking out, a big black woman in blue jeans and a smock. My father doesn't say anything to her. My mother says hello brightly and the maid nods.

At its middle, the hallway gives onto a small balcony. As soon as we step out, my father announces, "There it is!" I think he means the ocean, which I see for the first time, storm-colored and uplifting, but then it hits me that my father never points out scenery. He's referring to the patio. Red-tiled, with a blue swimming pool, white deck chairs and two palm trees, the patio looks as though it belongs to an actual seaside resort. It's empty but, for the moment, I begin to see the place through my father's eyes — peopled and restored, a going concern. Buddy appears down below, holding a paint can. "Hey, Buddy," my father calls down, "that tree still looks brown. Have you had it checked?"

"I had the guy out."

"We don't want it to die."

"The guy just came and looked at it."

We look at the tree. The taller palms were too expensive, my father says. "This one's a different variety."

"I like the other kind," I say.

"The royal palms? You like those? Well, then, after we get going, we'll get some."

We're quiet for a while, gazing over the patio and the purple sea. "This place is going to get all fixed up and we're going to make a million dollars!" my mother says.

"Knock on wood," says my father.

Five years ago, my father actually made a million. He'd just turned sixty and, after working all his life as a mortgage banker, went into business for himself. He bought a condominium complex in Fort Lauderdale, resold it and made a big profit. Then he did the same thing in Miami. At that point, he had enough to retire on but he didn't want to. Instead, he bought a new Cadillac and a fifty-foot power boat. He bought a twin engine airplane and learned to fly it. And then he flew around the country, buying real estate, flew to California, to the Bahamas, over the ocean. He was his own boss and his temper improved. Later, the reversals began. One of his developments in North Carolina, a ski resort, went bankrupt. It turned out his partner had embezzled a hundred thousand dollars. My father had to take him to court, which cost more money. Meanwhile, a savings and loan sued my father for selling it mortgages that defaulted. More legal fees piled up. The million dollars ran out fast and, as it began to disappear, my father tried a variety of schemes to get it back. He bought a company that made "manufactured homes." They were like mobile homes, he told me, only more substantial. They were prefabricated, could be plunked down anywhere but, once set up, looked like real houses. In the present economic situation, people needed cheap housing. Manu-factured homes were selling like hotcakes.

My father took me to see the first one on its lot. It was Christ-mas, two years ago, when my parents still had their condominium. We'd just finished opening our presents when my father said that he wanted to take me for a little drive. Soon we were on the high-way. We left the part of Florida I knew, the Florida of beaches, high rises and developed communities, and entered a poorer, more rural area. Spanish moss hung from the trees and the unpainted houses were made of wood. The drive took about two hours. Finally, in the distance, we saw the onion bulb of a gas tower with "Ocala" painted on the side. We entered the town, passing rows of neat houses, and then we came to the end and kept on going. "I thought you said it was in Ocala," I said.

"It's a little further out," said my father.

Countryside began again. We drove into it. After about fifteen miles, we came to a dirt road. The road led into an open, grassless field, without any trees. Toward the back, in a muddy area, stood the manufactured house.

It was true it didn't look like a mobile home. Instead of being long and skinny, the house was rectangular, and fairly wide. It came in three or four different pieces which were screwed together,

290

and then a traditional-looking roof was put in place on top. We got out of the car and walked on bricks to get closer. Because the county was just now installing sewer lines out this far, the ground in front of the house — "the yard," my father called it — was dug up. Right in front of the house, three small shrubs had been planted in the mud. My father inspected them, then waved his hand over the field. "This is all going to be filled in with grass," he said. The front door was a foot and a half off the ground. There wasn't a porch yet but there would be. My father opened the door and we went inside. When I shut the door behind me, the wall rattled like a theater set. I knocked on the wall, to see what it was made of, and heard a hollow, tinny sound. When I turned around, my father was standing in the middle of the living room, grinning. His right index finger pointed up in the air. "Get a load of this," he said. "This is what they call a 'cathedral ceiling.' Ten feet high. Lotta headroom, boy."

Despite the hard times, nobody bought a manufactured home, and my father, writing off the loss, went on to other things. Soon I began getting incorporation forms from him, naming me vice president of Baron Development Corporation, or the Atlantic Glass Company, or Fidelity Mini-Storage Inc. The profits from these companies, he assured, would one day come to me. The only thing that did come, however, was a man with an artificial leg. My doorbell rang one morning and I buzzed him in. In the next moment, I heard him clumping up the stairs. From above, I could see the blond stubble on his bald head and could hear his labored breathing. I took him for a delivery man. When he got to the top of the stairs, he asked if I was vice president of Duke Development. I said I guessed that I was. He handed me a summons.

It had to do with some legal flap. I lost track after a while. Meanwhile, I learned from my brother that my parents were living off savings, my father's IRA and credit from the banks. Finally, he found this place, Palm Bay Resort, a ruin by the sea, and convinced another savings and loan to lend him the money to get it running again. He'd provide the labor and know-how and, when people started coming, he'd pay off the S & L and the place would be his.

After we look at the patio, my father wants to show me the model. "We've got a nice little model," he says. "Everyone who's seen it has been very favorably impressed." We come down the dark hallway again, down the stairs, and along the first-floor corridor. My father has a master key and lets us in a door marked 103. The hall light doesn't work, so we file through the dark living room to the bedroom. As soon as my father flips on the light, a strange feeling takes hold of me. I feel as though I've been here before, in this room, and then I realize what it is: the room is my parents' old bedroom. They've moved in the furniture from their old condo: the peacock bedspread, the Chinese dressers and matching head-board, the gold lamps. The furniture, which once filled a much bigger space, looks squeezed together in this small room. "This is all your old stuff," I say.

"Goes nice in here, don't you think?" my father asks.

"What are you using for a bedspread now?"

"We've got twin beds in our unit," my mother says. "This wouldn't have fit anyway. We've just got regular bedspreads now. Like in the other rooms. Hotel supply. They're OK."

"Come and see the living room," my father tells me, and I follow him through the door. After some fumbling, he finds a light that works. The furniture in here is all new and doesn't remind me of anything. A painting of driftwood on the beach hangs on the wall. "How do you like that painting? We got fifty of them from this warehouse. Five bucks a pop. And they're all different. Some have starfish, some seashells. All in a maritime motif. They're signed oil paintings." He walks to the wall and, taking off his glasses, makes out the signature: "Cesar Amarollo! Boy, that's better than Picasso." He turns his back to me, smiling, happy about this place.

I'm down here to stay a couple of weeks, maybe even a month. I won't go into why. My father gave me unit 207, right on the ocean. He calls the rooms "units" to differentiate them from the motel rooms they used to be. Mine has a little kitchen. And a balcony. From it, I can see cars driving along the beach, a pretty steady stream. This is the only place in Florida, my father tells me, where you can drive on the beach.

The motel gleams in the sun. Somebody is pounding somewhere. A couple of days ago, my father started offering complimentary suntan lotion to anyone who stays the night. He's advertising this on the marquee out front but, so far, no one has stopped. Only a few families are here right now, mostly old couples. There's one woman in a motorized wheelchair. In the morning, she rides out to the pool and sits, and then her husband appears, a washed-out guy in a bathing suit and flannel shirt. "We don't tan anymore," she tells me. "After a certain age, you just don't tan. Look at Kurt. We've been out here all week and that's all the tan he is." Sometimes, too, Judy, who works in the office, comes out to sunbathe during her lunch hour. My father gives her a free room to stay in, up on the third floor, as part of her salary. She's from Ohio and wears her hair in a long braided ponytail, like a girl in fifth grade.

At night, in her hotel-supply bed, my mother has been having prophetic dreams. She dreamed that the roof sprung a leak two days before it did so. She dreamed that the skinny maid would quit and, next day, the skinny maid did. She dreamed that someone broke his neck diving into the empty swimming pool (instead, the filter broke, and the pool had to be emptied to fix it, which she says counts). She tells me all this by the swimming pool. I'm in it; she's dangling her feet in the water. My mother doesn't know how to swim. The last time I saw her in a bathing suit I was five years old. She's the burning, freckled type, braving the sun in her straw hat only to talk to me, to confess this strange phenomenon. I feel as though she's picking me up after swimming lessons. My throat tastes of chlorine. But then I look down and see the hair on my chest, grotesquely black against my white skin, and I remember that I'm old, too.

Whatever improvements are being made today are being made on the far side of the building. Coming down to the pool, I saw Buddy going into a room, carrying a wrench. Out here, we're alone, and my mother tells me that it's all due to rootlessness. "I wouldn't be dreaming these things if I had a decent house of my own. I'm not some kind of gypsy. It's just all this traipsing around. First we lived in that motel in Hilton Head. Then that condo in Vero. Then that recording studio your father bought, without any windows, which just about killed me. And now this. All my things are in storage. I dream about them, too. My couches, my good dishes, all our old family photos. I dream of them packed away almost every night."

"What happens to them?"

"Nothing. Just that nobody ever comes to get them."

There are a number of medical procedures that my parents are planning to have done when things get better. For some time now, my mother has wanted a face-lift. When my parents were flush, she actually went to a plastic surgeon who took photographs of her face and diagrammed her bone structure. It's not a matter of simply pulling the loose skin up, apparently. Certain facial bones need shoring up as well. My mother's upper palate has slowly receded over the years. Her bite has become disaligned. Dental surgery is needed to resurrect the skull over which the skin will be tightened. She had the first of these procedures scheduled about the time my father caught his partner embezzling. In the trouble afterward, she had to put the idea on hold.

My father, too, has put off two operations. The first is disk surgery to help the pain in his lower back. The second is prostate surgery to lessen the blockage to his urethra and increase the flow of his urine. His delay in the latter case is not motivated purely by financial considerations. "They go up there with that Roto-Rooter and it hurts like hell," he told me. "Plus, you can end up incontinent." Instead, he has elected to go to the bathroom fifteen to twenty times a day, no trip being completely satisfying. During the breaks in my mother's prophetic dreams, she hears my father getting up again and again. "Your father's stream isn't exactly magnificent anymore," she told me. "You live with someone, you know."

As for me, I need a new pair of shoes. A sensible pair. A pair suited to the tropics. Stupidly, I wore a pair of old black wingtips down here, the right shoe of which has a hole in the bottom. I need a pair of flip-flops. Every night, when I go out to the bars in my father's Cadillac (the boat is gone, the plane is gone, but we still have the yellow "Florida Special" with the white vinyl top), I pass souvenir shops, their windows crammed with T-shirts, seashells, sunhats, coconuts with painted faces. Every time, I think about stopping to get flip-flops, but I haven't yet.

One morning, I come down to find the office in chaos. Judy, the secretary, is sitting at her desk, chewing the end of her ponytail. "Your father had to fire Buddy," she says. But before she can tell me anything more, one of the guests comes in, complaining about a leak. "It's right over the bed," the man says. "How do you expect me to pay for a room with a leak over the bed? We had to sleep on the floor! I came down to the office last night to get another room but there was no one here."

Just then my father comes in with the tree surgeon. "I thought you told me this type of palm tree was hardy."

"It is."

"Then what's the matter with it?"

"It's not in the right kind of soil."

"You never told me to change the soil," my father says, his voice rising.

"It's not only the soil," says the tree surgeon. "Trees are like people. They get sick. I can't tell you why. It might have needed more water."

"We watered it!" my father says, shouting now. "I had the guy water it every goddamn day! And now you tell me it's dead?" The man doesn't reply. My father sees me. "Hey there, buddy!" he says heartily. "Be with you in a minute."

The man with the leak begins explaining his trouble to my father. In the middle, my father stops him. Pointing at the tree surgeon, he says, "Judy, pay this bastard." Then he goes back to listening to the man's story. When the man finishes, my father offers him his money back and a free room for the night.

Ten minutes later, in the car, I learn the outlandish story. My father fired Buddy for drinking on the job. "But wait'll you hear *how* he was drinking," he says. Early that morning, he saw Buddy lying on the floor of unit 106, under the air conditioner. "He was *supposed* to be fixing it. All morning, I kept passing by, and every time I'd see Buddy lying under that air conditioner. I thought to myself, Jeez. But then this goddamn crook of a tree surgeon shows up. And *he* tells me that the goddamn tree he's supposed to be curing is dead, and I forgot all about Buddy. We go out to look at the tree and the guy's giving me all this bullshit — the soil this, the soil that — until finally I tell him I'm going to go call the nursery. So I come back to the office. And I pass 106 again. And there's Buddy still lying on the floor."

When my father got to him, Buddy was resting comfortably on his back, his eyes closed and the air-conditioner coil in his mouth. "I guess that coolant's got alcohol in it," my father said. All Buddy had to do was disconnect the coil, bend it with a pair of pliers and take a drink. This last time he'd sipped too long, however, and had passed out. "I should have known something was up," my father says. "For the past week all he's been doing is fixing the air conditioners."

After calling an ambulance (Buddy remained unconscious as he was carried away), my father called the nursery. They wouldn't refund his money or replace the palm tree. What was more, it had rained during the night and no one had to tell him about leaks. His own roof had leaked in the bathroom. The new roof, which had

cost a considerable sum, hadn't been installed properly. At a minimum, someone was going to have to re-tar it. "I need a guy to go
up there and lay down some tar along the edges. It's the edges, see,
where the water gets in. That way, maybe I can save a couple of
bucks." While my father tells me all this, we drive out along A-1-A.
It's about ten in the morning by this point and the drifters are
scattered along the shoulder, looking for day work. You can spot
them by their dark tans. My father passes the first few, his reasons
for rejecting them unclear to me at first. Then he spots a white
man in his early thirties, wearing green pants and a Disneyworld
T-shirt. He's standing in the sun, eating a raw cauliflower. My
father pulls the Cadillac up alongside him. He touches his electronic console and the passenger window hums open. Outside, the
man blinks, trying to adjust his eyes to the car's dark cool interior.

At night, after my parents go to sleep, I drive along the strip into
town. Unlike most of the places my parents have wound up, Day-
tona Beach has a working-class feel. Fewer old people, more bikers.
In the bar I've been going to, they have a real live shark. Three
feet long, it swims in an aquarium above the stacked bottles. The
shark has just enough room in its tank to turn around and swim
back the other way. I don't know what effect the lights have on the
animal. The dancers wear bikinis, some of which sparkle like fish
scales. They circulate through the gloom like mermaids, as the
shark butts its head against the glass.

I've been in here three times already, long enough to know that
I look, to the girls, like an art student, that under state law the
girls cannot show their breasts and so must glue wing-shaped ap-
pliqués over them. I've asked what kind of glue they use ("Elmer's"),
how they get it off ("just a little warm water") and what their boy-
friends think of it (they don't mind the money). For ten dollars, a
girl will take you by the hand, past the other tables where men sit
mostly alone, into the back where it's even darker. She'll sit you
down on a padded bench and rub against you for the duration of
two whole songs. Sometimes, she'll take your hands and will ask,
"Don't you know how to dance?"

"I'm dancing," you'll say, even though you're sitting down.

At three in the morning, I drive back, listening to a country and
western station to remind myself that I'm far from home. I'm
usually drunk by this point but the trip isn't long, a mile at most,
an easy cruise past the other waterfront real estate, the big hotels

and the smaller ones, the motor lodges with their various themes. One's called Viking Lodge. To check in, you drive under a Norse galley which serves as a carport.

Spring break's more than a month away. Most of the hotels are less than half full. Many have gone out of business, especially those further out from town. The motel next to ours is still open. It has a Polynesian theme. There's a bar under a grass hut by the swimming pool. Our place has a fancier feel. Out front, a white gravel walkway leads up to two miniature orange trees flanking the front door. My father thought it was worth it to spend money on the entrance, seeing as that was people's first impression. Right inside, to the left of the plushly carpeted lobby, is the sales office. Bob McHugh, the salesman, has a blueprint of the resort on the wall, showing available units and timeshare weeks. Right now, though, most people coming in are just looking for a place to spend the night. Generally, they drive into the parking lot at the side of the building and talk to Judy in the business office.

It rained again while I was in the bar. When I drive into our parking lot and get out, I can hear water dripping off the roof of the motel. There's a light burning in Judy's room. I consider going up to knock on her door. Hi, it's the boss's son! While I'm standing there, though, listening to the dripping water and plotting my next move, her light goes off. And, with it, it seems, every light around. My father's timeshare resort plunges into darkness. I reach out to put my hand on the hood of the Cadillac, to reassure myself with its warmth, and, for a moment, try to picture in my mind the way to my room, where the stairs begin, how many floors to climb, how many doors to pass before I get to my room.

"Come on," my father says. "I want to show you something."

He's wearing tennis shorts and has a racquetball racquet in his hand. Last week, Jerry, the current handyman (the one who replaced Buddy didn't show up one morning), finally moved the extra beds and draperies out of the racquetball court. My father had the floor painted and challenged me to a game. But, with the bad ventilation, the humidity made the floor slippery, and we had to quit after four points. My father didn't want to break his hip.

He had Jerry drag an old dehumidifier in from the office and this morning they played a few games.

"How's the floor?" I ask.

"Still a little slippy. That dehumidifier isn't worth a toot."

So it isn't to show me the new, dry racquetball court that my father has come to get me. It's something, his expression tells me, more significant. Leaning to one side (the exercise hasn't helped his back any), he leads me up to the third floor, then up another, smaller stairway which I haven't noticed before. This one leads straight to the roof. When we get to the top, I see that there's another building up here. It's pretty big, like a bunker, but with windows all around.

"You didn't know about this, did you?" my father says. "This is the penthouse. Your mother and I are going to move in up here soon as it's ready."

The penthouse has a red front door and a welcome mat. It sits in the middle of the tarred roof, which extends in every direction. From up here, all the neighboring buildings disappear, leaving only sky and ocean. Beside the penthouse, my father has set up a small hibachi. "We can have a cookout tonight," he says.

Inside, my mother is cleaning the windows. She wears the same yellow rubber gloves as when she used to clean the windows of our house back in the suburbs. Only two rooms in the penthouse are habitable at present. The third has been used as a storeroom and still contains a puzzle of chairs and tables stacked on top of one another. In the main room, a telephone has been installed beside a green vinyl chair. One of the warehouse paintings has been hung on the wall, a still life with seashells and coral.

The sun sets. We have our cookout, sitting in folding chairs on the roof.

"This is going to be nice up here," my mother says. "It's like being right in the middle of the sky."

"What I like," my father says, "is you can't see anybody. Private ocean view, right on the premises. A house this big on the water'd cost you an arm and a leg."

"Soon as we get this place paid off," he continues, "this penthouse will be ours. We can keep it in the family, down through the generations. Whenever you want to come and stay in your very own Florida penthouse, you can."

"Great," I say, and mean it. For the first time, the motel exerts an attraction for me. The unexpected liberation of the roof, the salty decay of the oceanfront, the pleasant absurdity of America, all come together so that I can imagine myself bringing friends and women up to this roof in years to come.

When it's finally dark, we go inside. My parents aren't sleeping up here yet but we don't want to leave. My mother turns on the lamps.

I go over to her and put my hands on her shoulders.

"What did you dream last night?" I ask.

She looks at me, into my eyes. While she does this, she's not so much my mother as just a person, with troubles and a sense of humor. "You don't want to know," she says.

I go into the bedroom to check it out. The furniture has that motel look but, on the bureau, my mother has set up a photograph of me and my brothers. There's a mirror on the back of the bathroom door, which is open. In the mirror, I see my father. He's urinating. Or trying to. He's standing in front of the toilet, staring down with a blank look. He's concentrating on some problem I've never had to concentrate on, something I know is coming my way, but I can't imagine what it is. He raises his hand in the air and makes a fist. Then, as though he's been doing it for years, he begins to pound on his stomach, over where his bladder is. He doesn't see me watching. He keeps pounding, his hand making a dull thud. Finally, as though he's heard a signal, he stops. There's a moment of silence before his stream hits the water.

My mother is still in the living room when I come out. Over her head, the seashell painting is crooked, I notice. I think about fixing it, then think the hell with it. I go out onto the roof. It's dark now, but I can hear the ocean. I look down the beach, at the other high rises lit up, the Hilton, the Ramada. When I go to the roof's edge, I can see the motel next door. Red lights glow in the tropical grasshut bar. Beneath me, and to the side, though, the windows of our own motel are black. I squint down at the patio but can't see anything. The roof still has puddles from last night's storm and, when I step, I feel water gush up my shoe. The hole is getting bigger. I don't stay out long, just long enough to feel the world. When I turn back, I see that my father has come out into the living room again. He's on the phone, arguing with someone, or laughing, and working on my inheritance.

The Burial

Stephen Dixon

GOULD'S MOTHER DIES and he makes plans for the funeral. Days before in the hospital when she was still lucid she said she didn't want any funeral-home service. "Too expensive. They charge a fortune to rent a chapel and a little side room and for all their employees to act as ushers and doormen, and it's also so unnecessary. Why should people, if they want to see the whole thing through, come to the chapel and cemetery both? And in addition some even come to the funeral home the night before just to view my cheap casket and pay their respects to you, and I want it to be the cheapest so you don't go broke for a stupid box and I also don't want you opening it once I'm in it. Have it at the cemetery only. Open air and light, even if it's raining, is better than the solemn nonsense and awful recorded organ music of a chapel. A few people I knew saying some brief things about me if they want or just praying to themselves or together from some little prayer book the cemetery could loan you or even staring at their feet or into space if they like, and then drop me in the ground between your father and brother and you go home. If the whole thing takes more than half an hour, starting from the time you get there till you leave, then it's taken too long. People's time shouldn't be wasted for things like that. It's already enough they had to get there." "That's why a funeral home might not be a bad idea, in spite of the expense, if we have to talk about it now," and she said "We do. If you're not going to be the practical one, then I have to, so what were you saying?" "I was saying I could find a home in the city. People wouldn't even have to drive their cars to it, if they lived there and weren't planning on going to the cemetery. They can come by cab or subway or bus, and for some who live on the Upper West Side, where I think the best place is, they can even walk. Then the ones that also want to go to the cemetery can go in my car or someone else's if someone else who comes has one, or even a limo I'll hire if there are that many people coming. I mean, how much can one cost, for the cemetery's not *that* far away, if I remember. The rest will feel they've paid their respects and did their duty and so on by coming to the service or to the funeral home the night before, if they also did that, and they can go back to work or home. But please let's drop the subject," and she said "Who are all these people you're expecting? If you get six, tops, it'll be a lot, or seven, eight, but don't look for a crowd. That's also why the funeral-home service makes no sense. You'll have to get someone to conduct it — a rabbi or some expert in Jewish religious services the home gets for you — and you want him speaking to a practically empty audience? The cemetery; have it all there. And don't let them do anything to my body for it. Just put me in the pine box straight from the hospital, store me for the night someplace — if it's got to be at the funeral home where you buy the casket, then let it be — ship me to the grave site the next day in the cheapest conveyance allowable, and that'll be it. All this is almost a favor I'm asking of you. But since I won't be in any position to argue, do what you want except to cremate me. Even though I'll be gone at the time — *dead*; why not just say it? What else do I expect will happen to me by the end of the week? — the thought of all that fire scares me. If you don't promise you won't cremate me, I swear it will kill me sooner. Worms and bugs and whatever else is underground don't make me feel that much easier, but I just think if there is a soul in your body and it doesn't get completely out of it once you die, it won't survive those terrific temperatures. Besides, I'm leaving you almost no money. I don't have much, that's why, since whatever I had or Dad left me was mostly used up to keep me alive the last few years and for someone to look after me. So why waste what's left plus some of your own on even a simple chapel service when you also have to go through one at the cemetery? I know the burial will also have to cost something. But so would anything you do — cremation; hiring a boat to drop me in the ocean, which by law you can't do — so we know there's a minimum you have to spend on this. You can't, unfortunately, I'm saying, just make me disappear. I wouldn't even have a rabbi or any kind of burial professional at the grave, since they can set you back a bundle too. Just ask the cemetery to get one of those little old religious guys who hang around the cemetery and who knows the right prayers for the dead, and slip him a twenty to read some passages over me and maybe to point something out for you to read. Or conduct it any way you want on your own, with you or whoever has come there, reading or speaking whatever you want. In the end, what's the difference? And I don't say that to you that way to make a joke. Let's face it, dead is dead, and I know that whatever you say and read and however you say it, even if it comes out fumblingly, is meant well."

He decides to have the body sent to that West Side funeral home, put in the cheapest pine casket they have there and with nothing done to the body, not even washed or reclothed, since once she's in the casket and it's closed nobody's going to see her again, and next morning sent by simple van to the cemetery for a short burial ceremony, though he doesn't know what he's going to do there yet. His wife's cousin and her husband will meet him there, same with his mother's best friend from her street, whose son will drive her and the woman who took care of his mother the last two years. Later that day someone from the funeral home calls him and asks if he wants her marriage bands removed from her finger — she added his father's band to her own when his father died — before she's put in the casket, and he says "Oh God, she never told me what to do about that, and I don't know. She should probably be buried with them, right?" and looks at his wife and points to his own band and she points to her chest and shakes her head she doesn't want them, and the man says "Look, yes or no, because we won't be able to get them off later without, if you'll excuse me, chopping off her finger. And that, unless it was absolutely necessary for some other reason, I'm not allowing any of my workers to do," and he says "Then okay, leave them on. They're hers, whatever that means, and eventually I'd just lose them."

The next day, on the way to the cemetery with his wife and two girls, he blurts out "Damn, just thought of something. I mean I've been thinking and thinking what I'll say at the ceremony after someone reads a couple of prayers, and simply decided to say what comes naturally but to keep it brief. But there's a poem she loved and though she didn't mention it when she talked the other day about everything she wanted and didn't want after she died, except for the wedding bands . . . do you think I made the right decision on that?" and his wife says "Too late, don't even think of it." "But the kids might have wanted them for when they're older," and his youngest daughter says "What?" and his wife says "Nothing, we're not going to talk about it. It'd be totally futile and it wouldn't seem right. What'd you start out to say?" and he says "I remember a couple of years ago when she was very sick and I was called to New York and we thought she was dying . . . we're talking about

Grandma, of course," to his girls. "And she said if there's one thing she wanted read at her funeral, but not by a rabbi, she added, it was an Emily Dickinson poem about dying. She gave the title but I can't remember it, though I probably wrote it down then," and his wife says "I don't think hers had official titles. They were all first lines of her poems, weren't they? Either she decided on titling them that way or someone did for her after she died and the poems were found. Wasn't that her?" and his oldest daughter says "Who, Grandma again?" and he says "Emily Dickinson, a poet of the last century, and it was her, I'm sure." "Oh, I know her. We read her in the CTY humanities class I took, but I can't remember any of them now or anything about them except they were all short." "There's one very beautiful one I recall," his wife says, "that starts 'Because I could not stop for death,' and then goes on 'so death stopped for me,' or something," and he says "That's it, her favorite, or one of them. She used to read me them when I was a boy. And for years she kept a copy of all the poems on her night table — there weren't many, or as Fanny said, they were all short. The collected works in one volume, plus the letters, I think, or some of them. I haven't seen the book around in a long time and before that one time in the hospital she hadn't brought up Dickinson in years. It's probably still in her apartment somewhere, or someone borrowed it and never gave it back — it could even have been me — or she just read it till it fell apart. No, I could never have taken it from her; it had been by her bedside for maybe ten years and you don't borrow a book like that, or loan it out. Did she say then that it was at home and I should get it from there? I don't remember. But I have to read that poem at the burial. It might be all I'll read or say, in fact, except that this was one of her favorite poems, maybe her favorite, and that Dickinson was her favorite poet, or certainly among her favorites and the only one whose book she had by her bedside so long, if I'm remembering right. And that she used to read them to me and I thought this one appropriate to read today, because of all I've said about it and its contents — the poem's — and so on. Do you remember the rest of the poem?" he says to his wife. "It's short, right? You can write it down for me, or one of the girls can; you can just recite it," and his youngest daughter says "I'll write it down — I've a pad and pen with me," and Fanny says "No, I will; I know her works, or read her, and those first two lines Mommy said I especially remember and won't need her to repeat," and he says "Either of you, so long as it's written clearly," and his wife says "I only know those two, I'm afraid; and the second's 'He kindly stopped for me.'" "That's right, that's right," he says. "Think, come on, remember; and Josie, get your pen and pad out," and his wife says "I can't; that's it, a blank. 'Because I could not stop for death' and 'He kindly stopped for me.'" "Then I'll stop in a town on the way — we've time — and buy it at a bookstore if there's one, or an anthology of some sort with that poem in it. It's one of her most popular, so it'd be in one. And every bookstore must have an anthology like that or a collection of her poems, or at a bookstore at a nearby mall where most of them seem to be now," and his wife says "But there could be people waiting for us already. I think even the receptionist in your mother's doctor's office said she was coming. And the funeral-home people with the casket in their van. They all expect you to be the first one there, and for the funeral people, probably for some paperwork to fill out or just sign." "Then this is what. I'll drop you all off. Anything to sign, you do it; you're my wife. If anyone's there or they come, tell them to wait, I'll be back soon. As far as the funeral-van people; well, they can just put the box over the grave, the rest is up to the cemetery. Good thing no rabbi though. If we had one and he was there he wouldn't let me go because he'd probably have a wedding to run in an hour or another funeral somewhere and he couldn't give us even five minutes more than what we hired him for. I'll go to the nearest store and buy the book. I won't be more than half an hour. If it takes more, I'll drop it. A half hour from the time I leave you might just be when I told everyone the service would start anyway. And tell them I'll keep the ceremony shorter than I had even planned to. *Ceremony, service,* whatever you want to call it; fifteen minutes, if that." "Please don't look for any book," she says. "Why not just talk about the poem, read the first two lines . . . read them twice, three times; they're that good and right for a funeral service. After that, say you don't know the other lines, but what Dickinson's poetry meant to your mother . . . the night table, reading them to you, all that. And how you wanted to read all of this poem; how you almost even started out from the cemetery to get the book at the last minute —" and he says "No, that's all circling around to avoid it, and dishonest — from my part — and lazy, because this is what she wanted. She told me it that first time two years ago and then again about a year later, I just remembered — I think we were in the waiting room of a doctor's office. Didn't say anything about it this last time in the hospital, but she was on drugs and not clear-headed—" and she says "What do you mean? You said she was about as lucid and articulate and well informed as you've seen her recently, using the big words she loved and with you having a long and absorbing personal conversation with her as you haven't had in years," and he says "She was still on medication, and I think a painkiller, and being fed intravenously, and anyway, not clear all the time . . . dozing off, sleeping a lot. Besides—" and she says "I don't know how much to believe you," and he says "Yes, believe me. Besides, maybe she thought I already knew about her poem wish and didn't want to repeat herself. That she didn't want me feeling she thought I had a lousy memory and that she had to say things over and over again for it to sink in. After all, she told me it at least twice before. Listen, you have to see how important this is to me. I don't want to put you and the kids in a bind, but this'll be my last good thing to her, or last chance to do it rather, besides how much it'll help me get through the day. If I can't find the Dickinson collection or that particular poem in an anthology, or one close to it on death or immortality or the ending of life and transmigration of the soul or something, I swear I'll give up after the first store and rush right back."

He drops them off at the burial site. Nobody's there yet, not even the van or the prayer reader he called the cemetery for late yesterday. A secretary in the cemetery office tells him how to get to town and says there are two bookstores there—"Lots of people must read around here, and perhaps there are two stores because the nearest mall is fifteen miles away," and he drives there in five minutes. Both stores are on the main street. The first is really just a used paperback shop, with mostly romances, spy fiction, mass paperbacks of every sort, and the only poetry is religious: St. Augustine is in this section plus several of the same editions of a book of poetry by the pope. The second store has an anthology of twentieth-century American poetry and books of poems by poets like Hardy, Whitman and Blake but no Dickinson. "I know we had one," the salesman says. "The Everyman edition—hardback, complete works, and only eleven dollars—a steal. Ah, it was sold, it says here," looking at the inventory record on the computer screen by the cash register. "Last week, May third. I could order a copy today," and he says "No time; I need it right away." "Try the library; they should have it if Miss Dickinson hasn't been assigned as a class project at one of the local schools," and he says "Great idea, why didn't I think of that?" and at the library down the street

305

he locates a volume of Dickinson poems with the one he wants in it and goes up to the main desk and says "Excuse me, I don't live in this area; I'm not even a resident of New Jersey. But I'd like to borrow this book just for an hour or so," and the librarian says "If you want to sit here and read it, that's fine, but we can't loan a book to a non–New Jersey resident." "Let me explain why I need it," and he does, points out the poem and she says "I'm sorry, I appreciate your reason and offer my condolences, but it's a by-law of our town's library system I'd be breaking if I loaned you the book. In the past we've had every excuse imaginable for loaning books to nonresidents, and if we see a fifth of them returned we call ourselves lucky. Try to imagine what that figure would be if —" and he says "Believe me, I'll return it. I'll drive back here after the burial. You can even call the cemetery—I have the number here—to see if my mother's being buried today," and she says "Whether you're telling the truth or not —" and he says "I *am*," and she says "Then even though you are telling the truth, which is what I meant to say, it's strictly prohibited to give loaning privileges to people without valid library cards of this town. If they have cards from other New Jersey localities, then that town's library has to request the book for them and it's sent to that library through the state's interexchange system." "Look, I have people waiting at the cemetery for me—the burial service was supposed to start five minutes ago. Not a lot of people—I don't want to lie to you—but my wife and daughters and my wife's cousin and her family from Brooklyn. They drove all the way from there to come to it, and other people—cemetery personnel, etcetera. Again, it was among my mother's favorite poems and to have it read at her funeral was really one of her last wishes. But because I was so distraught at her death yesterday—confused, everything—I forgot, and we didn't— I didn't; I'm the only surviving child—have a regular funeral . . . this is the only ceremony we're having. And when I was driving to the cemetery I suddenly realized—" and she says "I wish I could. What if I photocopied the poem for you?" and he says "I thought of that as a solution. But I want to hold a book—not a Bible, not a prayer book, since she didn't go for that stuff at funerals or really anywhere, but a book of poems—and read from that. Look, I'll leave a deposit. Ten dollars, twenty, and when I return the book I'll donate the money to the library," and she says "This book," turning to the copyright page, "is . . . more than forty years old. In excellent condition for a book that's been circulating that long.

Maybe it's the delicacy of the poetry that makes readers handle the book delicately, though I don't want to engage in that kind of glib speculation here. I don't know what it originally cost, nor do I know what this copy's worth now. Fifty dollars perhaps, though more likely five, but around twenty to replace. I'm not a rare book collector, so that's not my point. We simply can't be loaning works to out-of-state residents because they're willing to give money to the library. That policy would mean only the more privileged among you can borrow from us, which wouldn't be the right perception for a library to give." "Okay, okay, I'll try and get the book somewhere else," and starts back to the poetry shelves with it and she says "You can leave it here, sir; I'll restack it," and he says "Nah, I've put you through enough already," and she says "Thank you then, but please make sure it's in the right classificatory order," and once there he thinks Take the photocopy; better than nothing. Have her copy two or three different Dickinson poems, they're all there in that last Resurrection and something section he just saw . . . No, you want what you said you did and that's a book to read from and not some flimsy photocopy sheet, and this edition particularly because it has a real old book look, and looks around, doesn't seem to be anyone else here but her, and sticks the book inside his pants under the belt. Feels it, it feels secure; he'll take it for the day, return it by mail tomorrow with a donation and his apologies, won't give his name or a return address of course. Though she can probably find out who he is, if she wants, from the cemetery, for how many burials can there be there at this hour in one day and he gave her enough information to give himself away. But what is she going to do, get the police to arrest him in Baltimore or New York for stealing a book for a day after he sent it back carefully wrapped and in the same condition and with a ten or twenty dollar bill?

Alarm goes off as he's leaving. She's looking at him from behind the main desk. "Oh Christ," he says, "who the hell thought you'd have these books electronically coded in such a small library. Here, take it, will ya," and sets it on a chair by the door and she says "Oh no, mister, you're not getting off as lightly as that. I don't believe your mother-burial story one iota now. And don't think of bolting or I'll follow you outside and take down your license number," and dials her phone and says "Officer Sonder? Well, anyone then, though he's the one I've dealt with so far for this particular problem. Amy LeClair at the library. I have a man here whom

I caught stealing one of our items . . . A book, but a potentially valuable one and I believe he knew it . . . Thank you," and turns to him and says "He says for you to wait; a police car will be right over," and he says "Call back and tell him I can't; to catch me at the cemetery on Springlake," and she says "Leave now and you'll be in even deeper water. We've lost too many books and documents as it is and this is the only way to stop this kind of petty crime that tallies up for us to grand larceny." What to do? Take the book, read the poem at the burial and then tell everyone what he did and wait for the cops there? Or leave it and go and just hope they don't come after him, or wait for the cops here? Surely they're not going to arrest him. "Do you mind, while I wait, if I call the cemetery to hold up the burial?" and she says "If that is whom you'll call," and he says "Then you dial for me — I have the number right here or get it out of the phonebook," and she says "I'd rather not waste any more of the library's money by using the phone, even for a local call. We have restrictions regarding that too. We're barely surviving, you know. People aren't exactly putting this institution in their wills." "Then will a dollar cover the phone cost?" and she says "I'd also rather not take money from you. Who knows what that'd imply." Just then a policeman comes in. Gould explains quickly. She says "Nothing for me to add; whatever his reasons for the theft were, he just admitted he was caught walking out with one of our books," and the policeman says to him "Looks like I'll have to write out a summons or even arrest you if Miss LeClair insists I do," and she says "I don't think we have to go that far, but certainly a summons." The policeman starts writing one out. "This means you'll have to appear in a county court in a number of weeks. Unless you check the 'no contest' box on the court notification you get and request to be fined through the mail and the judge accepts it," and he says "Okay, but please hurry it up. I don't mean to sound disrespectful but there are all those people waiting at the cemetery for me and I still have my mother to bury," and the policeman says "No disrespect meant either, sir, but I can do it much faster with machines at the station house if that's what you want."

Only his wife and children are at the cemetery when he gets there, sitting on a bench several plots away; casket's on a few planks above the open grave. "By the time your message got to us," his wife says, "Rebecca and everyone else had left. They all had to be somewhere later this afternoon and didn't know when you'd get back. They were concerned about you, paid their respects to you through me and said a few words of their own to your mother. You'll tell me it all later, all right? Now we should get the cemetery people to help us get the coffin in the ground." "Did you get the poem, Daddy?" his youngest daughter says and he says "Oh, the poem; Jesus, I even forgot to get it photocopied. I could have before but this librarian, you can't believe it, she gave me the option to but I wanted to hold the whole book, this beautiful old hardbound copy of Dickinson's, as if it were a religious book, rather than read from this skimpy transient sheet—" and his wife says "What are you talking about?" and he says "The poem. 'Because I could not stop for Death.' There's a capital D in the death. The prayer guy ever show up?" and she says "He waited awhile, then said he had to go to another grave site, and made some prayers over her casket and left." "So let's do it ourselves, though we'll have to get the cemetery workers to lower the box once we're done. Maybe that's all it should be anyway, since we're the only ones left of her family who are still semisound."

He drives to the office, returns with a cemetery official and two gravediggers in a truck behind him, and standing in front of the grave says "Please, now let the funeral and burial and service and everything else begin. Sally, do you have anything to say?" and she says "Just that we all loved you, Leah, very much. You were always wonderful to be around, wise in your ways, delightful to the girls, and because you're Gould's mother, special to me, and we're profoundly sorry to see you go. Kids?" and the oldest shakes her head and starts crying and the youngest says "No," and then "Yes, I have something. Goodbye, Grandma. I wish I knew you longer and when you were younger, and I feel extra bad for Daddy. And I love you too and am sorry to have you die and be buried." "Thank you, dears," he says. "As for me, if I mention the word love and how I feel I'll blubber all over the place and won't be able to continue. So to end the service, because I've kept everyone here way too long, I'd like to read something—I mean, recite—and very little because it's all I know. I tried to get more but that's another story, Mom, so just two lines of an Emily Dickinson poem you liked so much. 'Because I could not stop for Death' . . . what is it, Sally?" and she says "'He kindly stopped for me.'" "Right. 'Because I could not stop for Death, he kindly stopped for me. Because I could not stop for Death, he kindly stopped for me. Because I could not stop for Death, he kindly stopped for me.' Amen. Now if you gentlemen will lower the coffin, we'll go home."

Confession of My Images
Barbara Guest

Confession of my images,

the protective varnish of the portrait in color,

dew mere dew kaleidoscopic.

After the barbarians
ballooning trousers tucked into their belts,

the sliding window

left agape, and

the centurions have made a mess of distribution—,
the neck does not swell
                an octave with ardor
is destabilized.

(i poeti che parteciperanno.)

Eros freed of the wooden seat

the crowd similarly, as

an elbow fits into the

ancient arm

touch
of the sweet vest

creating furor,

to create sweet furor

(without missing)

of query and cultivation, vases not known.

And degrees of ignorance, an inheritance
even as the known voice so is the smothering —

eye to whom there is no appeal.

gli poeti   poeti

Barbara Guest

The third page
floats on knobbled water *in perpetua*

debris in its atrium —;

and to visit Leopardi in Naples

not breathing in
the same idiom
the way it now is.

TIME AND SUPPORTIVE LILIES

in Spoleto: *"i poeti che parteciperanno"*
Pound, Elmslie, Brainard — the Austrian,
Bachmann — the addio, addio.

From The Negro-Lover
Joyce Carol Oates

1.

TO SHOW THE FLY THE WAY OUT OF THE BOTTLE was the
life's hope of Ludwig Wittgenstein but the truth is that human
beings don't want a way out of the bottle; we are captivated, enthralled by the interior of the bottle; the bottle is the perimeter of
our experience and our aspiration; the bottle is our skin, our soul;
we could not survive outside the bottle; or tell ourselves, in the
glassy-echoing confinement of the bottle, that this is so.

2.

As the ancient Jewish people, persecuted by their enemies, interpreted history and the random events of nature moralistically,
believing that catastrophes of even weather and geology were
consequences of man's evil, so in times of emotional distress we
are inclined to ascribe to whatever happens a moral significance.
We cease to believe in chance, and cling to a belief in design; we
can't accept that we don't in some way deserve what happens to
us; we prefer a wrathful, capricious god to no god at all. Like children we try to influence what can't be influenced; we beg to be
treated mercifully. When I was in love with Vernor Matheius in
the winter, spring and summer of that year I became twenty years
old, and when, for a while, it seemed to me that Vernor Matheius
to some inscrutable degree was in love with me, or behaved as
if this might be so, I carried myself like easily shattered glass; I
seemed to understand that my behavior was madness; yet I could
not alter my behavior; I did not want to alter my behavior; for
that would have been to abandon the madness, the hope of being
loved by him; that would have been to abandon the glassy-echoing
confinement of the bottle; that would have been to die. I was convinced that my connection with Vernor Matheius was a force outside my volition as it was outside his; it would consume us both,
like wildfire. Therefore every glance, every facial expression, every
word, every gesture of mine had to be controlled. There was a way

313

of behaving that was good, decent, virtuous and blameless; I'd known as a child that "good" behavior would save me from harm, yet I had not cared; for the worst had already happened, my mother had died; as a child I could not perceive otherwise than *My mother's death happened to me;* it was difficult to comprehend that my mother's death had happened to her. Perhaps I have never been able to comprehend that simple melancholy fact. So now I understood: if I were good, decent, virtuous and blameless I would be rewarded with Vernor Matheius's love; if not, not. There was no God monitoring such behavior; I did not believe in God; I was contemptuous of God; I despised God; the Lutheran God presented to me, drilled with lackluster diligence into me as a child, seemed silly, contemptible; a fantasy figure of my elders, whom in any case I did not respect. (To hear my German grandmother mumbling her prayers with a pursed, prissy, pained expression on her time-raddled face, her fattish fingers twined in reverence, was to be tempted, oh so dangerously tempted, to break into laughter.) Yet I'd become increasingly superstitious; as in the childhood of our race spirits and demons were believed to populate the invisible world, obsessively concerned with human affairs, so it seemed to me, in love with Vernor Matheius, that invisible forces were on my side, or against me; I had to placate them at all times; I could not ignore them; I could not risk defying them; I had to guard against impulsive wishful thoughts; constantly I was warned *If you think a thing, that thing will not happen;* thinking for instance *He will see me tonight, we will make love in his bed* fatally assured that this would not, could not happen. My thoughts were powerless to control my fate yet my thoughts were omniscient controlling my fate. To counter *wish-thoughts* all my thoughts had to be monitored. To counter *wish-thoughts* all my behavior had to be monitored. There was a way of walking, standing, breathing, chewing my food; even a way of sleeping; a way of relating to other people; I was in a constant state of anxiety that I would violate it; I was required, for instance, to smile at everyone with whom I came into contact, whether friends, classmates, strangers; I was required to smile at all persons in authority; I was required to be warm, gracious, courteous even when the effort was exhausting; even when my heart was breaking; even when I wanted to die, to extinguish myself utterly, to be free of my love for Vernor Matheius, to be free of love.

Is something wrong? is something wrong with your face? one of them was asking, a girl in the residence hall who'd imagined herself a friend of mine. I was hurt, I was angry; I stared at her my eyes shining with tears like shards of glass, *what do you mean? what is wrong with my face?* and she said, embarrassed, meaning to be kind, *your face seems frozen sometimes, you smile with just one side of your face.*

3.

> *Love for any one thing is barbaric for it is exercised at the expense of everything else. This includes love of God.*
>
> — Nietzsche

When he was bored and depressed, when his thoughts (he said) backed up like a sewer he could taste then he wanted me; wanted Anellia whose true name he'd never cared to learn. *C'mon girl sing for me!* — that wide damp glistening smile, the gap between his two upper front teeth glistening too, and I would protest laughing I couldn't sing and Vernor would say with mock sobriety like the schoolteacher he'd vowed he would never become *I'm telling you, girl, sing! You can save your life if you sing for me.* So barefoot there on the splintery floorboards of Vernor Matheius's room (blinds drawn, windows open a few inches to dispel the airlessness) I sang what flew haphazardly into my head, shut my eyelids singing the imperfectly recalled lyrics of a long-ago popular love song of yearning, shameless female yearning heard on the radio in another lifetime, my mother's lifetime perhaps; and Vernor would clap his hands impatiently *Faster, girl! Speed up the beat!* and out of my astonished mouth would burst snatches of songs heard during those months of torment I'd lived in the Kappa Gamma Pi house, songs I'd detested at the time and had pressed my hands over my ears to keep from hearing, maddening records of "The Kingston Trio" my Kappa sisters played again, again and again and another the calypso-beat *Hey c'mon kitch let's go to bed, I gotta small comb to scratch your head* and Vernor burst into loud laughter hearing this, such smut; such brainless idiotic smut; clapping his hands and regarding me, for a moment, before he rose to take hold of me, with almost tenderness.

Desire rising in a man's eyes like a swiftly lit flame.

When he was bored and depressed. When he was in one of his shitty moods.

Two kinds of moods: the inspired and the shitty. Swinging back and forth between them he said like a monkey on a bar.

Certainly he disapproved of *moods*. There was no category of *mood*, no account of *mood* in Spinoza, Descartes, Kant; *mood* as a category in serious philosophical inquiry did not exist. A philosopher succumbing to a *mood* no longer existed as a philosopher but as something other, lesser. In such *moods* he despised himself and in a sense did not know himself.

When he was bored and depressed his thoughts backed up like sewage and he didn't want to see newspaper headlines pushing away scattered pages of the local paper left behind on a table in the coffee house or in a pub where we'd arranged to meet, didn't want to know of the civil rights marches that spring in Alabama, Georgia, Mississippi, the police attack dogs, the Ku Klux Klan bombings, arrests of civil rights volunteers; he wished the volunteers well, he hoped they would succeed he said but he hadn't time to spare for such activism, even the contemplation of such activism. *Time is an hourglass running in only one direction* he said. I did not say *I think they must be very brave, some of them very reckless living in time, in history* for perhaps these thoughts had not crystallized in my mind, perhaps the words were not there.

Love for any one thing is barbaric (so Vernor Matheius quoted Nietzsche of whom generally he did not approve) *and yet more contemptible is lust, yet more contemptible than lust the habit of lust, the addiction.* The body's compulsion, grovelling in another's flesh. As if redemption, meaning, might be found in another's flesh. That warm eager leap of seed (which, at least, most of the time Vernor could thwart, with trembling fingers tugging a condom on his erect, bobbing penis). Like drinking (yes damn it Vernor admitted he was drinking more than he'd ever done), like smoking (yes he was smoking more, too, chain-smoking cursing such a foul filthy expensive habit an ashtray on his desk overflowing with ashes, butts spilling onto the floor). When he was bored and depressed. When his thoughts backed up like sewage. When he was in one of his moods. Angry, impatient with himself. Shouldn't blame Anellia, poor sweet Anellia who loved him when it was himself to be blamed; when his work wasn't going well; when he was praised nonetheless (by his dissertation advisor who was perhaps intimidated by Vernor Matheius though twenty years his senior) though his work wasn't going well; when he lost faith in his work; when he lost faith in philosophy; gripped by the *philosophical puzzlement* of which Wittgenstein spoke; tragic lacerating Wittgenstein for whom the posing of unanswerable questions was a strategy for the postponement of suicide; when he lost faith not in philosophy nor even in the vision of his work but in his ability day by day, hour by hour to execute his work; when he lost faith in the very concept *faith*; when he despised me for adoring him; when he despised himself for being adored; how like an addiction was a man's sexual desire; a man's sexual need; that weakness he'd believed he had conquered years ago; yet now it had returned as if in mockery of him; in mockery of the Vernor Matheius he'd become; how like a sickness that need for Anellia whose true name he did not care to know, the slender pale-gleaming body *a white woman's body* in to which he could fall, fall, fall. Stripping me bare studying me with scholarly objectivity adjusting his wire-rimmed glasses that glinted like frost. Brushing away my crossed arms and hands where I tried to hide myself, embarrassed of his scrutiny. *Don't pretend, Anellia. It's too late for that.*

Come here he would say quietly.
Lie down he would say. Or *Take off your clothes.*
Sometimes whispering words I could not hear, words of angry endearment or obscenities or curses not for me to hear; his voice was hoarse, cracked; it was not Vernor Matheius's voice, it was not the voice I'd originally loved; he seemed no longer to trust his voice; often he would say nothing at all as if desire choked his throat, rendered him mute; nor did he trust himself caressing me; running a thumb hard against the pale blue vein at my hairline, framing my face in his hands both his thumbs dangerously close to my eyes *You have beautiful eyes, Anellia* as if he'd never seen them, or me, before *how can you trust me, don't you know I could gouge out your eye in an instant* but of course I trusted him, I never flinched even when he squeezed my breasts as if hoping to squeeze liquid from them, squeezed my thighs, my buttocks smooth-cupped in his hands whispering what he would not say aloud *Your cunt your skin the color and texture of your skin are repulsive to me, don't you know? can't you guess? how can you do these things with me, how can you abase yourself so?* Never would he have said *I love you*; though often in my dreams he said *I love you*; he would cover my mouth with his to suffocate my words, my cries, my breath; if I felt sexual pleasure rising in me in

317

rhythm with his own, if mesmerizing pleasure burst between my
legs he did not want me to scream; he did not want his neighbors
to hear me scream; if he closed his fingers around my neck he did
not want to hear me scream; if he spat into my mouth that seemed
to him in orgasm ugly and gaping as a fish's mouth he did not
want to hear me scream; he would fill my mouth with his tongue;
he would fill my mouth with his cock; my dry anguished mouth
filled with his immense tongue; my dry anguished mouth filled
with his immense cock; he would spill himself into me, that I
might choke and drown; he would whimper almost saying *I love
you*; as if these words were snatched from him as his seed was
snatched from him he would whimper almost saying *I love you*.
In his strong fingers he would grip my back, my hips and buttocks
so that the angry imprint of his fingers would remain for days,
overlaid upon earlier bruises; he would arch his backbone above
me, he would collapse upon me sobbing and groaning falling from
a great height; he would bury his burning face in my neck; he
would bury his burning face between my breasts that were chafed,
aching; he would lie exhausted in my arms as if defeated; I would
stroke his tight-curly oily hair I loved; I would cradle his heavy,
handsome head I loved; I could not see his eyes I loved but it was
to his eyes, his vision I spoke; I spoke softly and quietly and un-
hurried now in the aftermath of our lovemaking as in the aftermath of struggle in which opponents embrace or sink together
to earth mutually exhausted, doomed; I spoke wonderingly to him
of things I had never seen, thoughts I had never had; the bright
sea rippling in sunshine where on a wide white beach of sand fine
as confectioner's sugar I ran splashing in the surf cutting
my bare foot on a seashell and my mother ran behind me lifting
me in her arms as I cried more in surprise than in pain; though
the pain came swiftly, throbbing through my foot; and my mother
kissed the bleeding cut, and made it well; I told him of my mother
whose face was beautiful and loving yet flimsy as rice paper to
be marred, torn almost by accident; I told him of my father who'd
been in life solid, heavy; heavy-hearted and heavy-footed; yet in
death as flimsy as my mother; his handsome ruined face now
smudged as in a charcoal drawing; once I had drawn him, in charcoal;
a childish face I'd drawn yet recognizable as my father's; I'd shown
it to him, and he'd laughed at first but later took the drawing from
me, tore it swiftly in two; always I would recall how he tore the
drawing swiftly in two; it had seemed just to me, I'd had no right

to draw my father in charcoal; if I cried my tears were the usual false tears for I'd known beforehand I should not have done it; I should not have transgressed; I had not the right; children have no power, and children have no right. Yet somehow my father's face was a charcoal-smudged face; it was not a face you could see clearly; my father who was *a big bag of guts* as once he'd spoken of himself in drunken good-natured disgust; *a big bag of guts with a love of beauty, good things; a big bag of guts* who'd wanted to be something more; not knowing what that might be; waiting like most men to be told what that might be; not knowing, and waiting, and not being told. Like most men simply dying when he'd worn out. These things I told my lover Vernor Matheius who lay warm, heavy and motionless in my arms; his face hidden from me; his eyes hidden from me; slowly I stroked his back, his knotty spine and ribs; this was the great happiness of my life holding Vernor Matheius in my arms stroking him slowly, in wonder; that which we do not deserve alone fills us with wonder; my voice was soft with wonder, a voice that surprised me with its clarity, and its authority; I told my lover how at night in the country often I'd heard Death outside in the cornstalks in the wind of October and November; I heard Death entering my grandparents' farmhouse too flimsy to keep Death out; I lay awake hearing Death moving across the creaking floorboards downstairs and I prayed that Death would pass me by, and the others in the house; I prayed that Death would pass me by, and take another in the house; I saw that all who lived lay very still in the terror of Death waiting for Death to pass by, and to take another; as in a herd terrorized by predators there must be the wish, the single flame-like collective thought *Take another! take another and not me!* This was a secret of which adults would not speak; it was a secret of which no one, not even the great philosophers, would speak; because it is so stark, so simple; it is a secret lacking a revelation.

And so we would drift into sleep. Vernor Matheius who was my lover at last, and I who was Anellia, his Anellia whose true name he never troubled to know; or, if he knew, never spoke. In those weeks, months of our love never spoke. Sharing a single cramped bed, a bed with a flat, trampled mattress, sagging in the center like a bent-back beast of burden this mattress, suffused with our sweat, the smell of his hair, underarms and feet, the smell of his stopped-up semen liquid and milky in the limp, sad condom drooping from his penis now quieted, subdued after sexual triumph which was indistinguishable from defeat; the individual that is the dupe of the species; the individual who resists all instincts, all urges and demands of the species; we would share this cramped bed, and this hour, but not the same sleep; for where Vernor Matheius drifted at last to sleep I did not know though jealously I would have wished to know, my fingers in his hair I drifted off at least to sleep, where he went I could not follow.

4.

> *The mind can neither imagine nor recollect save while in the body.*
>
> — Spinoza

And what of my life in those months that was not Vernor Matheius, what of the vast world that was not Vernor Matheius, what of a girl whose body I inhabited who was not "Anellia," what connection, what vision seen through her eyes, had she no future, had she no hope, did none of this exist?

Yes. But no.

Instructing the Devouring Locust
{Forties 123}
Jackson Mac Low

— in memorium David Rattray

Instructing a Judo class in his Eastern real-time childhood
returned to music   ludic-on-a-harpsichord distinctively voiced
becoming invisible through happiness translated by amphétamine
funnelled his friends to their líves through a black   hole that *was*
    Nervál   displacing anger   corresponded ardently   egregiously
    wróng and in pain
discovered gnostic craziness

Certainly no pleasure in the sickness or the lancinating agony
there in the practical gap between presence   and absence   we see him still
troubadour-anachronism singing with poison   soaring inside unresisted
blazing on a peak amid dark towers that gleamed like audience
    teeth   entwined in unaccountable death on the
    polished   blackened   ground
pointing with a gesture or a wave

Stabbed in the knees   enwrapping the shoulders of nothing   with
      delicate tiny steps
missed after going far from friends   no more
      multifoliate-pícture-correspondence
inscribed with Sanskrit proverbs   poked in the eye from-the-beyónd
near a stream beside Mount Adams   on a ferry in open water melted
    continually away   set-óut   tethered for jailyard
    exercise   vision's   scrim   warped
in dark   tufted knots

Lineage revealed in a joke   weakly bound-to-one-another-catastróphically
floating over beaches uncurated   transmuted time into poetry outside
humorously aware of horror   thanks-to-relentless-generósity
stepped aside from the pulsing nose of the dog   sunken in ghost-ridden
    mud where a rabid   bear   sat at a treasured pyrámidal table
growing like corn in a field

Singin' in the kitchen with Dinah in the crudely triángular hospital basement
fell into a well   guided by an all-too-human-fáce without music
played an In Nomine on a harpsichord covered with
        question-marks-and-scórpions
invoked by giddy wrath in Nessus' shirt neither rising nor falling
    in-an-effort-to-make-sénse overflowing with germs   prospered
    on an island
stood in line for Mont Blanc

Witnessed the universe's disregard with simple normal passivity
across from an open window displaying an estimable figure
suspended in a cell over a whispering líght-table   discriminated
    nothing from nothing
where a viscous cloud enfolded with ease   demonic-putrefáction
    immaterially imprinting molten glass   with tiny
    Republican eyes
that implanted themselves unobserved

Bathed with spatial fire   a crystalline   constellated   skeleton
stood in skinny sunrise wrapped in segmented spiral veils
stretching and snaking through toxic syllables of flaring color
reeking of thyme - and - garlicky spasms   protecting paven dreams
    of clear   gels   turning in space   exploding in
    blackness regained
when Lucifer carried-out-the-Wíll

Jackson Mac Low

Responding to a poem gone réd-again   like a russet potato recalled
played-back-as-if-it-ówned the place as the frontispiece owns the book
when similes-pile-úp-on-themselves   defying existence's miserly
    gauntness
shouted that Bodhisáttva vows   were keeping the Dalai Lama
    contaminated-with-hábits   presence   and earthbound as a pope on a
    merely-inward-súmmit   suspended in wind
like the devouring locust

Silences and/or prolongations: 3 en spaces [   ] = 1 unstressed syllable;
    6 en spaces [   ] = 1 stressed syllable or beat.

Nonorthographic acute accents indicate stress rather than vowel quality.
Each hyphenated compound is read as one extended word:
a bit more rapidly than other words, but never hurried. Spaced hyphens [-] indicate
slowed-down compounds. Indented lines conclude verse lines begun above them.
Breath pauses at verse-line endings ad lib.

New York: 1 May 1994; 12–30 August, 9 September 1996

323

James Doc Holiday, circa 1880. Photo courtesy of Western History Collections, University of Oklahoma Library.

The Pure, Scalding Light of Tombstone, 1881

Paul West

SEVERED FROM HUMANITY except for a tenuous lifeline to his nun in Savannah, Doc tended the nasty plant devotedly, not that a cactus needed much. Not until he quit his hovel for the bright lights of the saloons and card-rooms did he recognize how little padding there was in his days, that the miscellaneous noise of the rabble — shots fired into oil lamps, horses ridden into stores, fireworks let off like exclamation marks in the midst of the general outcry, screams of affront and howls of pain, long slithery sounds of throwing up, undisguised groans of disgust as hangovers bit home — all this kept him chipper, out of himself, away from the sullen recognition that most of his life he had lived against the odds, delighted usually to wake each morning, not much afraid to go to sleep, never in much need of company so long as he heard the racket of the mob, the untuned pianos, the strident fiddle, the click of gambling chips, the diminutive clatter of cup on saucer, the tiny suffocated ping of fork on plate, and could, with Wyatt say, stride out along Allen Street munching one of Pucette Romany's redhot morning buns. Where her name came from, what book of half-hatched handles, he did not know, but to eat the things was a juggling act as, too hot to handle, they bounced from one hand to the other, a smidgen of civilization although not of the South.

Landladies he had had here and there, best of all in Atlanta where a Mrs. Pomeroy had ministered to him, red-cheeked and insultably polite, never quite certain if he was being sarcastic or sentimental (she never knew him quite well). This landlady had a booby-trap called Miss Amelia, her sister, some dozen years older, and Miss Amelia liked to explain the firedrill in case the house went up in flames. She showed all guests the long, coarse rope, thicker than her wrist, and told them to tug it three times for her to come and guide them (she was almost blind), and to slide down it as far as possible while she was coming up. Doc could only imagine the bedlam on the stairs if the firedrill ever went into operation.

His worst/best experience with Miss Amelia had been in his first week, when, sleeping late, he had been in bed when she came upstairs on her sleepwalking household chores. Making his bed with him still in it, and wholly unaware of his presence, so numb her hands were, she covered him over with a winding sheet of her own devising. That clinched it. He could not let go such a novel incessant interlude, shocking him with humdrum surprises daily, so much so that he longed to be in Miss Amelia's inchoate neighborhood, ready to escape conflagration with her as they slid down the rope together toward its soaped noose. That kind of company, of gifted unselfconscious eccentrics, he had always needed and would go far to get, never dreaming of course that it would take him as far as Tombstone and into such real peril as distinct from the mythic kind.

Little matter that the bodies of the dead from the O.K. Corral had been cleaned up a little and then put on display in open boxes in the window of the Tombstone hardware store. What bothered Doc like an incubus, sitting in his mind and daunting him, was the image of short, stocky Ike Clanton who, having run up to Wyatt and grabbed his left arm, had been repulsed, thereupon mustering to his own purposes the energy in Wyatt's left-handed shove and bolting away into the lodging house, then through the rear door to the back landing, past Sheriff Johnny Behan skulking there with six-gun at the ready for who knew what, over the top of Billy Claiborne also skulking there, low and prudent, into the famous photography gallery itself, after which he sped down the hallway, thence to the back, right around the gallery corner, over the intervening fence, between the dismal, worn-out outhouses, clean across Allen Street, beneath a freight wagon like a collapsing greyhound, around the card tables, right through the active, astounded fiddle-player, through the rear door, all the way down the unwanted alley and into Alfred Henry Emmanuel's building on Toughnut Street, where while trying to think of how to go into hiding next he ensconced himself behind a barrel of mescal. He behaved like someone trying to create a record of propulsion and adaptation. Always, Doc told himself, Ike Clanton hiring somebody to talk against somebody. How many times had he or Wyatt run into Ike Clanton in the street, only to hear about yet another deal in the wind? If you remembered anything in detail about anybody, such as the peppermint candy that Virgil liked, or the huckleberry ice cream that lured Wyatt, it was the miasma of verbiage that haloed Ike Clanton's face: Ike the survivor, the self-exempted, the floater. No trace of his passage from Corral to mescal barrel, Doc lamented, nor of anybody else either, souvenir hunters having collected up both guns and empty shells (or savvy allies trying to help). He would not go so far as to say it was as if the Corral battle had never been, but had taken place out in the desert, in a purer form where there was no medical help, no cheering, no spectator, nor, he winced, any gunshop for outlaws to buy bullets at, nor a butcher's such as Bauer's where outlaws could sell their rustled beef. Out on the flank during the gunfight, and therefore a late starter, Doc had not even been called to testify at the trial; he felt one of the unnecessary, deemed so by their eminent lawyer Tom Fitch, a former editor and politico, without whom, Wyatt argued, they would have been sunk. It had been Tom Fitch who, invoking habeas corpus, had got them out of jail after being suddenly calaboosed halfway through the trial and having paid their bail. If a man needed a Fitch to survive in Tombstone, what would he need in Frisco? Doc, as he miserably recognized, had a bad name, and Fitch had thought it best to bury him as a despised phantom, good when the chips were down and the trigger fingers itchy, but a liability when people had gotten self-righteous and wanted a necktie party to add to the ongoing circus the town had turned into, with gun battles in its midst, corpses on view, and a huge, elongated trial swallowing both people and time, words and sleep. No one had, yet, said that this had been a show-down between Republicans and Democrats, but the slander was in the air; Wyatt was a self-proclaimed Republican, but did he think of himself in that light when having breakfast, peeling back his no doubt huge and ponderous foreskin, loading his Colts for the day's excitement? Doc saw himself as a freebooter, a man who lived for himself in his own terms, who never apologized. He had no politics save those of a patrician gentility, but he was surely, in his nerves and tendons, an aristocrat, transplanted and grown crooked but still a son of the South. Who or what else would respond gladly to the convent letters of a sequestered Mattie, who entered the nunnery almost as soon as he quit the South?

Wyatt, not one given to intimidating guesswork, had said to Doc that the bullet which struck him in the holster would have smashed his spine had it been an inch farther over. Doc felt it

327

whizz past him, made almost virtuous by luck; it was not he but Albert Bilicke, owner of the Cosmopolitan, who had seen Tom McLowery holding a gun as he came out of a store, and others had seen Ike and Billy Claiborne buying cartridges at Spangenberg's gun-shop. Everybody had something to contribute to the horn of plenty of knowledge, even those who had witnessed nothing at all. Nobody wanted to be left out, even to the point of slandering Doc (he liked to kill the healthy, they said), he would slice you from belly to dick for a mispronounced vowel, and he was addicted to the melody of money. He would go any distance, they said, for a five-dollar gold piece. Of course, nobody mentioned his passion for letter-writing, letter-receiving, and his gradually intensifying pagan religiosity fanned by his nun. He was a more private man than they knew, with a noxious flower, a lung-frenzy, and a critical devotion to Wyatt Earp, who seemed to him not quite enough of a gentleman but certainly enough of a lawman. Often enough, Doc's mind was on the most recent sentence he had read in a Mattie letter, or on something else she had sent all the way from sultry Savannah. She had recently confessed to him that she had widened her studies again, had sought to go back to being a poet, at least had begun writing new poems, not quite the poems she herself would have expected from a near-nun, based on readings or medi-tations that surprised her about herself as, tentatively, she bur-rowed into ancient literature, fired by some rusty old tome in the convent library (too boring to be censored, apparently) into at-tempting the monstrously difficult form of old India known as the *ghazal*, no sample of which she had yet sent him ("still slaving at it," she wrote), abandoning for the time being the little prayer she had mentioned earlier, and now, as if having at last found a ques-tionable — *most* questionable — form for her blazing sensitivity, voicing a statue of the poet Ovid in a Rumanian town — something she called "The Poet Ovid's Prayer from the Black Sea." So, she was back to prayer again, but in a most abandoned way that would surely have got her expelled had she circulated the poem.

> *Please make the huge red hibiscus my dinner plate*
> *All grubby again while I, black bird-limed statue*
> *In a Rumanian square, hunched on a giant plinth*
> *Bearing contemptible insignia while a hesitant boy*
> *Crosses the road, beg for a tent to cover me,*
> *A quotation from the piratic winds wobbling*

In the uproar above my skull. I was unsafe to know,
So let me once more wind a tapeworm around
My throat, in homage to treason.

It was the closest Doc had ever seen her to theological suicide, fixing on that rapscallion Ovid, whom he recalled distantly for the spicy *Ars Amatoria,* passed from sticky hand to sticky hand at school. Why she had chosen Ovid she did not say, though any reader could see rebellion stewing in her lines, in the last one especially. Heavens: perhaps she had in mind an entire series about Ovid and his rank behavior, designed to get her crucified, at least to the extent that nuns suffered any such thing. His Mattie was busting out, he could see that, but only within the confines of a letter, a poem. It was as if she had taken up boxing in the chapel. As poems went, her Ovid poem was not half bad, he thought, too garish perhaps (but she often had been) and, depending on how you read it, weighted with a too blatant pathos. Her early poems, which he had read at ease on his back in a Georgian valley, had been less acrid, less historical, more swooning and fertile. So this was what postulation, or whatever they called it, might do for a young woman left to her own devices, still dickering about the devotional life. It did not sound as if she had quite taken to it, not if her Ovid was any indication. Anyway, where were the *female* Roman poets? Had there ever been any? He knew of none. Her dilemma, he sensed, had to do with the faint difference between doing God's work as prescribed by an institution and God's work as permitted to the free-ranging imagination: duty and desire, the pernicious twins. Oh hell, why did he have to go through all this? Why now? Just when he thought he had her in exact focus, she had moved on, or sideways, not so much becoming another woman as turning into a different abstraction. He had really doted on her in their teens, and now she was sea-changing at speed, not even matching up to his notion of The Nun, but behaving more as if she had gone on to some supreme graduate school into which he had the brains to follow, but hardly the impetus, and certainly not from an enormous distance with killings all around him, his friends dead or wounded, his future very much in doubt. He had still not gotten over the white gloves encasing the hands of the three corpses before they were wheeled away for burial. The same town, that put its dead on show in the hardware store window like so many shoes in boxes, offered Paris dresses to those who could

afford them, and many could, fortune-hunters who had come good
on the silver platform that Tombstone provided. Remnants of events
tugged at him, matters he should have been able to dismiss, but
which occupied him with all the force of cadavers. W. B. Murray
had offered Virgil twenty-five armed men "at a moment's notice.
If you want them, say so." Had he and the Earps not needed them,
even if only to spread the blame? Had Virge really answered that
it was all right for the outlaws to be armed in the O.K. Corral because it was not illegal to carry arms in a livery stable? Why had
they had any part of the right on their side? The horse with its
head in the window of Spangenberg's bothered him, especially
when Wyatt as deputy city marshal, if that, decided to pull the
offending animal off the sidewalk. As he seized the bit to back the
horse, Frank McLowery charged outside and grabbed the reins.
Virgil came to help and he and Wyatt both watched the cowboys
slotting bullets into their gunbelts, as if nothing were going to
happen. What part had the crowd in front of Hafford's played in
the shootout, egging on the Earps? Would we not have done it, Doc
wondered, without popular support? Were we putting on a show
for the rabble? Did we really need to do what we did? Yes. The
town was rife with feuds, between town and country cowboys and
miners, maybe even, if you could track it down, between poets
and consumptives, bards and lungers. They should all have settled
for a five-cent bottle of iced beer to blur their prejudices, although
the effect of beer on the likes of Ike Clanton was extraordinary:
no help. Yet Ike Clanton had remained unarmed. Maybe there was
a connection between beer and helplessness. What had he said, the
worst among all the preposterous things he came out with? "Fight
is my racket. All I want is four feet of ground." He was lucky not
to have found six feet, buried in the correct cowboy rig for the
great last day: stockman style, as they called it, shotgun chaps,
Mexican loop holster for the .45, high-heeled boots, vest and dark
shirt, wide flat-brimmed hat. A general look of natty, pragmatic
splendor, all for the grave. The Earps looked so much alike that
Tombstone had weighed them, the differences being minimal,
none of them above 158, Virgil the oldest the heaviest, Morgan
a touch heavier than Wyatt, each with wavy light-brown hair,
periwinkle blue eyes that never twinkled, and copious mustache.
Indeed, those firing in the O.K. Corral could not have known who
they were shooting at, the point being of course that he Doc was
the deadliest marksman, in fact and by repute, yet he had been the

last to shoot just because of circumstances. He might not have been there at all but finishing off the last hour of innocent sleep. Had they weighed *him*, he would have come out light on account of all the blood he'd spat over time. Give a horse to Morgan and Wyatt would end up with it even though it properly was Virgil's. Why, Doc mused, even if they had compared penises, the Earps would have been identical, although, come to think of it, could the other two like Morgan that day have vaulted the Alhambra lunch counter to lead him, Doc, out into the street before he got into worse trouble with the profuse Ike? Out in the street, bickering and yelling, they attracted the attention of City Marshal Virgil Earp, who never kidded about his job, having already arrested Mayor Clum for speeding in a buggy and his own brother, Wyatt, for brawling. If they refused to quit their indoor and open-air row, Virgil said, he'd calaboose them both, and it would cost them dough. So Doc sidled away, muttering, and Ike headed for the Grand while Virgil went back to the Occidental and Wyatt, having had his lunch, marched over to the Eagle Brewery where he had a faro game going. As he did, he walked right into the bad penny, Ike Clanton, who invited him to walk with him a piece, during which conversation Wyatt told Ike there was no money in fighting. Come to think of it, Wyatt had always been more interested in money than in fighting. Laughing about the 1880 territorial census, they had all joked about what they put down as their Tombstone profession, Wyatt a farmer, later to become saloon-keeper, James Earp also saloon-keeper, Morgan and Warren Earp laborers, Doc a dentist, Virgil correctly as a U.S. deputy marshal. Therefore, Doc noted, *ergo*, during the O.K. Corral gunfight, Wyatt was a saloon-keeper deputized as a deputy town marshal by Virgil expressly for shooting duties and he, Doc, the deadly dentist also roped in and deputized. He would have loved to wear the star just once — the shield, the badge, whatever it was known as in the profession. Doc dreamed about U.S. Marshal Crawley P. Dake, officially blamed for not keeping order in Cochise County, arriving in Tombstone with a trunkful of badges to pin on all brave and willing men, Doc among them. It could all have been more glamorous, and perhaps it would be again, once the corpses had cooled. In the meantime he owed Mattie a poetry-sensitive letter on the occasion of Ovid's prayer and his statue in Rumania.

Paul West

My dear Mattie,

It is so long since I have seen one of your poems, this one as startling as I have seen, arriving in this turbulent town like a well-trained dove from an order of being, a dimension, of sweet deliverance. As you know only too well, Tombstone has been in the news in the worst possible light, and people are leaving town. More will have gone by the time this reaches you. Those of us remaining feel as if a spell has broken; not only do we feel like survivors, as survivors should, if indeed we still are that, but we feel both elect and doomed at the same time. Wyatt is still in Arizona, thank goodness, out and about on various missions, and I may soon join him. If he is not prospecting, he is looking people up or tracking the missing.

I had never realized you had a fondness for Ovid, whom I remember from grammar school for some risqué things about love. I find, now, that addressing a nun is no different from addressing Vosper, the acting governor of Arizona with whom I once roomed. I do not have to be delicate or abstemious: just tell the truth. After all, as I understand the veil, at least as well as I do the cloth and silk, nuns exist to assist people in dealing with their own abominations. So it is not a matter of protecting people from the bad things in life, but of helping them to deal with them. The nun, out in practice in everyday life, dips her hands in the dreadful without becoming contaminated. Unless, of course, we are dealing with nuns who devote themselves to things metaphysical and never go out. I sometimes do not know which type you intend to be.

Back to your poem. It has gorgeous images, as always, and some arresting shifts of voice. I like that hesitant boy crossing the road—he might be the young Ovid or an epitome of the young braveling, a foretaste of the rotten things that could happen to an outspoken poet.

He paused as some clatter began on the stairs, no doubt a new arrival carelessly lugging his belongings alongside him, heedless of others' repose or of those intent on attempting an appreciative letter to a gifted nun with a poetic gift.

332

In the end, the strongest image I find is that of the tapeworm around the throat, a gross metaphor for all outspoken people. It might have been around almost anything else, but where it is makes you gag as being throttled along with him. This takes me back to the huge dinner plate in the first line, one an image of plenty, the other one of strangulation. I love the notion of the big flower (they are a foot wide, aren't they, some of them?) being a dinner plate: you eat the perishable off the perishable. My own flower, mate or buddy, is the carrion cactus, not easy to sniff at, but, once you get used to it, cordially encouraging. This is how we were taught to read poetry in the old days, quite instructive I used to think, and now it stands me in good stead. Your poem is not one to puzzle over, however, unless you get lost in speculation, say about how the petal plate got grubby again, perhaps from a second helping? You never know. Nivver, we used to say around here. I sit here at the end of an era, telling myself, oddly enough, I am on my own again with my own disease, as one is when reading poems. I like Ovid for wanting a tent over him; I know that feeling, Mattie (nunlike?), and I relish his thought about being unsafe to know, which has been true of yours truly.

Now the battery from the stairs became another noise, mobile, more aimed, a clomping shuffle that preceded a knock on his door, then two more, followed by a series of impatient increasingly fast ones, in the humiliating vocative: *"Doc?"* He did not answer, but, sucking inspiration from defiance, cocked both pistols and arranged himself against the pillows to face the door, which was not locked (it did not lock, it was a door that had seen better days and more rambunctious knockers). On he wrote, hectic, nervous, piqued, managing to get a sentence further before it all became too much and he bellowed a response.

I wanted to tell you how I responded to the piratic winds, so [he left a space for the mot juste, now feeling too harassed to decide on it], *and I had to think about that one, it is almost more rich than I can bear. Someone at the door, sorry, I will resume.*

"What? Who the hell?" He bellowed, but his throat was dry, his vocal cords had tightened from the sheer concentration of writing the letter, and what he yelled was hardly audible even to him — unneeded, however, as the door burst in, with almost the intemperate speed of someone drawing on him, and Parsons the diarist appeared in the doorway, lucky to miss the bullet that hummed past his neck and buried itself in the wall across the corridor.

"Jesus, Doc, you didn't have to shoot!" Parsons's life was a series of near-misses, all dutifully recorded in his little book. Panicked as he was, he marveled to see Doc clearly interrupted in the act of writing, yet with a gun in either hand, one emitting a haze-blue curl of smoke.

"You almost got me that time," Parsons said, unoffended but austere. Doc might have seemed to have been cheating at poker (Parsons loved games, discerning in them perhaps a model of Tombstone itself: life as a gamble, a prank, an exercise in mindless distraction). "Please don't."

"You sure got better at ducking, you old fart," Doc told him. "I wouldn't go around knocking on doors and then barging in. Wyatt will buffalo you, but some of the surviving badmen will drill you for sure."

"I came to tell you," Parsons began, mustering a broken smile, but Doc interrupted.

"I don't want to hear. You write your diary and I write my letters. Would you care to exchange roles for a week? What do you know of Ovid the Roman poet?"

"Smutty," Parsons told him with an almost disdaining leer. "Your Latin is better than mine."

"Tot homines, quot sententiae." Doc was getting into the mood.

"Misquoting again," Parsons bluffed. "All we need is Johnny Ringo and we'll have a triumvirate of classical scholars. God forbid." Parsons palped between finger and thumb his recently healed broken nose, an injury sustained by accident in one of Tombstone's swarming crowds; an elbow had caught him and laid him low, back into his diary, where he had written "Hurts like the devil. Can't blow it."

"You're a messenger, I take it?" Doc had suddenly realized this was not a social call on Parsons's part, gregarious as he was, especially toward people in power. By now, however, Parsons had thought fast about the messenger's being killed in the old Greek tradition and was almost on the point of not delivering. Yet, in tough times of heavy lifting from office to office — heavy ledgers and boxes of carbon copies — his colleagues had called him a Trojan, so it was as a doughty Trojan that, clear of all involvement with Latin, he said what he had come to say. As he did so, he wished he could have done it in Latin, thus creating an aura of doubt as to the exact message.

"They want you down in Bisbee."

"No they don't," Doc quipped, suddenly aware of why this man irritated him: not with his incessant diary, about which he talked all the time like an invalid discoursing on an irreversible disease, but with his use of the sobriquet "Doc" to indicate Doctor Good-fellow, Tombstone's best. This purloining of his own local copyright had always bothered Doc, and right now he was not in specially genial humor. "No they don't," he snapped, "and they can't have me anyway. I have to be leaving town." He already had in mind Silver City, Rincon, New Mexico and Colorado, along with Wyatt and whoever else wanted to come along, leaving the George Parsonses behind.

"You're wanted for sure," Parsons told him. "There was an accident. A shooting."

"None of my work," Doc said. "I'm retired, you know."

"What is that stench?" Momentarily distracted, Parsons had succumbed to the carrion cactus, backing into the doorway that now framed him, the very personification of a man about to depart or deliquesce, perched on the very edge of being temporary, wrinkling his almost-healed nose. Laconic in his diary entries, often to the point of omitting verbs, Parsons was becoming that way in conversation too, almost a fugitive from Dickens, *The Pickwick Papers*, say, which he had read and allowed to form his prose style, wishing he did not live in Arizona and could emulate Dickens in his apparently simple-minded relish of such English things as roaring fires, slipping on ice, a haunch of roast beef at Christmas, and elementary love affairs. Samuel Weller the pithy cockney boot-black who was his progenitor might have found a richer vocation in Tombstone. Again Parsons tried to deliver his message. Now he gave Doc the wire that had just arrived downstairs in the lobby.

Puzzled by the scrawl, Doc got up, walked to the window and winced at the disappearing soreness in his back. Mildly injured, he felt the wound's traces still. He was wanted in Bisbee to assist in an investigation of a death: Big Nose Kate was no more. He felt no grief, but an almost arithmetical pang for the woman who, in the end, in a drunken fit, had tried to frame him as an outlaw. She had taken her thousand dollars and gone, and he had never expected to see her again. Now they wanted him to come and view her remains, with the gift of her cactus still prickling his nostrils. He would rather go the other way, northward, out of the whole damned area, but something from an old honorable Southern tradition nagged at him; she had not died, she had been killed, but by whom? Pestered by Parsons, who was always keen on gossip, he at length got himself dressed under those deliberate eyes and invited the diarist along for the twenty-mile ride to Bisbee, where Kate had died in infamous Brewery Gulch, a victim of ill-fortune, far too young for this.

After a brisk series of gallops without conversation, Doc and Parsons were in Brewery Gulch by noon and conducted to the squalid little shed in which she lay in state naked on a wooden slab, bosomy and buttocked as ever, hardly the worse for wear, with no sign of a wound. It seemed that some hothead drunk had entered the saloon, shooting at random as cowboys often did, an event that Doc had often witnessed without even looking up from faro. It had always struck him as the loudest form of crude conversation. Those in the know, Kate included, had gone for the floor while the bullets whirled until the cowboy ran out of ammunition and his little paddy was over. They all arose save Kate, who had remained there on the floor in her ungainly sprawl, inert and unblemished, dead perhaps of a heart attack. Or so the locals thought, lacking any kind of a doctor to check her out. Now they had a former dentist, far from ideal, but many of them would have let a veterinarian examine them, none too fussy about the dividing line between animal and human.

"Look," Doc said to the aghast diarist, already making notes he would later write up without the verbs. "Nothing." He looked again, turning Kate over onto her front, trying not to hear gurgles from within or notice an aroma not that of carrion cactus, but akin. Then he saw what nobody else had seen in their cursory first and final look: a tiny fleck of blood on one buttock, a dab, a bloblet, congealed of course but firmly attached almost like a blister. They brought him the razor he asked for, and as best he could he performed partial autopsy, confirming that, when the shootist drunk had entered the saloon, Kate had dived for the floor with her butt toward him and taken an invisible hit in the rectum, an area of little or no resistance. The bullet had travelled all the way up to her heart, rending her entrails as it went. Doc removed the bullet with an agonized sigh and patted the remains in bewildered pain. He felt distorted, called upon to perform on his old beloved an act so gross it shocked even Parsons the diarist, and Doc depending on medical knowledge long rusty had gone right only through a series of mistakes. It was grotesque to be paddling around in the penumbra of the parts that had given him so much pleasure not that long ago. He felt sickened by the sheer meatish quality of human life and he agonized, right there in the presence of her remains, about the lyricism that celebrated the private parts of women, what dear old Milton had called the "zone," adored, revered, coveted, fondled, licked, buffeted, hymned, only to come to this last favor. Who could tell now what bliss her parts had given, even to him alone, or what jealousy they had provoked, what lust, what hatred? He could not bear to think about it, even in one who had betrayed him. Why had she behaved so badly toward him after behaving fairly well? Now she was — nowhere. She still had seepages, of course, and an almost peaceful contemplative look with closed eyes, as if old Buda had come to mind one last time and she was thinking of trying life once again from scratch, from a different starting point, heading into Russia instead of the United States (a term that immigrants dreaming of America never used).

"Accidental death," Parsons suggested, licking his pencil's point. "Misadventure."

"All of that," Doc told him. "They used to say that, if you found yourself among bullets, the best thing was to hoist your keister into the line of fire and trust to luck. It was the least lethal place to be hit. So much for maxims. Poor Kate, buggered by a bullet."

"Bulgarian?"

"Hungarian, actually."

"Oh," whispered Parsons, disappointed, having hoped for a structural pun of some kind. How little we knew of those eastern countries, some of them only just created out of a loose amalgam that united states, provinces, areas, principalities, and puppet monarchies. Kate had come from there to an ignominious end, raw material for the diarist, the autopsy man, the peerer and leerer, ripe for a dirty joke in the saloon. In later years, the rumors would begin, bringing her back to life, hailing her origin (this time in Pest), and a host of impostors would surface, claiming to have known Doc and seen him at the O.K. Corral on that accursed day. No doubt the very gun that killed her would reach antique-stores with a ticket dangling from its butt, worth a fortune even while

337

the sublime meat of her body had almost completely rotted away. By then, though, they would be saying that Doc suffered from syphilis; indeed, he did not put it past Parsons to do just that, ever alive to something picturesque and scandalous.

What happened to Big Nose Kate, though, was more than Parsons could stomach: one side of him, the sensationalist, doted on the approach to her the slug had made, almost like fate retaliating, whereas the other side winced and looked away, unhappy that any human could suffer a destiny so gross. He was no killer or shootist, that was plain, unaccustomed to seeing men in extremis, and less able to handle the gruesome spectacle than your average nun. Armed with the slug that finished his Kate, Doc left Bisbee in short order, having seen to her burial and arranged for a suitable cross. How would Mattie have handled this? He did it just so, trusting in his divination of her tact. Whatever Kate had done, whatever she had taken her wages for, she had done with it all now and her name must be left in peace and honored — honored for what, he wondered. For the dignity of having been used and idealized. He instantly regretted all the times he had yelled at her, called her names and otherwise abused her (just as he deplored, and then forgave, her own version of the same thing). He fixed on the romantic interludes, most of them conducted in a vaporous glow from a red light, when he persuaded himself she never went off whoring to pay the rent. It took some effort to achieve that degree of oblivion, but at times he had risen to it, sharply sealing off their situation from any outside event. He had almost learned, from Napoleon perhaps, how to make his mind a chest of drawers; when a drawer was closed, he did not think of its contents. So there were hours when his cough did not plague him, and her promiscuity did not wound him. Try not to think of God, he would tell himself, and he almost managed it, at least until he recognized that God was in everything, at the heart of Kate's misbehavior even. That stopped him, at least until he saw that the universe accommodated everything without the least ripple; it left moral judgments to human beings, who of course were part of the universe in any case.

Back in Tombstone, he set the death slug in the pot that held his carrion cactus and bowed it welcome, wondering what would join it next. He asked the diarist if he might read about various events, most of all the gunfight at the O.K., but Parsons refused, saying he might let Doc look at his entry on going to Bisbee to see the end of Big Nose Kate, an entry that as far as Doc could tell he never made, out of dithering shock or an all-enveloping fastidiousness.

When he got back, Doc found a letter for him in which Mattie described the convent, drawn into it by a reference to their orchard which doubled as a cemetery, with the obvious implication that dead sisters nourished the fruit, if such a thing could be. There were pews for visiting nuns, a hospice, an almonry, a bakehouse for guests (with a better menu), a kiln or drying house, a special room for the preparation of sacramental elements, a refectory, a bath, a *latrina* as she termed it, a cloister garth, an old room once consecrated to leeching and now an infirmary, a barn with a threshing floor, a guest house (he smiled), a school, and what tempted him most: a scriptorium and library. What premises, he thought, worldlier by far than where he had lived and spluttered in Dodge, Las Vegas, Prescott, and Tombstone. *He* was the deprived one, eking out a living in restricted quarters. He looked again, hard, having missed one item because his eyes had skipped, eluding the penmanship imperative of her bold, announcing hand: *calefactory,* he read. Ask her what a calefactory is. Something to do with heat, where things are warmed up, perhaps? She went into the practice of painting frescoes into wet plaster—while it was still "fresh," and he loved the idea. What on earth would they have done with Big Nose Kate impaled on a bullet? Would the resident doctor have quailed? Not a bit of it; she would have rendered back unto God God's own creature without the least sentimental obfuscation. And what was an almonry? He would have to ask, perhaps mentioning his journey to Bisbee, just to see what she would say. Maybe the soul of Kate had arisen in a flash, like the corposant that showed sometimes in a ship's rigging. He had not been there, and if such a thing happened it took place in the first few seconds after death, did it not? Could a pure soul have ascended from Big Nose Kate, the depraved courtesan? He did not doubt it, sensing she had gone to a celibate Tombstone worth idolizing, gunless and cardless and whiskeyless. Not a bad start.

Chihuahua
Toby Olson

A SOCIETY WOMAN on the streets of the Zona Rosa in Mexico City. She's come from New York and her husband, a businessman, has given her the day for shopping. She's done that, eaten a light lunch, and now she's bored. The clothing and the pieces of fine jewelry she's bought as souvenirs for friends make but a small bundle and a light one and she has only a broad shoulder purse and a sturdy shopping bag for toting. So she sets off into the back streets of the Zona, down into those byways where only Mexicans live.

The streets are empty, it's siesta, and deep in a shadowy alley between a bookstore and artist's studio, she glimpses a sliver of movement as she passes. She stops, pauses, then returns to the alley's mouth, and there, growing increasingly visible as it limps forward from the shadows, is a dog.

It's a very small dog, short haired, with large oval ears and a pug snout. Its color is a dirty white, and over the foreleg it holds limply above the ground, its chest is a row of bird bones, and its eyes, its protruding eyes, like those of a just born calf, are rheumy and running, and it's those eyes that get her.

A chihuahua, she thinks, poor thing, and she squats down gracefully, places her shopping bag to stand alone on the broken pavement beside her, then reaches her palm and her opening fingers out toward it. The dog limps from the final shadows and to her hand, extends his snout tentatively and sniffs her fingers. Then, his mooning eyes in her eyes, protruding from his small skull as if they might pop out should he stare much longer, his salmony tongue slides through his lips and touches the tip of one of them. Her fingers curl back quickly. She's a little startled, but she's undeterred, and she takes the silk scarf from her neck, makes a kind of hammock out of it, then reaches down and lifts the dog, light as a single tortilla, swaddles it and stuffs it gently down into her shoulder purse, among the jewelry, cosmetics and air freshener.

This is a good woman, you can see, and unapproachable, so when she does not tell her husband about the dog, smuggles it aboard the plane, it is no wonder she is successful, given her husband, her fine clothing and demeanor. The dog leaves the bag only when the two have reached the woman's apartment in New York City, the guest room that her husband never enters.

But the dog will not eat. The woman tries everything, and still it fails. Soon it no longer limps, though it might stand shivering beside the guest bed. And its eyes are closing, victims of an oozing infection.

Veterinary medicine? She's tried that, pills and potions gathered from friends surreptitiously. And every imaginable hard food and liquid sustenance too. It's sipped only at a saucer of milk, and this briefly, but that gives her the idea, mother's milk. She's heard it somewhere, a thing about animals, and she sets out with efficiency to find it, and she does.

The dog drinks and drinks again, and for a few days he's limping, his eyes seem to be opening. But then he takes a turn and is failing again, even more quickly than before. No longer can he stand now, and his rheumy eyes have closed completely. He begins to resemble a premature fetus, a small dirty bladder of some kind, curled into a shallowly panting bit of wet empty flesh at the foot of the guest bed.

The woman, in desperation, calls the family doctor, who recommends a veterinarian of stature. Then she calls him and makes a special appointment for the afternoon. She goes then to the dog and lifts it, in a thin rubber pillowcase this time, and settles it gently on a bed made of dishrags deep in a cloth satchel.

They arrive at the doctor's office on time and are ushered right into the examination room, where the woman takes great care in lifting the dog out of the bag. She places the small rubber package on the shining surgical table, then steps away, and the doctor steps forward and peels back the swaddling.

The dog has become nothing to the woman, nothing surprising that is, so when the doctor jumps back, a little shaken at the sight, she is offended. It's only a dog, she says, though a very sick one. Ah, well, the doctor says. But did you feed it mother's milk? I did, the woman says, and they both look down at the dog, only now recognizing that its eyes are half open and completely glazed over and that it is not breathing.

My poor, poor dog! the woman cries, her hands fluttering near her face.

Poor, yes, the doctor says, that is true. But this is no dog,

341

chihuahua or otherwise. This is a Mexican slum rat, numerous in those cities. Did you find it there?

The story unfolds no further, since the point has been made. It's the weakness, cowardice and filth of the Mexican and his representative dog, which is really a rat, or often mistaken for one and vice versa. But this has been a modern version of the story and a reversal is coming, which is not really part of the story but is suggested by it.

In the version just told, the woman is like the woman in any such story, elegant and refined, but though she is these things, and kind, she is also useless. There are no details in her life here, but for her concern with shopping, and though she is possessed of certain efficiencies she had no place to put them, but in the service of the failed resuscitation of a rat. The woman's husband is completely absent in this version, a piece of reality and social commentary, since that's the way it is up north.

And you might notice too a hint of the commercial quality of the fine main streets of the Zona Rosa here and how these are in contrast to those invisible byways behind it where the Mexicans live. The woman finds the dog in a dark alley and the concrete is cracked. But the alley is between two shops, one a depository of intellect, the other of art, those two crucial elements of the survival of a culture, the *real* Mexico here, *el corazón* of the healthy beating under the drumming of commerce.

And in the reversal the story has not quite ended though the point has been made, because the doctor was wrong. The thing left on the examination table was no rat at all, but a chihuahua of mixed strain, one who had drunk of pure mother's milk and was not dead but was rising up in the night, his blood cleansed by that milk in the way Mexico might be cleansed, returning to the children of the Indian mother. For the pure chihuahua is an Indian, one who came down from those mountains behind us where I came from. He's preening and turning in slow circles, his nails clicking on the slick metal, free now of the attentions of woman and doctor and the manipulations that might come from them. It's dark in the room, and the dog shakes its bum leg and stretches, its eyes blinking then opening wide as small saucers as it stares down over the table's edge. It licks its lips. Then it jumps into the void of blackness below.

Its feet hit, its pads thumping on the hardwood of this floor. There it is now, returned to the female through its mother's milk.

In our candles' light it searches the room for something it might never find. See it? It's passing low over the carpet there. It looks like a piece of fruit. I think it must be the Indian phoenix that could rise again, redeeming a rodent and the meaning of a hue. This is why I have named my chihuahua Rata and why I have colored her yellow.

The Berlin Sonnets
Robert Kelly

1.
As if it were hard to begin. But one has already begun,
the air is there, the song, the smoke above the Norman plain
going up from Joan's funeral pyre while the English stand around —
I saw the sky still smudged from it when I passed on the bus
years ago, passing by bus through famous places. Here Goebbels
was photographed with a cigarette and pretty woman,
here Paul Valéry stopped to light his pipe and peered
absentmindedly at a window full of soap, here Dvořák
fed pigeons on his windowledge and spoke English. And so on,
all in the same comic book called History, or,
Our Dream of What Must Have Happened To Make Things
The Way They Are and Hurt So Much. Or are they?
There's something about Saturdays and politics, as if the flesh
knew it for what it is, a sinister tragic sort of golf.

2.
But I sat on the bus fingering my ticket — good for two hours
of nonstop riding and changing and going — I could visit the poor
and still come back to the Zoo. I was in the middle of something,
a sky so clean it looked like they scrub it down with sand.
O blue Berlin you dream beneath my body! Or I am riding now,
remember, and the pretty aqua bridge across the Spree
coaxes me to alight and interview the swans. And the birds
— even these cultured and poetic drowsers — are all
that is free of history. Nothing ever happens where they are
except themselves. To live in the sky! They hardly notice us,
we are the ghosts in their lofty liberty, down here
in the cellar, where ghosts belong, where when I was young
they groaned all night behind the cellar door, choked me
breathless before I lost that soft virginity of fear.

3.

One sits in one's seat and listens to the conversation
as if the bus runs on words. Streets pass neatly,
traffic is mild. Why isn't anybody worried? Not even me.
Look at our faces in the glass, a face is a vertical landscape,
a study of the distant heart, becalm thee, maiden,
there is hope among the wheels. No one is close,
no one far. Every person in the bus is enduring
a different city, each one mapped on all the others,
inexpressible, terrible, remote. The woman beside me,
jolly, with rucksack, fresh from flying, is in a city
further than Lhasa, unreachable, sacred to her,
her Berlin, her little neighborhood, I'll never find it,
she'll never find mine. Wherefore are we all Ishmael
to each other, vague drifters, sand and rain and rabble
and we are war. Fifty years ago all this was just a fire.

4.

Bloody history. Who knows what you mean.
The mind that carries is also carried,
there is a galaxy that moves these things around

Go ahead and seem. Forgive the meaning.
Everything sweeping towards Sagittarius,
wise man with a beast's body, arrow in his hand.

We used to think we spoke the consonants
that shaped some everlasting vowel,
howl or groan or moan or sigh of time

but I don't know. Things come and go
without arriving or departing.
We are archers curiously void of arrows,

anxious in a targetless universe. We twang the bow
only for the music's sake, I guess.

Robert Kelly

5.

The summing up — such a long trial — begins. The evidence
died before any of us was born, the wind still smells of it
sometimes — a lawyer does what he can. The gold.
A morning sun reminds us, moonlight deludes us —

under every shadow we suspect the moon's been buried
and we dig. Theology, geology, logic, analytics,
acoustics, optics, astrophysics — not one
from Galilee to Ganges does much good.

Witnesses shuffle and mutter in their chambers
weary of the trial they once volunteered to guide
with fine speeches and rememberings towards the real.
Who would be a lawyer in such weather?

In my poor dining room, hardly room to eat,
row after row of metal cabinets stuffed with truth.

6.

Habe nun, ach . . . ! No need to mention all
the unprofitable fetishes and disciplines the heart
took for its master, then later broke
or forsook or ran right through the other side

into that clear blue absence of commodity
empty of discourse: the Actual.
The sky before we flew in it. Just read
the floating lights of fairies and divinities,

water drops and rainbow-lings, the gold
angel on the Victory Column winking
her eye to catch my glance, I see, I see,
that's where all the trouble starts,
I try to touch what the eye, that holier hand,
already touched and measured, loved and let go.

7.
And something was enough to say. Angels
interviewed by churchbells
answer with clouds. Little airplanes
bumblebee across the valley.

Every creature wants to go down.
I remember the fullness of your arms
while we wept and talked of Dachau and ate well —
I wondered at us — are we strange crows

grieving and feasting at once on a ruined world?
We are only an opera.
The names are forgettable,

what is remembered is the interval —
the heart leaping up a ninth, say,
or bathers in the surf up from an amazing wave.

8.
Not when it is spoken to but when it speaks.
Landgraves and tyrannies, little counts and servitudes,
there is a goldfinch to my seed. Would she stop
if I asked her to begin? There are churches
where no matter how many visitors are stirring
the shape makes you alone with mind — Pieter
Saenredam painted them, Haarlem, the stones
give light — and in such dedicated spaces
I have silenced hungers that the mind lets go.
That's why volcanoes speak, why Jewish women
have red hair, why summer night's so long.
Something is stirring to be loose, or less, or lost
into the strange altitude we used to call heaven,
just Japanese businessmen hurrying in big jets.

9.

Now everyone's offended. We have one mother and some fathers,
we come from clan. O the poverty
of our identity, to be so proud of what we guess we are.
I am a church of that. Of such weightless stone
I build my plinth, with color alone. And set you on it one by one,
you victors in the heart's olympiads, I medal you
with the bronze of my body's shadows, silver
of my deep water, gold of my vague eyes. I adore you
in the empty measures. There is no music yet,
it has not found the way to be. If it came to us
it would be formal and would grant us space
to dance inside it or alongside or not to move at all,
just watch it pass, can music pass, a train of conquerors,
what the not so ancient Greeks called a holy throng
and heard them leaving the doomed city all night long.

10.

Sixty years ago the stadium filled up with song.
Two hundred thousand voices sang the opening hymn
the famous Richard Strauss had written for this day,
my favorite composer, here at the hub of hell.
I have a record of them doing it, how can you count
each voice in all that ardor, the orchestra
blatant as an airplane overhead. Yet over the years
I've come to hear and recognize them all, the born
and the unborn, music grants no exemptions to the dead,
a girl who won't be born till Saturday, she
was singing loudest, and all the bitter athletes
black and yellow in that nightmare time, they
were singing too. Sometimes there's really nothing else to do.
Music is the actual politics by which we're ruled.

11.
For it lusteth to take hold, and constrain
all the lads and maidens of the town to dance
midnight naked round the broken chapel
for no delight but its delight, no harvest
to its hoe-down. It is a kind of manacle
slips round your soft pale wrist and pulls
by pulsebeat to the chaffy floor
where one way or another dancing does.
And does it to us whether we'd be done or no.
And deadbeat elders huddle in their beds
refusing to be flesh among such eldritch liturgies
yet their minds can think of nothing but
do not listen to this music, do not listen darling
for music means nothing but manipulation.

From Doubt Uncertainty Possibility Desire
Mary Caponegro

> —*Every shoot and every fruit is produced above the insertion (in the axi) of its leaf which serves as its mother, giving it water from the rain and moisture from the dew which falls at night from above, and often it protects them against the too great heat of the rays of the sun.*
>
> —Leonardo Da Vinci

Set yourself to describe the beginning of man when he is created in the womb.
And why an infant of eight months does not live.

Interventional treatment of the fetus before birth has been applied in such life-threatening conditions as hydrocephalus (fluid buildup in the brain) and hydroephrosis (a blockage of the urinary tract). The computer-enhanced image illustrates injection that passes through abdomen, uterus and into fetal bladder.

What sneezing is.
What yawning is.

A picture made with ultrasound in the sixth month of pregnancy shows the face of a healthy fetus with mouth open in a yawn. "By this point the fetus does just about everything it will do after birth," said Dr. Christopher Merritt of New Orleans, who obtained the image. "It yawns, blinks and even sucks its thumb."

In the year 1473, Leonardo assists his master Verrocchio with the painting The Baptism of Christ, in which two angels kneel together beside a standing, praying figure whose feet and ankles are submerged in water. The angel on the left, painted with astounding delicacy and fineness, by the apprentice, far surpasses the angel on the right, by the master. This moment is said by many in Verrocchio's and other Florentine studios to be the beginning of Leonardo's painting career.

Probing painlessly, sonography uses sound waves to look within.

It is also the moment, in a sense, of my birth, although my actual birth was a decade later, for the angel painted by my master, Leonardo, bears an uncanny resemblance to my perpetually youthful self, whom he would discover on the streets of Milan at age ten, twenty years after executing that depiction, and rescue from poverty by taking into his home and training as servant, pupil, protégé, whatever term you choose. Labels matter little. My given Christian name, for example, is Giacomo, but you will know me by another name, with which my master rechristened me. Frankly, though — I'm accused of lying all the time ma questo sincero, senti: I don't give a shit about painting. It makes me yawn.

In trouble before birth, Joseph Ward was found to have a tumor growing in his throat that forced him to keep his mouth open inside the womb.

> Somewhere, in what had been up until then a near perfectly harmonious community of some one hundred trillion cells, a normal cell becomes a cancer cell.

Trembling.
Epilepsy.
Madness.
Sleep.
Hunger.

My master eats no meat, and I, today, eat only candy: some aniseed sweets I was craving, and who would be so cruel as to take candy from a little boy? (A boy, moreover, with the appearance of an angel.) All right, I admit that I stole the money he had put aside to make my jerkins with. Have you never had a craving?

Sensuality

To spy on the brain in action, PET scanners watch the way brain cells consume substances such as sugar. The substance is tagged with a radioisotope brewed in a small, low-energy cyclotron.

His name for me, Salai, means limb of Satan. As to which, the name or my behavior, is chicken and which is egg, I cannot say. I leave to you.

. . . stating which part of it is formed first, and so successively putting in its parts according to the periods of pregnancy until birth and how it is nourished, learning partly from the eggs laid by hens.

He says I break his heart when I make mischief. But he has never thrown me out or threatened to.

The heart of itself is not the beginning of life but is a vessel made of dense muscle vivified and nourished by an artery and a vein as are the other muscles.

The heart of the system is a piezoelectric crystal 1) that converts electric pulses into vibrations that can penetrate the body. The sound waves are reflected back to the crystal, which reconverts them into electric signals. Echoes from the fetus are translated into faint signals, which are processed by the computer into a video image 3).

When women say that the child is sometimes heard to cry within the womb, this is more likely to be the sound of wind which rushes out. . . .

What about your mother, master? Who sang to you and gave you milk?

To generate a US image, a transducer in the shape of a small rodlike microphone is placed in contact with the surface of the body. A signal of high frequency in the range of 2 to 10 MHz (millions of cycles per second) is transmitted through the skin. . . . The time delay between sending the pulse and receiving the reflection determines the depth of the target.

Why the thunderbolt kills a man and does not wound him, and if the man blew his nose he would not die.

How many profiles can you list? My master has a handsome collection of noses, but not all of them handsome, capito? Are you in a bulbous mood today? Lunedì, aquiline; martedì, straight; mercoledì, pointed; giovedì, concave; venerdì, snub; sàbato, round; doménica, regular? Shall we review? Take a deep breath and then take up your pencil.

It is impossible to breathe through the nose and through the mouth at the same time. The proof of this is seen when anyone breathes with the mouth open taking the air in through the mouth and sending it out through the nose, for then one always hears the sound of the gate set near to the uvula when it opens and shuts.

A padded compression plate is lowered from above and gently squeezes the breast to facilitate better imaging of the entire breast. The patient is told to hold her breath as views are taken of each breast.

Because it hurts the lungs.

The radiologist in this case is looking for a pulmonary embolism (a clot in the lung's blood supply). Ten percent of cases of pulmonary embolism are fatal, so quick detection and therapy are usually of urgent concern.

My master hops from patron to patron to keep us fed. But every time one of them dies, he takes an interest in that particular disease and seeks to understand its workings, thus adding new distractions to his painting projects. If he were quicker with his work, this wouldn't be a problem. Perhaps they died of waiting, I say, surely there's a cure for that: just make art, Leonardo!

The classic form of Kaposi's sarcoma is rare and tends to strike men of Italian, Mediterranean and Eastern European Jewish heritage from their fifties to their eighties. It also occurs as an endemic form in African men.

Figure to show from whence comes the semen.
Whence the urine.
Whence the milk.

Lurking deep within the lobes and ducts of the breast, abnormal cells are detected by mammographic screening. In the color-enhanced image to the left (side view of a breast) the small black dot surrounded by a contour of colors indicates a malignancy.

"I fed you with milk like my own son," you complain, in a voice that deserves the accompaniment of your infamous lira da braccio, ready to break into sobbing. You make it sound as if I sucked it straight from your tit. Let's get it straight; are you my mother or my master?

Whence come tears.
Whence the turning of the eyes when one draws the other after it.
Of sobbing.

Stop bawling! Send me home. Go find a wife; go have your own son.

353

Mary Caponegro

To get a firsthand idea of just how difficult (but very rewarding) the film inter-
pretation process can be, I traveled to Rochester, New York, to spend a day
with Dr. Wende W. Logan, one of the busiest mammographers in the country.
Her patients call her "Eagle Eye" for her ability to see things that others cannot.

*The light, or pupil of the human eye, on its expansion and contraction, increases
and decreases by half its size. In nocturnal animals it increases and decreases
more than a hundredfold in size. This may be seen in the eye of an owl, a nocturnal bird, by bringing a lighted torch near its eye, and more so if you make it
look at the sun.*

From the back of a great swan, my master says, a man shall
someday fly, and so he builds and treats and smears and plans:
with pine upon lime, feather on canvas, sized silk; fashioning
platforms and rudders and cables and windmills and undercar-
riages and something that looks like a giant shoe, the last of which
is of least use to me as I cannot steal it to sell to the shoemaker for
aniseed sweets. What will be next? Madonna! It's another original
contraption by Da Vinci, get out of the way; stai attento, vai via!
before it crashes against the palace wall!

*Then you will observe the pupil which previously occupied the whole eye, diminished
to the size of a grain of millet.*

The smooth patches of skin that characterize Kaposi's are described
by doctors as nodules, plaques and macules; they vary in size from
that of peas to that of large coins.

There are many kinds of breast cancers, Dr. Logan told me. Some are as small
as fine grains of sand that "pepper" an area of the breast.

*With this reduction it compares to the pupil of man, and the clarity and brightness
of objects appears to it of the same intensity since at this time they appear to man
in the same proportion because the brain of this animal is smaller than the brain
of man.*

The planning of 3-D treatment uses new techniques such as the "Beam's Eye
View." It is as if the human eye were placed at the exact position of the origin
of the radiation and watched where it went.

*Sight is better at a distance than near at hand with men who are somewhat ad-
vanced in years because the same thing transmits a smaller impression of itself to
the eye when it is remote than when it is near.*

354

What do you want from a street urchin? You always seem surprised that vulgar things should issue from these cherub lips? But
you don't know the viler things the Milanese say. (All eyebrows
raise immediately, of course.) Everyone knows I'll never make a
painting on my own, that these wasted hours of instruction only
allow you to gaze in my angelic eyes. But in the master one cannot
excuse incompetence. It doesn't take much talent, Zio, it doesn't
take a second sight or even a trained eye to see that the painting
you've been working on for years still isn't finished yet. Just like
the one before it, and . . . . . shall we name names, and dates?

*All things seen will appear larger at midnight than at midday and larger in the
morning than at midday.*

Shall we begin with March 16th, 1478, at St. Bernard's Chapel:
the absent altar painting, which despite the receipt of twenty-five
florins (and some persuasion on your father the notary's part) you
never created — this first adult commission a striking contrast to
your first work as a child, when your alacrity sustained the stench
of decomposing animals in your room as you assembled a dragon's
face so fierce your father sent you straight away to study with
Verrocchio, ostensibly to mine your talent subito — but I think
otherwise: your father was afraid of keeping such bizarre imagination in his own house, alive inside his little bastard, what's more!
In any case, the Madonna, in maturity, did not sustain your inspiration in the same way. Admit it, you prefer a dragon to a
virgin!

*The wrinkles or folds of the vulva have indicated to us the position of the gate-
keeper (portinario) of the castel which is always found where the meeting of the
longitudinal wrinkles occurs. However, this rule is not observed in the case of all
these wrinkles but only in those which are large at one end and narrow at the other,
that is, pyramidal in shape.*

The opening of brothels is no deterrent, is it, for the Florentine
perversion known in certain studios, so prevalent in fact it needs
no mention. And yet there is sufficient interest from my master to
design a brothel so discreet that clients have at their disposal
secret staircases to exit, enter. Artisans might climb such stairs, if
only with intent to draw, observe and draw still more into the
night. Perhaps he'll slip himself between the putta and her client,

355

then whip out his pen: "Per piacere, Signorina, open, if you would, your thighs; my study lacks a female organ and I must, if only in duty to nature, be thorough."

The epidemiology of cervical cancer is extensively documented (*The Walton Report*, 1982). Increased incidence is associated with early intercourse, multiple sex partners, early pregnancy, large families, low socioeconomic status and poor personal hygiene. It is rare in nuns and Jewish women. . . . Three types of viruses are commonly associated with cervical cancer: herpes simplex type 2 (HSV2), cytomegalovirus and papilloma viruses.

But how peculiar it looks, master: this souvenir you sketched: like an unadorned aperture: a lipless mouth, no fleshy rim to feel the sensation of a kite's tail tapping, tapping, gently tapping. More like the mouth of a cave.

The woman commonly has a desire quite the opposite of that of man. This is, that the woman likes the size of the genital member of the man to be as large as possible, and the man desires the opposite in the genital member of the woman, so that neither one nor the other ever attains his interest because Nature, who cannot be blamed, has so provided because of parturition. Woman has in proportion to her belly a larger genital member than any other species of animal.

It has occurred to me at last, master, the formula for finishing that you lack. There is no mare, no donna to dispel fatigue, and thus few paintings ever proceed beyond the inevitable impasse at which you weary yet again of the brush.

For I once saw a mule which was almost unable to move due to the fatigue of a long journey under a heavy burden, and which, on seeing a mare, suddenly its penis and all its muscles became so turgid that it multiplied its forces and to acquire such speed that it overtook the course of the mare which fled before it and which was obliged to obey the desires of the mule.

A stand-alone, dedicated machine (a "mule") may be assigned the task of testing all new software coming into the firm. The security measures applied to the mule must be impeccable because the consequences of an undetected infection on this machine will be severe: all incoming software will be infected. Physical security is also essential: access should be limited to the mule's operator, and the machine should be locked when not in use.

Non importa, obviously you have no time to cultivate these conventional appetites and perceptions. Already you must make up for lost time. Into every Milanese ear it has been whispered that the coating you put on the wall of the Santa Maria della Grazie is as water to the walnut oil with which Christ and the apostles are painted; thus they are destined to fade and peel, already disappearing. You might have spared yourself the effort of The Last Supper. There will be no feast on the table for posterity, Leonardo.

Thus the liver becomes desiccated and like congealed bran both in color and in substance, so that when it is subjected to the slightest friction, its substance falls away in small particles like sawdust and leaves behind the veins and arteries.

The positrons collide with the electrons, and the two annihilate one another, releasing a burst of energy in the form of gamma rays. These rays shoot in opposite directions 1) and strike crystals in a ring of detectors 2) around the patient's head, causing the crystals to light up.

As ever, against convention, you allowed Judas a halo — after procrastinating over a year before arriving at his proper face, while receiving two thousand ducats as annual salary (non c'e male) — because such distinctions were too crude for an artist of your sophistication, preferring to mark the traitor by posture and expression. I, however, if you like, could piss the nimbus round the traitor's head to make it apparent to the philistines who can't discern these subtleties. I'm just trying to make myself useful, as you've taught me.

That sound which remains or seems to remain in the bell after it has received the stroke is not in the bell itself but in the ear of the listener, and the ear retains within itself the image of the stroke of the bell which it has heard, and only loses it by slow degrees, like that which the impression of the sun creates in the eye, which only by slow degress becomes lost and is no longer seen.

For a long time, maybe twenty or thirty years, the cancer cell divides again and again. Even when the descendants number in the billions, the body exhibits no readily apparent sign or symptom of what has by then become a semi-independent mass with its own blood supply.

I suppose you acquired your taste for preposterous projects from the first of Verrocchio's you witnessed: the gilded ball and cross atop the bell tower of Santa Maria del Fiore in Firenze, long before my birth. Giotto, who had made the bell tower itself, you wrote, *was not content merely to emulate his master. Nor are you, Leonardo, except in taking on ridiculous ambitions, which you, moreover, often can't bring to fruition. (As for me, allora, I have better things to do than emulate you. But here's a secret your Salai will never whisper in your ear: he wishes he could steal some of your perseverance. I am ashamed that nothing seizes my attention, except demanding your attention, any way I can.)*

The Doppler effect was first explained by the Austrian physicist Christian Johann Doppler in 1842, and refers to the change in the frequency of sound as an object moves in distance and velocity from a given point. If you are transmitting sound waves through a blood vessel, the way the sound is returned can signify subtle changes in blood flow.

If a man jumps on the points of his feet his weight does not make any sound.

Dr. Kaposi reported that, until death occurred, the most persistent symptom for which his patients required treatment was "the feeling of tension and pain in the hands and feet."

I'll jump up and down and stamp my feet until you tell me who that woman in our house is, with a name I've never heard before. The new housekeeper is all you'll say. Where did she come from though? From Vinci? Boys I am accustomed to in your house but a woman, this is something new. Is she your mother, this Caterina? The mother of my bastard master? I'll shake the house, I'll hold my breath until my face turns blue! Chi e la donna nuova? Dimmi!

Write why the campanile shakes at the sound of its bells.
Where flame cannot live no animal that draws breath can live.

In this case, a radioactive gas makes a picture after the first breath; more pictures are obtained after several minutes of inhaling and after the gas mixture has been exhaled and the patient is breathing room air. (Embolism, pneumonia, asthma, bronchitis, emphysema and even cancer can be diagnosed by perfusion and ventilation scans. Radiation here is again at a very low level.)

I say that the blue which is seen in the atmosphere is not its own color, but is caused by the heated moisture having evaporated into the most minute imperceptible particles, which the beams of the solar rays attract and cause to seem luminous against the deep intense darkness of the region of fire that forms a covering above them.

Researchers say severe childhood sunburns and teenage sunburns are more than twice as likely to lead to skin cancer.

The new image is displayed on a TV monitor and each density is assigned a color. As an example, pure black can be changed to blue, pure white can be displayed as bright orange. Other colors can fill in the intermediate densities; assignments of color can be arbitrary or standardized.

I say that the pink my master wears is silly, and I say he's a sissy, but if he wants to dress me up in green velvet ribbons and silver cloth and parade me all around Milano with him, why should I object? Why not be pretty as a picture for the painter?

Every element of a virtual world is a design decision. What colors, shapes and sounds should you use? What effects will your choices have on the user? How do you make something appear realistic, and does that really serve your purposes? How do you structure an application when you can make it do anything you want? How do you guide users when they can do anything they want — or anything might happen?

How the first picture was nothing but a line which surrounded the shadow of a man made by the sun upon a wall.

Although it is likely that breast cancer has been around since man first scratched on the wall of his cave, the real thrust of organized research in this country began only in 1970.

Man has progressed from cave painting to canvas to camera and now to machine vision.

I am sick of your lines, figures, your studies, your instructions; Io, Giacomo, Io, Salai, sono stuffa! Sick of your bodies, your elegant insufferable doodles, dappertutto ogni pagina, your limbs and bones and lines, your wombs and vessels. Voglio vomitare. Capisci? I want to puke! And you do not deserve to know, but I am jealous of your grotesque faces, grim cadavers, for I believe at times they fascinate you more than I do, than my bland beauty. It is obscene to be so drawn to beauty as my master is, in all and in its most peculiar forms. Bellezza is his mistress; I am merely his inadequate apprentice. I want to leave this place, this post I never asked for, and crawl into a cave.

I was curious about the omission of breast cancer from the cave and wall scratching of primitive man, and most of the authorities I asked about this said it was probably because women died of other cancers long before they reached the vulnerable breast-cancer age.

359

You accuse me of rudeness, but how polite is it to stalk a face
il tutto girono? I've seen you follow some poor unsuspecting jaw
or brow or nose, fixing your eyes upon that arbitrary face until
surrender. How many victims, for instance, did you seize in the
Borghetto before Judas was filled in? L'Ultima Cena senza l'ultima
testa per tante mese — ridiculo!

*What nerve is the cause of the eye's movement and makes the movement of one eye
draw the other?*
Of closing the eyelids.
Of raising the eyebrow.
Of lowering the eyebrows.

Try closing one eye and picking a point on an object within two to three feet
of you. Now, starting with your finger on the tip of your nose, try to touch
the point on the object. Try doing the same thing with both eyes open. In the
first case, it's difficult to judge if your finger has traveled far enough or not.
In the second case, your finger moves rapidly to the spot without hesitation.
The same holds true for similar tasks in the virtual world.

Of shutting the eyes.
Of opening the eyes.

You roll your eyes at me affecting indignation. But we both know
I get away with anything — almost. We both know it is our destiny
that we be strangely linked, like breath to flame, like hand to kite.
Your destiny is to be always seeking flight, and mine: to pull you
down to earth, to make you roll in dirt, or worse. This game de-
pends on your participation. You remain eternally enamored of
possibility, and I, at every moment, your desire's doubt.

*Why as the image of the light of the candle diminishes when it is removed to a
great distance from the eye the size of this light does not diminish but it lacks only
the power and brightness of this radiance.*

The radiologist can alter brightness and contrast, and zoom into specific areas,
magnifying as well as reducing image size.

Sometimes I wake to find my master staring over me. I spit on
him. Must I endure your probing when I'm still asleep? Couldn't
you ask permission? Your face in innocence, he says, is all I wanted,
as he sketches, before you distort its sweet natural expression with

your vile grimaces. I want to hold the startling beauty of your fair radiant eyes, no less than when the sun from darkness rises. It's too early for poetry, caro Zio, I'll close these heavy lids again and turn my back on you, OK? If you can't bear to leave, just sketch my ass.

Radiologists have been studied for longer than any other defined population to assess the late effects of exposure to ionizing radiations received as a consequence of their occupation.

Of raising the nostrils.
Of parting the lips with teeth clenched.
Of bringing the lips to a point.
Of laughing.
Of wondering.

The most natural of expressions on the mysterious face of the woman on the balcony, do you recall it? I promise I will never tell the world how you contrived it with a band of revelers and musicians in the studio daily provoking Monna Lisa, Francesco del Giocondo's wife, to curve her lips ever so slightly, enigmatically, nearly imperceptibly. . . . And did you finish even so? Four years went by with brushstrokes missing from the robes and landscape, left for your pupils to be responsible for—O don't look at me, I wouldn't dare, all are aware I do not work to excellent effect. But don't think I'm complaining, I'd prefer you be occupied with these interminable labors or join her singing revelers than that you serenade me in my bed!

Like the director of a chorus, an MR scanner conducts the "singing" of hydrogen atoms within the human body. The scanner surrounds the body with powerful electromagnets. Supercooled by liquid helium, they create a magnetic field as much as thirty thousand times stronger than that of the earth.

Let the earth turn on which side it may, the surface of the waters will never move from its spherical form, but will always remain equidistant from the center of the globe. Granting that the earth might be removed from the center of the globe, what would happen to the water?

Couldn't we just once play an ordinary game, as children do?— not a perspectograph, not strange inventions, not artist's tools, not rotting creatures (sempre qualcosa schifo), not something to learn from or marvel at—but something simple, divertenta, as even my poor father found the time to use with me, and with my sister?

Mary Caponegro

Spinning like tops, the protons normally point in random directions. A. But inside the scanner's magnetic field B they align themselves in the direction of the field's poles. Even in alignment, however, they wobble, or precess, at a specific rate, or frequency. The stronger the magnetic field, the greater the frequency.

In reading right to left his never-ending notes, sometimes with the assistance of a mirror, I feel as when my sister and I would grasp each other's hands and spin around until we were so dizzy we would fall. We laughed then, now I scratch my head and blink instead. But ogni tanto I wonder what would become of little Giacomo were Leonardo suddenly to cease creating. What would my waters have to crash against without his earth?

When the scanner excites these protons with a radio pulse timed to the same frequency as their wobbling, it knocks them out of their alignment.

My master confided to me that as an infant in the cradle he felt the tail of a kite against his lips, and I at a slightly more advanced age often feel the tip of a pen or a silver-point pencil (it's true I've stolen one or two from other of his pupils) or brush, always scratching or stroking uncomfortably near to my skin. Absurd, you say, a tactile sense so sensitive, but my master has said, the greater the sensibility the greater the suffering, and I may as well use that to my advantage with him. For the gala festivities of the many pageants he has prepared, Leonardo has created an animated heaven and a cannon that spews forth a flaming actor; for the Masque of the Planets, the first that I observed, he made a giant egg surrounded by signs of the zodiac. In each he tries to include me, put me on display. I do not mind the admiration, for which, in preparation, Leonardo takes his brush and paints my lips; the bristles tickle me.

Cancer therapy can cause dental and oral complications so severe they can compromise cancer treatment and recovery, dental experts said today in recommending that cancer patients get thorough oral examination before treatment.

But other times, art bruises little Giacomo. Cruel master, I am quick to say on these occasions, keep my fine apparel, give me back to poverty. Dove e mio povero padre? Poor father had no soldi, and no schola, not a learned man but decent; at least he left me in peace. Signor Caprotti, al meno un huomo normale, I miss you! Why did you steal me from him, cradle snatcher? And you call me a thief! Wait . . . come back. I didn't mean it, master. Please come back and sing to me.

> *This plan of mine of the human body will be unfolded to you just as though you had the natural man before you. The reason is that if you wish to know thoroughly the parts of a man after he has been dissected you must either turn him or your eye so that you are examining from different aspects, from below, from above and from the sides, turning him over and studying the origin of each limb; and in such a way the natural anatomy has satisfied your desire for knowledge.*

Master, put aside your studies; why must you wonder about everything? Come sing to your Salai. Please don't stay away.

The current conventional techniques of 2-D radiation therapy employ multiple radiation fields aimed at the tumor from various angles built in a single plane of the body. . . . With the aid of specialized computer programs, we can precisely reconstruct the 3-D configuration of the tumor, look at it from any side and geometry, define its borders and determine its relationship to other organs.

> By this time some tiny "gangs" of cancer cells have broken away from the original mass and have started thriving colonies in the brain and in the lungs, places to which the "colonists" were carried by the bloodstream.

> *The rumbling of the cannon is caused by the impetuous fury of the flame beaten back by the resisting air, and that quantity of the powder causes this effect because it finds itself ignited within the body of the cannon; and not perceiving itself in a place that has capacity for it to increase, nature guides it to search with fury for a place suitable for its increase, and breaking or driving before it the weaker obstacle it wins its way into the spacious air; and this not being capable of escaping with the speed with which it is attacked, because the fire is more volatile than the air. . . .*

The Department of Defense has long used image enhancement in evaluating aerial pictures in camouflage detection, and more recently this equipment has been applied in medical imaging.

Kaposi's sarcoma, it turned out, was probably the most important single clue to the discovery of AIDS in New York in 1981, and it remains an integral part of the baffling investigation of its cause, cure and prevention.

Mary Caponegro

AUTHOR'S NOTE

"Doubt Uncertainty Possibility Desire" is a collage consisting of materials assembled by the author from the following sources: *The Notebooks of Leonardo da Vinci,* compiled and edited from the original manuscript by Jean Paul Richter, Dover; *Medicine's New Visions,* by Howard Sochurek (1987), Mack Publishing Co.; *Dimensions of Cancer,* by Charles E. Kupchella (1987), Wadsworth Publishing Co.; *Breast Cancer,* by Rose Kushner (1975), Harcourt Brace Jovanovich; *Cancer Risks and Prevention,* edited by M. P. Vessey and Muir Gray (1985), Oxford University Press; *Virtual Reality,* by Ken Pimentel and Kevin Teixeira (1995), McGraw Hill; *Managing Computer Viruses,* by Eric Louw and Neil Duffy (1992), Oxford University Press; and *The New York Times.*

The only voice of the author's creation is that of the fictional apprentice Salai.

The different systems of indentation serve as a guide to the reader in distinguishing the voices: Salai's passages are indented in the fashion of conventional paragraphs, each of Leonardo's lines is indented to form a wider margin and the "found material" is not indented, with one exception.

The title, "Doubt Uncertainty Possibility Desire," derives from the Italian subjunctive mood, the *conjunctivo,* which is used to express hypothetical conditions and convey expressions of emotion, doubt and uncertainty.

NOTES ON CONTRIBUTORS

ROBERT ASHLEY's opera, *Balseros* (about the Cuban raft people), commissioned by the Florida Grand Opera, Miami Dade Community College and the South Florida Composers Alliance, will be premiered in Miami in May 1997. "Yes, But Is It Edible?," one of *The Immortality Songs* (forty short operas for television), will be completed for South German Radio (Munich) in the summer of 1997.

NEIL BARTLETT is artistic director of the Lyric Theatre, Hammersmith, London. His other collaborations with composer Nicolas Bloomfield include *A Judgement in Stone, Sarrasine* and *Night After Night*. His most recent novel was published in the United States as *The House on Brooke Street*.

MEI-MEI BERSSENBRUGGE's collaboration with Kiki Smith, *Endocrinology*, has been published by U.L.A.E. A trade edition is forthcoming from Kelsey St. Press, which will also publish her book of poems, *The Four-Year-Old Girl*.

PHILIP BLACKBURN is producing a series of publications based on the Harry Partch archives, entitled *Enclosures*. He is an experimental composer, has written extensively on Vietnamese music and is program director of the American Composers Forum.

NICOLAS BLOOMFIELD, composer, arranger and performer, is a founder member of Gloria and will visit the United States this autumn with a tour of *Lady Into Fox*. His other compositions for Gloria include *The Picture of Dorian Gray* (available on CD from Gloria, Lyric Theatre, King Street, London W6 0QL), *A Judgement in Stone* and *Sarrasine*.

The excerpt from MARY CAPONEGRO's "Doubt Uncertainty Possibility Desire" that appears in this issue of *Conjunctions* is from the final piece in her collection of stories titled *Il Libro dell'Arte* to be published this fall by Marsilio.

JULIO CORTÁZAR (1914–1984) is the author of *Hopscotch, Blow-up and Other Stories, Cronopios and Famas, Around the Day in Eighty Worlds* and numerous other books. "For Listening Through Earphones," which appears here in English for the first time, is from his collected poems, *Salvo el crepúsculo (Save Twilight)*, a selection of which has been edited and translated by Stephen Kessler.

STEPHEN DIXON's *Man on Stage: Playstories* was published by Hi Jinx Press in November 1996. *Gould: A Novel in Two Novels* was published by Henry Holt in February 1997. "The Burial" is from a work in progress, *Here and Then So Far: The Gould Stories*.

JEFFREY EUGENIDES is the author of the novel *The Virgin Suicides*. His fiction has appeared in *The New Yorker, The Paris Review, The Yale Review* and *Granta*.

ALICE FARLEY is a choreographer/director, costume and illusion designer. Alice Farley Dance Theater is a resident company of LaMama, E.T.C. in New York. Recent productions include *Daphne of the Dunes* (with music by Harry Partch performed by Newband), *Imaginary Ancestors, ANGGREK, the human life of plants* and *Black Water (dancing below the light)*.

THALIA FIELD is a writer of prose, plays and music theater works, and joined the editorial staff of *Conjunctions* in 1995.

SUSAN GEVIRTZ's books include *Domino: point of entry, Linen minus, Taken Place, PROSTHESIS : : CAESAREA* and *Narrative's Journey: The Fiction and Film Writing of Dorothy Richardson* recently out from Peter Lang.

ANN T. GREENE has collaborated on music, dance theater and opera works with Blondell Cummings, Chambliss Giobbi, Fred Ho, Leroy Jenkins, Bill T. Jones, Roberto Pace and Dominic Taylor. A cantata version of *The Negros Burial Ground* had its workshop premiere, under the direction of Dominic Taylor, at The Kitchen in May 1996.

BARBARA GUEST has a new book of poems published by Post-Apollo Press, *Quill, Solitary Apparition;* also out is a reprint by Sun & Moon of her novel, *Seeking Air*.

ANSELM HOLLO's most recent books are *Corvus* (Coffee House Press) and his translation of *The Poems of Hipponax of Ephesus* (Tropos Press). *And How on Earth* (acronym *AHOE*) is a work in progress whose first installment, *Survival Dancing*, is the final section of *Corvus*.

MAUREEN HOWARD is the author of the novels *Natural History, Bridgeport Bus* and a memoir, *Facts of Life*. Her new novel, *ALMANAC; A Winter's Tale*, will be published early next year by Viking.

RONALD R. JANSSEN teaches modern literature at Hofstra University. He is translating Zhang Cheng Zhi's *A History of the Soul*.

LEROY JENKINS composed the dance opera *The Mother of Three Sons* with writer Ann T. Greene and choreographer Bill T. Jones. Recent recordings include *Leroy Jenkins Live* (Black Saint, 1993) and *Themes and Improvisations of the Blues* (CRI, 1994). His multimedia theater piece, *The Three Willies*, had its premiere at Philadelphia's Painted Bride, and will be performed in Chicago and New York during the 1997/98 season.

ROBERT KELLY's most recent books are *Red Actions: Selected Poems 1960–1993* (Black Sparrow Press) and *Queen of Terrors* (McPherson & Company). He is editing a new collection of poems 1994–1996, and a fifth gathering of his short fictions.

STEPHEN KESSLER's poems, essays, translations and journalism have appeared variously in the independent literary and alternative press since the late 1960s, most recently (or forthcoming) in *Exquisite Corpse, Hambone, Oxygen, Poetry Flash, Press* and elsewhere.

JACKSON MAC LOW and his wife, Anne Tardos, presented their collaborative work *Provence*, for video and two speakers, at The Kitchen (New York) in November 1996. His most recent publications are the CD *Open Secrets*, realized by Tardos, seven instrumentalists and himself (Experimental Intermedia, 1993), *42 Merzgedichte in Memoriam Kurt Schwitters* (Station Hill, 1994) and *Barnesbook* (Sun & Moon, 1996).

RUTH E. MARGRAFF is currently working on her libretti *The Elektra Fugues, Centaur Battle of San Jacinto, Locket Arias* and *The Cry Pitch Carolls* for theaters in New York, Texas and Minnesota.

MIKE McCORMACK hails from the west of Ireland. His first book of short stories, *Getting It in the Head* (Jonathan Cape, 1995, and forthcoming from Henry Holt) won the Rooney Prize for Literature. This is his first appearance in print in this country.

MEREDITH MONK, composer, singer, filmmaker, director and choreographer, has created more than one hundred works since 1964. Her latest compact disc, *Volcano Songs*, will be released by ECM New Series in March 1997.

JOHN MORAN's first opera, *The Jack Benny Program*, was produced in 1987 by Ridge Theater. Since then he has penned an opera a year, including *The Manson Family, Everyday Newt Burman* and *Matthew in the School of Life*. His latest opera, *The Cabinet of Dr. Caligari*, was presented by the American Repertory Theater in Cambridge in 1997. His next project will be a new opera commissioned by Lincoln Center.

BRADFORD MORROW's latest novel, *Giovanni's Gift*, is just out from Viking. The novels *Trinity Fields* and *Come Sunday* were recently published in paperback by Penguin.

JOYCE CAROL OATES is the author most recently of a novel, *We Were the Mulvaneys*, and the novella *First Love*. An opera adaptation of her novel *Black Water*, for which she wrote the libretto, premiered in Philadelphia in April. She lives and teaches in Princeton, New Jersey.

TOBY OLSON's "Chihuahua" is from his recently finished novel *Tampico*. His two most recent books are *At Sea* (Simon & Schuster) and *Unfinished Building* (Coffee House). Chihuahua's story is also the basis for a chamber opera libretto.

JENA OSMAN is author of *Jury* (Meow Press), *Amblyopia* (Avenue B) and *Twelve Parts of Her* (Burning Deck). She edits the interdisciplinary arts journal *Chain* with Juliana Spahr.

HARRY PARTCH (1901–1974) grew up in the remote Southwest, where he heard Indian music, Hebrew chants for the dead, Chinese lullabies and Congo puberty rites. In California, he attended Chinese opera. Endeavoring to mimic the exact inflections of the dramatic spoken voice, he resurrected ancient Greek microtonal scales and built or adapted new instruments to play them. For twelve years, he lived as a hobo, turning the everyday life of the world around him (graffiti, train rides, the speech of fellow transients) into music on an Americana theme. His notion of Corporeality, an integrated ritual drama involving the total commitment of every player as mover, actor, musician, characterizes his later works, such as *The Bewitched* (1957), *Revelation in the Courthouse Park* (1960) and *Delusion of the Fury* (1966).

RIDGE THEATER is best known for bringing the works of John Moran to the stage. John Moran and Artistic Director Bob McGrath were awarded an OBIE in 1994 for Sustained Excellence in Collaborative Creation.

JOANNA SCOTT is the author of the novels *Arrogance* (Simon & Schuster), *The Manikin* (Henry Holt) and from Owl, *The Closest Possible Union* and *Fading, My Parmacheene Belle* as well as a collection of short stories, *Various Antidotes.*

GILBERT SORRENTINO has published thirteen novels, the most recent of which is *Red the Fiend* (Fromm, 1995).

NATHANIEL TARN's CD *I Think This May Be Eden* (Spoken Engine, Memphis/ Nashville) is available from Small Press Distribution. His *Scandals in the House of Birds: Shamans and Priests on Lake Atitlan* is expected from Marsilio in late spring.

Acclaimed composer-saxophonist HENRY THREADGILL is widely considered one of the most important composer-instrumentalists working in jazz today. Repeatedly voted "Best Composer" by *Downbeat* magazine's critics and readers, he tours widely and has recorded over twenty albums. His most recent recording is *Where's Your Cup?* on the Columbia label.

YASUNAO TONE's CD, *Musica Iconologos* (Lovely Records), was released in 1994, and his album *Solo for wounded CD* will be released later this year. He is currently working on a CD ROM project, *Musica Simulacra,* an interactive sound piece based on *Manyoushu,* an eighth-century Japanese anthology of poems.

DAVID FOSTER WALLACE's most recent novel is *Infinite Jest.* A collection of his nonfiction, *A Supposedly Fun Thing I'll Never Do Again,* was published by Little, Brown in February.

PAUL WEST's novel *The Tent of Orange Mist* was runner-up for the National Book Critics Circle Award for 1996. In the same year, the government of France made him a Chevalier of Arts and Letters. His most recent book is the novella *Sporting with Amaryllis,* and his next novel, due in late summer of 1997, will be *Terrestrials.*

ELIZABETH WILLIS is the author of *Second Law* (Avenue B, 1993) and *The Human Abstract* (Penguin, 1995).

CAN XUE's *The Embroidered Shoes* is forthcoming from Henry Holt in 1997. This is her third book in English (all translated by Ronald R. Janssen and Jian Zhang).

JIAN ZHANG is assistant chairperson of the Communication and Arts Department at the Brentwood Campus of Suffolk Community College, SUNY.

Back issues of
CONJUNCTIONS

"*Conjunctions* offers a rich collection of fiction and poetry with a definite sylistic bent toward language-loving authors."

The New York Times Book Review

CONJUNCTIONS:9 William S. Burroughs, Dennis Silk, Michel Deguy, Peter Cole, Paul West, Laura Moriarty, Michael Palmer, Hayden Carruth, Mei-mei Berssenbrugge, Thomas Meyer, Aaron Shurin, Barbara Tedlock, and others. Edmond Jabes interview. 296 pages. ISBN 0-941964-15-9.

CONJUNCTIONS:10 *Fifth Anniversary Issue.* Walter Abish, Bruce Duffy, Keith Waldrop, Harry Mathews, Kenward Elmslie, Beverly Dahlen, Jan Groover, Ronald Johnson, David Rattray, Leslie Scalapino, George Oppen, Elizabeth Murray, and others. Joseph McElroy interview. 320 pages. ISBN 0-941964-21-3.

CONJUNCTIONS:11 Lydia Davis, John Taggart, Marjorie Welish, Dennis Silk, Susan Howe, Robert Creeley, Charles Stein, Charles Bernstein, Kenneth Irby, Nathaniel Tarn, Robert Kelly, Ann Lauterbach, Joel Shapiro, Richard Tuttle, and others. Carl Rakosi interview. 296 pages. ISBN 0-941964-23-X.

CONJUNCTIONS:12 David Foster Wallace, Robert Coover, Georges Perec, Norma Cole, Laura Moriarty, Joseph McElroy, Yannick Murphy, Diane Williams, Harry Mathews, Trevor Winkfield, Ron Silliman, Armand Schwerner, and others. John Hawkes and Paul West interviews. 320 pages. ISBN 0-02-035281-6.

CONJUNCTIONS:13 Maxine Hong Kingston, Ben Okri, Jim Crace, William S. Burroughs, Guy Davenport, Barbara Tedlock, Rachel Blau DuPlessis, Walter Abish, Jackson Mac Low, Lydia Davis, Fielding Dawson, Toby Olson, Eric Fischel, and others. Robert Kelly interview. 288 pages. ISBN 0-02-035282-4.

CONJUNCTIONS:14 *The New Gothic,* guest-edited by Patrick McGrath. Kathy Acker, John Edgar Wideman, Jamaica Kincaid, Peter Straub, Robert Coover, Lynne Tillman, Bradford Morrow, William T. Vollmann, Gary Indiana, Mary Caponegro, Brice Marden, and others. Salman Rushdie interview. 296 pages. ISBN -0-02-035290-5.

CONJUNCTIONS:15 *The Poetry Issue.* 33 poets, including Susan Howe, John Ashbery, Rachel Blau DuPlessis, Barbara Einzig, Norma Cole, John Ash, Ronald Johnson, Forrest Gander, Michael Palmer, Diane Ward, and others. Fiction by John Barth, Jay Cantor, Diane Williams, and others. Michael Ondaatje interview. 424 pages. ISBN 0-941964-32-9.

CONJUNCTIONS:16 *The Music Issue.* Nathaniel Mackey, Leon Botstein, Albert Goldman, Paul West, Amiri Baraka, Quincy Troupe, Lukas Foss, Walter Mosley, David Shields, Seth Morgan, Gerald Early, Clark Coolidge, Hilton Als, and others. John Abercrombie and David Starobin interview. 360 pages. ISBN 0-941964-33-7.

CONJUNCTIONS:17 *Tenth Anniversary Issue.* Kathy Acker, Janice Galloway, David Foster Wallace, Robert Coover, Diana Michener, Juan Goytisolo, Rae Armantrout, John Hawkes, William T. Vollmann, Charlie Smith, Lynn Davis, Mary Caponegro, Keith Waldrop, Carla Lemos, C. D. Wright, and others. Chinua Achebe interview. 424 pages. ISBN 0-941964-34-5. (OUT OF PRINT)

CONJUNCTIONS:18 *Fables, Yarns, Fairy Tales.* Scott Bradfield, Sally Pont, John Ash, Theodore Enslin, Patricia Eakins, Joanna Scott, Lynne Tillman, Can Xue, Gary Indiana, Russell Edson, David Rattray, James Purdy, Wendy Walker, Norman Manea, Paola Capriolo, O. V. de Milosz, Rosario Ferre, Jacques Roubaud, and others. 376 pages. ISBN 0-941964-35-3.

CONJUNCTIONS:19 *Other Worlds.* Guest-edited by Peter Cole. David Antin, John Barth, Pat Califia, Thom Gunn, Barbara Einzig, Ewa Kuryluk, Carl Rakosi, Eliot Weinberger, John Adams, Peter Reading, John Cage, Marjorie Welish, Barbara Guest, Cid Corman, Elaine Equi, Donald Baechlor, John Wieners, and others. 336 pages. ISBN 0-941964-36-1.

CONJUNCTIONS:20 *Unfinished Business:* Novels-in-Progress. Robert Antoni, Janice Galloway, Paul Gervais, Ann Lauterbach, Jessica Hagedorn, Jim Lewis, Carole Maso, Leslie Scalapino, Gilbert Sorrentino, David Foster Wallace, Robert Creeley, Ben Marcus, Paul West, Mei-mei Berssenbrugge, Susan Rothenberg, and others. 352 pages. ISBN 0-941964-37-x.

CONJUNCTIONS:21 *The Credos Issue.* Robert Olen Butler, Ishmael Reed, Kathy Acker, Walter Mosley, Robert Coover, Joanna Scott, Victor Hernandez Cruz, Frank Chin, Simon Ortiz, Martine Bellen, Melanie Neilson, Kenward Elmslie, David Mura, Jonathan Williams, Cole Swensen, John Ashbery, Forrest Gander, Myung Mi Kim, and others. 352 pages. ISBN 0-941964-38-8.

CONJUNCTIONS:22 *The Novellas Issue.* Allan Gurganus, Lynne Tillman, Robert Antoni, Arno Schmidt, Harry Mathews, Robert Olen Butler, Wendy Walker, Stephen Ratcliffe, Kevin Magee, Barbara Guest, John Barth, Donald Revell, James Surls, and others. 384 pages. ISBN 0-941964-39-6.

CONJUNCTIONS:23 *New World Writing.* Eduardo Galeano, Claudio Magris, Abd al-Hakim Qasim, Coral Bracho, Nuruddin Farak, Faiz Ahmed Faiz, Harold Schimmel, Bei Dao, Joachim Sartorius, Nina Iskrenko, Juan Goytisolo, Friederike Mayröcker, Botho Strauss, J. Rudolfo Wilcock, and others. 336 pages. ISBN 0-679-75820-8.

CONJUNCTIONS:24 *Critical Mass.* Yoel Hoffman, Mark McMorris, Githa Hariharan, Barbara Guest, Kathleen Fraser, John Taggart, Thalia Field, Lydia Davis, Bernard Hoepffner, Guy Davenport, Douglas Messerli, Myung Mi Kim, Marjorie Welish, Donald Revell, Meridel Rubenstein and Ellen Zweig, Leslie Scalapino, Peter Gizzi, Paul West, Jason Schwartz, Cole Swenson, D. E. Steward, Mary Caponegro, Robert Creeley, Mei-mei Berssenbrugge, Martine Bellen, William T. Vollmann, Louis Ferdinand Celine. 344 pages. ISBN 0-941964-29-9.

CONJUNCTIONS:25 *The New American Theater.* Tony Kushner, Suzan-Lori Parks, Jon Robin Baitz, Han Ong, Mac Wellman, Paula Vogel, Eric Overmyer, Wendy Wasserstein, Christopher Durang, Donald Margulies, Ellen McLaughlin, Nicky Silver, Jonathan Marc Sherman, Amy Freed, Romulus Linney, Keith Reddin, Joyce Carol Oates, Arthur Kopit, Doug Wright, Robert O'Hara, Erik Ehn, John Guare, Mark O'Donnell, Harry Kondoleon, David Ives. 360 pages. ISBN 0-941964-41-8.

CONJUNCTIONS:26 *Sticks and Stones.* Angela Carter, Ann Lauterbach, Rikki Ducornet, Paul Auster, Arthur Sze, Elaine Equi, Nathaniel Mackey, Forrest Gander, Robert Coover, David Mamet, Diane Williams, Thalia Field, Ben Marcus, Rick Moody, Brian Schorn, Lois-Ann Yamanaka, Terese Svoboda, Brian Evenson, Shelley Jackson, Gary Lutz, Timothy Crouse, Dawn Raffel, David Ohle, Craig Padawer, Ronald Johnson, Norman Manea, Liz Tuccillo, Michael Palmer, Martine Bellen, Robert Kelly, Laynie Browne, Lynn Martin, Fanny Howe, Mei-mei Berssenbrugge, Paul West, Rae Armantrout, Anna Maria Ortese. 360 pages. ISBN 0-941964-42-6.

CONJUNCTIONS:27 *The Archipelago.* Gabriel Garcia Marquez, Derek Walcott, Adam Zagajewski, Cristina Garcia, Wilson Harris, Olive Senior, Senel Paz, Ian McDonald, Kamau Brathwaite, Julia Alvarez, Nilo Cruz, Juan Bosch, Manno Charlemagne, Bob Shacochis, Merle Collins, Antonio Benitez-Rojo, Rosario Ferre, Arturo Uslar Pietri, Adrian Castro, Severo Sarduy, Edwidge Danticat, Madison Smartt Bell, Linton Kwesi Johnson, Fred D'Aguiar, Marlene Nourbese Philip, Glenville Lovell, Kwado Agymah Kamau, Mark McMorris, Mayra Montero, Lorna Goodison, Robert Antoni. 360 pages. ISBN 0-941964-43-4.

Send your order to:

CONJUNCTIONS
Bard College
Annandale-on-Hudson, New York 12504
Phone 914-758-1539
Fax: 914-758-2660
online: bergstei@bard.edu

All issues are $15.00, shipping included.

Milton Avery Graduate School of the Arts

BARD COLLEGE

ANNANDALE-ON-HUDSON, NEW YORK 12504
(914) 758-7481 • e-mail: Gradschool@Bard.edu

MASTER OF FINE ARTS

MUSIC•FILM/VIDEO•WRITING•PHOTOGRAPHY
SCULPTURE•PAINTING

Our unusual approach has changed the nature of fine arts graduate education:

- One-to-one student-faculty tutorials are the basic means of instruction.
- Students meet with faculty from all disciplines.
- Eight-week summer sessions.
- Three years of summer residencies and independent winter work fulfill the requirements for the MFA degree.

SUMMER 1997 JUNE 9–AUGUST 1

Faculty: Peggy Ahwesh, Nancy Bowen, Alan Cote, Dorit Cypis, Lydia Davis, Cecilia Dougherty, Stephen Frailey, Kenji Fujita, Arthur Gibbons, Regina Granne, Charles Hagen, Peter Hutton, Ann Lauterbach, Nicholas Maw, Pat Oleszko, Yvonne Rainer, Leslie Scalapino, David Shapiro, Matthew Stadler, Lynne Tillman, Stephen Westfall

Recent Visiting Faculty/Critics: Vito Acconci, John Zorn, Polly Apfelbaum, Mowrey Baden, Ericka Beckman, Charles Bernstein, Tom Butter, Peter Campus, Mel Chin, John Corigliano, Petah Coyne, Michael Dougherty, Kenward Elmslie, Wendy Ewald, Larry Fink, Richard Foreman, Tom Gunning, Gerry Haggerty, Ann Hamilton, Jane Hammond, Dave Hickey, Susan Howe, George Kuchar, Bradford Morrow, Lorie Novak, Judy Pfaff, Lucio Pozzi, Denise Riley, Andrew Ross, Judith Joy Ross, Jonathan Schell, Beverly Semmes, Joan Snyder, Michael Joan Tower, Ursula von Rydingsvard, Jessica Stockholder, James Welling, Constance DeJong, John Divola, Barbara Guest, Jake Berthot, Laura Newman, Ellen Phelan

burning deck books

Paul Auster: WHY WRITE?
Haunting and humorous by turns, these personal essays reveal the matrix of an art that is inseparable from the writer's life, an "art of hunger," of need, and of community. The book also includes photos of a kinetic sculpture by Jon Kessler on a text by Paul Auster.
64 pages, offset, smyth-sewn ISBN 1-886224-14-5, paper $10;
-15-3, cloth $20.

Lisa Jarnot: SOME OTHER KIND OF MISSION
"This impressive newcomer builds graphic meta-logics to dislocate the myth of history. The sudden jumps and quirky mappings may leave some heads spinning. Her visual poems, in particular, are resonant and haunting, requiring and rewarding second and third looks."—Tom Clark, *San Francisco Chronicle.* Poems & visuals, 112 pages, offset, smyth-sewn ISBN 1-886224-12-9 original paperback, $ 11

Jaqueline Risset: THE TRANSLATION BEGINS
[Série d'Ecriture No. 10, transl. Jennifer Moxley]
A poem on Diana and Actaeon, on Eros and Language, on dismemberment. By an important French poet from the "Tel Quel" group.
96 pages, offset, smyth-sewn, ISBN 1-886224-09-9, original paperback $10

Jessica Lowenthal: AS IF IN TURNING
Biblical texts, Euclidean geometry, the language of definition, are all transformed in this first book of poems. As if in turning, words re-sound as warped echoes of their sources, guiding us, like the cave swiftlet, through dark corridors.
36 pages, letterpress, saddlestitched in wrappers, ISBN 1-886224-17-x, $8

Mark McMorris: MOTH-WINGS
On a ground of inclusive geographies, running from the sugar fields of the Caribbean, through Ethiopian camel caravans, to caravans of hallucinatory cities, the ordinary is a joke. It presents no resting place though it welcomes the migrant human into its house of death. Taken far enough, meaning and hardship coincide.
Poem, 44 pages, letterpress, saddlestitched in wrappers ISBN 1-8816224-10-2 $8

Thanks to the Fund for Poetry and the Rhode Island State Council on the Arts, Craig Watson and Chris & Jeanne Longyear.
Order from Small Press Distribution, 1814 San Pablo Ave., Berkeley, CA 94702 (800-869-7553)

Enclosures: Harry Partch

a full-length portrait of an unconventional life...

• **Enclosure One** (*innova* 400): four films by Madeline Tourtelot with music by Harry Partch—**Rotate the Body, Music Studio, U.S. Highball, Windsong.** 74', VHS/NTSC. 12-page booklet included.

• **Enclosure Two** (*innova* 401): four-CD set of archival recordings of Speech-Music from the 1930's and '40's, including settings of Li Po, his hobo journal, **Bitter Music**, and a sound documentary.

• **Enclosure Three** (*innova* 402): 500-page, limited-edition artbook, a bio-scrapbook of Partch's own documents: 300 photographs, correspondence (with Anaïs Nin, W.B. Yeats, Edmund Dulac, Alwin Nikolais, Martha Graham, Kenneth Anger, Lou Harrison, and many more).

• **Enclosure Four** (*innova* 404): two films—**Delusion of the Fury**, the ritual theatre work that established his reputation, and **The Music of Harry Partch**, a 1968 TV special.

• **Harry Partch: The Early Vocal Works, 1930-33**. Bob Gilmore (British Hary Partch Society, 1996), 208 pp. The first in-depth discussion of Partch's Speech-Music works.

Series producer: Philip Blackburn

Contact: American Composers Forum,
332 Minnesota St. #E-145, St. Paul, MN 55101-1300
compfrm@maroon.tc.umn.edu
http://www.tc.umn.edu/nlhome/m111/compfrm
Fax: 612 291-7978   Tel: 612 228-1407

The 1997 Mississippi Review Prize

$1000 awarded to the winning story
$500 to the winning poem

Winners and all finalists in fiction and poetry will be published in print and online editions of *The Mississippi Review*.

1997 Jurors
Fiction: Padgett Powell
Poetry: Angela Ball

DEADLINE & ENTRY FEE: Deadline is May 30, 1997. Nonrefundable entry fee is $10 per story, limit two stories per author ($20), or $5 per poem, limit four entries per author ($20). Make check/money order payable to Mississippi Review Prize. No ms returned. Contest open to all US writers except students or employees of USM. Previously published or accepted work ineligible. **FORMAT:** Fiction--maximum 6500 words (25 pages), typed, double-spaced. Poetry--each entry a single poem no more than ten typewritten pages. Author's name, address, phone, plus story title and "1997 Mississippi Review Prize Entry" should be on page one of entry. Do not send cover sheet. **ANNOUNCEMENTS:** Include SASE for list of winners. Winners will be announced November 1, 1997. The Prize Issue will be available to competitors at a reduced rate ($5). Issue scheduled for late fall 1997. These are complete guidelines. AA/EOE/ADA

send entries to:
1997 mississippi review prize
box 5144, hattiesburg, ms 39406-5144

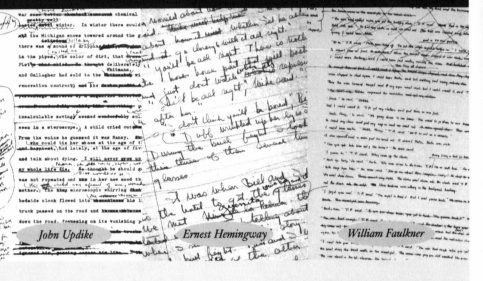